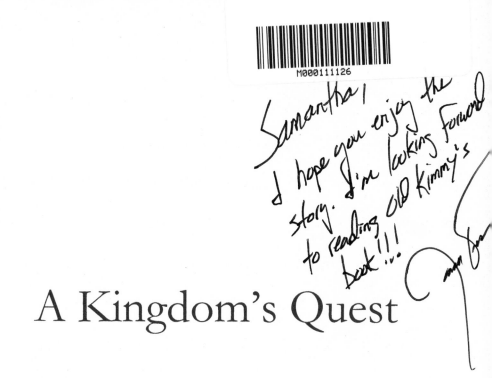
A Kingdom's Quest

James D. Troe

DEDICATION

To Carrie, who agreed to let me cut my hours at work to pursue this gigantic bucket list item.

CONTENTS

ACKNOWLEDGMENTS

Thank you to my editor, Jeremy Corey-Gruenes, who taught me things about English that I should have learned in school, and who kept me confident with his encouragement. Thanks also to the Park Avenue Authors, who listen, share and sharpen.

Author's Introduction

To my great-grandchildren,

They say an author should write to an audience. Well, you're my audience. I don't know if I'll meet any of you. I certainly won't meet all of you.

I started writing a book once, back in college. It was called *Green Lake*, and the protagonist's name was Samuel Myran (my mother's maiden name). Unfortunately, after several paragraphs, I discovered I didn't have enough book-worthy thoughts to continue. That, of course, surprised me. I knew everything back then.

About ten years ago, I tried again—this one's title: *Beyond Color*. The protagonist's name was *Truth*. As you can probably guess by that name, I again thought I knew something. My intended audience for *Beyond Color* was me. It was an internal journey. When I was about seventeen chapters in, I joined a writer's group, and asked someone to critique what I'd written so far. "Your characters are flat, and I don't like your protagonist," she said. "At fifty years of age, he's way too immature."

A little miffed at first, I then realized I could solve that problem. And with the wave of my fictional wand—POOF, my protagonist was a young man—someone you'd expect to stumble around.

I now understand that I don't know that much. But I finally know myself pretty well. And to some extent, I'm alive in you. So I've condensed my most valuable lessons into one fast-paced summer adventure. By the time you finish this book, you'll know me a lot better, and you might know yourself a little better, too. Remember: You don't have to learn *everything* the hard way.

Thanks for being willing to share some time with me.

Grampa

A Kingdom's Quest

CHAPTER 1

"Jens, follow me to the tower."

The tower?

I'd been nervously awaiting Thoren's appearance, standing near the palace doors, expecting something a bit more formal. He was the king, after all. He was also my childhood friend, whom I hadn't seen privately in the five years since his crowning. My father, Jacoby Berrit, had served as an advisor to Thoren's father, King Kristoffer. But now our fathers were dead, Thoren had taken the throne, and I had fallen into obscurity.

I'd been anticipating this day from the moment I received the summons, wondering what it was about and how I should act. Would he treat me like an old friend? At first, I thought so, but then I didn't know. I'd best approach him as a king.

"Are you coming?" he yelled, disappearing through the stone archway leading to a long hallway. I started after him, suddenly feeling like we were children again.

By the time I passed the archway, Thoren was at least fifteen paces ahead, and gaining speed. This hallway was familiar. As children, Thoren and I spent many winter days running up and down its long expanse, only because the servant assigned to his care couldn't shoo us outside. He loved to kick a pebble and keep it from me, using speed and finesse. I wasn't good at keeping up with him then either.

Following behind, I realized what a specimen he was. The wild blonde curls of his youth had turned gold, tamed with oil, making them glimmer like a crown. His athletic shoulders seemed carved to wear the royal cloak. He had a determined stride. He'd always walked that way, but I'd never considered it a kingly pace—he just seemed in a hurry. The muscles and veins in his calves bulged and relaxed with each step, quickly leaving me in his wake.

By the time we reached the chapel, the distance between us had lengthened. But the chapel was no place to run. I hoped the holy ground would slow him somehow. It didn't, of course. It never had.

When I reached the side aisle of the chapel, my eyes lingered on the vaulted stone wall, where two banks of organ pipes hung like gigantic lungs above the carved altar. My memory drifted back to when we were children, sitting in the stiff-backed wooden pews. I remembered once rubbing goosebumps off my arm after the pipes had blasted a holy note, seeming to draw the Creator into our presence. I'd nudged Thoren, asking if he felt it.

"Feel what?" he whispered back.

I pointed at my goosebumps. "You're daft," he replied. I didn't talk much about the Creator after that. Now, watching him breeze past the altar, I wondered if the weight of his crown had ever forced him to his knees before the polished rail.

Slipping out the back of the chapel, I entered the parapet walk, barely in time to see Thoren disappear into the spiral staircase of the tower. Being alone on the parapet, I made an undignified sprint for the tower door, entering just in time to see the king striding up the circular staircase, devouring two stairs with each step. I followed at a more composed one-stair-per-step pace, which I eventually abandoned to catch up, my view of him obscured by the curved walls.

The tower was illuminated only occasionally by a window, tiny in size. Even with the frantic chase, these small portals tempted me to stop and peer out. The increasing elevation brought stunning beauty to the kingdom. I wondered if Thoren chose the tower's roof to escape the aggravation of ground-level existence. In all the time I'd know him, he had no patience for the mundane or the status quo. Thoren was a progressive king, unwilling to steer gradually toward his envisioned future. He embraced change, fully intending to march Tuva forward, kicking and screaming if need be.

Though I couldn't see him, I was relieved to hear the slowing of sandals. Finally, the clapping of leather on stone ceased altogether, replaced by the sound of Thoren tinkering with a latch. As I rounded the final curve, the king pushed open the door, blinding me with intense sunlight. I stopped for a moment, waiting for my sight to adjust, and when my vision came back, Thoren was stepping onto the roof. I quietly followed, watching him closely. Allowing his shoulders to sag, he dropped his head, slowly filling his lungs with fresh sea air. Then, as if releasing all the tension from the morning, he looked up at the clear blue sky and exhaled.

"How are you, Jens? I've missed you."

"I've missed you too."

Neither of us seemed to know what to say next. I waited awkwardly for Thoren to carry the conversation, but when he only stared at me, I began speaking without knowing what would come out. "I often wonder," I stammered, "what it's like for you . . . shouldering the responsibilities of the crown."

"Responsibilities?" Thoren took a step closer, his face inquisitive. After an uncomfortable moment, he released me from his scrutiny with a laugh. "Ha! Responsibilities . . . That's what makes you curious? You've always been the responsible one, Jens."

"No, it's just that—"

"Jens, if you were king, I'd have something interesting to be curious about."

"Like what?"

"I don't know . . . Like learning your secrets, or finding out who your bravest soldier is, or whose head you'd like to chop off . . ." He turned his back to me and walked to the rail, mumbling the word *responsibilities* again.

I fell silent. Our friendship had grown rusty, and I'd forgotten how it worked. I was one of the few people who appreciated his vision. Thoren had a knack for seeing what *could be*. My gift to him had always been to listen and inquire, letting him paint a canvas for me from nothing but blue sky. Now, I'd broken the rules by releasing a ground-level word.

There was a pile of stones sitting alongside the turrets. Thoren selected one the size of a walnut and stepped back a few paces. Tossing it up and down in his hand to make a careful study of its weight, he gathered his energy. Then, in a violent flurry, he hurled it toward the horizon. I joined him at the turret to watch it soar.

"DAH!" he cursed, as the stone landed short of the water, "Strong breeze today . . . I need more weight." He kicked the pile flat to make a better selection.

Amused by his sport, I asked, "Who stockpiles your throwing stones?"

"There are certain tasks a king must do himself," he replied. "I'm afraid this is one of the responsibilities I must shoulder." Then he winked at me. This time, he selected a stone the size of an apple, tossing it to me, saying, "Give it a bath, Jens."

From our vantage point, the throw to the sea looked deceptively easy. Unfortunately, my attempt fell unimpressively in the grass below, failing even to reach rocks of the cliff. Thoren groaned. With his brow furrowed, he yelled, "You've wasted my best stone!"

"Sorry."

"Oh well. I didn't summon you here to throw stones."

"Why did you summon me?"

Thoren studied me for a moment. "How are you at bargaining? I understand you bargain with shepherds."

He was right. Since my father's death, I'd found employment with a merchant who made his living selling woolen products. He had scores of widows spinning and sewing, making garments, blankets, and rugs, sold in his shop in the Royal City's commercial district. It was my task to purchase his wool. It wasn't much of a position, but it provided a meager income. Of course, the wealth went to the merchant, who padded his margins by underpaying me and the poor widows. Having few options to provide for ourselves, we couldn't complain. My work made me feel like a stray arrow shot from my father's noble bow.

"Yes, I'm a wool buyer. Why are you interested in my bargaining skills?"

Thoren's eyes locked with mine. "Jens, the world is changing."

"What do you mean, *changing*?"

"It's been explored," he replied, turning a full circle with his arms raised as if I could view the entire earth from the tower. "It's becoming smaller. The shipyards no longer build sleek vessels to cut through the sea quickly. No, they build wide-hulled ships to haul cargo. The world is like a young child, finally weaned from its mother's breast—ready for new foods."

"New foods?"

"I'm not just talking about food, Jens. Don't you understand? It wasn't just the land the explorers discovered—it's what they brought back. They've awakened an appetite for things we didn't even know existed."

"What things?"

"Foods, spices, weapons, jewels, the list is endless." Thoren looked south, surveying the city. "My father, and the kings before him, only worried about Tuva's protection and independence. They had no vision for the future. We've never had the strength to conquer new lands or to become great. We've relied on our geography to protect us. Look at this fortress."

Thoren paused, inviting me to survey the landscape. The Royal City was located in the northeast corner of the kingdom, with the Sea of Temis to the north, its southern shore splashing on the jagged rocks far below. From where we stood, the shoreline was nothing but a sheer cliff, impossible for harboring ships until reaching Tuva's northwest border, where the rough terrain gave way to a gradually sloping trough leading down to the sea. This bay area is called *The Crucible* for its bowl-like appearance and is considered Tuva's one geographic weakness—the one place an invading army could harbor their ships. But it was a three-day march from The Crucible to the Royal City, and the Royal City was protected on three sides by either mountains or sea. An invading army could only approach from the south, and even there, the long incline leading to the city would give the king's archers ample opportunity to decimate an oncoming troop from the rocky crags on both sides of the slope.

Remembering a lesson from my past, I said, "My father told me there's no city like this, where mountains and sea so effectively defend its people. He estimated that a squad of fifty archers could defend this place."

Pacing now, Thoren chose his words carefully. "That may be true, Jens. I'm not questioning the wisdom of our forefathers. This city was designed for its time, but that time has passed. This is the seventeenth century. If we want to progress from being a gnat on a horse's ass into a modern nation, we need to assess our strengths and weaknesses differently."

"I don't understand. Nations still have armies. If the world is becoming smaller, wouldn't the threat of invasion be greater?"

Turning his back to me, Thoren scoffed, "You sound like the wretched advisors I inherited from my father. Come over here."

I hesitated, realizing he could throw me from the tower without consequence. "What?" I mumbled, approaching the turrets.

Placing his arm around my shoulder and turning my body to face the northwest, Thoren pointed to the distant horizon over the sea. "Jens, do you know what the great kingdom of Gladon would take from us if they were to invade?" Without waiting for an answer, he turned me to the east. "Do you know what the king of Sagan would take from us?"

I thought for a moment. "The land, I suppose. We have good farmland."

"No, Jens. Gladon and Sagan would sooner buy our crops than grow them. They're building merchant fleets—ships that travel the world to buy and sell. If they took anything from us, it would be The Crucible. Do you understand what I'm saying? The bay our fathers considered a great weakness is now our greatest strength. It's one of the best winter harbors on the sea. But they'd not need to take it from us if we built a glorious port ourselves and invited their ships."

Releasing my shoulders, he began pacing again. "Jens, if we lose The Crucible, we'll lose our connection to the outside world and be forever lost in the past."

While he had his back to me, I said, "I've heard talk of your port. It's rumored that it will one day bear your name."

Thoren turned and sighed. "I suppose that sounds arrogant, but yes, I've taken over the fishing village of Keenod. It's centered in The Crucible. I've built a summer palace there, along with docks and warehouses for cargo. Already vessels from Gladon and Sagan are using the harbor. Sagan's king has even sent a crew to Keenod to build me a ship."

Thoren waited for my response. When I didn't say anything, he continued, "Jens, I believe this port will be my legacy. My advisors say I'm wasting Tuva's resources, placing the kingdom in jeopardy, tempting invasion, but time will prove me right. Future generations will remember my name. I'll be vindicated when the world speaks of Port Thoren in Tuva."

"What does this have to do with me?" I asked.

"You're not wrong about our farmland, Jens. There's no soil like Tuva's. If our farmers could be convinced to grow crops for export, we could turn food into gold. The mines won't last forever. I want to use what remains of Tuva's gold to harness our true wealth: The Crucible and the soil. When our gold leaves the mountains, it's gone forever, but the soil is generous. It brings new wealth to the surface each year."

I nodded. "So, you want me to negotiate with farmers. You want me to purchase crops to ship from your port."

"Exactly."

"What crops?"

"That's a discussion for later. First, I need to know if you're willing to help me. I'll give you a post in my administration. You'll be my Minister of Agriculture."

Minister of Agriculture? A title? I'd lost hope of having one. A man's identity and occupation flow through his father. My father's work was teaching, but he'd broken away from it to serve the king, taking the title of Special Advisor. Unfortunately, he died without forging a path that I could follow. Never in my wildest dreams could I have imagined how quickly his death would fling my ladder from the wall, toppling my future. From the muddy hole in which I landed, I was lucky to secure my employment with the merchant. He had no sons, and no paternal affection either. No doubt, he saw in me what he saw in the widows—desperation, and an opportunity to take advantage. Slowly, my soul had shrunk to accept this injustice—until now.

My gaze went south, taking in the Royal City and the countryside beyond. My father loved the nation of Tuva. He was a curator of its history, treating names, dates, and events like an eternal record meant to outlive the earth. What if I could attach my name to an extraordinary accomplishment?

"When can I start?" I asked.

"We'll perform an induction ceremony tomorrow at noon. The day after that, we'll travel together to The Crucible. We'll make our plans there."

Looking out over the sea, I watched a swarm of seagulls spiraling in the breeze. At a certain point, they glistened white, the sun sparkling off their feathers. I looked at my arms, where goosebumps had suddenly appeared.

Thoren noticed my smirk, "What are you grinning about?" he asked.

"Nothing."

CHAPTER 2

Standing on the platform in the chapel, I faced Thoren. Behind him, I imagined the people of Tuva, represented by row after row of empty pews. Indeed, the only bench occupied for my induction was the one nearest the platform, where Thoren's advisors sat in starched black robes.

Organ music played before my vow of loyalty could be pronounced. I stood waiting, Thoren sat waiting, and the advisors glared at the platform as if witnessing the beheading of a notorious criminal. Great beads of sweat had gathered on Thoren's forehead and, although he tried to give me a reassuring look, I could see the tension spreading across his face like cracks on plaster. In front of me, the black pack of advisors radiated their disapproval. Even the music sounded like a funeral dirge.

When the organ finally fell silent, the court orator approached the platform with an open book, pronouncing vows one sentence at a time, then waiting for me to repeat his words. When I spoke, I didn't know whether to cast my eyes on the king or his advisors, so I chose instead to speak to the empty seats, the invisible people of Tuva.

When the vows were complete, the book was closed with a reverberating echo. King Thoren rose without looking at me, striding from the platform to the rear door of the chapel, leaving me alone with his advisors. Unaccompanied I wasn't allowed to go through the back door to the parapet walk, so I descended the platform, nodding at the advisors, then hurrying down the central aisle toward the front entrance. Just when I thought I was in the clear, I heard the brisk cadence of starched fabric closing on me from behind.

"A word with you, young man." The sour voice crawled up my back before registering in my ears. Wanting to run for the door, I instead stopped and slowly turned, waiting for the skinny old advisor to approach. "I'm curious," he went on, his words curt and precise, "to learn more about your post. What exactly does a Minister of Agriculture do?"

"I'll be contracting farmers to grow crops for export."

He moved a step closer, only inches from my face, where his words could be smelled as well as heard. "And what qualifies you for such an assignment?"

"Well, I—"

"Certainly not your nobility. Your father was a teacher, after all."

The starched relic spoke the word *teacher* with contempt. I wanted to flatten his pointed nose. My father was indeed a teacher—one of the best in the kingdom. His knowledge of history won him the post with King Kristoffer, who wanted his critical decisions informed by the past. The other advisors on the king's council were members of noble families, many of whom selfishly used their roles to sway the king's decisions in their favor.

"I've spent the last few years bargaining with shepherds," I said, "buying wool for a merchant."

The old man laughed. "And this qualifies you to be Tuva's Minister of Agriculture?"

"I didn't choose that title, but I am capable of the responsibilities. Now if you will excuse me, I have a great deal to do before tomorrow."

"Tomorrow? What happens tomorrow?" He kept moving toward me as I backed away.

"I'm sorry, but if you're interested in the king's plans, you should speak with the king."

"If the king would take the time to confer with his advisors, I'd have no reason to speak to the son of a school teacher, would I?" Then he stuck his finger in my chest. "Hear me on this, young man, even your father would advise against opening a harbor to foreign ships. Search his history books and see if you can make a case for a tiny country like Tuva engaging in such foolishness."

"I need to leave, sir."

While making my exit, I heard his voice from behind. "Remember your oath. You swore to serve Tuva. Don't betray this kingdom!"

I ran down the steps, whispering the advisor's newly invented cuss phrase, "Son-of-a-school-teacher." It had a ring to it.

Not knowing when I'd return home, I moved my things from the small room above the woolen shop. The merchant considered use of this room a portion of my pay—a furnished apartment. An old mattress and a three-legged table were its furnishings. The merchant raised his eyebrows when I gave him the news of my new post. Then he muttered, "You'll likely be back."

Happy to leave my old life behind, I brought my crate of worldly belongings to my old bedroom at my mother's house. I had the remainder of the day to get situated before leaving in the morning for Keenod with King Thoren.

Rummaging through the crate, I found a sling my father bought me when I was eleven. I remembered the man who made it. He traveled from place to place, demonstrating this deadly weapon by exploding clay jugs with nothing more than a pebble. He made it look so easy, but after begging my father for one, I discovered that the stone's speed and my throw's accuracy were at odds. My mother finally confiscated the weapon, trying to save what remained of her windows.

Wondering if my coordination had improved with age, I looked around the room for something that might serve as ammunition. Spotting the untouched bowl of radishes my mother foolishly left for me, I grabbed one and loaded it in the pouch. Spinning the sling, I was hoping to strike the crate from across the room. But as I was about to let the radish fly, my mother pushed open the door. "Put that thing down. Your father isn't here to fix my windows."

I dropped the sling into the crate and continued rummaging for treasures. My mother remained in the doorway. "Now, tell me again about this post. What exactly will you be doing?"

My mother, Hedda Berrit, had little regard for royalty or nobility, blaming the pressures of my father's post for his untimely death. His immense favor with King Kristoffer fueled toxic jealousy among the other advisors, who came from noble families. They undermined his efforts at every turn, continually reminding him of his lowly birth. In truth, I don't know if my father even noticed. A history teacher through and through, he taught those who were willing to listen and ignored those who weren't. My mother, on the other hand, took note of every slight. Her intense loyalty to my father made it difficult for her to hold her tongue, and sometimes she didn't.

"I'll be working with farmers," I told her, still bristling from my earlier conversation with the advisor. But the last thing I wanted was to upset my mother. She knew I was being stingy with information, so I avoided her probing eyes, pretending to still be exploring the crate.

"When will you be leaving?"

"In the morning," I replied, trying to slide on a leather glove that was too small for my hand.

"I see." She backed away from the door to swing it closed.

"Mother . . . How do you think father would feel about all this?"

Leaning against the doorpost, she folded her arms across her chest. "That depends."

"On what?"

"If you inquired of him as your father, or as a teacher."

I laughed. "There's a difference?"

"Jens, your father marveled at you." She smiled a sad smile, looking at the floor to revisit her memories. "You've always been apprehensive, and yet you've been inclined to attempt things in spite of your fear. Your father's only interest was to study and inform. He had no ambition to explore anything other than words on a page. He told me once that he didn't know how to raise a boy like you, other than to give you some tools for your journey. I think you have what he intended to give you." With that, she closed the door, leaving me alone with my thoughts.

That night, my father visited me in a dream. I was a young boy, and he'd brought me to The Crucible to swim and play in the sand. I spent the day transforming the beach into a kingdom, hauling water from the sea in a pail to make the sand suitable for building. My father sat alongside me as an advisor, offering suggestions. But while I was building, the tide came in, leveling my work. I glared pleadingly at my father, expecting him to save the kingdom.

"What have you learned, son?" was all he said.

I couldn't take my eyes off the waves. Finally, my father grabbed hold of my shoulders, turning me to face him. "What have you learned, Jens?"

"Waves are cruel!"

"Yes, but they've given you a new beginning, a chance to start over, to apply what you've learned." Just then, a gigantic wall of water rolled over us, smashing us into the sand. Scrambling to sit up, I gasped for air as I reached for my father. Then my eyes popped open to a room lit pink by the sunrise.

Later that morning, Thoren and I set off in his carriage for The Crucible. I could see where new gravel had filled potholes and ruts, I suppose to make the king's ride more comfortable. It was quite a contrast to my bone-jarring wagon rides on sheep paths, searching for shepherds. The stuffed leather cushions softened the few bumps we did encounter. Inside the carriage, I sat facing Thoren, but our conversation had been sparse. Bedraggled by stress, the king was more interested in sleeping than talking, and when he was awake, he only stared out the window.

Looking to the south, I noticed a farmer harnessed to his mighty horse. Clods of black soil belched from last season's stubble as the man coaxed his beast onward. The spring sun was gaining strength, and it wouldn't be long before planting. It felt too late to get started—like I was already behind in my work. How could I move fast enough to sway their decisions if they were already in their fields?

I interrupted the king's reverie, "How much progress do you hope to make this season? They're already working in their fields."

Thoren's eyes were distant. "I'd rather not discuss this here, Jens. I have my notes in Keenod."

I turned to look out the north-facing window, where the jagged mountains were beginning to subside, melting gradually into foothills. "I'm looking forward to seeing it," I said.

"Seeing what?"

"Your palace, the docks, The Crucible . . . It must excite you to be there, amidst the progress."

Thoren sat up. "You have no idea. The air in the Royal City is no longer suited for my lungs but at the port . . . Well, you'll learn soon enough. We're nearly there."

A few moments later, Thoren cracked open the carriage door and yelled for the driver to stop. Then, swinging the door fully open, he pointed to the northwest where the foothills had disappeared, and the land seemed to fall away into a great void. "We'll ride with the driver the rest of the way," Thoren announced. "You won't want to miss this view."

The two of us climbed up with the driver on the bench. As we neared the rim of The Crucible, the first thing to appear on the horizon was the tranquil sea. I gasped, surprised by the unusual shade of aqua. "Whoa . . . Why is it colored so differently?"

Thoren laughed. "I had the same response the first time I laid eyes on her. It's shallow here—the sun reaches the bottom. She's beautiful, isn't she?"

"She?"

"Ha! I guess I've grown accustomed to listening to sailors. They speak of the sea as their moody wife. She can be frigid and unforgiving, but not here. Here she's friendly."

It was indeed a welcoming color, and unlike the harsh blue that churned far below the cliffs of the Royal City, here a person could wade in its surf.

When we reached The Crucible's rim, we could finally see the smooth terrain from the carriage to the sea. Thoren commanded the driver to pull back the reins so we could enjoy the view from this grand elevation. To our right was an overgrown cart path leading to the nearest coastal village, but now a more prominent road had taken its place, pointing instead to the central town, where a white stone palace gleamed amidst gray shacks in the afternoon sun. The view was breathtaking, as though the entire slope had been turned on a gigantic potter's wheel, gently bending not only to the sea but also to the east and west, forming half a bowl. The scene looked like a child's painting to me, too simple, and the colors exaggerated. This place was overly fashioned for human habitation, unlike the Royal City, where men and mountain goats dwelled together.

"I can guess which village is Keenod," I said.

Thoren smiled, but didn't say another word until we'd arrived at the palace and he'd led me down a long hallway with white stone floors to a nondescript door. "These are my living quarters," he said.

I stepped inside the spacious bedroom, where in front of me, a large window overlooked the port. To my left, a massive fireplace nearly filled the west wall, leaving only enough room for a small bookshelf. The king approached the shelf as if to take down a book, but when he pulled the binding a latch clicked, and the entire shelf swung open. "And this is where I work," he said, extending his hand as a gesture for me to pass through the secret door into his study.

I'd never seen anything like it. The room seemed too large to be a private study. A massive table occupied the center, with only two chairs, one on each side. Floor-to-ceiling windows covered a long wall facing the sea, flooding the room with afternoon sunlight. Outside, a private balcony with a couch gave the king a bird's-eye view of the harbor's activity. The wall we'd passed through shared a two-sided fireplace with the king's bedroom, and the west and south walls were made entirely from slate, covered with chalk scrawling in Thoren's unmistakable handwriting. There were arithmetic calculations spread haphazardly on the back wall, but the sidewall was more orderly, listing objectives in sequence. My name appeared in several places among these objectives, so naturally, I began to study them.

"I'm glad you're eager to get started, Jens, but let's save the work until morning. Tonight we will feast."

The king opened the door to the balcony, and a salty breeze pushed into the room. When I stepped outside, unfamiliar noises met my ears. Beyond the din of the harbor, the rhythmic waves were crashing to shore. Gulls screeched like spoiled children, fighting each other for scraps in the tide and jostling for the best perches on the docks. Shore-men and sailors barked orders at one another, exchanging banter laced with colorful expletives, all of it charged with energy, a symphony of contested progress.

The king closed his eyes, inhaling deeply. "Why is it that I need busyness to find peace? That chaos down there," he said, pointing to the nearest dock, "is like medicine to my soul. This port is Tuva's one artery, Jens, and these ships are our blood."

"How have you accomplished all this?"

The king laughed. "It hasn't been easy. My advisors have no love for this project. In truth, they hate it. All of Tuva's expenditures pass through the advisors, so needless to say, finding the gold to complete the work has been a challenge."

"How then is it going forward?"

The king gave me a wry smile. "Fortunately, I control the army. Pirates abound on these seas, and ship owners pay me handsomely to protect their cargo. Many of these ships come here only to collect my soldiers."

I gave a slight bow to his genius. If nothing else, Thoren was resourceful. But as I thought it through, I could understand the advisors' animosity. They feared Thoren was inviting an invasion by opening our harbor and, to make matters worse, he was funding his project by exporting the very soldiers who were paid to protect Tuva. Thoren must have believed his plan was worth the risk. If our tiny kingdom indeed had one artery, he wasn't about to let his advisors pinch it off. He was leveraging everything for a plan that had my name all over it.

We stood together for a time, watching men unload crates with ropes and pulleys. Finally, Thoren offered me his couch. "Relax for a while," he said. "The air will do you good. I have some things to look after on the docks. The fishermen will be returning with their catch shortly. I'll choose the best of the sea for our supper."

After Thoren left, I stood at the rail surveying his achievements, amazed by what he'd accomplished in the face of opposition. After a while, I heeded the king's suggestion and reclined on his couch, allowing the sea breeze to cool my face. But, try as I might, I couldn't relax. The ship moored to the pier in front of me was incredibly massive. I tried to imagine how many farmers it would take to fill it with crops. What a task. My mind began racing back and forth between Thoren's conflict with his advisors and his lofty expectations of me. But after a while, the warm sun and the rhythmic crashing of waves offered my reluctant soul a measure of relaxation, and I slowly drifted off to sleep.

CHAPTER 3

I heard my name like the tail of an echo. Then it came louder, and I felt my shoulder jostled. Overhead, a gull screeched, and my head sprung from the pillow.

"Hungry?" came the voice again, this time from the same world. I blinked, and Thoren's face came into focus. He was standing over me, nibbling some fish. The balcony door was open, and the savory aroma had followed him out.

"Starving."

When I walked through the door, I was surprised to see Thoren's study transformed into a dining room, his working table cloaked in white linen. Two golden candleholders flickered to life under the patient care of one of the king's servants, who held a flaming wooden splinter to the stubborn wick. The mellow sun was now hiding from the windows, showing its fading presence by an orange sheen on the calming sea. How long had I been napping? The dimming room emboldened the candles to provide a warm yellow glow over the silver serving trays, which held enough food for ten men.

"A feast from the sea," Thoren announced, extending his hand toward the food.

With eyes riveted to the display, I asked, "Was this your business at the harbor?"

"In part. The fishing boats make shore in the afternoon. If you meet them on the beach, you can purchase the best of their catch before they reach the market. It was a good day for the fishermen. Have you eaten from the sea before?"

"Only pickled fish from the commercial district," I replied, approaching the table to get a better look.

Thoren became my guide. White fillets covered the nearest tray. "Cod," he said, pointing. Then, moving his index finger across the table in a sweeping motion, he introduced the other delicacies. "Sea trout, crab, shrimp, and clams."

"I'll need a lesson," I said. "Some of your prisoners are still wearing armor."

"Yes. I'll train you to conquer the shells, but it starts with drink." The king lifted a large decanter, filling two goblets with wine. Handing one to me, he said, "We must keep these full. I have a story for you, and it tells better drunk." Extending his goblet toward me, he offered a toast. "To Tuva's new Minister of Agriculture."

Clanking his goblet, I added, ". . . and to our future."

We drank and Thoren poured more. Pointing to the chair with a view of the sea, he said, "You sit there. I am always privileged to the view. Before long, the moon will come out, and the water will shine like gold."

Thoren took the seat directly across the table, where he could attend to me. Grabbing a crab leg and tearing it from the creature's body, he popped off the claw and wrenched open the pincher, revealing a tuft of white meat. Extending the claw over the table, he instructed me to pull the meat from the shell and dip it in the melted butter. The fibers were sweet and fell open in my mouth. I smiled with delight. I could feel the wine going to work, cloaking my anxieties, bringing my senses to the surface. I hoisted my goblet for another swig, settling in for the king's story. "I'm all ears, Your Majesty."

Thoren reached for the white fish. Ignoring the serving fork, he pulled off a piece with his fingers, dipped it in butter, and raised it over his cocked head before dropping it into his mouth. Chewing impatiently, he reached for his wine to clear his throat. Then he held out his goblet to show me its design, saying, "Do you see these gems?"

I nodded. The orange, somewhat translucent stones were familiar, found in Tuva's mountains. Most women possessed one, dangling from a necklace. They were available in the commercial district at a reasonable price.

The king continued, "I was standing on the dock one day, holding this very goblet, when a merchant approached, obviously from a distant land. His skin was brown, and his beard was like black wool flecked with gray. It was hard to tell his age, but his eyes gleamed with adventure. It's strange how you can see that in a man. 'Your Highness,' he said, 'my name is Akeem. May I inquire of the gems mounted on your chalice?'"

I told him they were found in our mountains and asked why he was interested.

He said he was a merchant, traveling aboard a Saganese ship. He explained that the ship's owner allows him to travel with the crew, buying and selling on his own accord. He pays something for the ship's unused cargo space until the owner can support the entire vessel on his own. Then he boards a new boat and starts the process again. In all, he's helped establish ten ships, filling his own pockets with great wealth.

"He gave me a leather pouch and said he'd pay me handsomely upon his return if I could fill it with the stones. 'I will see what I can do,' I said. In truth, I had them already. My gold miners find them in the mountains and hold them aside. I sell them to the jewelers in the commercial district. But I didn't tell him I had piles of them, wanting him to think them rare."

"Ha! You're a merchant at heart."

Thoren filled our empty goblets. Then he grabbed a smooth rock that sat on the platter and violently pounded one of the severed crab legs. Pulling out a long chord of meat, he ripped it in half, giving me the larger piece. I beat him to the saucer of melted butter, nearly knocking over the small candle keeping it warm. Then I punched the crab into my mouth in a single bite.

Thoren laughed, "You learn quickly, Jens."

As delicious as the food tasted, I didn't want to be distracted by eating. I placed an elbow on the table, resting my chin on my hand as a signal for Thoren to continue. "What happened next?"

"Nothing happened for quite some time. Then one day, Akeem found me again on the docks, 'King Thoren,' he called, 'Have you collected the gems? Your payment awaits onboard.' He was pointing to the ship moored to the very dock on which I was standing. I went to the palace to fetch the leather pouch, which had long been filled with the orange stones and met him on the pier. I expected gold or maybe gems in return, but I did not expect what I received."

"What did you receive?"

"It wasn't one thing, but many. The old merchant was wise enough to seize the opportunity to lure me into a trading relationship, to show me his wares, so to speak. He brought me strange things from distant kingdoms. Akeem trades with a prince from the east, who collects gems of every kind. The prince was unfamiliar with our orange stone, and was willing to part with a great deal to acquire the pouch."

"What did he give you?"

"The rug under this table, for one thing."

I looked down at the tightly woven carpet extending a handbreadth beyond the table legs. I'd already admired its intricate weaving. I knew something of rugs from my days with the woolen merchant, but this one stood out—its reds and blues stunningly vibrant, and its design intensely detailed.

"Very nice."

Eager to steal my attention away from the rug, Thoren continued, "He also gave me an array of musical instruments. The prince is said to have sixty wives, who dance for him to strange music. Their dancing is strong medicine to soften his moods. Akeem said there are even dances to provoke desire."

"Have you played them?"

"The instruments? I have no music in me, Jens. You know that." I laughed at the thought of Thoren trying to sit still long enough to learn an instrument. "No, I've not found anyone to play them. What good would it do? They would only play the music of Tuva." Thoren again filled the goblets and grabbed four clams, throwing two on my plate. Then he wedged a knife in the slit separating the two halves and pried one open, using the knife to stab the meat. This time, Thoren ate it himself. Smirking in defiance, he said, "I'll not feed you like a baby anymore."

Clumsily, I went to work on one of the clams, now feeling the full effect of the wine. The seam of the shell seemed to move about, my knife staggering over the clam's exterior like a sailor on a storm-tossed deck. Finally, I found the slit, but stabbed overzealously, poking the blade through the clam and sticking the point into the palm of my hand.

Thoren roared with laughter. "I've given you one assignment—against a defenseless clam and you've stabbed yourself."

As I held my hand to the candlelight to see the extent of the wound, a woman slipped quietly into the room through Thoren's secret door. She was wrapped in light blue silk from head to toe, the sheer fabric separated between her forehead and nose, revealing only her dark brown eyes and some black hair, which shimmered in the candlelight as much as the silk. A lower opening in the silk exposed the brown skin of her stomach, her naval decorated with an inset gem. Her eyes were both sad and beautiful, and she kept them downcast as she approached with a decanter of wine, the silk slipping over and around her curves, which themselves danced unrestrained beneath the fabric. Spellbound, I watched while she placed the wine on the table, retreating then like an evening breeze into Thoren's private chamber.

Looking down, I noticed my blood leaving a scarlet stain on the white tablecloth. When I looked up, Thoren was extending his handkerchief with a devilish smirk. "She was also part of my payment from Akeem."

"What? One of the prince's sixty wives?"

Thoren widened his eyes as if sharing my confusion, "His wife? His daughter? His enemy's wife? I don't know. She doesn't speak our language. If I had someone to play the instrument, I'd have her dance for us. Perhaps a calming dance for you, though. Your desire seems already aroused."

The thought of men trading gems for a woman twisted my stomach, but her fragrance lingered in the room, tickling the vile recesses of my imagination. Recollecting the details of Thoren's story, I asked, "Was that the extent of the trade then—the girl, the rug, and the instruments?"

"No, there was more—spices, tea, medicines—things Akeem thought would sell in our commercial district. I give him credit. He netted me like a fish."

Our conversation continued well into the night, Thoren sharing stories he'd heard from ship owners and sailors. Clearly his appetites were propelling Tuva into uncharted waters. As enjoyable as it was to listen to his exploits, in the back of my mind, I wondered where this would lead. Did the lusts of their king advance all kingdoms?

I thought of Thoren's father, King Kristoffer, who'd intentionally yoked himself to my father's advice, steering the kingdom by what he considered a reliable chart—history. Unlike his father, Thoren was an explorer, the kind of pioneer who views history as an unnecessary bridle, a constriction of instincts. Still, at times his unveiling of the future poured forth earnestly, logically, with no discernible self-interest, causing my devotion to him as my friend and king to ebb and flow. It seemed a dangerous game he was playing, but the picture he painted was compelling, and I felt the pride of his trust in his invitation to add my brushstrokes. It was the first time I felt important since my father's death.

When the second decanter was empty and each of the trays was disturbed by our nibbling, Thoren stood, wobbling to a gradual balance. "It's time to retire," he announced. "We have a great deal of work to do tomorrow. Let's get some sleep."

He led me through the secret door into his unlit bedchamber, where I discreetly surveyed the darkness, hoping to catch another glimpse of the mysterious woman. In front of the king's bed stood a wooden table holding a large brass dish where a glowing ember was sending up a wisp of the fragrant smoke that held her aroma. The light from the ember was just enough to obscure my eyes from whatever lay beyond—a stalking tiger, or a scared fawn. The thought of her peering at me through the darkness sent a cold chill through my body, and I reluctanly gave up my search.

Once Thoren had me in the hallway, he summoned a servant, and a weary-looking man escorted me to my room.

CHAPTER 4

I was startled awake by Thoren's pounding on my door, his impatient voice jeering through the wood, "Jens, we need to get to work!"

I sat up, disoriented. The bedroom was sunlit, and my head was pounding. I quickly dressed and shuffled down the hall, finding Thoren's door open. Inside, the king was standing by his clever bookshelf, waiting. Seeing me, he opened the secret door, allowing my passage before encasing us together inside.

"Sorry for sleeping late," I said. "The wine—"

The king lifted his hand to halt further explanation, and nodded toward a plate with a sweet pastry. "I brought you breakfast. You can eat while we work."

We sat across from one another at the table, but this time Thoren had my back to the sea, probably so I'd have a view of his slate wall. While staring at my breakfast, the king slid a dirty beet across the table. I didn't know what to make of it. Surely, he didn't expect me to eat it.

"Thank you, but the pastry will be enough."

Thoren squinted curiously, then snorted in laughter. "You can be so witless, Jens. That's not your breakfast. It's your future."

"My future?"

Reaching across the table, he grabbed the beet and dangled it from its long root. "Do you know what beets sell for in the commercial district?"

Although I'd never bought one, I prided myself in tracking the price of everything sold in the commercial district. It was a game for me. Pulling some coins from my pocket, I selected the appropriate sum and tossed them on the table. "This would purchase six. More when they're in season."

Thoren smiled. "Impressive." Then, reaching for his coins, he pulled together a sum worth three times what I'd presented, slapping them on the table next to mine. "Akeem will pay this for the same six."

"Why would he pay such a price for a dirty vegetable?"

"Because, Jens, they aren't vegetables everywhere."

"I don't understand."

Thoren held the beet in his open hand like a giant ruby. As if enchanted by its splendor, he spoke his words with his eyes fixed on his treasure. "Akeem tells me of a kingdom where they are used to dye fabric a deep red. He tells me of another kingdom where healers grind them into medicine to soothe the stomach. In a third kingdom, they're used for cosmetics, making their women more beautiful. The juice is even pressed by diviners in one far-off place to concoct a love potion. Akeem told me it's the favorite nectar of their goddess of love."

I tore off the tiniest crumb from my pastry and held it on my tongue, not sure if my stomach was prepared for me to eat. Thoren seemed to be waiting for my soul to soar with his, to recognize the potential of his discovery, but my head was still pounding, my thoughts running thick and slow. My apathy seemed to puncture his trance. "The point is, Jens, Akeem will sell Tuva's beets at some ghastly price for things other than stew."

Remembering all the evenings of my youth, when I'd sat alone at the supper table, defiantly refusing to choke down a bowl of my mother's soup, I said, "I agree they're worthless to eat, but why do these kingdoms need Tuva's beets? Can't they grow their own?"

"Yes, of course, but Akeem assures me they're nothing like ours—not as big, or as red. Beets thrive in our soil, Jens."

Then Thoren turned in his chair, grabbing a burlap sack and dumping its contents on the table. What fell out had the shape of beets, but they were smaller and pinker than the impressive Tuvan specimen standing in their midst. "These were grown in the East. Akeem brought them to show me the difference."

"How many of ours could Akeem sell?"

Thoren's eyes lit. "Who knows? He seems confident he can sell whatever we supply. I'd like to fill my ship with them."

"Your ship? The ship that's now under construction?"

Thoren pointed to the west. "The Saganese craftsmen are working on her as we speak, not a mile from here."

"I'm curious to know how you convinced the king of Sagan to build you a ship."

"Sagan is mostly coast and mountains. They possess the most wretched soil. The king owns cattle and horses that are a nuisance to feed in the winter. I offered to provide him five years of winter hay."

"In exchange for a ship?"

Thoren nodded. "The king has commanded his men to finish her by fall so we can deliver the first installment of hay before winter. Not a bad trade, in my estimation."

"No doubt. But how will you acquire the hay?"

Thoren's brow lifted. "How will I acquire it? That's a foolish question coming from you."

"Oh . . . I see. I'll need to convince the farmers to sell you their hay."

"Yes," said Thoren, dangling the beet again by its root, "and you'll also need to convince them to grow these. Offer a premium over what the local merchant's pay if you must."

I finished his thought, "Enough to coax them to dedicate a field or two without giving away too much. I'm familiar with that game."

The two of us spent the day together, Thoren schooling me. He had an impressive mind for commerce, using the slate wall to formulate five-year projections. They were aggressive, very aggressive, but not impossible. There was nothing illogical in his reasoning—if things went just so. The greatest challenge in my mind was how to get started.

Finally, the king set down his chalk, allowing me an opportunity to voice my concerns. "Thoren, the farmers are already in their fields. Is it realistic to think we can make much progress this season?"

Thoren's face signaled his irritation. "Of course. Progress will always be contested—if not by time, then by people. Look around, Jens. This village would still be a collection of shacks if I'd respected the obstacles. I've built this port under far worse circumstances than you'll ever face."

"I know, but—"

"No *buts*, Jens. All my work is for naught if we have nothing to trade."

Surprised by his intensity, I sat speechless, suddenly understanding the difference between a minister and an advisor. As an advisor, my father was valued for his opinion. But my opinion held no value at all—especially when it flew in the face of results. I was expected to get my hands dirty.

My mind raced to think of a single accomplishment to qualify me as the kind of man to take the bull by its horns and wrestle it to the ground. I wasn't like Thoren. I felt like an imposter. Then, from the deep recesses of my thoughts, my mother's words came back to me: *"Jens, your father marveled at you. You've always been apprehensive, and yet you've been inclined to attempt things in spite of your fear. He told me once he didn't know how to raise a boy like you, other than to give you some tools for your journey. I think you have what he intended to give you."*

Lost in my reverie, I didn't notice Thoren's growing impatience. Finally, he broke my spell by leaning over the table and growling at me through teeth that were nearly clenched. "Are you the right man, Jens, or shall I find another?"

His words set me on edge. The question he was asking didn't seem to be, "Was I *the man*?" But instead, "Was I *a man*?" Propelled forward in my chair, and forgetting who I was talking to, I narrowed the distance between our faces. "I'm as much a man as you, Thoren." I could feel the muscles twitching around my jaw. "I am not looking for a way out. I'm looking for a way forward."

We stared at each other for a quiet moment, our breathing labored. Then Thoren leaned back and mellowed his tone. "Well, you'll be glad to hear that I've been working ahead of you for quite some time."

"What do you mean by that?"

Thoren hesitated. Then, lowering his voice, as if to skirt the ears of an invisible listener, he said, "I'll need your promise to keep a secret."

The room was silent for an uncomfortable moment while he waited for my promise, but I just sat there stubbornly, not able to release my anger as quickly as he. Finally, I gave him a reluctant nod, which was enough to set him pacing alongside the table. "I've been involved in certain . . . *commercial activities.*"

Waiting for him to continue, I suddenly realized his confession was made. Apparently, a king shouldn't also be a merchant. But Thoren had already confessed to renting Tuva's army to fund his port, and selling our jewels in exchange for personal keepsakes—not the least of which was a woman—so I didn't understand the distinction.

"Is it forbidden as a king to conduct commerce on your own accord?"

"Not expressly, but it would be viewed by many as a conflict of interest. In any case, it isn't my subjects that worry me. It's my damned advisors. I've told you how they scrutinize my every move. The only power they possess is to approve my spending, and that practice goes back to Tuva's beginning. Dah! I wish King Tuva would have populated his army with peasants. If he could have foreseen what an anchor these noble families would become . . . Did you know that I'm still bound each year by that ancient covenant to pay them an allotment of gold for supplying fighting men to King Tuva?"

"Do they still supply soldiers?"

"No! Not for a hundred years. Those damn advisors pretend they're protecting Tuva by denying my spending at the port, but they're only protecting their purses."

"So, you've found other ways to fund your port."

Thoren nodded. "Jens, I am like a damn beggar, scrambling to find the money to build a respectable kingdom. A kingdom needs a king, not a castrated bull." He gripped the backrest of his chair, gathering himself before continuing. "Do you understand why I need your discretion?"

I felt like I was standing on a ledge, gathering the nerve to leap a chasm. Whatever Thoren shared with me now, if I held it secret, would make me his accomplice, the consequences for which I couldn't imagine. No doubt, it would be a long fall. On the other hand, he said he'd been working ahead of me, and I needed that information to be successful.

Thoren must have recognized my dilemma because, uninvited, he launched into his story. "Jens, three years ago, I began sending Tuvan soldiers with Gladonese ships to protect their cargo from pirates."

"Yes, I know. You told me that already."

The king held up his hand to gain my silence before continuing. "There was a man from Gladon on that first ship—a trader. He'd traveled the orient and discovered a plow without wheels that can be pulled by a single animal. He told me the Orientals use it to work their wet fields. The secret of the plow's ease through the soil is the curve of its shear. Our blunt shears need a team of four draft animals to break the ground.

Remembering the farmer that I'd watched from the carriage only the day before, I interrupted, "I saw such a plow yesterday."

"Yes, they're now everywhere in Tuva. I purchased the design—just some drawings on scroll from the Gladonese trader. Then I anonymously enlisted a blacksmith in Tinsdal to build one for me."

"Anonymously?"

"Yes, I'll get to that. Anyway, the plow seemed to work, so I had the blacksmith make a few more, asking that he distribute them, free of charge, to some prominent farmers to try in their fields."

"It must have been a success."

"More than I could've imagined. Word spread like wildfire. Farmers travel to Tinsdal from every corner of Tuva to purchase this plow. I think they number their sons and their beasts and purchase a plow for every pair. Several fields can now be prepared at once. In any case, the blacksmith pays me a certain amount for each plow he sells."

"How do you keep track?"

"That's tricky. As I told you, I've done this anonymously. I've never met the blacksmith, and he doesn't know I'm the recipient of his payments. He delivers the money to the innkeeper across the street from his shop. The innkeeper is the brother to my port manager. I compensate him to collect my payments and to keep a watchful eye on the blacksmith. Essentially, he counts the plows leaving the blacksmith's shop."

"And your advisors know nothing of this?"

Thoren laughed. "Well, they know about the plow. They've discussed it in council. They think it's a Tuvan invention. In fact, they cite it as an example of our ingenuity. Ha! It's all I can do to hold my tongue. I want so badly to tell them the idea floated into my port."

As the king spoke, I began to grow impatient, thinking he was only using the story to boast, giving me a lofty example to follow. As he filled his lungs for what I guessed would be more bragging, I interrupted, "—and how is this to help me?"

For a moment, it appeared like Thoren might disregard my interruption and go on with his story in whatever meandering way he'd planned to tell it, but then he drew back his breath, changing tactics, becoming more direct. "John is the name of the blacksmith. His shop is in Tinsdal—the heart of Tuva's richest farmland. He's endeared himself to the farmers, and obviously, he owes his prosperity to me."

"But he doesn't know it's you."

Ignoring me, the king continued, "I've penned a letter as his anonymous benefactor, asking for his assistance in identifying and recruiting farmers to grow crops for export. He probably thinks I'm a merchant, having something to do with the port."

A ray of hope entered my soul. I felt bad for mistaking the motive behind Thoren's story. "Thank you," I said. "That letter was a good idea. I'll need the blacksmith's help. When shall I set off for Tinsdal?"

My gratitude seemed to renew Thoren's goodwill. "First thing in the morning. You can take a room at the inn across the street from the blacksmith shop. That inn is another of my commercial interests. It can be your base of operation while you're away."

"What? You own the inn?"

Thoren's chest puffed again. "I am afraid so—a share of it, anyway. The innkeeper's an odd fellow. He has an inflated opinion of his importance to me as a spy, but I've come to trust him less than the blacksmith. He approached me a year ago, asking for an investment. He needed to add rooms to his inn. The number of farmers traveling to Tinsdal to acquire the new plow is staggering, and he couldn't house them all. I really had no choice but to make the investment. He's the only man, besides you and his brother, who knows of my connection with the plow, and I didn't want him soliciting investors for fear he'd let my secret slip."

"Loose lips sink ships," I replied, quoting the old proverb.

"Yes, well, my ship hasn't even floated yet, and I am not about to have an innkeeper sink it. But I fear I've made a mistake—I should have cut him a straight loan, but I let him talk me into a half-share in his inn. Now, instead of being repaid, I am entitled to half the profits. I think he hides revenue from me. It's probably a trivial sum, but still, I don't trust him."

Thoren's growing paranoia struck me. I'd never seen it before. Suddenly, an impish spirit came over me. Thinking myself witty, I said, "I suppose you could hire the stable boy to spy on the innkeeper while he spies on the blacksmith."

"Do you make light of me?" Thoren snapped, his eyes suddenly fiery.

"I only meant it as a joke."

"This isn't a joke."

A long pause ensued, Thoren waiting for an apology, and my stubborn soul refusing him the courtesy. After all, he thought nothing of poking fun at me—and now he'd pulled me into his sticky web with the appearance of corruption. At that moment, I didn't feel I owed him my manners. Finally, I asked, "Are we finished?"

Thoren's eyes narrowed a little, but then his irritation seemed to dissipate. "Yes, we're finished. Now get some sleep. I'll be pounding on your door much earlier tomorrow. I have a surprise for you."

CHAPTER 5

That night, I flailed under a ragged blanket of worry, my state of half-sleep keeping my problems fresh and unsolvable. Thoren's question repeated itself over and over in my mind. *Was I the man?* A better man would have simply confessed he wasn't. He'd make his own way, create his own adventure. Now, in the throes of the night, my commission seemed like a clever trap, baited with my desire for importance, and it was too late to free myself.

I thought of the polished altar rail in the Royal City, wondering if Thoren had indeed steered clear of it—even in his private moments. Was there never an occasion to bend his knees before the Almighty? Did he ever seek a will higher than his hunger? I wondered if I'd forfeited my right to pray by throwing in with him. I wanted to believe that Thoren's grand scheme had at least a seed of Divine inspiration, but it didn't seem likely. Staring up at the ceiling, I realized there wasn't even a chapel under this roof—just a slate wall with the king's plan drawn in chalk.

In the wee hours of the morning, long before sunrise, I remembered Thoren's promise to wake me early. My words pierced the dark room, "No, you won't." Throwing off the blanket, I slid from the bed to my knees. Kneeling wordlessly, I waited to see if courage would enter my legs before anxiety stirred me to action. The great enemies held each other at bay, neither making a decisive move, and the chapel-less roof seemed to shield me from any Divine thing falling from above. My knees finally grew sore, so I stood and groped the darkness to find my pants. Remembering the wall-mounted torch across the hall, I found the door and pulled it open for some light. To my surprise, in the doorway was a neat pile of clothes, complete with shiny new boots.

"This must be the surprise Thoren had for me," I whispered to myself.

Hurriedly, I dressed with the door open, throwing on tan trousers, tight to the calf, designed to be tucked inside the proud black boots, which rose nearly to my knees. The white linen shirt had small brass buttons descending from its collar to my chest, over which I slid a blue jacket with two rows of its own shiny buttons. Cut to the waist in front, the coat then angled down to create two blue flaps over my buttocks. I felt ridiculous— like an imposter who'd stripped a dead soldier of his uniform. But admittedly, my other clothes had grown threadbare, and my wardrobe would be an embarrassment to the king.

With still no hint of the morning in the windows, I decided to walk the empty halls, trying out the boots. When I reached what seemed to be a ballroom, the sound of my footsteps amplified with the higher ceiling, and I judged my gait too timid. So I upped the determination of my stride, walking the perimeter of the room until the walls echoed with confidence. Like it or not, I had to be the man.

Shortly after the pale glow of morning smudged the horizon, Thoren opened his door and found me sitting in the hallway, packed and ready to travel. Startled, he said, "Jens. What are you—Ah, you found the clothes. What do you think?"

"I'm growing used to them."

Thoren smiled. "Well, the clothes are only part of the surprise. Come with me." We took a couple of steps, and then Thoren abruptly stopped. "Wait, I need to get something from my study." He stingily reopened his door—barely enough to squeeze through, but like lips parting, the room exhaled the woman's exotic fragrance, smelling to me like blue silk. Thoren quickly reemerged, carrying a leather pouch and some scrolled parchments.

We walked together down the long hallway, exiting the palace through the servant's door on the east where a cobblestone driveway led to the stable. In front of the stable, two groomers were working in the strange glow of a posted lantern mingling with the first orange beams of the sun. The men were fitting a wagon to a stately pair of horses, the muscled creatures appearing mythical in the dramatic light. Thoren smiled and extended his arm in presentation.

"This is the rest of your surprise."

The massive bodies of the horses were rich brown with manes and tails that might have been blonde at midday but were presently collecting the dawn's rays and glowing orange. One of the beasts pawed at the cobblestone with an eager hoof. They looked battle-ready, and the wagon seemed too small for even one of them.

Thoren approached the apparition, and I followed reluctantly. If my clothing didn't stir the attention of onlookers, I was sure to be a spectacle now.

"I had this wagon crafted especially for you," said the king, sliding his hand along the glossy black sideboard until it reached the round Tuvan crest affixed near the driver's seat.

"I'm used to a decrepit cart and an old mule," I mumbled. "I don't know what to think of this."

Thoren set the leather pouch and the scrolls atop the driver's bench. Pinching one of the parchments, he said, "These are maps of Tuva. They're the same maps the tax collector's use, with property lines and names." Moving his hand to the leather pouch, he continued, "There's enough money here to cover your expenses." Then he set his face toward the rising sun. "If you leave now, you'll make Tinsdal by evening."

Noticing my reluctance, Thoren relieved me of my bag, tossing it over the sideboard into the bed. Then he slapped the driver's seat, coaxing me to mount. I climbed onto the bench and one of the groomers handed me the reins. Through a bushy white mustache, his invisible mouth gave me instructions. "She lists to the right a little. That one's a bit bigger." He was pointing to the ass-end of the horse furthest from me. Then, backing away from the wagon, the three men waited for me to flick the reigns. I did, and the stately creatures set off in a high-stepping trot, as though aware of the king's presence.

Time went by unnoticed as I traveled south, my mind too full of thoughts to pay attention to the scenery. The horses had stopped showing off by the time I reached the rim of The Crucible. After that distance, they must've discerned they weren't harnessed for a parade and graduated to a more efficient stride. The sound was soothing, the rhythmic thumping of hooves stabbing the loose gravel, each step followed by the squeak of the leather harness stretching and retracting to yoke the powerful beasts in a unified effort. In obedience to the groomer, I gave constant attention to the rein in my left hand, seemingly reprimanding the weaker horse for the stronger one's power. I was amazed that the slightest tug could again set the wagon on course.

What if they decide to rebel against the leather and each go their own way? The thin straps could never rein-in a wayward horse. The bit and bridle were mere suggestions to their strength, relying on the creatures' tractable nature—a nature very different than Thoren's. He was an intractable king, spurning the wishes of his advisors, who were now realizing that their covenantal reins were an illusion. And here I was, harnessed with Thoren, the two of us trying to pull Tuva into the modern age, I the weaker horse.

By dusk, I'd made Tinsdal, where a collection of shops lined both sides of the gravel road. The village was the liveliest of any I'd passed along the way, their recent prosperity displayed by freshly painted storefronts. Unfortunately, my destination rested on the south end, forcing me to drive the wagon down the town's main street at the very time the merchants were closing their shops for the day. According to Thoren, visitors frequented Tinsdal, but the attention I received from onlookers reminded me that, even with a thick coat of dust, I was no ordinary traveler. Of course, the damn horses noticed the attention too and resumed their high-stepping, happy to have finally reached their parade route.

At the inn, I steered the team onto a grassy path leading to a shelter in the back. The moment the stable boy heard the commotion, his head spun, and he came running, fearlessly confronting the horses and blocking their way forward. The young man's baby-face and narrow shoulders belied his long legs and man-sized feet. His growth must have been recent because his pants failed to cover his ankles. Without looking at me, the boy nodded toward the inn, yelling, "I've got them, sir!"

"Let me get my bag before you stable them."

The boy looked at me as if I'd broken a rule. "I'll bring your bag to your room."

Reaching into the leather pouch, I pulled out a coin, probably worth a day's wages, tossing it to the young man before dismounting. His eyes lit, and his smile revealed two rows of perfectly crooked teeth. "Thank you!"

Approaching the door, I wondered if the purse of gold belonged to the king or me. In all our planning, we hadn't discussed my pay. Thoren didn't think like that. He considered everything his; nothing beyond reach. A wage would seem foreign to him. I, on the other hand, liked to see how far I could stretch things. I wondered if I scrimped to conserve the gold if I'd be allowed to keep what remained. No, I needed to stop thinking that way. My mind had grown used to scarcity, but there'd be no compassion from Thoren if I failed my assignment without employing all my resources. The stable boy was ample proof that a coin could buy a friend, and I needed friends. Reminding myself that I no longer worked for the thrifty merchant, I resolved to be uncomfortably generous. Before opening the door to the inn, I pulled out two more coins.

The foyer smelled like fresh lumber, reminding me of King Thoren's equity stake in the inn's expansion. There were still unfinished areas—lath walls constructed without the fineries of plaster or paint. Oddly, portraits adorned the unpainted walls, as if trying to hide their nakedness. It looked as though occupancy had trumped completion. Like the stable boy, the inn was making do with clothes that didn't quite fit.

The innkeeper appeared anxious to greet me. "Are you Jens?"

"I am."

"My name is Heskett, Emil Heskett. I've been waiting for you to arrive." His voice sounded too formal against the rough backdrop. "We have a cut of lamb simmering in the kitchen. You may dine here or in your room." He pointed to a spacious but stark eating area with tables and chairs strewn about in no particular order. Then, leaning forward, he whispered, "I've arranged for a courier to be available to shuttle correspondence between us and King Thoren."

"Us? The king didn't say anything to me about a courier."

Acting as though he didn't hear me, his formal voice returned. "Your room awaits. I think you'll find it to your liking. Let me know if you need anything."

"Thank you," I replied, placing the coins on the desk. "What room will I occupy?"

The innkeeper glared at the coins, frowning. "The king himself is compensating me for my trouble. You may keep your coins." He slid them back across the desk as though repulsed by the paltry offering.

With my façade of sophistication dismantled, I returned the coins to the pouch. The man considered himself at least my equal. "I'll dine in my room. What room did you say?"

"I didn't say. I'll keep you nearby." He pulled a key from a line of crude hooks on the wall behind him but refused to place it in my outstretched hand until he was finished with me. Pointing toward a narrow hallway on the far side of the dining room, he said, "First door on your right. Breakfast at six. What is your plan for tomorrow?"

I hesitated, remembering Thoren's comment about this nosy man's inflated sense of importance. "I'll cross that bridge in the morning. Right now, I'm anxious to eat and get some sleep."

"Of course. I'm sure you're tired—probably not used to this kind of work. You can let me know in the morning."

My face grew hot. Had Thoren commissioned his spy to keep tabs on me? Thinking back to our discussion, he was intent that I make this my base of operations, but he also confessed that he didn't trust this Emil Heskett. Maybe he didn't trust me either.

Tainted with contempt, I critically surveyed the unfinished walls, wondering what Emil had done with the king's money. In my mind, I practiced an accusatory sentence. *Perhaps you should be more worried about your plaster and less concerned about my plans.* No, I couldn't afford to pick a fight. But I wasn't going to share anything with this snitch either, and if he pressed me, I'd have some questions for him.

Suddenly, I was sickened by the whole affair. We were like two scrawny roosters, squabbling over a status neither of us deserved. I reached for the key that dangled from Emil's fingers.

CHAPTER 6

I held back a biscuit and some jam from supper so I'd have breakfast without leaving my room. No doubt the innkeeper expected me in his dining hall, but I had no appetite for his company. Poking my head through the window, I had a partial view of the blacksmith shop, obscured only to the north by the corner of the inn. Straddling the sill so I could lean out, I watched for the blacksmith while I ate. The morning air felt unusually warm on my bare foot, reminding me that spring was advancing and I needed to move fast. My hope for success rested on this meeting.

Within minutes, three men entered the shop, each too young to be the proprietor. Thinking that perhaps the blacksmith was already inside, I started to climb down from the window, but then I heard whistling and the drumming of boots marching down the boardwalk from the north. I froze like a hunter in a tree, waiting for my prey to emerge. When I saw him, I knew it was the blacksmith—barrel-chested, wearing a leather skull cap with curly hair protruding from the back. When he reached the door to his shop, he turned toward the street, addressing two young men walking his way.

"On time today," he yelled. "You boys musta left some ale in Ruby's barrel last night." Waiting for them to reach the door, he grabbed one of them by the shoulder and shook him. "Maybe I can get an honest day's work outa ya."

The young men seemed to welcome his attention, one taunting the other. "Tell him, Luke. Tell him why you left early." Then, not waiting for Luke to answer, he continued, "Ruby sent him home, John. She quit serving him. Got sick of him lookin' down her dress."

"S'not it," Luke protested, "I just wasn't thirsty no more." They laughed, and the bantering continued as the two followed the blacksmith inside. Climbing down from the window, I rummaged through my bag until I found the letter that Thoren had penned as the blacksmith's anonymous benefactor. Sealed with wax, I had no way of reading the note, but I was hoping the words contained enough power to secure the blacksmith's cooperation.

Avoiding the innkeeper, I pulled on my boots and escaped the room through the window, trotting alongside the building like a thief. When I reached the street, I could see the little village waking up—the merchants busying themselves with brooms near their doors. I started to cross over to the blacksmith shop in front of an oncoming wagon but then thought better of it, realizing its speed. Instead of passing me, the wagon's driver pulled back on the reins. "Whoa now!" he yelled. The horse threw back its head and stiffened its legs to obey the unreasonable command. When the dust cleared, I noticed a plow in the back of the wagon.

The farmer hurried inside, and within seconds walked out again with the blacksmith on his heels. I stayed on the far side of the street, watching, leaning against a wooden column. Upset by his inconvenience, the farmer was nearly yelling. "I was breaking some new ground," he said. "Hit a rock, and she snapped like a bad tooth."

The blacksmith studied the shear. "We can fix it before you finish breakfast," he said, nodding toward the inn, and bringing their attention across the street to where I was standing. The blacksmith's eyes narrowed a bit when he noticed me watching.

"Na, I'll stay and help," replied the farmer.

The blacksmith squared off with the man. "Andrew, I'm gonna put one of my boys on it, and you'll just stand over him and make him nervous." Then he slapped him on his shoulder. "Now go on over and get some breakfast. I'll send someone when it's ready."

At a loss for words, the farmer reluctantly shuffled across the street, passing me as he entered the inn. Alone now, the blacksmith threw a final glance my way before re-entering his shop. I swallowed hard and crossed the street.

After slipping through the door, my eyes needed a moment to adjust to the dim shop. Two small windows on each end of the building produced barely enough light for an unaccustomed eye to see from one end to the other. My father had brought me to a blacksmith shop in the Royal City once for a lesson in weaponry, and I learned that the craft requires a degree of darkness to discern the necessary shades of oranges and yellows in the hot iron, something to do with forging at precisely the right time.

Once I could see, I spotted the blacksmith in the corner, giving instructions for repairing the plow to one of his apprentices. The other young men were about their work, drawing, forming, and punching iron plates into curved steel plow shears. On the far side of the room, a man was grabbing the finished shears from a pile, one at a time, sharpening them on a large stone grinding wheel spun by his right foot pumping a wooden pedal. Slowly, I approached the blacksmith as he was finalizing his orders to his underling. "Let me see your work before you bring him back over here, and let's sharpen it for him."

The young man didn't realize I was standing behind him. Without looking where he was going, he turned on his heels and piled into me. "Sorry," he grunted, taking a moment to inspect my uniform before leaving to fetch the broken plow.

The blacksmith wasted no time with pleasantries. "My name is John. What can I do for you?" he asked, giving me a sideways glance while scanning the shop with a critical eye. With the young men on the clock, John's playful spirit had been cast aside like a jacket too warm for the sweltering room, replaced now with the brashness of industry.

"My name is Jens. I work for the king. May I have a few moments of your time?"

The blacksmith squared off with me, just as he had moments earlier with the farmer. "The king? What's this about?"

I handed him the letter, which he quickly opened and read to himself with some difficulty in the dim room. Then, inspecting the parchment, first front, then back, he asked, "Who's this from?"

"The man who owns the drawings for the plow."

The blacksmith took a step closer. "What does he have to do with the king?"

"As you probably know, sir, the king is developing his port in Keenod, and many will stand to profit from trading there. Tuva has good soil, and there's an opportunity for growing crops for export."

The blacksmith handed the letter back. "I still don't understand what this has to do with me?"

"Well, you know the farmers, and—"

"And they'll do what I say. Is that what you think?"

I took a step backward, regaining a comfortable distance. "Your benefactor thought you might be willing to help me."

"And who is that?"

When I didn't answer, the blacksmith turned away, saying, "*Benefactor* . . . That's quite a word." Then he spun and looked me square in the eyes. "What makes him my benefactor?"

"Well, the plow. You clearly don't lack work."

The blacksmith gave me an unhappy smile. "Yes, the plow . . ."

Surveying his shop again, he let his eyes settle momentarily on each of his apprentices in turn. The crowded room was filling with smoke, muting the white glare of the three forges. The fires looked like demonic mouths with tongues of orange iron flapping in their center, pinched by the tongs of busy men. Finally, the blacksmith suggested we go outside.

Once outdoors, the chirping of birds and the soothing radiance of the morning sun softened the blacksmith's countenance. He leaned against the side of the building and scratched his whiskers, staring up at the sky. With his sleeves rolled to his elbows, I watched his forearm muscles dance as he scratched his face. Thankfully, his rugged frame was offset now by a gentler voice.

"My father was a blacksmith," he said, "and his father before him. I became an apprentice at thirteen, learning my father's secrets—secrets handed down from one generation to the next. We've lived simple lives, my family, not wealthy but respected." He stopped and stroked his beard some more before continuing. "My oldest boy is nine years old today—still too young for this work, but already I have five apprentices."

"I can see that. All this business—is it due to the new plow?"

"It is," he mumbled, looking off in the distance. Then, seemingly waking from a dream, he held up all of the fingers of his right hand. "Five apprentices. Think about that."

"Well, you seem prosperous—and the town, too."

He stared at his shoes. "I don't know . . . I don't know if I'm building my son's future or giving it away. Hopefully he'll step into a successful business, but I fear I might be training his competition. My apprentices are local boys—sons of farmers. There might come a day when one of them opens a shop of his own."

The blacksmith stopped momentarily, gazing down the street, probably envisioning another blacksmith shop. "Either way, my son's life will not be simple—not like my father's or grandfather's. So you tell me: Is the new plow a blessing or a curse?"

"I don't know. Some might say, '*Make hay while the sun shines.*'"

"Yeah, that's what they say." Then he looked at me as if noticing my clothing for the first time. "What do you call yourself, anyway?"

"What do you mean?"

He reached out and pinched one of the brass buttons on my jacket. "Do you have a title?"

My words came out sounding sheepish. "Minister of Agriculture."

"Ah, a farming expert."

I couldn't lie, not after he'd been so open with me. What good would it do? Any question about farming would expose me. "No, I'm not a farming expert. I grew up with King Thoren."

Amused by my confession, the blacksmith pushed his shoulders from the wall. "You don't say? The king's playmate, huh? And now you're the Minister of Agriculture." Leaning against the wall again, he chuckled.

I was at a loss. The letter didn't produce its intended result, and now I had blown the cover of my uniform. I only had one choice left. If my friendship with the king had landed me this assignment, then maybe building a rapport with the blacksmith could help me carry it out. Quietly, I took my place beside him, both of us leaning against the wall, staring across the street toward the inn. "John, I need your help."

I could now feel the blacksmith's eyes looking at me, but I kept my gaze fixed across the street while continuing, "My only real qualification for this position is that I have the king's trust. At least, I think I do. I need to fill a ship bound for Sagan with hay, and somehow convince farmers to grow beets."

"Beets?"

"Beets."

We stood quietly for a moment. Finally, the blacksmith straightened himself and cleared his throat. "I need to get back to work. I appreciate your honesty, and I'm not looking for trouble with the king. I wish you the best, but I don't have time to go around visiting farmers."

"But—"

John placed his hand on my shoulder. "Listen, I'll make you deal: I'll give you a couple of names if you agree to meet me at Ruby's tonight. I want to hear your stories about young King Thoren—secret for secret."

"Fair enough. When may I have the names?"

"Right now—Carl Lundgren and William Strower."

Committing the names to memory, I waited for him to continue.

"Lundgren is an odd man, not good around people, but smart— incredibly smart. Safe to say, you haven't met the likes of him. He knows the secrets of the soil—keeps plenty of it on his skin. I don't know when he last took a bath. Anyway, he probably grows more beets than anyone in Tuva."

"That's encouraging."

"Yeah, he claims he feeds them to his cattle as fodder."

"He claims? What do you mean by that?"

"Let's just leave it there."

"And the other is William . . ."

"Strower. He's the opposite of Lundgren—smart with people. Could talk a squirrel out of his nuts in the fall. Damned ambitious. Has a knack for getting things done. He has quite a few men working for him."

"May I use your name when I talk with them?"

"Won't do you any good with Lundgren. He's mad at me."

"Why?"

John took a deep breath and exhaled slowly. "Well, Carl designed a plow not very different from the one I'm selling—had me build it for him years ago. He farms peat ground, soft soil. Of course, ol' Carl, he noticed farmers using a plow like his and thinks I took his design as my own. He wants to be paid something for his idea. I can't blame him for thinking it. Anyway, I told him it wasn't his design—that it came from someone else. He wanted to know who. What was I supposed to say to that? I couldn't say anything with all this damned secrecy."

"Is that where it ended?"

John shrugged. "Well, he hasn't been back asking for money. But he told me he'd find out the truth. He travels from one end of Tuva to the other and talks with all kinds of people."

"Why does he travel so much?"

"Enough talking. That ain't none of our business. Do you need directions to their farms?"

"No. I have maps in my room."

John looked at the inn and then back at me. "How's it going over there with Emil?"

"The innkeeper? I'm trying to steer clear of him."

"Hah! You and I have more in common than I thought. That imp is over here a couple of times a day, nosing around, counting plows. He's the worst damned spy. Can't keep a secret for anything—spills his guts to Ruby, thinking she'll take a shining to him if he makes himself out to be someone important. But me and Ruby, we grew up together like brother and sister. She won't keep secrets from me."

I stood quietly, pondering how much Ruby had already told him. I had a feeling he knew the king was his benefactor, and if he did, I wondered how many others had found out.

"Any chance Emil will be at Ruby's tonight?" I asked.

John shook his head. "No, Saturday is his night. He walks Ruby home at closing time—makes her skin crawl. He thinks she might invite him in. That'll be the day. Anyway, you're safe tonight. I'll see you at sundown."

With that, John retreated into his shop, and I climbed back through my window to get the maps.

CHAPTER 7

Studying the maps, I discovered that Lundgren and Strower both farmed south of Tinsdal. I could've reached Lundgren's farm in less than an hour, but when the stable boy asked where I was going, I lied and told him I was heading west to visit farmers. Of course, this deception required a meandering route, first north to the center of the village, where the roads intersected, then west to the countryside, then finally south again. I had no good reason to lie, other than to frustrate the innkeeper. I didn't want his nose in my business.

Since Lundgren's farm was closest, I decided to visit him first. It made me nervous that he was on such mean terms with the blacksmith, so I spent most of my time in route practicing a workable introduction. Since Lundgren was a beet grower, I planned to show him the pathetic beets Akeem had brought from across the sea. Maybe I could appeal to his pride, offering him a chance to sell his crops all over the world.

From the crest of a hill, I spotted Lundgren's land nestled in a broad valley, where fresh spring grass had pierced the tan mat of winter. A swollen river divided the valley, reminding me of a gigantic snake sunning itself. The inner radius of the river's curves formed an array of near-perfect circle plots. These plots dotted the valley like dropped coins, plowed black, the soil laid open to bake in the sun. I sat wondering if this collection of round gardens could fill Thoren's ship with beets.

A ridge sprang up at the far side of the valley, covered with trees. According to the map, Lundgren owned that ridge as well. Although I couldn't see his house, I guessed its location by letting my eyes follow a cart-path that started at the road, then went down through the southeast corner of the valley, and finally up the ridge, where it disappeared into the canopy.

"There you are, Mr. Lundgren," I said to the hillside, snapping the reins. Taking the road down the steep hill, I veered east when I reached the cart path. Once on the trail, I discovered the grass taller than it appeared from the top of the hill, nearly reaching the horse's shoulders. The path's course meandered back and forth to skirt wet patches of standing water, waiting like spider webs to waylay an unsuspecting traveler.

Finally, I reached the incline and rode uphill, disappearing into the trees, where yellow sunlight turned greenish-gray, and the sound of happy birds gave way to foreboding caws, the damned crows seeming intent on passing along news of my arrival.

The trail led to the top of the ridge, but it wasn't until I was a stone's throw away that Lundgren's cabin came into view. There was no clearing for his homestead, nor a lick of paint giving evidence of human habitation. It looked like his little shack and assortment of small outbuildings had taken up residence wherever they could find space amongst the trees, making the farm look more like a hideout than a home.

Apprehensively, I dismounted the wagon, hoping to find the cabin unoccupied. It seemed safer to find Lundgren in his fields where I could face him in the bright sunlight.

My boots creaked across the porch floorboards. At the door, I tapped the worn wood softly with my knuckles, startling the eery solitude. Any noise seemed out of place here, except for the crows.

I stood dead still, listening carefully for stirring inside, but all I could hear was the thumping of my own heart. Turning from the door, I stood on the rickety porch, surveying my surroundings. This unwelcoming place was the lair of a hermit, and I was having second thoughts about venturing further. On the other hand, John's description of Lundgren had given me a burning curiosity. Carl Lundgren knew the secrets of the soil, and if the two of us could hit it off, there'd be no end to what I could learn. He specialized in beets, after all.

While I stood on the porch, trying to figure out which way to go, a thought crept into my mind. I couldn't understand why the river was flowing to the top of its banks. It had been a dry spring, and I hadn't yet observed a river or creek flowing to even half its bank. I wondered if Lundgren had built a dam of some sort, giving irrigation to his circle-plots—what an ingenious idea if he had. From the road, the river disappeared to the south behind the hill. I thought if I walked to the end of the ridge, I might have a view of the rest of Lundgren's farm from the safety of the trees and maybe even spot Lundgren in one of his fields.

Abandoning the wagon, I proceeded on foot. The ridge was like a horse's back with a walking trail for its spine. The thick canopy wouldn't allow the sun to produce much undergrowth, so it was an easy hike. Looking down the side of the ridge to my left, I could see Lundgren's cattle lying lazily in the shade toward the base of the incline with the tall grass and refreshing river right below them. No fences were necessary on this property—the cattle had had everything they needed right there.

The trail descended at the end of the ridge. The thick canopy of trees obscured my ability to see anything from my elevated perch, but I could hear the sound of rushing water, the noise seeming to coincide with the direction of the trail. Slowly, I made my way down toward the valley.

I stopped my descent at the treeline. I was still at a slight elevation and could finally see the object of my curiosity. Stepping off the path, I stood behind a massive oak, gazing into the valley. I was right—Lundgren had used rocks, wood, and earth to build an impressive dam. On the downstream side, built into the far bank, a wooden door gave entrance to an earthen cavity of some kind. On the nearest bank, a smokestack jutted strangely from a pile of rocks, leaking smoke, hardly noticeable in the breeze.

To the left of the dam, I saw two more circle-plots, but no Lundgren. I wanted to mount the dam and see what sort of apparatus he'd built into the near bank, and despite my fear, I still hoped to meet the man. John was sure I'd never met anyone like him, and now I could see it was true. There was nothing about this property a typical farmer would envy, but somehow Lundgren was making it work.

Finally, I convinced myself to step out of the trees, remembering that vulnerability was my only path forward with the blacksmith. Who was I to say I couldn't make friends with this strange farmer as well? I hurried down the trail and mounted the walkway on top of the dam. Now with a view of the nearside bank, I noticed it too had a wooden door, but this door had a window, probably to bring light to the underground cavern.

Scampering down the rocks, I approached the door. Holding both hands to the glass, I tried to shield my eyes from the bright sunlight while pressing my face against the window, but before I could see anything, I heard a human squeal over the sound of splashing water. I spun on my heels to see a grubby little man standing in the doorway on the other bank. Dropping his armload of wood, he picked up a hatchet and began swinging it in the air like he'd gone berserk. "Git off my properdy!" he screamed.

"No! Wait. I work for the king." I yelled across the river.

"I told you once—I feed my beets to cattle!" Then he ran with startling swiftness up the far bank, racing to get across the dam, all the while pumping the hatchet overhead.

I bolted from the cavern doorway and sprinted up the piled rocks, trying to beat him to the trail. Twice I stumbled, painfully catching myself from falling with my hands. By the time I reached the path, Lundgren was only a short distance behind—close enough to hit me with his hatchet if he decided to toss it. Dodging back and forth to make myself an elusive target, I ran full-speed up the path.

"I told you what would happen if you came back!"

My mind was racing as fast as my feet. What is he talking about? He must think I'm someone else. But I couldn't straighten him out with him waving that hatchet.

At the top of the ridge, I quickly glanced back to see if Lundgren was still chasing me. To my surprise, he'd disappeared. The long incline had taken all my strength. So, without the immediate fear of having a hatchet lodged between my shoulders, I slowed to a trot, my lungs burning. Traveling along the ridge's spine, I had the advantage of seeing down both slopes. Other than the mocking of crows from high in the trees, there was no movement. Still, I raced to the wagon as fast as my wobbly legs would allow.

Panicked as I was to get away, I nearly climbed out of my skin while trying to turn the wagon back toward the road. There were trees everywhere. I wondered if there was some command to get the horses to back up. Instead, I had to forge a route around the cabin with barely enough room between the trees to squeeze through. It was slow going—so slow I almost left the horses to fend for themselves.

When I finally had the wagon aimed in the right direction, I snapped the reins, and for the first time yelled at the beasts, "Hya! Let's go!" In unison, the majestic creatures drew back their ears and galloped down the wooded path as if charging into battle.

Once I'd escaped the clammy gray canopy and exploded into the sunlight, I breathed a sigh of relief. With only the curvy trail of tall grass to navigate before reaching the main road, I slowed the horses so our speed wouldn't take us off course and get the wagon stuck. Then I heard a frantic rustling in the grass. I hoped it was only a cow, but it occurred to me that Lundgren may have skirted the ridge and ran through the soggy valley. My mind raced for a plan, but before I had time to react, the grass parted, and Lundgren shot out, letting his hatchet fly.

THUNK.

The blade of the hatchet struck the side of the wagon right next to my leg, sticking into the king's crest. I must have pulled on the reins when I lunged backward to avoid being hit, causing the horses to stop. Lundgren ran up to the wagon, attempting to dislodge his hatchet. Instinctively, I dropped the reins, grabbing hold of the handle too, and by the time the weapon came free, all four of our hands were gripping it for dear life.

Refusing to take my eyes off the shiny blade, I grappled for control, keeping the sharp end as far from my face as possible. I had the advantage of elevation and tried to keep the handle above Lundgren's head so he couldn't use leverage to wrench it away, and after a hard jerk, the hatchet was mine. Scared by what I might do with it, I threw it into the weeds. Then the two of us stood scowling at each other—me in the wagon and Lundgren on the ground. He was filthy and unshaven with holes in his clothing revealing his hairy skin, but what commanded my attention most were his eyes—emerald green, with whites like fresh snow. Even the dirt couldn't disguise his intelligence. But at that moment, I had something more than brilliance staring at me—a wild fury that I desperately wanted to escape.

"Didn't I tell you?" he panted. "Didn't I tell you what would happen if you came back?"

"I've never been here."

"Liar!"

"I'm not lying, Mr. Lundgren."

"Well, maybe *you* haven't been here, but your friends have."

"What friends?"

"Tax collectors."

"I'm not a tax collector. I'm here to see if you'll grow beets for export."

"I feed my beets to cattle. I told you."

"You didn't tell *me* anything."

Lundgren stood silently for a moment with his eyes closed. I considered grabbing the reins and sending the horses down the trail, but he was slowly regaining possession of himself, and something wouldn't let me leave.

"Why are you here?" he finally asked.

"My name is Jens. I'm the Minister of Agriculture for King Thoren. The king is developing his port in Keenod, and he would like to export beets."

"The king is a thief," grunted Lundgren, his agitation returning.

"What?"

Ignoring the question, Lundgren took a step closer. "Who gave you my name?"

I opened my mouth, but then remembered that Lundgren and the blacksmith were on rocky terms.

Now more insistent, Lundgren asked again, "Who gave you my name?" The look of insanity was returning to his eyes.

"John the blacksmith."

"He's a thief too! Get off my property, and don't come back."

Slowly reaching into the wagon's bed, I grabbed the sack and pulled out one of the small beets. Lundgren's eyes grew larger. "Where'd you get that?"

"It came from across the sea. A trader brought it to King Thoren to show him how superior Tuvan beets are. The trader claims he can fetch a handsome price for our beets and sell them all over the world. They'd use them for paint and all kinds of things other than food. That's why I'm here, Mr. Lundgren. I'm not a tax collector. I'm here to ask if you'd consider growing beets for the king."

Lundgren held out his hand. "Let me see those."

I handed him the sack, and he glanced at its contents. Then he slung it over his shoulder. "I want you off my land."

"May I have the beets?"

He turned and disappeared into the tall grass in the same direction I'd thrown his hatchet. Though I couldn't see him, I heard him. "Get off my land, or I'll butcher your horses."

Picking up the reins, I coaxed the horses forward, twice looking back to see where he was. The second time, he had reemerged onto the path, hatchet in hand, and the king's beets still slung over his shoulder.

CHAPTER 8

When I reached the main road, I turned north, back toward Tinsdal. I had a mind to head to Ruby's and wait for John. It was only noon, but I'd sit there and load myself with ale or maybe something stronger. Then, at sundown, when the blacksmith showed up, I'd take a swing at him. He wouldn't see it coming. I'd knock him right off his stool. "Was that your idea of a joke?" I'd ask. He'd probably been laughing to himself all day, thinking how it'd go with Lundgren. He could've simply refused to help, but no, that wasn't cruel enough. Damn him.

The pain in my right hand was excruciating. I didn't notice it until I yanked on the reins. I'd caught myself from falling on the sharp rocks and sliced it open.

I drove only a short distance in this anger-induced trance, but at the river-bridge I began to get my wits back. Looking down at the moving water, it occurred to me I should stop and clean the wound. So I turned onto an elevated path on the far side of the bridge and parked the wagon.

Jumping to the ground, I yelped, realizing I'd injured my foot, too. My big toe hurt too much to squat on my haunches at the river's edge, so I fell backward in the grass, pulling off my boot and bloody sock to discover my toenail was barely attached. I must've kicked the big rock I tripped on. Until now, I was too panicked to feel the pain.

Thanks to Lundgren's dam, the water was flowing near the top of the bank. Pulling off my other boot, I rolled up my trouser legs and poked my feet and hands into the river, waiting for the coldness to numb the pain. My nerves were shot, and I eventually began shaking. At first I thought it might be from the frigid water, but then tears started streaming down my face. *What's happening?*

The tears made me feel like something foreign had invaded my soul. I hadn't cried since my father's death, and since then I'd never quite recovered the ability to feel anything very deeply. But now I missed my father with a yearning sharper than anything I'd felt for a very long time. I missed his logic, his ability to pull a problem apart and reduce it to principles. I missed his presence, the confidence he gave me. He was gone, and for the first time since his death, I could feel the severity of that wound. Contrary to what my mother thought, he hadn't given me enough—not enough to get me through this mess.

After a while, the tears subsided. Whatever advice my father would've given me, it wouldn't have allowed self-pity. Looking up from the water, I realized I hadn't put much distance between myself and Lundgren. I pulled my feet from the river and limped to the wagon, one boot in each hand. Again, I'd parked stupidly, having no way to return to the road without making the dammed beasts back up. I stood before the team, staring into their eyes, hating them. If they'd have backed up earlier, I would've beaten Lundgren down the path and avoided the struggle for the hatchet.

"Back up!" I yelled.

Both horses looked on with infuriating disinterest. "Back up!" I yelled again.

Nothing.

I slapped my boots together. "Back up!"

Still nothing. A violent wave of anger came over me, and I swung my boot, the heel clunking one of the horses on the jaw with a hollow thud. "Back up, dammit!" The horse only snorted, swiping at the ground with its massive hoof, barely missing my injured foot. With ears turned forward, the great beast's eyes opened wider.

"Have it your way!" I shouted, limping back to the wagon. Throwing my boots on the floor, I climbed onto the seat and yanked the left rein. "H'YA!"

The wagon plunged off the raised path, sogging the horses to their hocks in black sludge. Swamp odor permeated the air. The wheels sunk too, almost to the axles. Fighting for progress, the horses strained forward, stabbing their legs into the long grass, water splashing, mud flying everywhere, each spastic thrust yielding only inches. But the horses wouldn't quit. Churning and heaving with great puffs of air spurting through their nostrils, they coughed encouragement to each other.

What if they give up? Lundgren would rope and tie me if he found me. But the horses had no quit in them. Fighting side by side, they finally reached the incline of the ditch. Once on dry ground, the wagon practically leaped onto the road, demanding a conciliatory grunt of suction from the defeated bog.

Resting in the center of the road, the filthy beasts stood gasping, nearly choking on their bits. I jumped down from the wagon and limped to the one I'd hit with my boot, throwing my arms around its wet neck. I stood there for some time, talking, petting their foreheads, and stroking their manes. They'd have died to honor my command. When I finally remounted, I realized the wagon was facing south—William Strower's direction. "So be it," I said, "I won't quit either."

From the road, Strower's farm had none of the ominous forebodings of Lundgren's place—no canopy of trees hiding his dwelling or crows signaling my arrival. The house and outbuildings stood freshly painted in perfect order at the end of a straight path. There were groves of trees here and there, but for the most part, Strower's property consisted of tilled soil.

The blacksmith had told me Strower had quite a few men working for him, and, at a glance, I spotted three separate teams working the fields, man and horse yoked together. The old blunt-faced wheeled plow would have taken four horses to work a single field, but now several tracts were being planted at once.

I wished I could tell Strower about Thoren's involvement with the new plow. If he knew, he'd surely feel obligated to grow some beets. Then it occurred to me that Strower might feel beholden to John for making his plows. It was the blacksmith, after all, who gave me Strower's name. Unlike Lundgren, William Strower probably thought the world of John. I decided to use this to my advantage.

With no idea where to find Strower, I headed for the house. Parking the wagon on the path, I limped across the yard and stepped onto a large porch, where several chairs were strewn roughly in the shape of a circle. I wondered if this was where Strower met with his men in the mornings, giving instructions for the day. Through an open window came the faint sound of a woman humming.

I knocked, and the humming stopped. "What is it?" the woman yelled from somewhere inside. She must have assumed I was one of their hired men or at least someone who wouldn't mind yelling back.

I moved from the door to the window. "My name is Jens. I work for the king. Can you direct me to William Strower?"

"One moment." After some banging of pots and pans, I heard her footsteps. When the door swung open, there stood a young woman. "Hello," she said, looking me over curiously. "Why are you searching for my father?"

"I'm Tuva's Minister of Agriculture. I'd like to talk with your father about growing beets for export."

She threw a quizzical glance at the muddy horses, then back at me. "What happened to your hand?"

Looking down, I noticed my wound had reopened, and I was dripping blood on her porch. "I'm sorry . . . That's a bit of a story."

"Tell it."

"Well," I stammered, trying to think of how to begin, "I was in a fight . . . and the man had a hatchet."

"A hatchet? You were sliced with a hatchet?"

"No, not exactly."

"Then how did you get hurt?"

"On a rock," was all I said. She was pretty, and I didn't want to confess running from a fight.

She moved away from the door. "Come in. Let me clean that cut."

She led me to the kitchen, where a tub of water sat on a stand beneath the window, next to a brick of lye soap. The pots she'd been clanging were now tipped upside down, drying on a towel. "Wait here," she instructed, disappearing for a moment before returning with some strips of cloth.

She laid the strips off to the side, and without permission, took hold of my wrist, plunging the wound into the warm water. I tried not to flinch. While my hand soaked, her slender fingers rubbed the soap. I watched with anticipation, almost glad for the injury. This kind of thing seemed to be a normal part of her life, but being this close to a young woman was rare for me. After a moment, she lifted my hand from the water and gently began cleaning the wound, her lips frowning in concentration while she opened the torn fold of skin, carefully removing some embedded dirt.

"You've done this before, haven't you?" I asked, studying her profile. She had soft freckles and untamed golden hair. While she worked, she positioned my hand to take full advantage of the light coming through the window, making her eyes a transparent blue.

"Yes, I do this often," she said, keeping her eyes on her work. "Some of my father's men are quite clumsy."

She wrapped my hand with the strips of cloth, carefully tucking in the ends. There was a slight mischievous gap between her unusually white front teeth, not at all unattractive, and her tongue played there while she inspected her work. Finally satisfied, she released my hand. "There. That should do it."

"Thank you. What is your name?"

"Carrie. My father is out clearing a new field. I can bring you to him if you'd like. I need to run food to the men anyway. She turned her head and nodded toward a small table, where a basket sat, loaded with food.

"I'd appreciate that," I replied, walking over to get the basket.

"Why are you limping?"

"I hurt my toe."

Giving me a pitiful smile, she began leading me to the door. "Who were you fighting?"

"A man named Lundgren."

She stopped. "Carl?"

"Yes. Do you know him?"

67

"You didn't hurt him, did you?"

"What? No."

"He's a sweet man. People don't understand him."

"Sweet? He tried to slice me with a hatchet!"

Looking worried, she led me from the house, across the porch, and into the yard, where she stopped a moment to think. Then she said, "I suppose it would be faster to take your wagon."

"Of course."

We mounted, and I set the basket on the seat between the two of us. Seeming agitated, Carrie directed me toward a distant grove. After a few moments of uncomfortable silence, I asked, "How do you know Carl Lundgren?"

Looking straight ahead, she asked, "What are your horse's names?"

"My horses?"

"Yes. What are their names?"

"I . . . I don't know."

"Really? You don't know their names?"

"I've only had them for two days."

"Still."

Her question reminded me of the sickening thud of my boot on the horse's jaw. If she knew, she'd send me away for sure.

As we neared the grove, Carrie instructed me to skirt west. After rounding the corner, we saw her father swinging an ax at a spindly trunk. A fit man, Strower's age was only evidenced by some gray in his otherwise dark hair. Working shirtless, the muscles and veins draping his lean body were all visible beneath his sweaty skin. Obviously, he was no stranger to hard work. Two young boys with glowing blonde hair were keeping him company, climbing around on the brush pile—identical twins, it seemed. When the boys saw the wagon approaching, they untangled themselves from the branches and came running. Strower looked up from his work, set the ax head on his boot, and waited for us to approach, his tanned face shining with sweat.

Before we'd even stopped, the boys circled behind the wagon and climbed into the bed.

"Magnus! Rasmus!" Carrie scolded. "Get out of there."

I turned to find them rummaging through my bag. Strower approached, using both arms to scoop out his sons. "What do we have here?" he asked, looking at me with the same penetrating blue eyes his daughter possessed.

Carrie answered for me. "This man works for the king. Ask him about his hand."

Strower looked at my bandage, which I quickly hid behind my back. "May I have a few moments of your time, sir?"

"Yes, of course."

With long strides, Mr. Strower quickly attended to the brush lying near him on the ground. Then he kicked away the small sticks, giving us a place to sit. After leaving some food, Carrie corralled the boys and set off on foot to feed the other men.

Extending his hand toward the food as an invitation for me to share his meal, Strower started the conversation. "What is your position with the king?"

"Minister of Agriculture."

"Huh, I've never heard of such a post."

"I belive that I'm the first."

Strower nodded, seeming impressed. "Interesting. What are your duties?"

"King Thoren has tasked me with finding farmers to grow crops for export. As you probably know, he's developing a port in Keenod."

Upon my mentioning the port, Strower leaned in like a child listening to a bedtime story. As I unfolded the details, he frequently interrupted, asking every question imaginable. His interest in me was disarming. I told him about my father's post, my friendship with Thoren, my installation as Minister of Agriculture, and the king's fascination with shipping. I even told him about Akeem, and the surprising trade he'd made for the jewels. The afternoon flew by.

Finally, the conversation flowed to the blacksmith and his recommendation that I visit both he and Lundgren. At the mention of Lundgren's name, Strower dropped his bread on the ground. "John recommended Carl Lundgren grow beets for the king?"

"Yes, unfortunately."

Staring off in the distance, Strower tried to absorb this knowledge. "John must have no concept of Carl's hatred for the throne. Carl would run a sword through his own heart before he'd help the king."

"I know. He threw a hatchet at me this morning."

"You've been to Carl's place?"

I nodded. Strower stood and began pacing back and forth. Then, pointing at my hand, he asked, "Did he give you that wound?"

"No. I fell on a sharp rock, but he buried his hatchet in the king's crest." I pointed at the wagon.

Strower walked over and ran his finger along the slit in the crest. "What did Carl tell you, Jens?"

"Something about feeding beets to cattle. He thought I was a tax collector. I had no idea what he was talking about."

Strower resumed his pacing. "I don't like this . . . John is right about Carl's farming skills—he is unquestionably brilliant, but he despises the king. I've listened to his ranting myself."

For a while, we sat quietly. I could tell Strower needed time to think. He had offered me food earlier, but I was too busy talking. Now, after flicking some ants from the bread, I began tearing off morsels and sticking them in my mouth, trying to stay occupied while Strower contemplated my situation.

Eventually, Strower stopped his pacing. "I think you need to come back here in the morning. You and I should go visit Carl together. He and I have known each other since we were children. He trusts me—as much as he trusts anyone. Where are you staying?"

"At the inn across from the blacksmith's shop."

Strower smiled. "Then you've met Keeps."

"Keeps?"

"That's the name they've given the innkeeper. Odd man."

"Yes, I've been avoiding him. I go in and out of my room through my window."

Strower exploded with laughter. Then, after a quiet moment, he said, "That gives me an idea. My oldest son was married last summer, and now I have an extra bedroom. Would you like to stay here for a while?"

"Would your wife approve?"

Strower stared at the ground. "She passed away two weeks before Will's wedding."

"I'm sorry."

"Thank you. We're making due. Carrie's an enormous help. She looks after the boys, and she feeds the men. It's too much, really. I don't know what I'd do without her."

"I would only add to the burden."

Strower considered my words. "Well, she has chores you could help with—butchering chickens, milking cows—and the king's Minister of Agriculture should have first-hand experience shoveling manure." He winked before continuing, "Schooling the twins wears her nerves thin sometimes. You're no doubt well educated. Perhaps you could help with their lessons."

Nodding slowly, I gave Strower's invitation careful consideration. He'd recently lost two people from under his roof—one to death and another to marriage—so he might've been lonely, but I think there was more to it. I felt it, too. The afternoon had disappeared without any sense of time passing. The two of us had quickly bonded. I wanted to accept his offer, but the words stuck in my throat. I certainly hadn't impressed his daughter, and I hated to think of her reaction to having me around, sharing her responsibilities.

Suddenly, Strower began gathering food fragments from the ground, seeming apologetic for putting me in an awkward position. When he'd cleaned up, he clapped his hands, knocking off the crumbs. Then, extending an arm, he pulled me to my feet.

"You don't have to decide now," he said. "The offer stands."

CHAPTER 9

By the time I reached Tinsdal, it was nearly evening. I'd been driving the horses slowly, contemplating my circumstances, and considering Strower's invitation. My father always said that a good man avoids sailing on the winds of emotion. Far better, he thought, to be led by wisdom and honor. Easy for him to say—an advisor can share his insight and leave the messy decisions to others. Wondering if my father would find anything honorable about my circumstances, I tried to force my mind to think logically.

Using sober judgment, I felt justified in my contempt for the innkeeper. A spy who can't keep secrets is more useful to his enemies than his friends, and I desired to be neither. It was Thoren's idea that I stay at the inn—to keep an eye on me—but he hadn't commanded it. He had his reasons for wanting me there, and I had my reasons for leaving. I could play innocent if he questioned me about staying elsewhere, and he'd have no good reason to accuse me of anything.

With no reservations about leaving the inn, I contemplated the benefits of staying with Strower. He was an industrious and influential man. If he genuinely wanted to help, I'd be a fool to turn him down. On the other hand, although I didn't know him very well, in the span of a few hours he'd coaxed me into spewing my life-story. If Strower somehow wanted to use me for his own gain, it'd make sense to have me under his roof—where I'd be easier to manipulate. Then again, what did I care if he prospered from my success, especially if he was instrumental in creating it?

Behind my thinking loomed a fascination with Strower's daughter, tickling my imagination each time I peered at my tidy bandage. We'd gotten off to such a great start, but Lundgren had spoiled everything. Would she welcome my help or resent the intrusion?

With at least an hour before sunset, I decided not to bring the horses back to the inn, fearing the stable-boy would announce my return to the innkeeper. I didn't need Thoren's clumsy spy hunting me down at Ruby's.

Instead, I headed straight for the tavern to wait for John, where I could think about Strower's offer a little longer, perhaps over a mug or two of ale.

Like most taverns, Ruby's stood off by itself, where hooting and hollering patrons wouldn't wake sleeping villagers. I'd seen the place while taking my earlier detour to the west, and now retracing the same detour backward, I was able to avoid driving the wagon past the inn.

A menacing oak stood behind the tavern, its branches draping the roof. I drove the wagon behind the building and tied it to the tree where the horses busied themselves in the long grass, ripping up clumps and chewing noisily, their bits still in their mouths. Backing away, I made sure the wagon would be out of sight from the road before entering the building.

Inside, the windowless room glowed dim, lit only by crude flickering candles, one at each table. It was early by tavern standards, and the place was quiet. When my eyes adjusted, I spotted a woman at the far end, lighting a candle at the corner table. Without looking up, she called out, "Hello there."

Guessing her to be Ruby, I approached. She was an attractive woman, nearing forty, by my guess, with a few strands of gray in her auburn hair and some friendly crow's feet in the corner of her eyes. Her contours, however, were perfectly preserved, augmented by the cut and fit of her dress. Thinking back to the story I'd heard through my window that morning, I could see why John's apprentice had such a problem controlling his eyes.

"May I sit here?" I asked, pointing at the table she was attending. I wanted to situate myself in the corner, facing the door.

While surveying the room for any unlit candles, she said, "I won't stop you. What'll you have?"

"Ale, please—when you have a chance."

Softened by my good manners, she finally looked at me. "I don't believe I've seen you here before. What brings you to Tinsdal?"

"John-the-blacksmith is meeting me here at sundown."

"Is he now? I don't see much of Johnny these days. He's such a busy fellow with that shop of his. He's been good for business."

"Ah, I suppose the farmers from out of town spend their evenings here."

"From all over Tuva," she replied, making a little circle with her index finger. "The farther they travel, the worse they behave. Not long ago, one of them dropped his pants and relieved himself in that corner." As she pointed to where it happened, her face expressed horror and disbelief, like she was watching it all over again. I enjoyed her eyes. They'd seen a lot, but they hadn't lost their twinkle. "The more respected they are at home," she continued, "the more they cut loose here. But it's slower now with fieldwork going on." Then she stopped, inspecting me more carefully. "You're not a farmer."

"That's true," I said, reluctant to say more. John had told me that Emil visited Ruby weekly, and I didn't want to reveal anything that might reach his ears.

Discerning my wariness, Ruby abandoned the conversation and went to fetch my drink, returning with a large mug that she held by its thick round handle. "Enjoy," she said, carelessly setting the drink on the table. A wave of ale slapped the rim, escaping down the side and forming a puddle. Unaware of the mess she'd made, Ruby scurried off to attend to some other patrons who'd just walked in.

Without realizing how thirsty I was, I drew several gulps before returning the mug to its puddle. With an empty stomach, it didn't take long before the brew went to work, unwinding layer after layer of worry. Eventually, my troubles with Lundgren and the innkeeper felt like trivial inconveniences, hardly worth worrying about.

"You were thirsty," Ruby observed, returning to fill my mug from a large pitcher she carried around. "You might want to slow down, though. That's strong ale . . . I don't want to clean up any puddles on the floor tonight." Then she winked and hurried off.

By the time John arrived, the place was busy, and I'd almost finished my third mug. Ruby rushed to the door to greet him, giving him an affectionate kiss on the cheek. After a brief exchange, she pointed to my corner, and John made his way to the table.

"Survive the day?" he asked, collapsing onto the wooden chair. "You've been missed."

"Missed?"

"Yes, your friend Emil was in the shop several times, like a mother looking for a lost child."

"Evil Emil," I said. "Strower calls him *Keeps*."

"Hah! We all do. You're becoming a local."

"Well, he's no friend of mine."

"Nor mine. Enough about him—I'm here for your stories."

I'd forgotten that he expected to hear stories about King Thoren. I'd intended to think up a few but was too distracted by the day's events. "How about I start with today and work backward?"

The blacksmith's chin dropped and his eyes lazily looked up at me from under his furry eyebrows. "Today, huh? Alright then—how'd it go with Lundgren and Strower?"

I set my bandaged hand on the table, palm up, where he could see the dried blood that had seeped through the white cloth. "Lundgren came after me with a hatchet."

The blacksmith sat erect. "A HATCHET?" His voice rose above the noisy crowd, causing some people to look our way. Then, pointing at my hand, he said, "He did that?" Together, we stared at the bandage. I held my tongue, letting him draw his own conclusions.

Just then, Ruby approached with a mug for John. "What's this about a hatchet?" she asked, leaning her hip against the blacksmith. Then she placed her arm around his thick neck and reached her fingers into his hair, pulling straight one of his curly black locks and swirling it onto her fingertip. Unaffected by her attention, John waited for me to continue my story. I froze. How could I talk about Lundgren in front of Ruby? If Emil learned what Lundgren had done, he'd probably inform the king. As much as I disliked Carl Lundgren, I still had hopes that Strower could talk him into growing beets for me. I didn't want to get him in trouble.

"How long have the two of you known each other?" I asked.

John looked up at Ruby's face, and they smiled at each other. "Ruby and I were playmates. Next to me, she was the toughest runt in Tinsdal—prettiest, too."

Playfully, Ruby tapped John's nose with her fingertip. "*Now* you notice I'm pretty?"

"Who could tell? You were always covered with dirt." Then, turning to me, he added, "She was like the brother I never had." Ruby's smile vanished. Pulling away from the blacksmith, she surveyed the room, asking if we needed anything.

I shook my head, hoping she'd give us privacy. When she was out of earshot, I asked John what he'd told Keeps.

"I didn't tell him anything," he said.

"Did you tell him you sent me to see Lundgren and Strower?"

"I didn't *send* you anywhere. I just gave you their names."

"I know, but is Keeps aware that you gave me those names?"

The blacksmith leaned forward in his chair. "I told you—I didn't tell him anything."

"I'm sorry. I just don't want him in my business." The ale was making me too outspoken, and I could tell I was getting on his nerves.

John pushed his shoulders into the backrest of his chair. "How'd it go with Strower?"

"He was helpful. He wants to go to Lundgren's with me tomorrow—thinks he might be able to straighten things out."

John smiled with half his mouth. "Good. He'll get it done. He's a good man."

"Is he?"

"What do you mean by that?"

Looking down, I started fidgeting with my thumb on the mug's handle. "Strower asked me if I'd like to move in with him for a while."

"Why not?"

"I don't know. It's just that I don't know him very well."

"You don't know Keeps very well either, but he sure wants to know you. Listen, I've known William Strower for a long time. He's a good man. You'd be stupid to refuse him."

"Let say I do it . . . How can I keep Emil from finding out where I've gone?"

"Why do you need to keep your whereabouts a secret?"

"I don't know. I just don't like him spying on me."

John sucked on his ale, peering at me over the top of his mug. Then he set it down on the table empty, raising his hand so Ruby could see he needed more. "What'd you do to get Carl so blasted angry anyhow? I mean, he's been cross with me too—over that damned plow—but he never came after me with a hatchet."

"I don't know. He wasn't in the cabin, so I snooped around and found his dam. Have you seen it? It's amazing. Lundgren came out of a cavern on the far bank where he stores his firewood. I was on the near bank, trying to see through a window. He's built something into that bank, but I couldn't tell what it was. He started yelling—something about feeding his beets to cattle. Then he chased me off his property. For some reason, he thought I was a tax collector."

Looking uncomfortable, John only nodded. Emboldened by the ale, I called him on it. "You know something, don't you?"

Contemplating his answer for quite a while, John finally said, "You've gotta keep this a secret, Jens. I mean, I feel like I owe it to you, getting you hurt and all, but you gotta promise not to say anything. Ruby's been keeping this a secret from Emil for quite a while."

"What?"

"Let me put it this way: If it hadn't been for tax collectors, we'd probably be drinking Carl Lundgren's rum right now." Then he stuck his thick finger through the handle of his empty mug and let it swing back and forth before my eyes.

"Rum? I don't understand."

"Carl Lundgren makes the best damn rum I've ever tasted. What you were trying to see was his still. Now, this goes back a few years, but I made the pieces for it, so I'm kinda stirred into this soup, too. I didn't know what the pieces were for at the time. Carl would show up at my shop with drawings scrawled on birch bark, asking me to make 'em. About a year later, Ruby starts serving this rum, really different from anything I've ever tasted, so I asked her where she got it. She wouldn't tell me for the longest time, but I finally got it out of her that it was Carl's. She'd kill me if she found out I told you."

"Secret's safe with me. Thanks for letting me in on it . . . but what do the tax collectors have to do with it?"

"Carl's been selling rum all over Tuva for a few years now. Of course, he doesn't claim the money he makes. The tax collectors caught on somehow. They want their cut. Ol' Carl, he won't own up to making rum. He claims he's feeding all those beets to his cows. I'm sure it's partially true—he probably feeds 'em whatever's left after he's finished makin' his rum. Beets make good fodder."

"Wait a minute. Are you telling me Lundgren makes rum from beets?"

John looked around, making sure no one was listening. "That's what I'm sayin'. But now he only sells it down south. If tax collectors start sniffin' around locally for evidence, he doesn't want them finding anything. Ruby can't buy it no more. Carl won't sell her any. It's a damn shame too. I miss it."

I sat quietly for a while, a little too drunk to make perfect sense of everything. Finally, I said, "Well, I guess that explains the hatchet."

John shifted uncomfortably in his chair. "I'm sorry about that. It's just . . . I thought Carl may have more beets than he needs—now that he doesn't sell locally. I feel like I owe him something, you know, after the plow and all. I still feel guilty about that. I shouldn't, but I do. I figured you'd drop my name, and he'd be grateful. I guess I was wrong."

Suddenly, I felt guilty too—for letting John assume my wound was from Carl's hatchet. But I couldn't' tell him now that I'd fallen on a rock while running from Lundgren like a scared rabbit. "Don't worry about it," I said. "I'm hoping Strower can straighten it all out. I appreciate you telling me. Who knows, maybe Lundgren does need someone to buy his beets. I guess we'll find out in the morning."

John nodded. "You gonna stay at Strower's?"

"I don't know."

"Listen, Emil will probably find out eventually, but me and the boys at the shop, we can tell him you headed—I don't know—east? That'll take him off the scent for a while."

"Tell him west. I went west this morning."

John scratched his head. "You went west to go south?"

"Yeah. I was messing with Emil."

The blacksmith laughed so hard that he started coughing. "Very well—west, it is."

Suddenly, it occurred to me that my bag was at the inn. "Dammit. How will I get my belongings without Emil knowing?"

"Where's your wagon?"

"Out back. Tied to that big oak."

"Well, I came here on my horse. She's tied out front. I'll take you back to the inn later tonight. You can sneak in and out of your room through the window. No reason you can't sleep here in your wagon."

"Thanks."

"Don't mention it. Now, tell me about growing up with King Thoren.

CHAPTER 10

A crow squawked from an overhead branch, waking me from a deep sleep. From the wagon's bed, I glared at the bird, wondering if it was the sentry that had announced my arrival at Lundgren's farm. Or perhaps evil Emil had changed form and was now following me as a crow. Wishing I'd brought my sling, I yelled, "Shoo!" and the bird reluctantly flew off.

I needed to get going. Strower wanted me at his place first thing in the morning, and I was already late. Noticing I'd used my traveling bag as a pillow, I winced, remembering how I'd reacquired it—riding bareback behind John on his horse, laughing uproariously, hanging on for dear life, and then clumsily crawling through the window at the inn. As loud and careless as we were, it'd be a miracle if someone didn't spot us. Too much ale.

More angst came over me as other memories resurfaced. Although drinking had greatly enhanced my story-telling abilities, it failed me terribly in the editing. John and Ruby, along with a handful of others, encouraged me too much with their laughter, inspiring wild exaggerations, all at King Thoren's expense.

With my head pounding, and my mouth as dry as cotton, I jumped from the wagon to untie the horses. They'd been harnessed all night without being watered. Neglecting to learn their names was the least of my crimes against these magnificent beasts. I vowed to have Strower teach me how to care for them properly, but now they'd have to wait. I didn't want my tardiness to give Strower a reason to change his mind. Slapping my cheeks to clear the cobwebs, I mounted the wagon and set off at a trot.

It was midmorning when I turned onto the path leading to Strower's farm. One of his hired men came running from a nearby field. "Mr. Strower couldn't wait," the man panted. "Said to tell ya he'd be workin' where you found him yesterday."

I thanked him, then cursed him silently as he trotted off. I was hoping to stop at the house and ask Carrie where I could find her father. I was reluctant to take Strower up on his invitation to stay until I could get some clue as to how Carrie felt about having me around. I was sure one brief interaction would tell the story, but the hired man had taken away my excuse to see her. Forcing the thirsty horses past the house, I headed for the grove.

The brush pile had grown significantly since I'd last seen it. Strower was adding another skinny tree to the prickly mountain when he spotted me. Grabbing his hat from where it hung on a branch, he came running to the wagon. Then, in defiance of his age, he jumped aboard before I even had a chance to stop.

"Follow that trail," he instructed, sitting next to me on the bench, pointing to an obscure cart-path serving as a shortcut to the main road. Obediently, I steered the horses onto the path, and the two of us rode together in silence until the farm was behind us.

After what seemed like an eternity of Strower manipulating his hat—first slapping off the dust and then reforming the curvature of the brim to his precise liking—he cleared his throat. "Carl Lundgren is a different sort of man."

A variety of unwholesome remarks shot like poison arrows through my brain, but I kept them to myself.

"He's smart in some ways, but in other ways, well . . ."

"I understand," I grunted.

After another long pause, Strower turned to me. "I need you to keep a secret."

Another secret. I nodded that I would.

"Carl makes rum. That's why the tax collectors are hounding him—he refuses to claim the income." Strower paused, waiting for me to respond.

What could I say? I'd already promised the blacksmith that I'd guard this knowledge. I kept my gaze straight ahead, waiting for him to continue, trying not to betray an ignorant expression.

"I think he started selling a little here, a little there." Strower held his thumb and index finger slightly apart to make his point. "I suppose every farmer hides a little income from time to time, you know, some horse-trading. But now it's a lot more. The man's been selling rum all over Tuva. Thing is, if he fesses up now, the tax collectors will want to go back to the beginning. That's a pile of money."

Turning my head, I made eye-contact, showing I was listening, and Strower grabbed hold of my arm to keep my attention. "Carl can't stand the thought of coughin' up all that money, and he doesn't have the kind of mind to think about what'll happen if he doesn't."

Releasing my arm, Strower settled back on the bench, letting me think about what he'd said. Curiosity had me wondering why Strower felt so responsible for Lundgren's actions. I decided to probe the topic. "Did you say the two of you grew up together?"

Strower nodded. "Yeah, Carl's grandfather and my grandfather were brothers. His parents were both dead by the time he was sixteen, so my father looked in on him as much as he could—even tried to get him to move in with us, but Carl wouldn't leave his farm. He's a loner and didn't want much lookin' after. Before my father died, he asked me to keep an eye on him. I'm afraid I haven't done much of that, especially since my wife passed. Amanda, she'd always make sure he came over for holidays and that sort of thing. She'd have the children make things for him. Anyway, I can't help but feel like this is my fault—a crime of neglect. My daughter's been worried sick that they'll lock him up for coming after you with a hatchet, and she doesn't even know about his trouble with the tax collectors."

Looking straight down the road, I said, "I won't do anything to get him in more trouble. You can tell your daughter that."

"I appreciate it, Jens. Carrie will too."

Deciding to take advantage of Strower's goodwill, I raised the topic weighing heavy on my mind. "Fact is, Mr. Strower, I was hoping you might convince Lundgren to sell me some of his beets."

Strower removed his hat to scratch his head. "I'm afraid it's not that easy, Jens. Carl's beets don't look anything like the beets you're after. He breeds 'em for rum. He took most of the red out. They're kinda pale."

"How'd he do that?"

"Danged if I know. I told you he's smart. Somehow, he knows how plants work. He doesn't have a clue about people, but when it comes to plants?—He breeds them like other farmers breed horses or cattle.

Suddenly, I remembered the expression on Lundgren's face when he saw the strange beets that Akeem had given King Thoren. He was like a man who'd stumbled upon a treasure. Now it made sense why he'd taken them from me—he'd have a whole new breed for his experiments.

"You're right," I agreed. "The king won't want a pale beet. The merchant is buying them for their color. He needs them red."

Strower thought for a moment, then sat up like he had an idea. "You know, Carl's probably not finished planting yet. If we could get him some seed, maybe we could talk him into growing some beets for you."

"How?"

Strower scratched his head again. "We need to make him see that he doesn't have a choice. Rumor is he hasn't been sellin' his rum locally. That means he probably doesn't need all those beets he's been growing. The thing is—rum gets better the longer it sits in those oak barrels, so I'm sure he's just stockpiling it somewhere, waiting for the tax collectors to forget about him. We need to give him a reason to grow beets for the king."

"Staying out of jail might be reason enough," I said. "We could let Lundgren think I'll report the attack if he doesn't cooperate. I'm not saying I will, but he doesn't know that."

Strower frowned. "It's kinda mean, but you might have somethin'. To Carl, money is more valuable than beets because he's never had any. Now the king wants to take it from him. But beets—he can grow them like nothing. Let's say Carl would agree to plant a couple of those round plots with your beets—do you think you could talk the king into calling him square on his back taxes? You know, take the beets as payment instead of money?"

"Sure. I think Thoren would take that trade, especially if Carl would agree to grow them every year. And if he really can breed beets, maybe he can figure out a way to make them even bigger and redder. That would endear him to the king."

Strower smiled. "So, we just need to convince Carl that we're saving his head from the chopping block."

It started to rain. Strower held open his palm to feel the drops. "This is good," he said. "The rain will send Carl to his cabin, so we won't have to look all over tarnation for him. Listen, Jens, you need to let me do the talking. It'll take a while to bring him around. You just stand back and look serious. Wouldn't hurt to let him see your hand either."

By the time we reached Lundgren's, the rain was coming down in sheets. Soaked to the bone, Strower and I turned off the main road. The curvy lowland trail leading to the canopy of trees was quickly becoming muddy, and the horses seemed nervous, their hooves sinking once again in the black soup. Speeding to a trot, we traversed the valley, heading up the side-hill until reaching the canopy, where overhead leaves hushed the patter of rain and amplified the sound of the hooves and the squeaking of wet leather. Lundgren would hear us coming.

When we reached the cabin, I saw a slight movement in the dingy gray material covering one of the windows from the inside. "He's in there," I told Strower.

Strower didn't wait for Lundgren to come out. Springing from the wagon, he ran toward the cabin. Reaching the porch, he jumped the single step onto the rickety platform and wrapped his knuckles on the rough-sawn door. "Carl, this is William. Open up."

"William?" came a voice from inside, crackling with apprehension. "Who ya got with ya?"

"The man you chased around your farm with your hatchet. Open up!"

"I thought he was a tax collector."

"Carl, if you go chasin' tax collectors with a hatchet, the king will hang you from the tallest tree in Tuva. Now stop makin' me talk through this door!"

A moment later, the door opened. After stepping inside, Strower turned to me, signaling with his hand for me to follow. By the time I entered the cabin, Strower had already pulled a rickety chair to the corner and sat facing Lundgren, also in a chair with his back against the wall, sharpening a nasty-looking knife. I wasn't exactly sure where Strower wanted me, so I walked to the center of the room and stopped. Then, using my good hand to hold my wounded wrist, I made a display of the bandage.

When Lundgren noticed me, Strower seized his opportunity. "See what you did, Carl?"

Squinting at my hand, Lundgren looked confused. "I did that?"

"He cut it on a rock, running from your hatchet."

"He shouldn't have been nosing around."

"He wasn't nosing around, Carl. He was looking for you. He had your name as one of the best farmers in Tuva. He wanted to know if you'd grow beets for the king."

Staring at the floor, Lundgren mumbled something only Strower could hear. The only word I could make out was—*king*. Strower lowered his face to meet Lundgren's eyes. "Carl, you can have your opinion, but you need to keep it to yourself. You're in some serious trouble, and that sour mouth of yours won't help you one bit. Do you understand me?"

Lundgren nodded slowly.

"Now, I've told Jens about the rum . . ."

Like a mountain climber desperate for a handhold, Lundgren's intelligent eyes frantically searched Strower's face.

Strower's voice turned tender. "Carl, I know you feel like I've turned on you, but it's for your own good. Those tax collectors, they won't go away, and your problem will only get worse. You'll end up in prison, and that'd make Carrie real sad. Do you understand?"

Lundgren's eyes floated across the room, where a cloth banner hung on the empty wall. It was a crude black horse with a white mane. On top, the material wrapped a whittled stick with a string tied to both ends and hung over a nail. The years had given it a dusty veneer.

Turning to see what Lundgren was staring at, Strower noticed the banner. "Do you remember when Carrie made that for you, Carl? She's been worried sick about you. She thinks they might lock you up for what you did to Jens. She's the one who bandaged him up. You gave him a pretty nasty cut. Carl, you can't split the king's crest with your hatchet and not expect something bad to happen."

Lundgren's face grew tortured. He looked at my bandaged hand and then turned back to Strower. "What am I gonna do, William? I just want to be left alone."

Using his thumb, Strower pointed at me over his right shoulder but kept his eyes fixed on Lundgren. "Jens and I have been working on that, Carl, and here's what we came up with: You're gonna plant two of your round plots with big red beets." Strower held up two fingers in front of Lundgren's eyes and paused a moment before continuing. "I'll have Carrie pick up the seed in Tinsdal and bring it out to you. She'll bring the boys too."

At this, Lundgren's eyes reclaimed some of their brightness. Strower reached out and grabbed hold of Carl's arm, causing Lundgren to recoil. Realizing the man didn't like to be touched, Strower quickly withdrew his hand, speaking as gently as one trying to coax a chipmunk to receive a morsel of food. "Carl, these beets will be shipped all over the world to make paint and dye and things like that. Jens has agreed to talk with the king and arrange a special deal for you—to call those red beets your taxes every year. That way, you can go about your business, and the tax collectors will leave you alone. You'll just deal with Jens here, and me, of course. But Carl, you need to start treating Jens like a guest on your property. No more threats. Do you understand?"

"Just the dirty beets?"

"What do you mean, Carl?"

"I ain't washin' 'em? Or haulin' 'em?"

Strower smiled, realizing that Lundgren's mind was already working out the details. Once again, he reached for Lundgren, who tensed, prompting Strower to clasp his hands on his lap. "That's right, Carl, just a big pile of dirty red beets. Jens will take care of the rest. Do we have a deal?"

Carl was choking on his words, so Strower rose from his chair, assuming his cooperation. "Carrie and boys will be over in the morning with the seed. Remember—two plots."

CHAPTER 11

"I'd like to drive that fancy wagon of yours," Strower told me from Lundgren's porch.

"Oh, of course." I'd parked it the same way as the previous day, and I wasn't looking forward to navigating the trees behind cabin again.

I mounted the passenger side and watched Strower approach the nearest horse, talking to it gently. "Magnificent creatures," he said, scratching the underside of the horse's jowl. Then, with his arms wrapping the animal's neck, he buried his shoulder into its massive chest and began pushing. The horse huffed, but then complied with a backward step, causing the other beast to obey the directive of the harness. Before long, Strower created enough space to circle the wagon in front of the cabin. Then, jumping onto the seat, Strower grabbed hold of the reins, sending the team down the hill at a gallop, quickly traversing the muddy trail. *Where were you yesterday?* I thought to myself.

On the main road, Strower set the horses to a leisurely pace. Aside from a few stray drops, the rain had ceased, and low gray clouds sped across the sky, racing to their next destination. I could tell by Strower's face that he felt lighter. The line of his jaw had mellowed, and his face now wore the same friendly demeanor he had when we first met. Pushing his hat back to expose his forehead, he lifted his boots, resting them on the front of the wagon. From this reclined position, he looked at the sky and spoke philosophically. "You know, Jens, I'm envious of you and King Thoren."

"Envious?" I grunted, my mind swirling to think of why that would be. Although I was grateful for Strower's assistance, I couldn't help but also feel a twinge of resentment. Somehow, the responsibility for Lundgren's rebelliousness was now mine. Strower had convinced me to entreat the king to make special arrangements for his taxes, and I'd have to do it soon— before one of the collectors made another visit to his farm. The image of a dismembered tax collector floating down the river came to mind. What had me worried is that I wasn't sure how generous King Thoren would be with me now, once he discovered I'd evacuated my room at the inn, leaving Emil clueless as to my whereabouts.

"Yes, envious—not in a bad way. It's just exciting, you know? The possibilities . . ."

"What possibilities?" I asked. At that moment, I was more attuned to the impossibilities. Even if Lundgren came through with two fields of beets, I still needed more. Plus, I needed to fill a ship with hay. Where was I going to find that? I was hoping to use our traveling time to discuss more practical matters.

Strower placed both reins in one hand while using the other to set his hat even further back on his head. The sun was now peeking out intermittently, its radiance baking through my wet clothing and warming my skin, but my soul was still shivering. Strower didn't seem to notice.

"What possibilities? For one, the possibility of using The Crucible to send Tuva's beets all over the world. Isn't it amazing to think that a Tuvan hermit like Carl will grow beets for a princess across the sea—to rub as red powder on her cheeks?"

Trying to give my weary mind permission to splurge its energy on such a lofty thought in the midst of my problems, I turned and studied my traveling companion. He was utterly relaxed. Only moments earlier, he was a soldier marching into battle, intensely focused and strategic. Now, with the battle won, he didn't seem to have a care in the world—imagining Lundgren's unplanted beets already crossing the sea. His countenance reminded me of the strange courage that overtook me at Ruby's—that opaque curtain, pulled into place by the ale, hiding my worries from me. In a way, his reclining was infuriating. I wanted him to understand that neither my life, nor King Thoren's, was nearly as enjoyable as he seemed to think.

"Yes," I said. "the port is an exciting place, I'll give you that, but—"

"I bet it is. You know, Jens, I've dreamt of ships and ports since I was a child—sailing the seas, hunting for treasure, meeting interesting people. I'd like to sit down with that trader you told me about yesterday. What was his name again?"

"Akeem."

"Yes, Akeem. I'd like to sit down with him and hear his stories."

"Well, there's two sides to every coin," I said, trying to pour cold water on his little fire. "The king has no support among his advisors. They see The Crucible the same way our forefathers did: Tuva's greatest weakness, an invitation for invasion. They think King Thoren is tempting a foreign army."

Strower smiled. "And yet, he continues to build his port."

"Yes, you'd be surprised at what lengths he's gone to circumvent their obstacles. He takes great pride in his tenacity."

"Hmmm. . . Tenacity or . . . Never mind."

"Or what?"

"I don't want to seem critical."

"I won't tell anyone. What were you going to say?"

"Only—is it wise for a general to march into battle by himself?"

"No, not if he wants to win."

"That's my point. Why can't Thoren get his advisors onboard?"

"I told you—they don't see the opportunity, only the threat."

"And whose fault is that?"

Suddenly feeling defensive, I clammed up. Strower's analogy—comparing King Thoren to a foolish general—was more accurate than I cared to admit, with one crucial detail missing: the general's gullible friend stumbling along behind.

"I don't mean to be disrespectful, Jens, but I think a king's dominion can be his worst enemy. Thoren is too smart to think he can succeed without the support of his advisors. His power must blind him."

"Perhaps. He's determined to push Tuva into the modern age, kicking and screaming if need be."

"Yes, but pushing a kicking nation is dangerous, especially if he could coax it along some other way."

After watching Strower with the horses, I was convinced he knew something about coaxing. "What would you suggest?"

"Well, I've had very little dominion compared to a king—just a few men working for me—so forgive my comparison, but my most important task is getting my men to understand what needs to be done so we can all work together. They need to see what I see. I spend considerable time every morning doing just that—helping them see. When they step off that porch, every man needs to understand his assignment. If I do a poor job leading, I'm the one who loses. And if my men don't respect my leadership, they could leave and go to work for someone else."

Strower paused, waving to a farmer working in a nearby field. "Jens, those simple realities keep me sharp. I think it's too easy for a king's crown to slide down over his eyes. That's all I'm saying. I'd bet my best horse Thoren doesn't sit down with his advisors more than he has to—probably even hides from them. Am I right?"

"There's no better way to describe it. That's half the reason for the palace in Keenod—to escape his advisors."

"Well, in his defense, he's stuck with those men, like it or not. The noble families feathered their nest pretty well at Tuva's inception, entitling their descendants to sit as the king's advisors. At least I have the freedom to kick a man off my porch if he won't follow my lead."

"Have you done that?"

Strower thought for a moment, then laughed. "No. Fortunately for me, their ideas are often better than mine."

"Really?"

"Why do you think I've been chopping trees? I'm not the smartest man on the porch when it comes to working with animals, and I'm not the smartest with crops either, but I am smart with people. I concentrate on putting the right man on the right task. Then, I find ways to help. Chopping down trees, that doesn't take any brains, but it gives me time to think. In the meantime, my men are engaged with the important work."

Suddenly, Strower sat up straight. "By the way, I've decided to plant beets in that grove I'm clearing. I'm still not sure whom I'll put in charge of that project."

"That's wonderful," I said. This news, however, made me even more apprehensive about staying with Strower. What if he placed me in charge of the beets? My lack of farming skills would become painfully evident. My title, Minister of Agriculture, probably made Strower think I had some talent to lend his farming enterprise.

As though reading my mind, Strower asked, "How about you, Jens? What is your area of expertise?"

"I don't know. I don't do anything that well. I was a wool buyer, but I don't think Thoren recruited me for those skills as much as the fact that we grew up together, and he trusts me. That's why I'm wearing this uniform. It doesn't suit me very well."

Strower chuckled. "You know, I could tell the moment I saw you that someone was making you wear those clothes."

"Really? How?"

"I don't know—they fit, but they don't fit *you*, if you know what I mean. But being the kind of man people trust is no small thing. You have a way about you, Jens. You don't have your guard up like most people. You let folks see who you are. I think that's why they trust you so quickly."

"Yeah, I guess."

"What I'm trying to say is King Thoren knew what he was doing when he appointed you. He's no fool. He needs someone who can quickly earn people's trust because there aren't too many people who trust him."

"That's true. How about you, Mr. Strower? Do you trust him? I won't say anything. I'm just curious."

Strower held up both hands as if to display a sky full of possibilities. "Thoren's the kind of man who can see what *wants to happen*," he said, smiling at his new made-up phrase. "I know it sounds strange, but that's how I am too. I can see things that want to happen. Then it's just a matter of placing the right people in the right positions and getting everyone working together. That port wants to happen. This thing with the beets wants to happen. I can sense it. Thoren has an opportunity to lead Tuva into the modern age, and I'm completely behind him. I think he chose the right man for the job, Jens, but you need to believe it too."

"Well, maybe people trust me, but that doesn't seem like enough."

"It's isn't enough. That's what I've been trying to tell you."

Feeling like a dimwit, I sat there quietly, hoping he'd clear things up.

"See how this wagon lists to the right?"

"Yeah, that horse is bigger," I mumbled, pointing to the rump of the larger of the two nameless beasts.

"That's right. When you harness animals for work, you want them as close to identical as possible—so they pull straight—but it's not that way with people. It's kind of a mystery, but if you want people to pull straight, you need to harness all different sorts."

I nodded ever so slightly, still a bit confused.

"Let me explain it this way," said Strower, momentarily handing me the reins. "First," he said, grabbing hold of his little finger, "King Thoren imagined something that *wants to happen*, so he harnessed you. Right?"

"Yeah, I guess."

Strower grabbed his next finger. "Then, you came to my place, told me your story, gained my trust, and now you've worked me into that harness. Right?"

"Hopefully."

Finally, Strower grabbed his middle finger. "Then, the two of us wrangled Carl into the harness. Do you see? The three of us are as different as can be, yet we're starting to make progress."

Nodding, I said, "I think I see what you're getting at."

93

"People aren't like animals, Jens. Each of us is great at certain things and terrible at other things. If you focus too much on what you're not, you'll lose track of what you are, and if we don't work together, we're snake-bit."

As much as my father taught me, he'd never covered this lesson. My father wasn't a man of action like Strower. He was a thinker and a teacher, but the world held still for my father because he studied the past. To get things done, I needed strategies to navigate the squirming present—something Strower seemed to offer. I could've contemplated our conversation for hours, but we'd nearly reached his farm, and I was hoping for more advice.

"What do you think I should do next?"

"You should relax. I can see you're tense. Can you stay for supper?"

"Sure. Thank you," I replied, realizing I still hadn't told him I was planning to move in. Then I added, "I know I worry too much."

"Listen, Jens, every day has its challenges. You need to learn how to celebrate the little things." Then he turned to me with sad eyes. "My wife taught me that."

"She must've been quite a woman."

"Oh, she was," replied Strower, swallowing hard. Then he used his shirt sleeve to wipe a tear. "It wasn't until she died that I fully appreciated her. She had a way of caring for people, seeing to their needs. With me, it was always about the work, pushing to get things done. It's easy for me to treat people like possessions. I've had to learn how to slow down and take notice."

Strower took off his hat, inspecting its shape before he continued, "I wasn't much different than the king, but I didn't have a crown over my eyes. With me, it was this." He held up his work hat before placing it back on his head. "Amanda always made sure people felt special. I figured the two of us made a great team. I could focus on the work, and she could worry about the people. Anyway, I've been trying to be more intentional about looking after people now. But I'm afraid Carl slipped through the cracks. That's why I was dead-set on coming along today." Then laughing, he added, "You probably know more about me now than you wanted to know."

I shook my head. "No. I'm glad you came along. I don't know what I'd have done without you."

"Well, we're in the same harness now, aren't we?"

"Yes. Speaking of that, is your offer for lodging still open?

Strower spun around to see my bag in the back of the wagon. "Of course. We're happy to have you."

"Maybe you could teach me how to care for these horses. When I was a wool buyer, I inherited an old mule from the man who had the job before me. The shepherds loved that mule so much that they kinda took care of her for me. I think they thought I'd give them a better price for their wool if they fed me and looked after my animal."

Strower shook is head. "You have a knack for getting other people to do your work, don't you? Very well, the horses will be our first order of business when we get to the barn." Then, winking, he added, "But I'm only doing it to fetch a better price for my beets."

CHAPTER 12

Strower's barn was like nothing I'd ever seen. I was familiar with the lean-tos the shepherds erected near their pastures, made from tree branches and pine planks. Strower's barn had a stone foundation with oak posts, beams, and planking, built as an inheritance from one generation to the next. The front third was open to the roof, where pigeons cooed from the rafters. In the back two-thirds, a clean, wide aisle divided the barn down the center, with oak stalls on each side and an open hayloft above, piled high with pleasant-smelling clover. Running overhead, an iron rail extended into the loft, on top of which traveled a device with wheels and a pulley. It looked as though the large open area was for unloading hay wagons indoors. I wondered if the blacksmith had built the contraption.

Strower drove the king's wagon into the open area and tied the horses to wall-mounted iron rings. After unhitching the wagon and removing the harnesses, Strower opened the lid to the tack box, pulling out two brushes. Then, climbing the ladder to the loft, he kicked down some hay, instructing me to set it in front of the horses. After sending me to the well to fill two large buckets of water, Strower brought me to the granary and showed me where he kept the oats.

"You gotta be careful with oats," he said. "A horse will overeat oats if you let them. They can eat themselves to death." Filling the pail three-quarters full, he said, "This much for the two of 'em."

Once the horses had food and water, Strower handed me a brush. Then, grabbing one for himself, he patiently showed me how to groom the animals. "No, you need to press harder. Push those bristles into their coat. They like it."

After we'd been at it for a while, Strower's twin sons came running into the barn, announcing supper would soon be ready.

"Have Carrie set another place," Strower instructed the boys. "Tell her Jens has decided to stay."

After looking at each other, one of the twins said, "Oscar is staying for supper too."

"Oh," replied Strower. This news stopped his brush mid-stroke. Then, placing both arms on the horse's back, he just stood there, deep in thought.

"Who's Oscar?" I asked.

"One of my hired men," mumbled Strower. Then, turning to the boys, he said, "Tell your sister we'll be in soon."

As the twins ran from the barn, Strower continued his meditation, leaning against the horse, taking off his hat to scratch his head.

I kept brushing, trying to mind my own business, but my curiosity finally got the better of me. "What's the matter, Mr. Strower?"

He opened his mouth as if to start a sentence, then thinking better of it, went back to grooming. After a few moments of uncomfortable silence, he slapped the horse on the rear. "Well, that's about all we can do today."

Untying the animals, we led them into stalls in the back of the barn. Strower told me to fetch two more armfuls of hay while he spread straw on the floor.

"You hungry?" he finally asked.

"Starving."

When we entered the dining room, everyone was seated. The chairs at the head and foot of the table were open for Strower and me. Carrie and Oscar sat next to each other on the far side, with the twins on the nearside. Strower approached the blonde heads of his young sons and placed one hand on each of their shoulders. "Why are these pirates sitting together?" he asked. Carrie's eyes fell to her plate.

Squatting low, Strower inserted his face between the ears of his two sons. "If you boys don't behave, I won't hesitate to make you walk the plank." The twins looked at each other, giggling as if their fate was inevitable. With that, Strower removed his hat, hanging it on a hook near the doorway, and claimed his seat at the head of the table, between Carrie and one of his twin sons, leaving me the chair at the foot, between Oscar and the other twin.

As I pulled out my chair, Strower introduced me to his hired man. "Oscar, this is Jens. He works for the king. He'll be staying here for a while."

"Pleasure to meet you," I said, extending my hand. Oscar's arm reached instead for the spoon in the stew pot, so I retracted my offer and sat down. Oscar had an intimidating presence. Although he didn't appear to be very tall, his shoulders were broad, his arms muscular, and his suntanned face terribly serious.

Embarrassed by Oscar's rudeness, Strower tried with flattery to draw a more civil spirit from his worker. "Jens, Oscar is one of my best men. In fact, of all the farmers I know, he is second only to Carl in his knowledge of crops. He's been working on something the farmers in Gladon call *rotation*—using one crop to prepare the soil for another, making it unnecessary to leave fields fallow. It has staggering potential."

Oscar glared across the table. "Carl Lundgren? You'd put me second to that worm?"

"Oscar!" Carrie scolded. "That's enough." Then, turning to her father, she asked, "How is Carl?"

Strower smiled. "Carl's fine. He's agreed to grow two fields of beets for the king. I'd like you to make a trip to Tinsdal in the morning with the boys. I told him you'd purchase the seed and drop it off at his farm."

Hearing that they'd be traveling to Tinsdal, the twins began celebrating, asking Carrie from across the table what time they'd be leaving. Ignoring her brothers, Carrie tried to learn the details of our meeting. "That's quite a change from chasing Jens with his hatchet. How did that come about?"

Before Strower could reply, the twins, who'd abandoned their hope of getting a response from their sister, began asking Strower if they could play outside after supper. Strower gave them an almost unperceivable nod, which was far too subtle for the young boys, so they continued their badgering. This distraction allowed Oscar to interrupt:

"Why does Lundgren need beet seed? That's all he grows is beets—and why send her?" Then, without the courtesy of eye-contact, Oscar pointed at me. "Why don't you have him fetch the seed? I don't want her going there alone."

"We're going with her!" squealed one of the twins. "Right, Papa?"

Carrie dismissed Oscar's concern with a wave of her hand. "I want to go. Carl's like an uncle. It's been a long time. He'll be amazed at how the boys have grown. I'll bake him something before we leave."

Oscar then turned his attention to me, glaring at my uniform. Taking a big spoonful of stew and chewing it only enough to reduce the chunks to a manageable size to talk through, he asked, "What's your title, anyway?" Then, turning back to his food, he acted as though he couldn't care less if I answered.

Strower answered for me. "Jens is King Thoren's Minister of Agriculture."

"What does that mean?" Oscar sniped. Then, leaning over his bowl, he scooped several more bites in rapid succession.

Again, Strower answered, but this time his eyes were set on Oscar like a hawk. "It means he is a guest in this house."

Staring at my bowl of stew, Oscar stabbed the table a few times with his index finger, speaking again with his mouth full. "Why are you staying *here*?"

"I'm here to recruit farmers to grow beets for export."

Oscar shrugged. "We don't grow beets."

"We *haven't* grown beets. That's true," said Strower, "but the land I'm clearing will grow them."

Oscar dropped his spoon into his bowl. "You haven't said anything to the men about this."

"I will in the morning. I was wondering if you'd be interested in taking on the project—it's a new crop."

"Pfff no. Why don't you make him do it?"

"Who? Jens? Are you suggesting I rent my land to the king?"

"No, but if he wants beets, make him do the work."

"He's paying me handsomely to grow them. Why would he do the work?"

"Well, what will he be doing?"

Strower pronounced his words slowly. "That's not your concern."

Red-faced, Oscar now aggressively attended to his stew, tearing off chunks of bread and tossing them into his bowl. Then, using his fork to poke them into the gravy, he fished them back out again, flinging them into his mouth. Savagely, he continued this odd ritual until he'd sopped all the gravy, and only the meat and vegetable remained at the bottom of his bowl. Then, using his fork to stab the meat, he left his vegetables untouched.

The tension in the room was thick enough to keep even the pirates from talking, and for a while only the slurping of hot gravy interrupted the silence. Finally, Oscar pushed his empty bowl toward the center of the table. Standing to leave, he nudged Carrie's arm with one knuckle. "I'll be on the porch."

Clenching his jaw, Strower stood, following Oscar toward the door. Stopping briefly for his hat, he turned to Carrie. "Go to Will's room and find some work clothes for Jens to wear tomorrow. His bag is soaking wet from the rain. I'll be in the barn." Then, looking at me, he said, "I'll set your things outside your door when I come in. Will's room is the first door at the top of the stairs. Take your time and eat. I'm sure Carrie has made something for dessert."

"Would you like some help?" I asked.

With his back to me, Strower raised his hand, rejecting my offer.

Now sitting between two vacant chairs, Carrie rose to her feet. "Excuse me while I dish up the pudding."

Sitting alone with the twins, I could hear Strower and Oscar arguing on the porch. "You're not a member of this family yet!"

"When? When will I be?"

"When I say so." Then a pair of boots—I guessed to be Strower's—stomped across the porch and down the wooden steps.

"What's the matter with me, William?" shouted Oscar. Then it was quiet.

Moments later, Carrie returned from the kitchen with three bowls of pudding. Distractedly, she set one in front of each of us. "I'll set the clothes on your bed," she announced, before disappearing from the room again.

While attacking their pudding, the boys studied me curiously with bright eyes.

"How do people tell you two apart?" I asked.

Looking up from his bowl with pudding around his mouth, the one nearest me said, "I'm Magnus, and that's Rasmus." Then, pointing at his brother, he added, "He has more freckles."

Sure enough, Rasmus had a nose so populated with freckles they blotched together, while the freckles on Magnus's nose sat apart. "Ah, I see it now."

"May we be excused?" Rasmus asked.

"Well . . . I suppose," I replied.

"May we play outside 'til dark?" asked the other, following his brother toward the door.

Amused by their ill-placed manners and imagining their potential for mischief, I suggested they ask their sister.

As Magnus disappeared through the doorway, Rasmus was already yelling up the staircase to Carrie. Sitting alone now, I slowly ate my pudding, wondering what to do next. It wasn't long before Carrie returned. "Your clothes are on the bed. I hope they fit. They should—you and Will are about the same size. My father said something about you helping with chores and teaching the boys?"

Relieved to know my stay wasn't a total surprise, I replied, "Yes if that's alright with you?"

"It's not my decision. How's your hand?"

"It's fine. Thank you. You did a good job with the bandage."

"And your toe? Is it healing?"

"I—I don't know. I haven't taken off my boot."

"Not even to sleep?"

With a shoulder-shrug, I avoided further explanation, remembering my drunken state when I'd finally crawled into the wagon at Ruby's. Removing my boots hadn't even occurred to me.

"Well, I noticed you limping when you came to the table. I can take a look at it tomorrow." With that, she left the room again.

Waiting until I heard the door to the porch open and close, I stood from the table and made my way up the stairs, ascending to Will's old room, where a neat pile of worn clothes sat on the bed. The room was stuffy, but I noticed Carrie had already opened the window to let in the cool evening breeze. I pushed the clothes to the floor, removed my shirt and, with some difficulty, my boots before falling onto the straw mattress. It seemed too early to go to bed, and I was worried that someone might open the door, so I kept my trousers on, lying on top of the covers, staring at my stocking, which appeared to be bonded to my right foot with dried blood.

Settling myself into a comfortable position, I finally became still enough to hear something other than the crackling of the straw mattress—it was Oscar and Carrie on porch beneath my open window.

"Why won't he give me an answer?"

"Any answer? Would you be happy with no?"

"Of course not, but why won't he give us his blessing? I work harder than any man here, and he knows it. Dammit, I'm a good farmer."

"I suppose he has other things to consider."

"What things?"

"I don't know, but mother's death hasn't been easy for him—for any of us . . . And he has the boys to think about. Maybe it's not the best time."

"What? You can't expect me to wait until the boys are older. You can still look after them when we're married. I'll be working here. There's no reason we couldn't live nearby and come here together—even if we have children of our own.

"And why did he invite that city-boy to stay here? He's too good to work the fields—can't get that uniform dirty. No, he'll stay near the house—with you. Your father doesn't think I'm good enough for you, does he? Dammit. That little skunk better not get in my way, or Lundgren will be the least of his worries."

"Ugh. Why do you talk like that? I shouldn't have said anything to you. You best get home before my father comes back from the barn. I haven't seen him this worked up in a long time."

I heard Oscar's boots take a few determined strides across the porch then stop. "I'm not going to sit around like a helpless little boy and wait for him to warm up to the idea. He needs me more than he thinks. He's gonna find that out." With that, his boots continued across the porch and down the wooden steps.

CHAPTER 13

I woke to the clanging of pots and pans downstairs. I hadn't slept much, tossing and turning, thinking about the conflict I'd brought to the Strower home. I'd still been awake late in the night when Strower ascended the creaky staircase, setting my bag outside the bedroom door. I doubted the animals were keeping him in the barn until that hour. He was more likely mulling over his problem, thinking about Carrie and Oscar. I felt terrible for Strower. He'd spoken in such glowing terms about his farming operation, all of his men rowing together in a unified effort. Now he had a hole in his boat.

The most honorable thing I could do was to go back to the inn. Having me out of the way, Oscar might soften his attitude toward Strower. I needed to pull Strower aside and share my decision as soon as possible.

Fetching my bag from the hallway, I confirmed that the extra clothes I'd brought were soaking wet. With barely enough pink light from the window, I pulled on Will's old clothes, relieved they fit, and stepped into the hallway. Descending the creaky staircase as quietly as I could, I hoped to make it to the outhouse without being delayed by a conversation. A warm glow softly lit the bottom of the stairs from a kitchen lantern, and I could hear Carrie's humming as she worked, her pretty voice mingling with the light and the aroma of freshly baked bread.

Heading down the hallway in the opposite direction from the kitchen, I aimed for the door leading to the porch but noticed something strange while passing the parlor doorway. Through the parlor window, I saw Strower sitting on the porch in the glow of a lantern. He was conversing with someone, but I couldn't see who it was because the window was only large enough to frame Strower's profile. But judging by the look on his face, he was having a serious meeting. Was he with Oscar? I hated to interrupt, but I had to get to the outhouse.

Tip-toeing to the end of the hall, I quietly opened the door and stepped onto the porch, intending to pass without disturbing the conversation. But halfway across, Strower greeted me from his glowing perch. "Good morning, Jens."

I turned and, to my surprise, he was sitting alone on a straight-backed wooden chair with an open book on his lap. A second chair faced him with no one sitting in it. It seemed unlikely that someone could have vacated the porch so quickly, and I couldn't see anyone in the yard.

Closing the book and setting it down by his side, Strower turned his chair slightly to face me. His voice was barely louder than the chirping crickets. "Did you sleep well?"

"Yes," I lied. Then, pointing to the back yard, where the outhouse waited, I added, "I need to—"

"You can use that bush. No one out here but me."

While I relieved myself, Strower said, "I've been giving our situation some thought."

"I have too," I replied, pausing to buckle my trousers. "Truth is, I didn't sleep much last night, Mr. Strower. I feel terrible about the way things went with Oscar yesterday. I don't want to cause problems with—"

As though he didn't want to hear Oscar and Carrie's names spoken in the same sentence, Strower held up his hand, stopping me from going any further. "What happened last night had nothing to do with you," he said, offering me the chair opposite him by pushing it out a few inches with his boot.

I sat down and met his eyes. "I just wonder if it wouldn't be best for me to go back to the inn."

"Suit yourself, but I've been working up a plan that will require some effort, and it'd be easier if you were here."

"You don't think my being here will cause—"

"Listen," Strower interrupted. "Oscar is upset with me. It has nothing to do with you. He wants to marry my daughter and," his voice fell to a whisper, "I'm having a hard time making a decision. That's all." Then, looking off to the east, Strower furrowed his brow as if the sun was behind schedule.

"It's none of my business, sir, but Carrie . . . does she want to marry him?"

Strower looked at his boots. "That's complicated. I think she'd say she does, but you'd have to understand the situation."

"You haven't asked her?"

Strower squinted for an instant, as if I'd pelted him with an acorn. "No, I've been trying to get my thoughts straight first. I'm worried I might say something I'll regret. This is the kind of thing Amanda always helped me sort out. She had a way of understanding these things."

I nodded. "What do you think she'd say? I mean, did she like Oscar?"

Strower folded his hands and then reluctantly laid them on his lap, forcing himself to consider the question. "Yeah, Amanda was like a second mother to Oscar."

"Really?"

Strower scanned the dimly lit yard to ensure we were still alone. Then he lowered his voice to something barely above a whisper. "Oscar's father was a drunk—a mean drunk. He's dead now, but he'd lie around and leave all the work to his wife. One day, she'd had enough. She came to Amanda and me, asking if we'd rent their land—before they lost it. She asked if we'd take on Oscar as a hired man. The boy couldn't have been more than twelve, but she was desperate. She said he'd work hard. She had some other children too, but they were younger."

"It seems to have worked out," I said. "You mentioned last night that he's unusually gifted with crops."

"He is, but he's so damned ambitious." The intensity of his own words seemed to surprise Strower. After glancing at the porch window, he slid to the edge of his chair, lowering his voice again. "When my son, Will, took his wife, he went farming with his father-in-law. His wife's father doesn't have any sons. Will's never said it, but I think he was fed up with Oscar. They're close in age, and Oscar was always trying to show him up. I suppose he was just proving himself. But now, if I let Oscar take Carrie as a wife, he'll want to run this farm after my time is up. I've always dreamed of handing it over to Will."

"Do you think Will might come back?"

Strower thought for a moment, then shook his head. "I don't think so—not with Oscar here. I've given Oscar some authority with the other men. He's earned it. But when he tries pushing me into his decisions, it sets me off." Strower shook his head. "My anger isn't right. I know that. If it were my own flesh and blood pushing me to make different decisions, it'd be another matter—I'd be proud of my son for having his own mind."

"What do you think your wife would say about all this?"

Strower looked at the pink sky. "I don't know. She's the one who could calm me down when Oscar got on my nerves. 'He's just like you were at that age,' she'd say. The thing is, Carrie overheard comments like that—more than once. It makes me wonder if she thinks that this marriage would have her mother's blessing."

"Do you think it would?"

Strower unclasped his hands, using them instead to rub his stubbly face. "I've been wondering that. She had affection for the boy, but as a husband for Carrie? I don't know. I have my doubts."

"What do you think her objection would be?"

"Well, you saw him last night—he's crude, and he's pushy. He's not a drinker, but still, I can't imagine Amanda ignoring his temper. No, I don't think she'd envisioned Oscar as a husband for Carrie. I don't give a damn what kind of farmer he is if he doesn't treat my daughter right."

"Has he mistreated her?"

"Well, he's on his best behavior, trying to court her and all. He's been in a few fights through the years when someone finally stood up to him, but I guess that's not so unusual. I was in a fight or two myself when I was young."

Strower was quiet for a moment, thinking, then he smiled. "And Carrie—she ain't exactly docile either. She don't back down. I'm sure she thinks she could turn Oscar into a more reasonable man—as Amanda did with me, but I don't know about that. It'd be an ugly battle."

"What do you think Oscar will do if you say no?"

"Good question. He's plenty capable of farming his family's plot now. I don't need to rent their land—I have enough ground without it. I think he'd be fine on his own, especially with the way he's learned to rotate crops. A man can get a lot more from a smaller tract."

Imagining Strower and Oscar squaring off for that conversation, I said, "He'd be mighty angry."

Strower raised his eyebrows. "Oh yeah, I'd have an enemy for sure. So be it, though. I can't let that sway my decision."

"I don't envy you, William," I whispered. "You have a lot to consider."

"I do. To be honest, I wonder how selfish I'm being, hanging on to her—probably making Oscar worse than he really is." Then Strower turned toward the parlor window, gazing into the dark room. "Carrie reminds me so much of her mother. It's hard to imagine this house without her. But even if Oscar is no different than I was at that age, Carrie deserves more . . . Amanda did, too."

Suddenly, as though someone had shaken him awake, Strower sat erect and slapped my knee. "I've known you for what?—two days, and I think you know more about me than any living human. I trust this stays between the two of us. Now, do you want to hear my plan or not?"

"Of course."

Leaning forward, Strower set his forearms across his knees. "Every fall, I throw a huge harvest celebration. We invite all the neighbors. We've done it for years. There's horse racing, wrestling matches, a baking contest. The local farmers look forward to it. Amanda thought it up, and it's grown every year."

"Sounds like fun."

"It is. Now I'm thinking about adding another celebration in the spring—a planting celebration. These farmers work hard to get their seed in the ground, and sometimes it doesn't go so well—you know, a man gets sick or hurt. Half the time, we don't find out about it until it's too late to get his crop in. A celebration would give us a chance to find out if anyone needs help. It might keep a family from disaster."

"Great idea."

"Well, here's the part you'll like—I was thinking in the barn last night that most of the farmers around here could still clear out a small plot to grow beets if you offered them a generous price."

"Sure. The king has given me permission to pay more than the local merchants, whatever it takes."

Poking his index finger around on an invisible map, Strower said, "If we could get thirty plots, it might go a long way toward filling that ship."

"No doubt—especially with what Lundgren has already agreed to grow."

"Exactly. Once we have all the farmers together at the celebration, I'll let you present the opportunity. We'll have the seed in hand. I think we'll get some takers."

For the first time since I set off from Keenod, something like real hope entered my soul. "Thank you, William. I'd be grateful for the chance."

"Well, it's not just for you, Jens. It's a good opportunity for us farmers. But there's much work to do to get ready—and not much time. Another week or so, and everyone will be finishing up with planting. That doesn't give us long. It'd be a lot easier if you stayed here until after the celebration."

"Yes, of course."

"I won't say anything to the men this morning. I have a feeling Oscar will fight it, and I don't want to wrestle him over it—not in front of the other men. But with Carrie and the boys heading to Tinsdal today, you and I will bring the noon meal around. That's when I'll introduce you to each of them individually. We'll tell them about the planting celebration. I think they'll be excited if Oscar isn't there to piss on my fire."

Then Strower leaned back in his chair with his arms folded across his chest. "What do you think?"

My mind was flooding with thoughts, making it difficult to choose one. Did Strower spend those sleepless hours in the barn planning my success? I'd envisioned him pacing the aisle between the animal stalls, wondering what to do about Oscar. Perhaps it started that way, but Strower's brain was wired for working. He'd told me as much when we were returning from Lundgren's place. Work was his domain, and relationships had been his wife's. Now Oscar was forcing him to bring those two worlds together, and Strower's mind was resisting, turning instead to my problem, one more easily managed. It was a stroke of luck for me, but in the back of my mind, I knew Strower's trouble with Oscar wasn't going anywhere, and Strower didn't seem any less conflicted about what to do.

"Yes, of course I'm on-board," I finally said. "What can I do?"

"There'll be plenty to do, but first, we need to plant my new field with beets. I'm sure Oscar will see to it that no one volunteers for that project, so I think you and I should do it. The experience will be helpful for you, and it's good for my men to see me working."

Smiling, I said, "You're always one step ahead, aren't you?"

"No. Two steps. Why do you think I run everywhere? It makes my men feel guilty for walking."

"Oh great, and me with a sore toe."

"Forget about your damned toe, Jens. There's work to do. You can let your toe heal after the celebration."

"What about me helping Carrie with the chores and teaching the boys?"

"We'll work around that."

"What about the hay? The king wants to fill his ship before winter."

"Yes, I know. I've been thinking about that. That's a more difficult problem. Most of the farmers were able to get three cuttings of clover last year, so our barns are quite full."

"That's good, right?"

"Yes, but they won't commit to selling you their hay this early—not until they see how the summer shapes up. Sometimes we only get two cuttings. That's when we need the extra hay in our barns. If we get three cuttings again, we won't have room to store it. We'd be happy to sell it."

Just then, Carrie's voice came through the window, "Breakfast."

Strower gripped the arms of his chair to stand up, but then, discerning my worry, remained seated. "I know that doesn't help you much now. It's entirely possible you could be empty-handed this fall. That's the hard truth. The king has given you a ridiculous task."

"I can't come up empty-handed. Thoren's made a promise to Sagan's king in payment for a ship—it's already under construction at Thoren's port."

"Well, he should have rented ground near The Crucible and seeded it in clover a year ago. Hay isn't easy to transport, you know. It should be grown on that gentle slope outside of Keenod."

I could hear my heart pounding in my ears. "That's a great solution for the future," I said, "but what am I going to do now?"

Strower stood up. "We'll pray for three cuttings. Welcome to farming, Jens."

As we marched across the porch, Strower talked with his back to me. "We can let the farmers know that you want to purchase their hay when we have them together at the planting celebration, but I'm telling you—they won't let it go until they've had that third cutting. It'd be a foolish decision on their part."

CHAPTER 14

At Strower's request, we gobbled our breakfast so we could get to work. I think Strower wanted Carrie and me away from the house before the men showed up. He probably didn't want the two of us walking across the porch together in front of Oscar during the morning meeting.

Before heading to the barn, Carrie sat me down on a kitchen stool to have a quick look at my foot. She lost patience with me, however, as I tried to remove my stocking, which had bonded itself to my toe with dried blood. Finally, having no regard for my wound, Carrie grabbed the sock and yanked it off. I yelped as fresh blood and thick puss escaped from my toenail, now attached on only one side. Without removing her eyes from my foot, Carrie grabbed hold of the toenail and pulled it off entirely with a quick pinch of her fingers and a flick of her wrist.

"Son-of-a . . . school teacher," I yelped.

Carrie squinted. "What?"

"A little warning next time."

"Pfft. Any farmer would have pulled it off himself. I guess you city-boys don't know that."

Taking hold of my ankle, she plunged my foot into the bucket of warm water that she'd used for washing the breakfast dishes, repeating the same process of cleaning and bandaging that she'd so skillfully performed on my hand, but this time without a shred of gentleness.

I swallowed my anger, reminding myself to be grateful for the medical attention. But now, traveling from the house to the barn, limping as fast as I could to match her ridiculous pace, I thought she was making sport of me. *City-boy*, she'd called me. Sure, I was from the city. So what? Why was she making me chase after her like a wounded puppy?

The twins had already reached the barn and were using their combined strength to work the latches and swing open the big doors. Carrie caught up with them, finishing the job. As soon as the doors parted enough for the pirates to squeeze through, they raced to the hayloft ladder, one chasing the other up the rungs, disappearing to play in the piled hay.

"Don't forget to feed the chickens!" Carrie yelled after her brothers. "We're not leaving until you two finish your chores."

Fastening each of the two open doors to the wall of the barn with a hooking latch, Carrie finally stopped long enough to address me. "Ever worked on a farm before?"

Sour as my attitude was, I didn't feel like talking, so I nodded that I had.

"When?" she asked.

"I've worked with sheep a little. In my prior employment, I was a wool buyer."

"Surely if you were only buying the wool, you weren't *working* with the animals." Then she turned away and walked into the barn.

I didn't like talking to her back, but I felt obliged to justify myself. "Sometimes, I'd show up early, and the shepherds had me pen sheep or bundle wool."

"It's good to be helpful," she said, not bothering to look back at me.

"I didn't really have a choice—I needed their wool, so—"

Spinning on her heels, Carrie probed my face with her eyes. "So you were forced to help—to get what you wanted. And what do you want from us, Jens, helpful as you are?"

The question left me speechless. The truth was I did need something from Strower, and that's precisely why I was helping with the chores. The fact that I found her curiously attractive only expanded my selfish motives.

"Have you nothing to say for yourself?" she asked, her eyes probing ever deeper.

Remembering Strower's earlier words—that she wasn't one to back down, I quickly forgot my resentment over her treatment of my toe, knowing I couldn't compete with her intensity. Conjuring the most reasonable tone I could muster, I said, "Yes, Carrie, your father has agreed to help me, and I appreciate his assistance. I couldn't move forward without him."

Her eyes narrowed to slits, seemingly interrogating my character. Finally, she turned and resumed walking toward the back of the barn. Craning her neck to see me over her shoulder, she said, "Oscar thinks you're placing my father in jeopardy—our family, too."

"What? I'd never do that." But even as the words escaped my mouth, uncertainty crept into my soul. Truthfully, I hadn't even thought about it— and that, in itself, was an ugly fact. Strower had placed himself between the king and Lundgren, and now he was counting on me to free Carl from his troubles. Who knew how that would go? Was Strower only sticking his neck out for me so I'd stick mine out for Lundgren? Maybe Oscar *was* the only one who could see things for what they were—but Oscar's attitude toward Lundgren was probably also tainted. For all I knew, it might have been Lundgren's rum that killed Oscar's father.

"Carrie, your father isn't one to let a young man like me push him around. He has his reasons for helping me. He's completely behind the king's plan to export beets. He thinks it will help farmers. Go ahead, ask him yourself."

Carrie walked down the barn's center aisle in silence before stopping in front of a stall. Then, turning to look at me, she gave me one more chance to plead my case. "Listen," I said, "Oscar's probably right—somehow, my problem became your father's problem, and Lundgren's problem somehow became your father's problem. But this is a great opportunity. Maybe Oscar just doesn't see it. He's like a watchdog—he only sees the threat."

At those words, Carrie turned away, attempting to hide a grin. Once she regained her composure, she said, "Don't expect him to be licking *your* hand any time soon."

"I'd be happy to avoid his teeth."

A gentle laugh suddenly broke through Carrie's hard countenance, and just like that, her eyes softened.

"Carrie, if you prefer, I'll go back and stay at the inn at Tinsdal. I've already made the offer to your father. I don't want to be in your way."

"What did my father say to that?"

"He said that he'd prefer I stay here until after the—" I stopped, realizing Strower didn't want me announcing the planting celebration until we'd talked with his men individually. Telling Carrie now would give her a chance to warn Oscar, who would probably try to sour the men's attitude before we could get around to them.

"After what?"

My eyes fell to the stone floor. "Your father is planning a planting celebration here for all the local farmers."

"A planting celebration? Why?"

"Well, his best reason is to check everyone's progress—to see if anyone needs help getting their crop in before it's too late."

"But why do *you* need to be here for that?"

"Your father is going to give me a chance to recruit farmers to grow beets."

"But the planting will already be finished."

"He thinks they could be convinced to clear a small plot. Perhaps next year, they could grow more. Please don't mention this to—"

"Oscar? My father wants to keep this from Oscar?"

"Only until the noon meal. He wants to talk to the men individually."

"Hah, so Oscar can't rally them against the idea—ever the strategist."

With nothing to add to her conclusion, I remained silent.

Grabbing a small three-legged stool and a pail, Carrie opened a stall door, motioning with her head for me to follow. Setting the stool next to the cow, she pushed on my shoulder, signaling me to sit. Then, kneeling next to me, Carrie placed the pail under the engorged udder. Grabbing the teats with her nimble fingers, she squeezed and pulled down, sending a thin spray of milk into the bucket. Alternating between her right and left hands, she worked until the bottom of the pail was white. Then, releasing her hands, she presented the udder to me.

Grabbing hold of the same two teats, I squeezed, but nothing came out. Carrie placed her hands over mine, showing me how to pull the milk through the teat. Before long, the tinny sound of short spurts splashed the side of the pail: TSHHHT, TSHHHT, TSHHHT.

Carrie stood watching me for a while. Then she abandoned my stall, grabbed a stool and a pail, and entered the stall next to mine. Before long, I heard the sound of milk spraying into her bucket as well. There were narrow gaps between the stall slats, and I could see strips of Carrie's blue dress on the other side of the boards. After a while, her voice came quietly through the slats. "What's your opinion of my father?"

"I have immense respect for him. John-the-blacksmith told me of his good reputation among the farmers."

"He does have that."

"He seems like a good father, too."

"Yes. He's a changed man since my mother died."

Wondering if I should pursue this sacred topic through wooden slats, I then realized that it was perhaps the separation that made her feel safe enough to share her heart. Cautiously, I continued, "Your father described your mother to me a little. From what he told me, she was an incredible woman."

No response, no words, just the sound of milk spraying into her pail, and then it stopped. "She was beautiful. People say I look like her, but she was much prettier."

Wanting to contest her assessment, but never having seen her mother, I said, "Your father told me he is still learning to appreciate her, especially what was on the inside. I wish I could have met her."

Again, it was quiet for a while. Then her voice came barely above a whisper, "My father took her death very hard. It's strange though . . . over the last few months, he's taken on some of her qualities. It's like part of her has taken up residence inside of him. Does that sound strange?"

"It sounds profound."

"I saw you this morning, you know—watching him from the parlor doorway."

"Oh, I'm sorry, I—"

"No, don't apologize. Was he . . . Was he talking?"

"Well, yes, that's why I stood there so long. I was trying to figure out if he could be interrupted. I had to use the outhouse—"

"But there wasn't anyone out there."

"That's right. What was he doing?"

"He was doing what my mother used to do. She would sit by herself, reading out loud from the Holy Book. In the summer, she'd sit on the porch. In the winter, she'd sit in the parlor. After she'd read a little, she'd have a conversation."

"With who?"

"Well, with the Creator, I suppose."

"I don't understand."

"I'm not sure I do either. Half the conversation must have been in her head. My father teased her about it. 'Why do you still read that book?' he'd say. 'You must have it memorized by now.' My mother would say, 'I'm not reading a book. I'm conversing.' Father just rolled his eyes."

"And now he's doing it."

"Yes, but he's taken it a step further—he pulls up another chair." Carrie let out an endearing chuckle.

"And he's becoming more like your mother?"

"Yes, he's taken on a measure of her gentleness. Before, he didn't care much about people. He didn't think about how we were doing. He only cared about work. He had a sharp edge, but I haven't seen that side of him for a while—not until last night."

"I'm sorry."

"I'm not trying to blame you for anything, Jens. I just don't know why he's helping you. I don't know if it's his ambition causing him to pursue this venture, or if his heart simply wants to help. It sounds strange, but I feel protective of him. It's almost as if my mother's death sent him into a cocoon, and he's just now coming out, his wings drying. It actually makes me happy to hear that he's scheming against Oscar. I guess he isn't completely vulnerable."

We both laughed.

"Oscar thinks he's gone soft. He prefers my father as he was—hard-driving, tough-minded. That's what he expects from men."

"What about you?"

"What do I expect from men?"

"No. Do you think your father's gone soft? Do you think these changes are permanent, or is he just—"

"Grieving? No, I think he's changing."

"Are you religious?" I asked.

"Not like that. I mean, I talk to the sky sometimes, but I don't expect an answer—let alone a conversation. But I've been trained in the book. My mother saw to that."

Just then, the cow I was milking kicked over my pail, making a loud clank. Instantly, two barn cats appeared, cleaning up the mess with their quick tongues. They'd been lurking nearby, I suppose, waiting for the mishap.

"Was that what I think it was?" Carrie asked.

"Sorry."

Suddenly, Strower was standing in the aisle between the two stalls, giving himself a view of both Carrie and me over the top plank. Startled, I nearly fell off my stool, my face reddening for having talked about him behind his back. Now, I was grateful the cow had kicked the pail over, interrupting our conversation when it did, but I wondered how much he'd heard.

"Your carriage awaits, Madame. If you want to make it home to cook supper, you need to get moving." Then, looking at the mess I'd made, Strower added, "Looks like you've endeared yourself to the cats."

Leaving her stall to join her father in the aisle, Carrie let out one of her infectious laughs. "Jens is a cat man—doesn't much like dogs. He's scared of being bitten."

"Is that true?" asked Strower.

Looking at Carrie, I held my tongue.

Strower's eyes scanned the barn. "Where are the pirates?"

"In the loft," Carrie replied, "They haven't fed the chickens yet."

"Let's round them up." As Strower walked away, he glanced at me over his shoulder. "Try to keep the milk in the pail, Jens. We don't want the cats getting too fat to catch mice."

Following her father, Carrie stopped momentarily in front of my stall. Raising her pretty face above the top slat, she let out a low-pitched growl. Then she smiled and ran off.

CHAPTER 15

The next few days were busy on the Strower farm. The ground dried, and we finished planting, including a small field of beets that Strower and I cleared and planted together. Each morning, Strower's men assembled on the porch to receive their instructions. I was included in the morning meetings because Strower wanted every man to see how his work connected to the whole. "Mistakes happen when a man can't see the big picture," he told me one day while clearing brush. "That means mistakes are my fault—for not painting the picture clear enough. An extra minute on the porch can save hours in the field."

I quickly discovered what made William Strower a great leader. He had a way of intricately imagining each day, and then vividly unfolding his expectations to his men, making the work seem alive, hovering over the farm, waiting for human habitation. There was nothing like toil at the Strower farm. Work was a calling, and Strower employed his imagination for every detail, expecting the same from his men. And when he found something to celebrate—some clever initiative, or a unique unleashing of someone's imagination to overcome an obstacle—Strower glowed.

One morning, Oscar suggested an enhancement to Strower's vision for the day, having something to do with planting—the direction of the rows in relation to the position of the afternoon sun. It wasn't a big thing, but by the nodding of heads, I could see the men preferred Oscar's idea to Strower's. Oscar had been quietly sulking since the evening of their argument, withholding any contribution to the porch meetings, so I found myself holding my breath, anticipating conflict. To my surprise, Strower's eyes lit with glee, and he began slapping the porch rail. Marching over to Oscar, Strower took hold of his broad shoulders. "You're a genius!" he shouted. "I've never considered that." Then, grabbing Oscar's hat from his head, he kissed it. The men laughed as Strower bowed, handing Oscar his hat back like it was a sacred brain-covering.

Not being the sort of man to abide folly, I thought Oscar would push Strower away, but he didn't. Basking in the compliment, Oscar gave him a half-smile. There was magic in Strower's encouragement, intoxicating magic. POOF! A fire was lit, shooting each of us like flames from his porch to lay hold of our work.

In the back of my mind, I wondered if Strower had made peace with the idea of having Oscar as his son-in-law, but I didn't dare ask.

After two days as my mentor, Carrie left me alone with the cows. Oscar must have envisioned a much shorter training period than I did, and I was sure he'd put his foot down after just two lessons. Strower allowed Oscar to stay each night for the evening meal—a concession, I think, made because I was living under the same roof as Carrie. Each night after supper, Oscar and Carrie retreated to the porch while Strower and I sat at a small table in the kitchen, making our plans.

Sitting with Strower by the lamp reminded me of the evening I spent with King Thoren at his palace in Keenod, cracking lobster claws and dreaming about the future. In many ways, Strower and Thoren were alike— always thinking about what could be, never dwelling in the past. They only differed concerning the present. Strower had the gift of embracing the here and now, generously sharing it with others. Perhaps it was Thoren's power and privilege that made him think it beneath his position to unveil his colorful dreams to those who needed to see them the most. He kept his canvas turned away from almost everyone, protected from scrutiny, unwilling to share paint with an artist who might use different brushstrokes.

I had little contact with Carrie in the days leading up to the planting celebration, other than helping Magnus and Rasmus with their studies. With my formal education, Strower thought his twins would benefit from sitting under my instruction, choosing the subject of history for me to teach. It was a smart choice.

I could still remember all the stories to the smallest detail as told by my teachers and retold by my father. My father wanted to be sure I learned the principles from the stories of old, whether moral or tactical. In the evening, he'd pull up a chair next to my bed, asking, "What did you learn today, son?"

He had me retell the stories, interrupting when I'd mispronounce a name or when I couldn't remember a date. Then he'd ask: "Why is this story important, Jens?" Every day, I'd come home with little patches of knowledge from which my father sewed together a larger quilt. He'd say,

"Knowledge is nothing without understanding, Jens. You need to piece it together carefully for the truth to surface." Then he'd ball his fist, holding it high above his head. "When truth dwells in your mind, it's a powerful force." He probably envisioned me filling his post one day as an advisor to Thoren, so he wanted me thoroughly equipped.

As important as education was to my father, it was no less important at the Strower home. One day, while waiting for Magnus to return from the outhouse before starting my lesson, Carrie told me the story of her mother. She'd been orphaned and raised by an uncle, a rural priest who went from village to village throughout Tuva performing religious ceremonies. As her uncle's right hand, Amanda received tutoring while they traveled, not only in religion but in other disciplines as well. Carrie said William and Amanda first met at the age of eighteen, after a religious ceremony in Tinsdal where William fell head-over-heels for the young woman with long auburn hair and cat-green eyes.

That summer, William traveled by horse all over Tuva attending the priest's ceremonies, causing his parents to believe he'd found religion. The truth was, he was trying to cultivate the girl's affection. When Amanda finally fell for Strower, her uncle was reluctant to let her marry a farmer. Not surprisingly, Strower's charm won the priest over by the end of the summer, but only after vowing to make education a keystone in parenting the priest's grandchildren. Strower had kept his promise by allowing time each day for study, even though it was Amanda who did the teaching. Now, since her mother's death, Carrie shouldered the responsibility of educating her younger brothers.

We settled into a routine where I taught the boys right after the midday meal. Carrie fed me with the twins, and then she'd leave us to our lesson while she delivered food to the hired men. The twins were sharp as tacks, loving my stories, especially the battles. At the supper table, Strower made a practice of asking his pirates to retell their lessons. Each night, they exploded into a story, using their utensils as characters.

Of course, Oscar minimized their education. "What good is all this learning out here?" he scoffed one evening, waiting behind an empty plate for the rest of us to finish our meal. "These boys should be learning how to farm."

Strower fueled Oscar's frustration by ignoring him altogether. "What else did you learn?" he asked the boys, mussing Rasmus's blonde hair. Oscar glared at Carrie, shaking his head in disgust.

Most days, Carrie delivered the midday meal to the men as quickly as possible, allowing her to sit at the table for a portion of my lesson. I couldn't tell if she was interested in history or if perhaps she enjoyed my company. Either way, I looked forward to those brief moments, extending the lessons as long as possible. She sat right next to me, listening intently while the boys sat across the table. I was fascinated by how her mind grappled with knowledge. She could rotate a concept the same way a child examines an interesting rock, interrogating the story from different vantage points. In my formal training, there'd been only one way to understand things—you didn't just pick up a stone of knowledge and study the underside. When Carrie did, it was like she'd lit a torch, pulling me by the hand through unexplored tunnels. I found it exciting.

Carrie went about the house barefoot. I don't think she liked the constriction of shoes. One day, while sitting next to me for the twin's lesson, she set her naked foot atop my boot. At first, I thought it was an accident, but I enjoyed the contact too much to move. After a moment, she crossed her right leg over her left, and the toes of her right foot began ascending the shaft of the old work boot that I'd borrowed from Will's closet, finally reaching my stocking underneath my pant leg. Then her toes climbed my stocking. At the pinnacle, they gently pushed against my bare leg and pulled my sock down to the top of my boot. Then, resting her toes there, she quietly listened while I tried to deliver a lesson to the boys. Since this happened under the table, the boys were clueless, but I was utterly disoriented, losing my place and staring helplessly at the table.

"Go on," she coaxed, her face holding only the slightest hint of mischief—a playful challenge—could I keep my senses at bay while engaging my mind? Forcing my brain to return to the story, I regathered the fragments, but every time I had them collected again, the slightest movement of her toes toppled the stack, sending me scavenging for my thoughts. Finally, she removed her foot and stood to attend to something in the kitchen. But before walking away, she placed her hand on my shoulder, giving it a slight squeeze. "I'll leave you three alone," she said. Magnus and Rasmus seemed to sense the energy. Looking at each other, they snickered.

As the day of the planting celebration approached, Strower and I began using the evening hours to prepare my presentation to his neighbors, encouraging them to plant a small field of beets. "Farmers are a strange mix of careful and risky," Strower told me while spinning his index finger around the perimeter of his cider cup. "I guess it makes sense when you think about it," he said. "There's so little we control. We place the seed in the ground with no sway over the elements. The precious few things we do control, we tend to hold tightly—even to our hurt. A new crop, a new market, it'll seem risky to them."

Maybe it was the way the shadows were playing on his face, but for the first time since I met him, Strower looked tired. It wasn't just the kind of tired a man earns from a hard day's work, but the weariness that comes from a burdened soul bearing too much weight for too long. I'd seen a similar heaviness with my father. I remembered my conversation with Carrie in the barn—he was changing, softening in some way. Why was he helping me? Carrie's initial fears about my motives—were they justified? Was I taking advantage of his vulnerable state? He'd worked a lifetime to build his reputation among his neighbors. Was it fair for me to ask him to risk it for this untested plan?

We were alone, sitting in the flickering light of an oil lamp. Everyone had long since retired. I knew I'd have no peace until I pulled back the curtain on Strower's real motive for helping me.

"William, can I ask you a question?"

Since I didn't make a practice of seeking permission to ask questions, Strower seemed to sense I wanted to talk about something deeper than farming. "What is it, Jens?" he asked, sliding his chair forward.

"Why are you helping me?"

"Why do you ask that?"

"I don't know. I guess I'm wondering if you really see this as an opportunity."

"Why would I do it if I didn't see it as an opportunity?"

"You have a big heart, William. Maybe you've been guided by some misplaced mercy."

With that, Strower looked at me for a long time. I couldn't tell if he was insulted by my speculation or if he was just now weighing his motives. "Jens, I've not possessed mercy long enough to know when it's misplaced, or if it can be misplaced." Pausing, he then stared at me again. There was more he wanted to say, but some kind of emotion was blocking his words. Finally, tears welled in his eyes. In a whisper, he said, "But if there's such a thing as misplaced mercy, I've been its recipient. The Creator has given me a chance at a different kind of life. I don't know where it'll lead, but I plan to see it through."

As I was thinking of some way to respond, Strower suddenly stood up. "I want to show you something," he said, walking over to the wooden stand and grabbing the Holy Book. Thumbing through the pages, he returned to the table and sat down. When he had the desired page, he slid the book in front of me. I didn't need to ask where he wanted me to read because he'd underlined the passage.

See that you take care of foreigners and strangers, for you also were once aliens in the land. You are my chosen vessel to look after their needs. Have I not looked after your needs during your stay on Earth?

I searched Strower's eyes for an explanation.

"I read that verse the morning you came to visit me," he said. "I underlined it because it seemed to hold a particular meaning that day. Amanda used to talk with the Creator in the morning. I thought she was silly. But after her death, I felt so empty and alone. I thought perhaps if I connected with the Creator, I'd somehow connect with her as well. So I talked but never heard anything—not until that day, not until I read that verse. I asked out loud, 'Who? Who is the stranger?' Then I heard it—a quiet voice from inside my soul, an impression, really—'Wait and see.' Later that day, you showed up."

"You could have fed me a meal, William. You could have sold me some hay. You didn't have to step out on this limb."

"Now you're talking like a fool, Jens. Your request was clear—you needed my influence. The Creator was asking me to surrender my ambition, my reputation, to serve you. I've never been one to do things halfway. Are you suggesting I start now? Do you think if I'd provided you a meal and sent you on your way, that this kind voice would have returned to me?"

"You've heard it since?"

"Yes."

"What did it say?"

Strower thought for a moment. "I'm just a novice, Jens. I don't know what's to share and what's to ponder in my own heart."

"I understand. It's none of my business, but has this voice given you a connection with your wife?"

Strower stared into his empty cup. "I'm ashamed of that motive now. I shouldn't have approached for that reason—not just to feel close to Amanda again. More misplaced mercy, I guess. The Creator used my emptiness, the void, to awaken a new hunger. So you see, Jens, I'm not just doing this for you."

After contemplating his words, I finally resigned myself to sharing common fate with Strower. My mind was full, and I longed for the unconsciousness of sleep. Finishing the conversation, I said, "So, we'll hope the farmers show up at the celebration feeling brave enough to plunge into our venture."

"Yes," said Strower as he stood, taking hold of the lantern's handle to lead us up the dark staircase to our bedrooms. Then he added, "Actually, I plan to coax their bravery a little."

"What do you mean?"

"May the Creator forgive me, but when I sent Carrie and the boys out to invite our neighbors to the celebration, I had her stop at Carl's. I told her to ask him to bring a barrel of his rum."

CHAPTER 16

On the day of the planting celebration, a warm breeze floated across Tuva's black fields, whispering hints of summer. Strower's men arrived at their usual hour, attending to the final preparations, including butchering a cow and preparing several fire pits along the pasture fence to be used for roasting meat.

Lundgren arrived around noon, hauling a barrel of his rum in the back of his wagon. Strower noticed him first, calling for my help before the hermit had even reached the house. "Let's get that barrel unloaded under that elm," he instructed, pointing to a huge tree. "Plenty of shade over there."

Strower waved at Lundgren. "This way, Carl. Do you have some wood to sell me?"

The question confounded Lundgren. "Wood?"

"Yes, like maybe an oak barrel."

"You just wanted the damn barrel?"

Winking at me, Strower replied, "Well, if there's rum inside, I guess I'll buy that too."

Grumbling unintelligibly, Lundgren spun around on the driver's bench and slid his compact body into the wagon's bed. Then, he carefully walked the barrel toward the rear by leaning it to the left and rolling it a few inches, leaning it to the right and rolling it a few more inches until he finally reached Strower and me at the back of the wagon. Strower handed Lundgren a fist full of money. Then he and I clumsily slid the barrel from the wagon, cradling it between the two of us, and staggered toward the trunk of the giant elm.

"That's a considerable amount of rum," I panted when we had the barrel placed next to the tree.

"It sure is," agreed Strower, sounding like he might've been second-guessing his decision to purchase an entire barrel. But it was too late to change his mind—the hired men were already making their way over to try a swig.

Carrie and the twins must have noticed Carl's arrival from inside the house because the door suddenly opened and out flew Magnus and Rasmus with Carrie on their heels. It had been bath day for the three of them, and Carrie had kept the boys clean for the celebration by caging them indoors until the first guest arrived, which happened to be Lundgren. The twins were more excited to watch the cow butchering than to greet their adopted uncle, but Carrie ran straight for Carl, barefoot, in a beautiful blue party dress, her golden curls tamed and arranged like a bride on her wedding day.

"Hello, Uncle Carl."

Hearing Carrie's voice, Lundgren stopped counting his money and jumped down from the wagon. It looked as though he'd also bathed for the occasion and shaved off his scruffy neck whiskers. He wore a nearly clean suit of clothes, terribly tight, with small circles of hairy skin showing between the strained buttons of his shirt. No doubt the clothes had fit him better when he was a younger man. He'd also slathered his cowlicked hair with what appeared to be lard in a fruitless attempt to make it conform to his skull. But despite the hair and tight clothing, Lundgren looked surprisingly handsome. He had a square jaw, a distinguished-looking nose, and emerald eyes—glowing with an uncompromising fusion of intelligence and insanity—that darted and refocused like an eagle watching field mice from a distant tree. He rarely made eye contact, but when he did, it was unnerving.

Carrie ran up to Lundgren and gave him a big hug. "Welcome," she said, kissing his cheek.

Wishing it was me she was kissing, I looked over at the hired men who'd gathered around the rum barrel. They were watching too, probably thinking the same thing—all except Oscar, who was instead watching me with eyes that almost matched Lundgren's in intensity.

By early afternoon, wagons dotted the landscape, traveling toward the farm from both directions. There couldn't have been more than an hour separating the first and last. They arrived in a festive spirit, two of the wagons even raced along the road, trying to be first to turn onto the path.

Tired as the farmers must've been from long hours of planting, they seemed ready to cut loose and have fun.

Once their wagons were parked, the family members went in three directions. Women and older girls, adorned in dresses, brought pies and cakes into the house, while the younger children congregated around Magnus and Rasmus, who were fixing to play games in the yard. After tying up their horses, the men and older boys sauntered over to the shade of the large elm and the rum barrel.

At first the men reclined, exchanging planting stories and sipping Lundgren's rum from cups. It wasn't long, though, before the younger men began pushing each other around like roosters establishing a pecking order. They'd come to wrestle, hoping to make a name for themselves among their elders. Now, filled with a little rum, the older men were becoming a boisterous audience, and soon the contests began.

Strower gave the job of overseeing the wrestling to Oscar. He'd won the event twice at the harvest festival, and all the young men looked up to him. I breathed a sigh of relief to see Oscar engaged as a referee because several nights earlier when he'd asked Strower at the supper table about wrestling, his words were directed at Strower, but his eyes at me. I'm sure he wanted to prove himself the better man to both Strower and Carrie. I'd mistakenly reasoned that he couldn't both officiate and wrestle, but Oscar showed more cunning than I thought.

Leading the young men to a grassy area with a shallow trench dug in a five-pace square, Oscar stood inside the square, and to my dismay, conscripted me as his mock contestant to go over the rules with the young men. Of course, his first order of business was to demonstrate illegal holds, which he then applied on me, roughly enough for the boys to witness my pained facial expressions.

I did my best to remain good-natured, trying to convince myself that as a mock opponent, I was only experiencing mock humiliation. As the demonstration continued, however, and the women came to watch, the embarrassment felt as real as the pain. When Oscar grabbed me from behind to demonstrate an illegal take-down, he clasped his hands around my waist, pinning my arms to my sides and lifting me off the ground. With no way to protect myself against what he'd do next, I panicked, pulling my right arm free and swinging my elbow wildly, catching him square in the nose. Suddenly, Oscar's hands unclasped, and I turned to see him kneeling in the grass, covering his face, blood dripping between his fingers.

My first instinct was to glance at the faces of the farmers. I didn't know if bloodying the nose of their champion would stir scorn or respect, but try as I might, I couldn't tell. Their glassy eyes were simply enjoying the show, most laughing, but Carrie wasn't laughing. Catching sight of her in the middle of the yard, she shot an icy glare, turned, and walked back to the house.

In Carrie's absence, two other young women eagerly filled her role as Oscar's nurse, quickly attending to his injury. Although he was jovial with the crowd, Oscar shot me a fiery glance, prompting my departure. With my crucial speech to give later, I headed to the barn to practice, reasoning that if Oscar needed to continue his demonstrations, he could recruit a different stooge.

Closing myself inside the barn, I climbed the ladder to the hayloft and made my way to the far wall where piled hay separated me from the rest of the world. Intending to practice my speech to an invisible audience of farmers, I noticed my hands shaking. Then my mind started racing. Had I jeopardized my friendship with Carrie? How would Strower react to what I'd done?

I lingered for some time, sorting my thoughts until the creaking ladder brought me back to the here and now. Thinking Oscar might be looking to even the score, I stayed still, listening, but I couldn't tell if I had company or not. Finally, disgusted with myself for hiding, I decided to face whoever might be invading my sanctuary.

Walking to the sidewall, I peeked around the pile of hay and saw Carrie standing at the edge of the loft, preparing to descend the ladder. She must've heard me because her head suddenly turned in my direction. "Oh, Jens, there you are. Are you hurt? I watched you come here from inside the house."

"I'm fine. I'm just practicing my speech to the farmers. I'm sorry about Oscar, I—"

"No! Don't apologize." She walked through the hay to where I was standing, holding out her arms as if to embrace me. "Are you sure you're not hurt?"

Grabbing her shoulders, I held off her embrace. As much as I'd envied Lundgren earlier, I didn't want her treating me like a child. "I'm fine. As I said, I'm practicing my speech."

Carrie took a step back. "It means a lot to you, doesn't it?"

"Of course. Your father has gone to great lengths to set this up. I don't want to let him down."

"I think I finally believe you."

"What's that supposed to mean?"

"It's just that I was so skeptical when you first arrived, questioning your motive for coming here. I'm sorry."

"No. You were right to question me. It forced me to examine myself . . . and your father."

"Really?"

"Yes. Your words hounded me until I finally asked him."

"Asked him what?"

"Why he's helping me."

"What did he say?"

"He told me he's been led to help."

"Led by?"

I nodded, feeling like I'd already said too much. Thankfully, the nod seemed to appease her.

Carrie smiled. "You know, I've been envious of you two."

"Who? Your father and me?"

"Yes, you sit together every night, and I can hear little bits and pieces of your conversation through the porch window. You two go off on such interesting tangents, and I'm stuck on the porch, listening to Oscar ramble on and on about rotating crops."

Sharing a laugh at Oscar's expense, we then fell silent.

Finally, Carrie glanced at the ladder. "Well, I better let you practice your speech. I waited in the house for everyone to head to the pasture to watch the horseracing before coming out here. Big Lars carried the barrel to the pasture on his shoulder, so I'm sure they'll be there a while."

"I'm glad I didn't have to wrestle *him*," I said.

Carrie reached out and squeezed my hand. "It was nice to have a few moments alone with you—without Oscar or the twins. My brothers are going to miss you—we all will. I'm sure you'll be leaving soon."

"I suppose so. Although, I've been so focused on this day, I haven't thought much about what lies beyond it."

"Well, good luck with the farmers."

As she walked away, I called her name, not knowing what I'd say next.

"Yes?"

"I'd take that hug now."

Making her way back through the hay, she threw her arms around me. After a few precious seconds, I felt her body convulsing. I couldn't see her face buried in my chest, but I could hear her weeping.

"What's wrong?"

"I don't know what to do," she moaned between sobs.

I led her to the piled hay, her face still hidden in my chest, and we sat down together. "What do you mean?"

"My father's warming to Oscar. I don't think it will be long before he gives him permission to marry me."

"What will you do?"

She looked into my eyes without attempting to wipe away the tears cascading down her face. "I don't know."

I'd never seen her this vulnerable. She was always so strong and confident—qualities I admired but her current state melted me.

"I'm confused. My mother always told my father that Oscar reminded her of him when he was young. I've clung to that, but mother never knew my father as he is now. Although, maybe she saw him from afar—she had sight like that. But I don't. I can't see what he'll become. And I'm not sure I'm willing to wait twenty years for him to grow into something other than a good farmer."

Wiping her eyes, Carrie suddenly sat straight. "I better leave you alone. I don't want to distract you with this."

I placed my hand on her shoulder. "Wait. To be honest, I couldn't concentrate anyway. I was worried you'd be upset with me for what I did to Oscar."

"Hah! I saw him out there, seeking attention from those two girls. They can have him for all I care."

Wondering now if she was merely jealous and had more affection for Oscar than she was letting on, I asked, "Will you marry him?"

Staring at the floor for a moment, she then cleared her throat. "Can we talk about something else?"

"Gladly. What would you like to talk about?"

"Let's talk about you."

"I'm afraid that's not a very interesting topic."

"Growing up with the king? That's not interesting?"

"Well, perhaps my circumstances have been interesting, but I think my opportunities could have been placed better with someone else, someone bolder—like your father."

"You really like him, don't you?"

"I do."

"Well, you're interesting to me, Jens. I'll tell you what—let me be the judge. Tell me something about Jens Berrit that no one else knows."

"What do you mean?"

She took my hand. "You know what I mean. Have you ever shared anything personal with a girl? Something from your heart?"

"Not really," I said. But her question reminded of the occasional conversation I had with a marble statue on the palace grounds, so I added—"not with a real girl, anyhow."

Carrie laughed. "What does that mean?"

Nervously laughing with her, I wondered if I dared tell her about my secret friendship with the statue. It certainly qualified as something intimate. I'd never shared it with anyone.

"Promise not to laugh?"

"I promise." She nestled into the hay alongside me, still holding my hand. Then, leaning her head on my shoulder, she whispered, "Go ahead."

"Well, there's this white marble statue of a woman just outside the palace in the Royal City. She's fascinated me since I was a child. It's only a woman's head and a naked torso with outstretched arms, not well-defined—the lines are very smooth, and the image is only a crude representation. She has no features at all on her face."

"Why does she captivate you so?"

"That's hard to explain. I learned only recently that the sculptor intended her to represent the nation of Tuva, calling her children to her breast."

"Is that the impression she gives you—a sense of home?"

"In a way, but more than that. I've always had an anxious soul—I fret over things. Not long ago, my mother told me that my father was amazed at my ability to try things—in spite of my timidity. I'm a terrible mix of ambition and fear, never really at rest."

". . . and this statue seems to offer you rest?"

"I guess she does—or comfort maybe. I've always wondered if she has a face—you know, for me."

Carrie looked into my eyes. "Thank you for that gift."

"Gift? What do you mean?"

"Well, if I marry Oscar, I'm certain never to hear anything like that from his lips." Then, touching my lower lip with her index finger, she added, "It was nice to hear it from yours. I've always wanted to share a moment like this with a boy."

"A boy?"

"Don't be offended, Jens. I've only recently become a woman. Do you think I've dreamt of men? Well, maybe now I will. I hope you haven't ruined me for—" She didn't finish the sentence.

I desperately wanted to kiss her. She smelled fresh from her bath, and I wanted to taste her lips, or just breathe the air she exhaled—see if I could draw life from her lungs. But if I did, what then? I didn't know *what then*. I only knew it wasn't fair to kiss her without being ready for *what then*.

Still holding my hand, Carrie settled back to ponder what I'd told her. Without looking at me, she said, "I wonder why men are such incomplete projects. Does every man need a woman to finish him?"

Before I could contemplate her question, the barn doors swung open, flooding our nest with sunlight. From our vantage point, we couldn't see who'd entered, but we could hear footsteps walking up the center aisle. Sitting deathly still, we waited for what seemed an eternity. Someone was stirring in the back of the barn, but we couldn't discern who it was or what they were doing.

Finally, I pushed Carrie on her back, covering her with hay so she couldn't be spotted. Looking worried, Carrie only nodded. Then I crawled to the front of the loft, lying on my belly near the edge. After a few moments, I heard horse hooves clomping up the stone aisle, making their way to the front of the barn.

When the noise was directly below me, I peeked over the edge to see Oscar riding toward the barn door atop one of the king's horses.

CHAPTER 17

Outside the barn, Oscar stabbed his heels into the flanks of the majestic animal. With a belligerent snort, the horse bolted toward the pasture.

Sitting up from her casket of hay, Carrie swatted leafy remnants from her hair, and together we listened to the pounding hooves, the sound gradually disappearing in the direction of the racetrack. "Who was that?" she asked.

"Oscar," I yelled, scrambling down the ladder. "He stole my horse!"

Carrie called my name, but I ignored her. Instead, I raced from the barn through the pasture grass, determined to address Oscar's blatant disrespect. Never mind that I'd been with his girl in the loft. Never mind that I hadn't even bothered to name the damned beast. Suddenly that horse was my prized possession, and Oscar swiping it was an unforgivable insult.

Cresting the hill between the barn and the race track, I spotted Strower already giving Oscar a piece of his mind, his arms flailing to punctuate the words I couldn't hear. Sitting like a general on a war-horse, Oscar ignored Strower's rant, watching the horserace instead, the current heat of five making their way around the track. But Strower extinguished Oscar's obstinacy by pulling the reins from his hands and pushing him off the horse.

Falling on his back like a lifeless sack of flour, Oscar struggled to get air back into his lungs before trying to stand. Strower removed the horse's bit and bridle, slapping the animal on the backside, sending it deeper into the pasture. Then he stood over his rebellious farmhand, who was staggering to his feet. Finally, wobbling to a squatting stance, Oscar balled his fists and took a drunken swing at Strower, which Strower easily side-stepped. The momentum of the victimless punch nearly fell Oscar again, but he caught himself, reeling clumsily to face his employer.

By this time, I was close enough to hear Strower's words. "Get off my property."

"Is that you talkin', William," replied Oscar, pointing an unsteady finger in my direction, "or are those words comin' from the king's jester over there?"

Strower took a step closer, bringing his lips within inches of Oscar's face. "Would you think so little of the king's power if you stood before him as a horse thief? Dammit, Oscar. I'm your employer. I'm responsible for your actions on this farm."

Oscar stood dumbfounded like someone had clunked him over the head with a brick. Then Strower's voice went soft, his eyes possessing a deep sadness. "I want you off my property."

Taking a moment to read Strower, Oscar stood like a shanty in a windstorm, tilting back and forth ever so slightly. I wondered what he was thinking. Was he contemplating how to save face with the crowd? Maybe he was reliving his past with Strower—the man who'd been more a father than an employer. He could've been wondering the same thing I was wondering: Did Strower mean for him to leave until he was sober, or did he mean forever? Or maybe, being a practical man, he was contemplating what the king would do to a horse thief. For all I knew, Lundgren's rum may have so scrambled his mind that he was only trying to focus his eyes.

Whatever Oscar was looking for in William Strower's face, he finally found it. A clarity came over him, even in his drunkenness. Picking his hat off the ground, he walked past me, staring blankly at the horizon. The on-looking crowd whispered among themselves as he wove a crooked line through the pasture toward the barn. While watching him leave, I spotted Carrie traversing the hill, making her way toward the track. When she saw Oscar approaching, she stopped, waiting for him to reach her. I looked on apprehensively, dreading what he'd do when he saw bits and pieces of hay in her hair. But Oscar didn't seem to notice her. He simply walked on by, leaving Carrie standing alone. Now looking confused, Carrie again turned toward the track, but her feet didn't move. Eventually, she turned away from the festivities and headed back toward the house.

Of course, this drama didn't dampen the liveliness of the farmers. There were six planned horseraces, the winner from each heat to square off in a final race to determine the grand champion. The horses were by no means thoroughbreds but rather draft-animals, unhitched from wagons and ridden bareback. By the end of the sixth heat, it wasn't so much a contest of whose horse was fastest but which rider could stay mounted. Howling with laughter, the raucous crowd cheered wildly during the final race, as limp bodies flew into the straw lining the outside of the track, too relaxed to sustain injuries. In the end, Strower had the decision of either giving the grand-prize to the owner of a white horse that crossed the finish line first, but without its rider, or the second-place horse who'd miraculously retained a passenger. To the crowd's delight, Strower chose the latter.

Before the crowd could disperse, Strower gathered the men, asking for their attention. His timing surprised me because we'd discussed having the meeting after the meal, but I think Strower was concerned about their mental disintegration. The rum had gone beyond its task of making them brave and was now making them stupid.

When everyone had assembled and a tolerable silence was achieved, Strower began. "Thank you for coming today, my friends. I think it's good to celebrate the completion of planting."

Everyone cheered as Strower hoisted his unused cup—nothing but a prop—high above his head, his eyes dancing with delight. "Planting is hard work—at least, on this farm it is." Then pausing for dramatic effect, he added, "However, I see some of you have taught your horses to do the work on their own."

With that, the crowd hooted, and the owner of the white horse bowed deeply, causing his hat to fall off.

When Strower had their attention again, he grew serious. "My friends, before we feast, I'd like to take a moment to share an opportunity. Some of you may have met Jens today."

Strower motioned for me to squeeze through the tight circle of farmers, joining him in the center. When I did, he placed a hand on my shoulder. "Jens is the new liaison between the king and us farmers. The king has discovered foreign markets for our crops and would like to build an alliance with us—to grow crops for export. He's willing to pay a handsome price to those who'll grow beets and hay for him. I, for one, intend to take advantage of this opportunity, and I thought you might be interested as well."

"How much you lookin' to purchase?" someone shouted.

"All you can spare," I replied.

The same man spoke up again, "I don't have no beets, and I won't know how much hay I can spare 'til I see how things go this summer."

Nodding, I said, "I understand your reluctance to sell hay this early, and I'll have to be satisfied to wait, but Mr. Strower has just now cleared and planted a small field for beets. If you men would consider doing the same, we'd have a nice pile of Tuvan beets at the port this fall. I've already secured the seed, and I'd be happy to send it home with you today—if you'll agree to plant this season.

"How much you willing to pay?" one of them asked.

"Two-fifths more than the merchants in the Royal City. I'll leave it to William to verify the market price."

"What you payin' for hay?"

"Same as the beets—two-fifths over the market price, verified by Mr. Strower."

Looking at the sea of faces, I felt encouraged. Strower's planting celebration had successfully summoned a brave spirit, and their hearts seemed open to risk. Guessing by their looks, they weren't contemplating *if* they should get involved, but rather *how*.

Glancing at Strower for a signal to either stop or continue, I judged by his smile and his slight nod that I'd said enough for the moment. Soon, the farmers were discussing among themselves how they might take advantage of this late-season opportunity. After a few moments, Strower asked, "Are there more questions for Jens?"

To my dismay, it was Lundgren who spoke up, "I have a question—"

Feeling the blood drain from my face, I tried to appear calm. "Yes, Mr. Lundgren?"

"How does that rascal of a king have time to worry about growin' beets when he don't have time to protect Tuva's border in the south?"

Lundgren's voice seemed remarkably calm for the moment, but I knew how his temper could escalate, and the image of that hatchet buried in the king's crest came rushing back. Suddenly, my mind went blank, and I looked at Strower, silently pleading for help.

Calmly, Strower raised his arms above his head, gaining the attention of the mumbling crowd. "Carl, this is news to me. What're you saying? What've you heard?"

"It ain't just what I heard, William—it's what I seen . . . I git down there some."

Muffled laughter arose from the crowd. It seemed everyone knew about Lundgren's not-so-secret life as a bootlegger.

"What's so funny?" Lundgren squealed, his feet shuffling, and his breathing becoming labored. He was on his way to another tantrum, and once started, there'd be no stopping it.

Fortunately, Strower quickly intervened. "Carl, no one's laughing at you. Now settle down and tell us what's happening down south."

"It's Dag! They're invading the farms down there, stealing their herds."

"Dag?" replied Strower. "They're nothing but a collection of backward tribes. How would they have the nerve to invade Tuva?"

"Been invading for a while now, but the king ignores it. He won't offer 'em no help. He gets paid to send his soldiers out with ships, protectin' cargo from pirates—why'd he want to protect his people? That don't pay nothin'. He's evil. Pure evil!"

Strower turned to me. "What do you know about this?"

"Nothing."

"Liar!" yelled Lundgren.

Like a toppled beehive, the crowd went abuzz, whispering among themselves, peering back and forth between Lundgren and me. Fortunately, an old farmer with a long white beard was standing right in front of me. Raising his bushy eyebrows, he cleared his throat, and with a calming voice, asked, "Son could these reports be true?"

The old man must've had everyone's respect because they all quieted down, turning their attention to my response.

"I suppose anything is possible, but, on my word, I've not heard such a report."

With that, the chatter from the crowd grew louder and more chaotic. I could see Lundgren trying to worm his way toward the center of the circle, probably hoping to spew more of his venom against the king, but before he could further incite the crowd, Strower spoke up.

"I have a proposal."

The crowd once again grew quiet, and Strower continued, "I propose that Jens, Carl, and I take a trip down south to see what's happening. If King Thoren isn't protecting the farmers, we might be in a good position to use leverage to get them the help they need. We can offer to sell our crops to the king in exchange for his commitment to protect farms from these invasions. Or, if there's nothing to these reports, we can put it to rest."

Strower's eyes scanned the wall of faces. "Well? What do you think?"

Everyone looked at the old farmer whose jaws seemed to be chewing on nothing other than his thoughts. After staring at the ground for a long time, he finally spoke up: "I like your plan, William. Those of us who work the land should stick together. If Dag is invading our southern borders now, who's to say they won't come here next? There's strength in numbers—but I'm like you, Carl. I don't much like the king's involvement with farming, but we're not going to stop that—and we'd be fools to make him our enemy."

Then, turning to Strower, the old man made his final assessment: "William, if you can use the king's desires to create leverage for us farmers—protection in the south and better prices for us—I don't think we have any choice but to go along with it."

Wisdom had spoken, and the younger farmers nodded in agreement. Why wouldn't they? The way Strower had explained it, they'd be helping their brethren in the south and lining their own pockets at the same time—not much of a sacrifice. But what no one seemed to understand was that Thoren wasn't one to let others dictate how things would go. What good is leverage against an immovable object?

Someone from the crowd asked Strower when he intended to leave. "No point in waiting. I propose we leave tomorrow." Then, looking at me, he added, "If that works for you and Carl . . ."

If it works for me and Carl? *There is no me and Carl.* That's what I wanted to say. I'd already committed to intervening on Lundgren's behalf—pulling his head from the noose of the tax collectors. In my estimation, King Thoren would likely honor that request as a favor—a necessity of engaging in commerce. But this was too much—accompanying this crazy coot down south to build a case against Thoren. And how long would this take? Too much time had already elapsed without giving Thoren any news of my whereabouts or my progress. I'm sure Emil-the-innkeeper was frantically trying to locate me, which he'd undoubtedly do now after this huge celebration. There'd surely be farmers discussing this little meeting around the innkeeper's breakfast tables in the morning.

Lundgren's scratchy voice interrupted my thoughts—"I'll go."

All eyes were now on me, exploring my face. I had no choice, no way out. "Very well, I'll go too."

Now Strower seized his opportunity to push for a commitment from the farmers. "My friends, if we're to use your cooperation as leverage, we'll need your written pledge to grow crops for the king. We can make your commitment to sell hay contingent on three cuttings this year, but we'll need something in writing."

The old man with the white beard gave a quick nod. "That's a fair thing to ask."

"Good. Let's eat! Jens and I will come around while you're feasting and get your signatures on a letter-of-intent. That'll give us something to show the king."

As the crowd headed back toward the house, Strower pulled me aside. "Jens, some of these men are substantially drunk. We need to get this letter-of-intent drawn up fast. We'll worry about writing contracts later, but if we don't get them to sign something today, half of them won't remember what they've committed to by tomorrow."

Together, Strower and I went to the house to find parchment for the letter-of-intent. Inside, the women were crowding the kitchen, trying to prepare their food for serving. Scanning both the kitchen and the parlor, I saw no sign of Carrie. Wondering if she'd perhaps left with Oscar, I glanced through the parlor window, and, to my relief, saw her sitting in the yard, playing with the young children. My eyes lingered. I wanted badly to talk with her to see how she was doing.

When Strower found the parchment, he ripped a large sheet in half and drew four lines with ink from top to bottom on both pieces, labeling the columns: NAME, BEET ACREAGE, HAY ACREAGE, and GROWER'S SIGNATURE. Handing one piece to me, he said, "This is all we'll have time for, Jens. Once they sit down to eat, you take one of these letters and cover the families on the south side of the path. I'll take the north."

Then Strower pulled out another sheet of parchment, ripping it into many small pieces. Handing half to me, he instructed, "Use these to write their commitments and give it to their wives. They'll make sure their husbands see to it after the rum wears off."

It was a beautiful evening with a light breeze keeping the insects at bay. In no hurry to leave, the families reclined on blankets in the grass, enjoying the meal. Strower and I frantically moved between blankets with pen and ink. By the time the families were piling into their wagons to head home, we'd talked with nearly everyone, save a couple of Strower's closest neighbors, whom William promised to visit in the coming days. Almost every farmer I spoke with committed to growing beets, some intending to plow the land between their outbuildings to gain the necessary acreage. We gave beet seed to the wives, along with the small squares of parchment, reminding them of their commitment.

Their willingness to sell hay, however, was a different story. True to Strower's prediction, the farmers were reluctant to make even a contingent commitment so early in the year. Once the families were gone, Strower coaxed me inside to compare notes. Mounting the porch, I saw Carrie sitting alone in a chair next to the parlor window. Strower stopped, looking at his forlorn daughter, but didn't say anything. In the silence that ensued, Carrie's chin began quivering, and she quickly looked away. Strower took a step in her direction but then decided instead to lead me inside the house, marching purposefully to the dining room table.

Placing both pieces of parchment side by side on the table, Strower scrolled the columns with his eyes, following the names and numerals with his index finger. After some consideration, he tapped the table with his knuckles. "I'll bet we'll nearly fill that ship with beets."

"Really?"

"I think so," replied Strower, yawning. "But we didn't get enough hay to choke a goat. I knew the hay would be a problem."

My heart sank. If Thoren didn't collect the hay he promised to Sagan's king, there wouldn't be a ship to fill with beets. "What will I do?" I asked, not expecting an answer.

"This might sound crazy," said Strower, rubbing his tired eyes, "but Carl may have solved your problem today."

"Lundgren? What do you mean?"

"Well, you've told me yourself that King Thoren was renting out his soldiers to protect Gladonese ships."

"Yeah, so what?"

"How did Carl find out about that? I don't think he's making up this story about the invasions."

"You believe him?"

"I do."

"Well, if it's true, how does that solve my problem? It seems like it makes matters worse."

"Jens, the only thing those farmers grow down there is hay. Their land isn't fit for anything else. They pasture their cattle on the grassy hillsides in the summer, and they cut the flat ground for winter hay. Now, if some of the farmers have lost their herds to rustlers from Dag, they'll have hay they can't use. The least the king can do is give them a good price for it. It's probably the only money they'll have to get through the winter."

Stunned by Strower's ability to spot an opportunity in the bleakest of circumstances, I asked, "Are you telling me you thought of all this since Lundgren spoke up?"

"I suppose so."

Letting Strower's assessment trickle through my mind for a moment, I whispered, "So, Thoren's neglect might turn out to be his salvation."

CHAPTER 18

In the darkness of night, Strower knocked on my bedroom door, asking if I was ready to leave. He didn't pose the sentence as a question, though, and his feet clomped down the staircase before I had a chance to respond.

I rolled out of bed and threw on my clothes by the scant light of the stars. Then I stood before the chest of drawers, wondering what to pack for the journey. I didn't know we'd be leaving at this hour. Strower had stayed up late with Carrie, and I'd gone off to bed early, so we hadn't even discussed our trip.

Suddenly, it occurred to me that my time at the Strower house was likely over. Swallowing the sickening realization that I wouldn't have a chance to set things right with Carrie, I opened each drawer, blindly sweeping the contents into my bag. With the last article, however, I hesitated, knowing that with its disappearance, the house was rid of me.

Even more sickening was the thought that I'd now be sharing space with the man who gave my wagon its scar. Reluctantly, I picked up my bag and blew air through my lips, as if extinguishing a flickering candle. Once in the hallway, I couldn't make myself shut the bedroom door. I didn't want to hear the clicking latch. Illogically, it seemed like an open door might call me back. So with an eerie creak, I pushed it a handbreadth shy of closed and headed downstairs where Strower stood waiting.

At the landing, I noticed a light emanating from the kitchen. Over my shoulder, I saw Carrie leaning against the cupboard, still wearing her nightgown, her long curls strewn in a tangle. She didn't appear to have slept much. Her sad eyes met mine for only a moment before dropping to the floor. More than anything, I wanted to comfort her and tell her how much she meant to me, but Strower was standing at the end of the hall, holding the door open, radiating urgency. It wasn't the time to start a conversation, so I simply spoke her name. When she looked up, I gave her a reassuring nod. Then, turning toward Strower, I lugged my belongings to the wagon.

Traveling to Lundgren's in the dark, Strower drove the wagon with his collar turned up and his wide-brimmed hat pulled down over his forehead, giving every indication he wanted to be left alone. I wondered what Carrie had shared with him after I went to bed. I wasn't likely a part of their conversation, but what if I was? What if she'd told her father about the hayloft? Honoring my instincts to sit quietly, I let the crickets carry the conversation. More than likely, Strower's mind was devising a plan, and he needed time to think.

The silence gave me time to contemplate things too. Much had happened in one short day, and I wanted to get my bearings. What would happen at sunup at the Strower farm? Would Oscar show up for work? Was Carrie hoping he would? I couldn't stop thinking about the hayloft. For her, it seemed to be an experience she'd wanted to have with a *boy*—a stolen moment, an indulgence to her youth before becoming a farmer's wife. But if the experience had given Carrie closure, it had the opposite effect on me. It woke a deep hunger. Carrie was glowing in my soul, and my desires now seemed to be conforming around her. I couldn't stop thinking about her skin, her hair, her smile. Even her tears were something I now wanted to touch.

Suddenly, I wondered if Strower could sense my thoughts, which seemed savory enough to permeate the air beyond my skull. Thankfully, one glance to my left told me he was still in his private world—that place his mind went to shape the future. As I was settling back into my thoughts, Strower startled the darkness. "It's probably best for you to surrender your seat to Carl," he said, turning onto Lundgren's obscure path. "He won't be much company for me, but he is your elder."

So I spent the day in the back of the wagon with my bag as a pillow, trying to use sleep as a tool to speed the trip, but the ruts in the road allowed only an exhausting catnap. Sitting next to Strower, Lundgren was merely a lump on the seat, giving incoherent grunts as his part of what could barely be called a conversation. If I didn't know better, I'd have thought the man was incapable of speech. But if that were the case, I wouldn't have been bouncing around in the bed of the damn wagon.

Trying not to think about Carrie, I forced myself to instead wonder about Thoren. I suspected by now he'd be frantic for news as to my whereabouts and a report of my progress. He'd instructed me to stay at the inn, where Emil could keep him abreast of my comings and goings, just as he kept watch over the blacksmith. I'd thrown a fly in the ointment by abandoning my room without leaving word. But if the innkeeper asked around, he'd soon know that I'd unveiled a proposal to more than thirty farmers, rewarded with preliminary commitments to grow beets. Thoren would take that as good news.

Unfortunately, the innkeeper probably also knew I was heading for Tuva's southern border to look into the king's alleged failure to protect the farmers in the south. I could only imagine the sense of betrayal that would stir. Thoren had sent me out as his ambassador, and here I was acting like an inspector, evaluating his competence to rule.

Was Thoren fit to rule? He was either a progressive king or a selfish tyrant, depending on whom you asked. His advisors hated him, but in my opinion, they were greedy tyrants in their own right. My father was the first and only advisor in Tuva's history who hadn't inherited his seat but was *invited* to sit at the table by Thoren's father, who sought his knowledge of history. All the other seats were occupied by ancient right, held by representatives from noble families whose ancestors fought alongside King Tuva at the nation's inception. Back then, the nobles wanted the power to rein-in a wayward king by controlling his purse. But when they sat down to draw the founding documents, King Tuva insisted on full reign over his army. He argued that they shouldn't muddle critical military decisions with the need to gain advisory approval. In the end, the nobles submitted to the king's request with the stipulation that military force is never used against them. A soldier who turns against noble blood commits treason, so the soldier's oath states.

Now, generations later, Thoren had discovered an opportunity to use his kingly prerogative to raise money. By renting Tuva's soldiers to foreign ship-owners, he was raising the funds needed to finish his port. Understandably, the advisors considered this a treasonous act, undermining their ability to limit his power. The Crucible had always been considered Tuva's greatest vulnerability. The advisors thought Thoren's port was an invitation to hostile ships. If an enemy sailed into Keenod, there'd now be docks waiting—and precious few soldiers to protect us.

In Thoren's mind, the port was a calculated risk. Tuva needed to press forward into the new age of trade, or be left forever in the dark ages. To his way of thinking, the port was Tuva's only hope, and if his advisors were too blind to see it, he'd simply work around them. And so the battle-lines were drawn, and Thoren's advisors were losing.

Now, Dag was supposedly invading from the south. News like that would have Thoren's advisors licking their chops. *"See?"* they'd scoff. *"If the backward people of Dag can invade Tuva, think what might happen at the port!"* They'd capitalize on that kind of news to whip up public dissension. I knew their hatred for Thoren. I'd felt it at my induction ceremony.

Strower bought Lundgren's story about the invasions, but I was struggling to believe that Thoren would turn a deaf ear to his subjects. It's easy to assume the worst. That's why rumors are so insidious—one part truth and three parts nonsense.

Suddenly, I began wondering what kind of rumors the innkeeper was spreading about me. One part truth—I was heading to Saleton with a man who hates the king. My mind raced with all the terrible things a paranoid ruler could fabricate from that. Thoren would not be happy that his spy lost track of me, and Emil seemed like the sort of man who'd gladly slander me to save his hide.

When I was little, my mother used to say, "Jens, you leave a mess everywhere you go." I guess not too much had changed. I took some solace, however, in the fact that the mess wasn't entirely of my making, and if anyone could understand how messy getting results can be, it was Thoren. He had his list of desires, and obtaining those desires was his sole focus—damn the consequences. High on that list was a ship, and to get that vessel, he needed hay. Without hay to feed the king of Sagan's livestock, Thoren would not only lose his boat, but he'd likely also gain a new enemy on his eastern border.

If Strower's hunch was right—if there were barns full of hay in the south without livestock to consume it—then south is where I needed to go. Over and over, I ruminated on this logic, perfecting it for when I'd stand before Thoren.

After a long day of traveling, we camped just off the road, near a stand of trees split by a peaceful stream. Strower asked Carl to build a fire and me to unhitch the horses and bring them to the creek for water. While Carl and I attended to our chores, Strower familiarized himself with the king's maps. When our work was finished, we sat in the grass next to the flames, where Strower opened a large picnic basket. To my surprise, the first thing he pulled out was my jacket, the one I kept on a hook next to the door. Strower flung it at me. "Carrie's looking out for you, Jens. Good thing, too. It feels like it might be cool tonight."

After supper, Lundgren and Strower situated themselves for sleeping on the ground next to the fire. I had my choice of either sleeping next to them or in the bed of the wagon. While contemplating, I slipped my hands into my jacket pockets. That's when I felt a small scroll. Not wanting Strower or Lundgren to see what I was doing, I examined the rolled parchment with my fingers from inside the pocket. I couldn't think of what it could be unless Carrie had written me a note. After loitering at the fire for a while, I announced I'd be sleeping in the wagon. Crawling into the bed, I positioned myself to gain discrete use of the light from the campfire. Then, reaching into my pocket, I pulled out the little scroll. It was Carrie's handwriting. I'd grown to admire it from our lessons with the boys.

Jens,

I'm not sure when or if we'll see each other again, so I thought I'd write. I want you to know that you bear no responsibility for what happened with Oscar. Maybe it was for the best.

I wish great things for you, although you're still such a boy – still hiding behind others.

Jens, if you must hide behind my father, please guard his back. Magnus and Rasmus still need him, and so do I.

I've been thinking about your statue, wondering your reason for telling me about her. I suppose I flatter myself, but if you've thought to give her my face, you'd be wrong. I can't give weight to your soul.

Carrie

I lie numbly, the crickets seeming to chirp their lonely chorus from inside my head. As much as I hated her calling me a boy, it was Carrie's final sentence that gutted me. I couldn't believe she'd written it. And the more I thought about it, the more confused and angry I became.

Hadn't she cozied up to me in the hayloft, begging to hear something intimate? My feelings about that statue were a mystery even to me. There was profound gravity in my hope that the woman had a face—like ballast buried at the bottom of a ship, keeping it from capsizing in a storm. I had a reason for sharing that memory—Carrie gave me the same sensation as the statue, but with flesh and blood instead of cold marble. To think that she'd discerned this, and dismissed it, left me incredibly empty. Why had I given her that power? I should never have called her back when she was leaving the loft.

Then, more of her words haunted me—the words she'd spoken before Oscar opened the barn door: *"I wonder why men are such incomplete projects. Does every man need a woman to finish him?"*

At the time, I stupidly thought she was talking about Oscar, but now I could see she was talking about me. Her mother spent twenty years changing William from someone like Oscar into a good man, and Amanda never lived to see it. I suppose Carrie was sitting next to me in the hayloft, wondering how long it'd take to fix me—to give me substance. At least with Oscar, a precedent had been set—twenty years. Then, she'd likely have something to show for it—like taking a pie out of the oven. Oscar was a twenty-year pie. And what was I? To her, I was a boy who might never gain the substance of a man.

Reading the note over and over, I finally crumpled it in my hand. Couldn't she understand that my nature is what placed me in awe of her most precious gifts? She made me feel adventurous and brave. She helped me see with better eyes. I thought she'd felt what I had—the sense of being transformed in the presence of a complimentary soul. Why had she invited my affection in the first place? Why did she run her toes up my stocking? It must've been a reckless game to see how much sway she held over me. Damn her. She and Oscar deserved each other.

I arose at first light to study the maps, trying to determine the best route to get where Dag's Valley of Ten Tribes shared its border with Tuva. I found a low area where the river separating Tuva from Dag cut through the steep mountains. If tribes from Dag were stealing livestock, they'd most likely drive them across the border at that point. Sure enough, it was in that corner, the southwest corner of Tuva, where I found the small town I'd heard Lundgren mention to Strower. The name of the village was Saleton. After memorizing the roads leading there, I began hitching up the horses.

My commotion woke both Strower and Lundgren, and by the time they'd worked the cricks out of their bones, I had mounted the bench and sat waiting for them to climb on board. Unaccustomed to being a passenger, Strower wasn't sure where to sit. His decision was finally made by Lundgren, who quietly crawled in the back, probably relieved that he'd no longer need to carry on a conversation.

We finished our journey in silence, except for an occasional observation by Strower, mostly involving farming. Driving the wagon, I sat as his student, listening and learning. It was a welcome distraction.

By mid-afternoon, we'd reached Saleton, hungry and tired. The cozy little river town sat nestled in the foothills with the grand mountains of Tuva's border as its backdrop to the south and west. Strower and I marveled at the view, but Lundgren concerned himself with more practical matters. "There's an inn up this street," he grunted, poking his stubby index-finger between Strower and me while hunching on his knees in the back of the wagon. "There's food and rum there."

CHAPTER 19

Saleton's inn stood on the outskirts of town, the last shred of civilization before the road terminated at the river. I felt like I was viewing the edge of the world. Up ahead, I could see the riverbank, and beyond that, the vast wilderness of Dag.

Generations ago, the people of Dag were forced across the river when prince Tuva, the ambitious second-born son of Sagan's king, sailed his ships into The Crucible to claim a kingdom of his own. With no collective army, Dag's small tribes didn't offer much of a fight. Most of the tribes now lived secluded, deep in the mountains to the south and west. But ten tribes chose to settle in a valley near Saleton, directly behind the mountain that we were now admiring. This region was aptly named *The Valley of Ten Tribes*.

Pulling the wagon alongside the inn, the three of us dismounted. "You two go in," Strower told Lundgren and me, "I'll be right there." Looking at each other awkwardly, the two of us obediently started for the door, but before we were out of earshot, Strower added, "Jens, you might want to keep your employment under your hat for now. I don't know what we're walking into here."

Lundgren entered the inn first, with me on his heels. The spacious front-room was lit yellow by the low rays of the setting sun. To our left stood a massive oak counter with bulky stools, and to our right, an assortment of tables, covered with white food-stained tablecloths, each adorned with a wilting flower arrangement hastily stabbed into an ale mug, the detached petals lying on the white cloth like dead soldiers in the snow. Further back was a darker, more private room, where I fully expected Lundgren to burrow, but to my surprise, he pulled out a stool and bellied up to the counter. With Strower still outside, I kept an open seat between Lundgren and me, sitting next to a man who appeared to be a fixture in the place. Like the flower arrangements, the man was trying to pull moisture from a dry mug, his drunken head bobbing up and down. "Hello," I said, but he didn't respond.

At the far end of the counter, the proprietor was busy separating a giant pile of silverware into neat stacks. Looking up from his work, he recognized Lundgren. "Carl," he called out, making his way over. "What brings you to Saleton? I still have two full barrels in my cellar, and I don't have the money right now to buy more."

Lacking the social etiquette to make a proper introduction, Lundgren only grimaced, signaling his unwillingness to discuss his rum business in my presence.

Clueless as to what the grimace meant, the proprietor turned his attention to me. "Are the two of you together?"

I hesitated, remembering that Strower had asked me to leave out a big part of my story. "Well, there's three of us, actually. William will be in shortly."

As if on cue, Strower threw open the door and bounded across the room with his signature gait, bigger than life. "Have you two ordered yet?" he asked, even before reaching us. "I could eat the south end of a north-bound skunk." Pulling out his stool, he extended his hand to the proprietor. "Hello. My name is William Strower."

Curiously eying the three of us, the proprietor seemed mildly entertained by the odd assortment we made. "What bring's you men down here? Carl, aren't you from up around Tinsdal? If you'd wait long enough, you'd get our north-bound skunks."

Everyone laughed, except Lundgren, who didn't seem able to shake his grimace. When we didn't reply, the proprietor added, "Well, we might be eating our skunks before long—if we keep losing our damn cattle."

With that, Lundgren slid his rear to the edge of his stool, as if ready to head back to Tinsdal. With his story confirmed, I suppose he thought there was nothing left to do.

Strower coaxed Lundgren back onto his stool by pulling on his sleeve. Then, with what pretended to be a mild interest, he asked, "Losing your cattle down here, huh?"

"You haven't heard? Warriors from Dag are rustling our herds." Then, pointing at the drunk sitting to my left, he added, "He was the last victim."

"That's too bad," said Strower, leaning forward on his stool and peeking at the farmer. The gray-faced man stared straight ahead, too far gone to know we were talking about him.

Acting as though he was ready to move on to another topic, Strower placed his hand on my shoulder. "Well, we're down here for a little adventure. Jens here has been working on my farm this spring, and now with the planting finished, Carl and I figured it was time to teach him how to drink."

"No rum in Tinsdal?" the proprietor quipped, smiling at Lundgren. "That's hard to believe."

Lundgren's grimace turned frighteningly scowlish, reminding me of what the blacksmith had told me in secret—that the tax collectors were bearing down on him, and the wily Lundgren wasn't selling his rum around Tinsdal anymore. I'm sure the proprietor was clueless of Lundgren's circumstances, but the innocent jab had triggered Carl's ire, and his berserker symptoms were kicking in.

Diverting the attention from Lundgren, Strower addressed the proprietor, "You can't train a boy how to drink near home. It could ruin his reputation forever."

Upon hearing the word *boy*, I felt a scowl of my own forming. Strower's daughter had already given me that title, and I didn't need to listen to it from him. In passive protest, I disengaged from Strower's little stage performance, turning on my stool to see what else was going on in the room. The place was quickly filling with dusty men, probably slipping in for the latest news and some spirited camaraderie before heading home for supper. Across the room, a table of four young men, about my age, had their eyes on me. Three of them looked down immediately, as if guilty of talking behind our backs, but the fourth waved, giving me a friendly smile. Then, standing up, he came over and parked himself between the herdless farmer and me.

"That your wagon outside?"

"Yeah."

"Never seen horses like that. What are they?"

155

Knowing I couldn't pass them off as ordinary draft animals, I told him I didn't know exactly, but they had some warhorse in them.

"I don't doubt that," he replied, extending his hand. "My name's Marcus."

"I'm Jens."

Marcus leaned over the counter far enough to receive the proprietor's attention. Once he had it, he showed him four fingers. This signal seemed to snap the proprietor from the trance Strower had him in. Suddenly conscious of his responsibilities to his patrons, he turned and pulled several mugs off the shelf. Then, looking at Strower, he asked, "Do you men want to start your drinking now, or you gonna eat first? It'll be a while before the skunk is ready. Most everyone around here likes Carl's rum—two fingers deep at the bottom of a mug of ale. It speeds up the process considerably.

"Well then, let the drinking begin," Strower proclaimed. "And draw one for yourself, too," he told the proprietor. "Jens has a purse full of money, and it's burning a hole in his pocket."

"This could be expensive," I whispered to Marcus under my breath.

"No doubt. Where you from?"

"Up around Tinsdal," I lied.

"Damn, I've heard that's nice farmin' country up there, but I didn't know you plowed with warhorses." Then, laughing at his own joke, he asked, "What you talkin' to Lloyd about, anyhow? You got 'im so distracted, he don't realize there's men dyin' of thirst back there." Marcus poked his thumb over his left shoulder to show me where *back there* was.

"Oh . . . He was just telling us about the rustling."

Marcus nodded, placing a sympathetic hand on the shoulder of the man sitting next to me, who still seemed oblivious to what was going on.

The proprietor set a mug in front of me, then went back to the barrel to work on Marcus's order. Before lifting the mug to my mouth, I apologized, "Sorry, I think you ordered first."

"No, no. The man with the biggest horse always drinks first."

"To big horses, then," I said, guzzling half the mug. It felt smooth going down, leaving a warm, prickly sensation in my throat.

Smiling, Marcus said, "Good rum, isn't it?"

Partially because the rum had stolen most of my voice, and also because I didn't want Lundgren to hear my compliment, I whispered, "That is good."

The proprietor then set four mugs in front of Marcus, waiting with an outstretched hand to be paid. Consumed by our conversation, Marcus hadn't thought to pull out his money. So I yanked the king's purse from my pocket, spilling out some gold coins—enough to pay for the entire evening. "I'll get those four as well," I told Lloyd.

"Thanks," said Marcus, trying to get his fingers through the handles of all four mugs.

"You're welcome," I replied. Then, stiffening, I blinked several times in rapid succession.

"What's the matter?" asked Marcus.

"I don't know. I hear buzzing."

"Hah! That's the rum. It's a pirate's drink, you know."

A pirate's drink, indeed. Had there been a mast nearby, I'd have climbed it for sure and dove from the crow's nest. Suddenly, I understood why Oscar stole my horse. He needed it. Case closed. For a little while, he was a pirate.

Free from my usual apprehension, I grabbed Marcus by the shoulder. "I have a question for you," I said, my numbing lips a little too close to his ear. "How do you know the rustlers are from Dag? Maybe someone else is stealing your cattle and blaming it on those savages to divert attention."

Quiet for a moment, Marcus then asked, "How'd you like to take a little drive in that fancy wagon of yours?"

I slapped his back. "You know, Marcus, you're not supposed to answer a question with a question."

"Oh, you'll get your answer."

"Then let's go."

Sliding off the stool, I made my way toward the door, mug in hand. After a couple of steps, I turned, realizing I should say something to Strower, who was still conversing with the proprietor. Holding my mug high, as if making another toast, I said, "William, I found some other *boys*." Taking another big gulp from my mug, I added, "I'll be back later."

With four drinks occupying his hands, Marcus motioned with his head for his friends to join us outside, and before anyone could make a protest, the five of us were through the door.

Outside, a pale pink blanket was rising over the western ridge, tucking in the little village before the snuffing of the sun. Approaching the wagon, Marcus ran his hand down the smooth black paint, stopping to inspect the honey-colored circle of bare wood where the king's crest had been. Strower must have removed it after he sent Lundgren and me inside. He was always thinking.

"What was here?" asked Marcus, still examining the circle, naked of paint.

"Oh, that? Strower had his family crest there," I lied again. "Took it off—thought it looked braggish." Then, trying to get Marcus's mind off the crest, I asked, "You wanna drive?"

"Of course."

With his three friends climbing into the wagon's bed and me sitting next to him on the bench, Marcus planted his mug between his legs, freeing his hands to take hold of the reins. Then, with a snap of his wrists, he dispatched the team. Responding with a trot that didn't suit Marcus at all, the horses then received a more violent snap. Sensing a general on-board, the horses exploded into a gallop, spilling some of my drink. Reaching for something to grab hold of, the three passengers in the back whooped and hollered, announcing our departure to the entire village.

At the river, Marcus pulled back on the reins, driving the wagon slowly off the road onto a grassy trail that followed the river's winding contour to the southwest. While quietly slicing through the grass, one of Marcus's friends poked his head between the two of us on the bench. "What kind of horses are these?" he asked.

"He don't know," Marcus answered. "They got warhorse blood in 'em though."

"Is that right? Huh, I've never seen nothin' like 'em. Look at 'em, Marcus. They *look* like warhorses."

"Yeah, they're something alright," I said. Then, trying to change the subject again, I asked, "Where are we heading?"

Marcus pointed straight ahead. "It's just up there."

Minutes later, he pulled back on the reins. Hopping down from the wagon, Marcus began scouring the path for tracks. "Here they are," he announced, becoming animated. "See 'em?" Then he started kicking the ground beneath some trampled grass. Marcus's friends jumped off the wagon to kick some sod for themselves, but I stayed on the bench, trying to decide if I wanted to see actual proof to verify Lundgren's story.

Pointing east, Marcus replayed the crime. "They drove the herd right along this tree line until they got here." Then Marcus planted himself at the spot where the tracks turned south, making a sweeping arc with his arm to show the change of direction. I could almost hear the bellowing of cattle as I imagined the animals on the outside squeezing the herd tight to keep from falling into the river. Marcus then walked the arc himself, stopping when he faced south. Making his arm straight as a knife blade, he bought it dramatically to a point on the horizon. "They crossed the river down there. See where that range slopes downward? The river slips between those two mountains. These tracks lead down there and disappear at the water's edge. I can show you if you want."

Dangling my right arm alongside the wagon, I spilled what little remained of my drink into the long grass. The bold feeling it gave me wasn't welcome anymore—not when I needed to think. Remembering Oscar's vacant stare while being commanded to leave Strower's farm, I tried desperately to get my wits back. Did I need to jump down and see the hoof prints? Did I need Marcus to show me where they crossed into Dag? No. Even in my dizzy state, I could see Lundgren's story was true. Dag was invading Tuva, and Thoren didn't seem to care.

No doubt the gray-faced man at the inn had a barn full of hay he didn't need. Maybe I'd be able to buy it. I felt guilty for thinking in such a cold-hearted way. When Strower had suggested there might be hay available in the south, he was considering how we might help the families survive the winter. I was only thinking about filling the king's ship, covering my backside. But before I could buy their hay, I'd have to get these farmers some help. Strower would see to that.

In my mind, I imagined Strower and Thoren sitting across the table from one another, both determined to get what they wanted, both expecting me to take their side. Unfortunately, I'd had too much of Lundgren's rum to figure out how I'd handle that situation.

Suddenly, my crippled thoughts were interrupted by Marcus. "Well," he asked, a bit impatiently, "you want to see where they crossed or not?"

"No. I believe you. Let's go back to the inn."

On the return trip, Marcus drove the wagon slowly, stopping several times to tell stories of things he and his friends had done. By the time we parked in front of the inn, only a sliver of light separated the distant mountains from the black sky. Marcus's friends jumped down, scattering for home. Waiting for them to leave, Marcus didn't move from the driver's seat. When the goodbyes were said, and his friends had disappeared into the night, Marcus turned to me. "I'd like directions to your place. I wanna come up there sometime and see what a real farm looks like."

"It's not my farm," I replied, hoping to discourage him from making the trip. Marcus was handsome, and I didn't want him bumping into Carrie. "I just work for Mr. Strower," I lied for the third time, "I'm one of his hired men."

"All the same. I'd still like directions."

My stubbornness finally relented, and I confessed to having maps in my bag. Who was I to dictate whom Carrie could see? She wasn't interested in me, and Marcus was a better choice than Oscar. Even wobbly from the rum, I could see that.

We had parked the wagon near a posted lantern, probably there to help tipsy patrons figure out whose horse was whose. Spinning on the bench, I reached into the wagon's bed for my bag and set it between Marcus and me.

When I pulled the bag open, there sat the king's crest, the gold leaf shining against the lantern's glow. Strower had hidden it in my bag. I looked up, momentarily locking eyes with Marcus before nervously flipping the crest upside down and reaching underneath to rummage for the maps. But the whole time, I could sense Marcus's cold stare.

"You work for the king, don't you?"

Not knowing how to respond, I abandoned my search for the map and looked up.

Shaking his head in disgust, Marcus stared off into the darkness. "These horses, this wagon . . . You don't even talk like a farmer. I guess I'm every bit the fool you took me for." Then, locking eyes again, he asked, "What are you doin' here? And don't lie to me."

As easy as lying was with the aid of Lundgren's rum, it was just as easy to tell the unfiltered truth. The rum seemed to have taken away my mind's ability to practice a sentence before it escaped my mouth.

"You're right. I work for the king. I grew up with him. My father was an advisor to his father. He hired me to entice farmers to grow crops for export. I've been working on William Strower's farm, though—that much is true. He's helping me recruit his neighbors. You said it yourself—the soil is generous around his place."

Slowly changing from angry to curious, the hard lines of Marcus's face softened a bit. "What you doin' down here? And why are you lyin' bout who you are?"

"Did you see that weasel sitting two stools down from me at the counter?"

Marcus gave me a slight nod without breaking his stare, waiting for me to continue. "Well, his name is Carl Lundgren. He's one of Strower's neighbors. He makes rum and sells it down here. It's his rum we're drinking. He knew about the invasions because he gets down here. But Strower and I weren't sure we could believe him. He has no love for King Thoren. He hates him."

"Why does he hate the king?"

161

"Well, if you ask me, most of his hatred comes from the fact that the king's tax collectors are on to him. They want to tax his rum sales."

"I see. They've got their hands in his pockets."

"Well, let's just say that they're reaching for his pockets, and if he keeps going the way he's going, they'll be reaching for his neck. That's why he only sells his rum down here—he's trying to cover his tracks. Anyhow, when I proposed an alliance between the king and the farmers up around Tinsdal—to grow crops for export—Lundgren started spewing accusations about the king's unwillingness to protect the border down here."

Marcus finished my thought, ". . . and the farmers won't commit until they know if there's any truth to Lundgren's story."

I nodded. "They figure if the king doesn't have any real concern for you down here, he probably doesn't bear any concern in them either—except for their soil."

Marcus pondered what I'd told him for a moment. "Why you callin' Lundgren, a *weasel?* He seems better than you." Then, after studying my face for a moment, he smiled. "He put ya in a bad spot, didn't he? Yer gonna have to find a way to help us." Slapping his knee, Marcus threw back his head, laughing.

Relieved that he was no longer angry, I laughed with him. Then, pulling out the crest, I showed him the hatchet scar. "Before you put a medal on Lundgren's chest, you might want to see this. He threw his damn hatchet at me. That's my biggest reason for calling him a weasel."

Marcus studied the crest. "He split it right down the center, didn't he?" Then, turning to his left, Marcus ran his hand over the honey-colored wood, considering the crest's location relative to the wagon's bench. "Looks to me like if Lundgren wanted to split your skull open, he woulda. Whatya gonna do now, Jens? That's your name, right?"

"Yeah, it's my name . . . I'm not sure. I think Strower and I need to visit the king. Maybe we can convince him to send some soldiers down here."

"You and Strower, huh? Yer not takin' the weasel to see the king?"

Holding up the wounded crest, I stared at Marcus like he'd lost his mind, but then his crooked smile made me realize he was only trying to get a reaction. Suddenly, I felt a wave of anxiety. I'd said way too much, and now I was at this man's mercy—a circumstance he seemed to be enjoying.

"Marcus, I've no right to ask this, but would you keep this a secret for now."

Becoming solemn, Marcus nodded that he would. "My mother's been prayin' every night at supper that we'd get some help. Maybe you're it, Jens—you, Strower, and that weasely friend of yours." He smiled when he included Lundgren, but then turned serious again. "But there are some men around here who'd probably tie you between two horses and pull you apart if they knew you worked for the king."

Feeling a clammy chill run up my spine, I hunched my shoulders, imagining my arms torn off as quickly as a man separates a wing from a roasted chicken. "Thank you, Marcus."

Jumping down from the wagon, my new friend leaned in, offering a handshake. "I farm just east of where we saw the hoof-prints. Only one farm separates our land from the river. That's where you can find me. You know, Jens, they drove those damn cows right through our property."

I shook his hand and tried to find some comforting words, but before I could think of any, he disappeared into the night.

CHAPTER 20

When I stepped into the inn for the second time, different men were sitting on the stools where I'd left Strower and Lundgren. From behind the counter, the proprietor motioned for me to come over.

"Where are my mugs?" he asked as I drew near.

Looking at my hands, I said, "Um, still in the wagon, I guess."

Narrowing his eyes, the proprietor wrote something on a piece of parchment. Then, slapping a key onto the counter, he pointed to a door in the back of the room. "Up the stairs—first room to the right. Your friends are across the hall."

"Thank you. I'll fetch those mugs in the morning."

"Don't bother. They're already on your bill."

"Ah, souvenirs from Saleton," I quipped, trying to lighten his mood, but he'd already turned his attention to a gigantic man standing next to me.

The inn's staircase creaked terribly, announcing my ascension. When I finally reached my room, Strower opened his door halfway and slid through the opening, obviously trying not to wake Lundgren. By the dim light from the wall-mounted lantern, I caught a glimpse of Carl's snoring carcass, face-up, gasping for air like a dying fish. Strower gently closed the door, but it barely muffled the sound of Lundgren's snoring.

"I can't imagine why you're still awake," I whispered.

"Make your jokes. It's not too late to swap beds. You only have a room of your own because I was worried Carl might try to kill you in your sleep."

"Thoughtful," I mumbled, turning away to unlock my door.

Speaking to my back, Strower asked, "Why'd you leave with those young men?"

Fumbling to get the key in the lock, I didn't answer him right away. But when the key finally found its home, I opened the door and once again turned to face Strower. "I don't know why I left, William. I guess it all started to get to me."

"What do you mean by that?"

What did I mean? I didn't like Strower calling me a *boy*, but I wasn't about to confess it. "I don't know—all this acting—I feel like I'm a pretender—pretending to be Tuva's Minister of Agriculture. That uniform feels like a disguise. Then, for a while, I wore your son's clothes—another disguise." Grabbing hold of some fabric from the shirt I was wearing, I said, "It feels good to be wearing my own clothes again."

Strower stared at me, looking confused and struggling with his balance. He'd probably drank considerably more than I had, so I decided to keep it simple. "It was the rum, William. After a couple of swigs, I couldn't keep everything straight. I had to get out of there."

"Where'd you go?"

Just then, the door opened and closed at the bottom of the stairwell, and a set of boots mounted the wooden steps, causing both of us to glare into the darkness, waiting for the emergence of a face into the scant light from the hall lantern. The boots caused what seemed like an unnatural depression in the wooden treads, straining the fibers nearly to the point of cracking. The groan of each sinking tread, mingled with a sigh of the one below it, created an eerie rhythm to accompany the man's low-pitched humming, a growl set to music. It was a drinking song. I could also hear the rubbing of fabric on plaster, which could only have been his shoulders, alternately brushing the two walls as he trudged upward. He was either very large or very drunk. I worried he might be both.

His face startled me when it broke into the yellow light, emerging even higher than I expected. His beard seemed more foliage than hair, and his deep-set eyes were only black shadows in the lantern's glow. I recognized him. He was the man standing next to me at the counter.

"Hellooo," came a rumbled greeting. He had a clay jug in each hand, dangled by their holes from his thick index fingers. He stopped, seemingly to devise a way past us in the narrow hallway. But like a well-oiled human gate, Strower fell submissively against his door, and I retreated one step into my room, offering him easy passage. Once he'd walked past, he turned, as if finally recognizing us.

"You're the farmers from up north."

Jumping to attention, Strower offered his hand. "Yes. William Strower's the name. I farm near Tinsdal."

"Thomas Beech. My friends call me Bear."

Performing an exaggerated imitation of himself, Strower enthusiastically shook the man's huge hand. "Well, sir, I'd like to be your friend." Then, laughing nervously, he added, "I wouldn't want to be your enemy."

Thomas Beech chuckled in a low rumble, not much different than a dog's growl. An uncomfortable silence ensued, which Strower finally interrupted by asking the obvious. "Staying here tonight?"

"I am," replied Thomas Beech, eying Strower like he was trying to decide if he'd make a decent meal. Then he said, "I heard you talkin' about Dag downstairs. I mine gold for the king. We've been working the mountain just north of the Valley of Ten Tribes. I know the raids have everyone here on-edge, but I've met one of the Daggites from the Valley. Grown fond of him. We all have."

"We?" inquired Strower.

"The men at the mining camp. We take turns comin' down here to purchase a barrel—except it's always my turn." The last part of his comment caused the big man to chuckle again, and I swear I could feel the floor vibrate. Then, holding up the two jugs, he added, "This is my private stash."

"How'd you meet the Daggite?" asked Strower.

"A while back, the king purchased some exploding powder from a trader. We use it to blow-up rocks, uncover gold. Well, the explosions caught this Daggite's attention, so he snuck up the mountain to see what the noise was. Right about then, we set off the powder. A rock came rolling down on him. Pinned his leg. Busted it up pretty bad."

"But he recovered?" I asked.

"Sure did. Daggites are tough. Our old cook took him under his wing and nursed him back to health. Some of us wanted to step on his neck while he was pinned under the rock—send him back to his gods, but the cook saved him. Get this—he taught him to speak Tuvan. He even taught him to read. He has a limp now, but he gets around good—helps with cooking and keeps the camp clean. The men like him. He's even taken some of us huntin'. You should see him sneak up on an animal. They can't hear him. It's the damnedest thing. But then, I'm not very sneaky."

With that, Thomas Beech, Bear, continued down the hall toward his room. While working his key in the lock, he started talking again, but now without looking at us. "There's this man who comes to camp every so often with supplies. He reports the latest gossip—what the king's up to. He told us Thoren sent out a fancy black wagon with a young man who's trying to round up farmers to grow crops for the king."

Then, facing us, he added, "I imagine it looks kinda like that wagon out front, but it'd have the king's crest, of course. Wouldn't it be a shame if that young man made a report that turned the king murderous against those tribes? They're gentle people, for the most part. There ought to be some way to stop these raids without butchery."

Stepping inside his room, he then poked his big head out. "If you men are heading north, you should follow the mountain road. Listen for the thunder—speshly if there ain't no clouds. The boys and me, we'd be happy to put you up for a night." Then, he shut his door, leaving Strower and me staring at each other.

"He knows who you are," Strower whispered.

"Yeah, and he's not the only one. I told one of those young men who I am . . . Well, I guess you could say he figured it out."

"How?"

"I opened my bag in front of him. He saw the crest."

Strower's head dropped.

"They showed me the cattle-tracks, William. They run along the river, not far from here. What should we do?"

"It's time for you to go talk with the king. He needs to know his success at the port hinges on his willingness to protect these farmers. My neighbors will never honor their commitments if Thoren turns a deaf ear to what's happening down here."

"Will you come along?" I asked. "You can be the voice of the farmers."

Strower nodded in a way that wasn't yes or no. "Let's try to get some sleep," he said. "We'll think up a plan in the morning." Turning toward his room, Strower then hesitated. "Did you stable those horses?"

I wanted to say I had, and then sneak down and do it, but I forced myself to tell the truth. "No."

"You know, Jens, you're a damn poor farmer."

"I know. I'll take care of it."

"No, I'll do it," said Strower, patting my shoulder. "You get some sleep. I need to think, and I think best around animals. They tend to listen better than people."

CHAPTER 21

The next morning, Strower and I sat in the wagon, waiting for Lundgren to return from the outhouse before heading back to Tinsdal. As far as I knew, we'd be dropping Carl off at his farm. Then I'd be heading to Keenod to meet with the king. Strower hadn't told me yet if he was planning to join me. The only thing he'd said concerning his plans is that he wanted to drive. So, while he sat studying the maps, I situated myself in the back of the wagon, trying to get comfortable for the trip.

While working the lumps out of my bag to make a decent pillow, Strower spun on the bench and lowered the map. "Jens, that mining camp can't be more than a couple hours from here." Then, turning the parchment so I could see it, he pointed to a road. "It looks like we'd take the main road north a short distance and then veer northwest on this trail here."

"Why do you want to visit the mining camp?" I asked.

Giving me an adventurous grin, Strower replied, "Well, Bear did invite us."

"Yeah, and I've been wondering why."

Strower rolled up the map. "There's one way to find out."

"What about Carl? Seems like he's anxious to get home."

Strower glanced at the outhouse, noticing Lundgren finally making his exit, still pulling up his trousers. "You leave Carl to me," he said, energized by the challenge of swaying the stubborn little man. Then, rubbing his hands together, he added, "I have until the road forks to convince him."

As soon as we left Saleton, Strower began telling Lundgren about our conversation with Bear, mentioning how fond the men at the mining camp were of his rum and how they blow apart rocks with exploding powder. Lundgren helplessly fell into Strower's trance, and by the time we'd reached

169

the place where the road forked to the northwest, he was eager to make the detour, even thinking it was his idea.

The morning sun shone silver on the sheer cliffs forming Tuva's western border, making it hard to discern where the mountain ended and the white-blue sky began. "Keep your eyes open for dust clouds," Strower told Carl. Like sentinels, the two of them fixed their stare at the mountains, while I rested my head on my bag, closing my eyes and settling into my private thoughts.

I couldn't figure out why Bear was so interested in having us visit the mining camp. He'd somehow guessed who I was. I suppose he saw my wagon sitting next to the inn and noticed the honey-colored circle of bare wood where the king's crest should have been. He said he'd heard of me from the man who restocks their camp supplies. Whoever that is, he has ears inside the palace, allowing him to keep the miners stocked with gossip as well as supplies. Although Bear never actually came out and said he knew I worked for the king, he wanted us to know that he'd put two and two together.

Another thing I couldn't figure out is why Bear was so worried that the king would turn murderous against Dag. I wondered if he'd heard something or if it was another of his two and twos. He thought Thoren was contemplating sending his army into the Valley to slaughter the tribes. It didn't make sense—especially since Thoren had supposedly turned a deaf ear to the farmers who'd only asked for a few soldiers to protect the border near Saleton. And if the king *was* planning to attack Dag, why would Bear assume he'd send me to Saleton? Surely, he'd send soldiers to spy the land, not the Minister of Agriculture. None of it made sense.

Then it occurred to me what Bear might have been thinking. Suppose Thoren wanted farmland to grow his own crops. He could use these invasions by Dag as an excuse to slaughter the tribes and occupy the Valley himself. He could use prison labor and grow crops for free. Bear probably suspected Thoren had sent me to Saleton to see if the Valley was fit for farming. If that were the case, it'd make sense for me to remove the king's crest and lie about why I was there. The king wouldn't want anyone to know what I was doing. If Bear had pulled the proprietor aside and asked what he knew about the three of us, he'd never believe we were in Saleton on a drinking binge—not in that wagon.

Thinking of it from Bear's perspective, if Thoren wanted to attack the tribes in the Valley, he'd likely ignore the farmer's plea for help until the situation became desperate enough to justify more drastic military measures. But he'd wait to attack until he knew for sure that the land was suitable for farming.

Was I letting my imagination run wild? I wanted to tell Strower what I was thinking and let him straighten me out, but I couldn't say anything in front of Lundgren.

What were we walking into by visiting the camp? It didn't exactly seem dangerous. After all, like me, the miners were employed by the crown. They couldn't mistreat me, not without consequences. Sure, Bear was an intimidating presence, but he didn't seem violent. Maybe he hoped I'd bring the king a bad report of the Valley—no good for farming. That is, if I had a heart to save the tribes. He'd taken a real liking to the Daggite who lived at their camp. I suppose he thought I would too.

If I was right about Bear's conclusions, I needed to find a way to calm his fears and let him know why I was really in Saleton before he started spreading rumors. Then I began wondering if an attack on the Valley had ever crossed Thoren's mind. Thoren is clever, and if he wanted his own farmland this would be one way to get it. Who knows, maybe I had stumbled upon his contingency plan for if I failed. One way or another, he'd get his beets. Of that, I was sure. The nation would likely applaud a bold military response to the invasions. They'd probably identify Thoren with King Tuva, the one who pushed the savage Daggites off the land in the first place. But did Thoren have enough soldiers left in Tuva to assemble an army? His men were traveling the seas, rented to foreign ships.

Mercifully, Lundgren interrupted my thoughts with an anxious grunt. Turning my head in the direction of his stubby index finger, I saw a dust cloud rising like a gray ghost from a distant ridge. Lundgren edged forward on the wagon seat, shifting his weight back and forth. Strower watched him for a long moment, then, glancing back at me, we shared a smirk, almost the way two parents exchange glances when witnessing some first in the life of their small child. Lundgren's mind was saved from all social conventions, allowing him to give extraordinary focus to the object of his curiosity. And at that moment, nothing existed in his world, save that dust cloud and the strange powder that caused it.

Although the distant gorge contained the sound of the explosion, the cloud lingered for a spell, allowing us to mark the location of the blast before it dissipated into the blue sky. Not long afterward, we came upon a well-worn trail heading up one of the mountain's gentler slopes. Confident the path would take us straight to the mining camp, Strower turned the wagon.

After an hour of hard climbing, we could hear faint voices over the wheezing of our horses, forming a dirty cloud of another kind—vulgar expletives that one might expect from a mining camp. A moment later, we entered a clearing, populated with several crude log cabins.

Shivering with excitement, Lundgren jumped down from the wagon before it stopped, spinning a quick circle in search of the miners. But it was midmorning, and the camp was empty. The voices we heard must have carried down the mountain from their worksite, wherever that was.

While dismounting, I noticed the camp's wagon sitting alongside one of the cabins. Although not painted like mine, it was built the same, with the king's crest affixed next to the driver's bench. That's how Bear recognized the missing crest.

As we prepared to search for Bear on foot, two men suddenly appeared from an obscure opening in the trees, carrying an array of cooking utensils. By my guess, they'd been washing them, perhaps in a stream further down the slope. One of the men was old and small-boned, wearing a gray beard and a dusty wide-brimmed hat. The other was young, perhaps my age, with very long brown hair and soft leather clothing. He was a handsome human-animal—not in the sense of lacking intelligence, but in having instincts different than I'd seen in men—sniffing the air and measuring his surroundings in light of our presence, acting like a deer. Strower and I exchanged glances, both understanding these men to be the cook and the Daggite.

Lundgren approached them first, boldly curious, asking what makes the powder explode. Studying Carl with cautious wonderment, the cook finally looked beyond Lundgren to Strower and me. "Curious about the powder, are you?"

With the same predictable ritual that I'd seen performed on every stranger he'd met, Strower marched toward the two men, his hand extended. "Hello. My name is William Strower. We came across Bear down in Saleton. Stayed at the same inn. He invited us up here to visit your camp."

Ignoring Strower's hand, the cook grumbled, "Indeed, he did. He showed up at camp this morning before we finished breakfast. Said we might have visitors today." Then the old man gave a wordless command to the Daggite, who laid down the cookware and slipped from our presence toward a trail at the far end of the clearing, probably to retrieve Bear.

Anxious to see an explosion, Lundgren followed the Daggite, leaving Strower torn between staying and chasing after him. He opted for the latter, leaving me alone with the cook.

I bent down, picking up the utensils the Daggite had dropped in the grass. "Can I give you a hand with these?"

"Suit yourself."

We walked together to an outdoor stove under a makeshift lean-to with a chimney protruding through its center. "May I help with anything else?" I asked, laying a large kettle in the shade of the lean-to.

The cook seemed to be wrestling within himself, trying to hold his friendliness at bay and keep his grumpy edge, but good manners were probably rare at the camp, and mine seemed to be whittling away at his crusty veneer. "How are you at cutting vegetables?" he finally asked.

"Compared to who?"

"Well, if I compare you with Joar," the cook postulated with an elevated chin, the way older folks sometimes do when they invoke their wisdom on younger people, "I imagine you'd be a miserable apprentice. But since I have, at the moment, no helper, your skills will have to do."

"Very well. Hand me some vegetables and something sharp to cut them, and we'll see how it goes."

For a while, we worked in silence, save an occasional plop from a skinned vegetable into the kettle. Finally, I spoke. "My name is Jens. I'm from the Royal City."

The cook didn't look up from his work. "Boy, I know as much about you as I care to. I understand that you're interested in learning about the Valley, but Joar is like a son to me, and his presence in this camp needs to remain a secret." Then, unwittingly, he pointed his knife at me, adding, "I don't want this visit to bring Joar any attention." When the cook noticed his menacing pose, he placed his knife back to work on the vegetables, mouthing a quiet apology.

"I understand your fear. I think I'd feel the same way in your shoes, but Bear might've misunderstood my reason for coming to Saleton. I was only there to purchase hay for export. I have no dealings in the Valley, and I won't speak to anyone about the Daggite."

"Why are you here then?"

"That's a good question. Curiosity, I suppose. I need to visit the king soon—report my progress. I'm supposed to be purchasing crops, recruiting farmers, and such, but after seeing what's happening around Saleton, I think I need to ask the king to send help down there—to protect the border. I guess we thought it'd be good to learn as much as we could before meeting with the king. Bear seems to think we'll gain something from this visit."

The cook looked up from his work. "Ah, yes, Bear."

"What's that supposed to mean?"

"Nothing."

"Well, it's probably a simple misunderstanding. Will you please tell Bear that the king hasn't said anything to me about bringing his army against the tribes? I was in Saleton on my own accord. I didn't even tell the king I was going. I think Bear may have built a story around seeing the king's wagon in town, with its crest missing."

The old man shook his head. "Well, it wouldn't be the first time Bear jumped to a conclusion. Do you know how he got his name?"

"Bear? I imagine it's because he looks like one."

"Nope. Believe it or not, that's not it. He's protective as a she-bear— loses all reason when someone gets between him and somebody he cares about."

"And he cares about the twelve tribes?"

"In a way. He's only ever met Joar, but he cares for him, and the twelve tribes are his people, so—" The cook left his sentence half-finished, opting instead to start a new one. "Bear and I had a spat this morning. I told him he's putting Joar in danger."

"Danger?"

"Yes, by telling you about him. We need to keep Joar a secret—especially now. I'm sure those farmers around Saleton would love to come up here and remove his head."

"Ah, I suppose. What did Bear say to that?"

"He said he'd kill 'em if they tried. Can you imagine the ruckus that'd start?"

"Well, for what it's worth, your secret's safe with us."

Looking up to search my eyes, the cook muttered, "We'll see about that."

For the next few minutes, we quietly cut vegetables, while I thought of some way to win his confidence. "I understand you've educated him."

The cook continued working, making me wonder if he'd heard my words, but as I was about to repeat myself, he breathed a quiet, "Yeah."

"Your own education is quite evident by your speech," I said. "Who schooled you?"

The cook stopped cutting vegetables for a moment, almost as if he was trying to remember. "My parents died when I was a small boy. I was raised in an orphanage by priests. If I learned their lessons, I ate. So I learned. When I was old enough, I ran off. Fate brought me to the mining camp as the cook's assistant. At that time they camped north of here. Not long after, the cook died, and I assumed his post. I've been cutting vegetables ever since. No one up here even knew I could read, not until I took Joar in. We make quite a pair, he and I."

"I guess you do. You've never had children of your own?"

The cook looked up at me. "Did you see any women on your way up the mountain?" Then he went back to cutting vegetables. "No, I never could understand why someone would bring an innocent child into this world. But when Joar was pinned under that rock, the look in his eyes was familiar to me—desperate, hoping for mercy. Bear was ready to kill him. I knew then it was my job to save him. But in truth, he's done more for me than I've done for him."

"You've never thought of bringing him back to his people?"

The cook's spine stiffened. "This might not make sense to you, boy, but there's a reason Joar was on this mountain alone. It brought me back to the time when I came up here by myself. If some well-meaning soul who couldn't understand my tongue had brought me back to my people, I'd have returned to those cold-hearted priests. Strange as it sounds, I had to teach him to talk before I knew the right thing to do."

"Was he escaping his people?"

"No. It's more complicated." Then, the cook placed his knife on a rock and wiped his hands on his trouser leg. "Joar is a spiritual soul. I've never met the likes of him. Have you ever met a truly spiritual person?"

"I suppose I have. I was taught by the high priest in the Royal City."

The cook explored my eyes. "Don't mistake religious for spiritual, boy."

"What do you mean?"

"Well, was your priest stiff as a tree and harsh as a mountain winter?"

"The high priest? That describes him perfectly."

The cook nodded. "The priests who raised me were no different— hardened by their religion beyond feeling. No, that's not what I meant by *spiritual*."

"Explain it then."

After thinking for a moment, he said, "Connected, I guess. I don't know how else to describe it. Joar was on this mountain to be with his Creator. Walking alone up here is where he feels at home."

My mind immediately went to Strower's wife, Carrie's mother, Amanda. The word, *connected*, describing her perfectly, from what they'd told me.

"I have to confess," I said, "if I've ever studied the religion of the Daggites, I've forgotten the lessons."

"They worship many gods. They practice all sorts of sacrifices to win their favor. Joar has no stomach for it. He believes that creation—" the cook stopped, pointing north to a high peak capped with snow, "is the work of one powerful God."

"Ah, and you learned all this after teaching him to speak our language?"

"Well now, that's the strange part. I had no means to teach him because I had no books. Then I borrowed the Holy Book from one of the miners who'd no use for it—his mother had sent it up here with him. I used that book for his lessons. But while Joar was learning to read and write, he was grasping the book—I mean, really grasping the book. More than once, he left me sitting with my mouth agape."

"So he's embraced our religion?"

"Not at all."

"I'm sorry, I'm confused."

The cook turned to face me directly. "Have you ever heard tales of pirate maps leading to a buried treasure?"

"Of course. I drew them all the time as a child—with King Thoren."

Unimpressed by my relationship with the king, the cook continued, "Then you know those maps require a key to decipher where the treasure is. Without that key, the map is useless."

"Are you suggesting that Joar possesses a key to our Holy Book?"

"I can't think of a better way to explain it."

Just then, Bear's imposing frame appeared at the trailhead, followed by Lundgren, then Strower and Joar.

As they drew near, Bear stopped short, deciding to rely on his booming voice rather than his legs to finish the journey. "Carl and I are heading back to the mine. He wants to see an explosion, and the men want to meet their rum-maker." As he spoke, he placed his imposing hand on Carl's shoulder. The expression on Lundgren's face was priceless—eyes squeezed closed, jaw clenched, but he dared not wiggle free from the giant.

177

As the unlikely friends disappeared again down the trail, Strower and Joar joined the cook and me at the lean-to.

"How did Bear find out that Lundgren was their rum-maker? I asked Strower.

"I couldn't think of a better way to transform ol' Carl from a nuisance to a hero." Then, taking a more serious tone, he added, "Jens, Joar has agreed to take us down the west side of the mountain. There's a Daggite village not far from here—at the north end of the Valley. We can watch people from a distance. If we leave now, we can be back here before dark."

CHAPTER 22

Quietly, Joar led Strower and me down the rugged west side of the mountain toward the Valley of Ten Tribes. Even with a slight limp, the Daggite's footfalls were utterly silent. Extraordinarily focused on what lay before him, Joar's head only swiveled backward when one of us snapped a twig or tripped over an exposed tree root. Each time he turned, his concern quickly blossomed to wonderment, seemingly amazed at how creatures designed so much like himself could be so clumsy. Being in a continual state of apology, I didn't try to start a conversation. And Strower was no better off. It seemed the more we concentrated on our walking, the more unmanageable our boots became.

We hiked for a couple of hours before the grade improved, giving Strower and me more control over our limbs. As we neared the Valley, Joar slowed his pace, becoming even more cautious. When we reached the bottom of the mountain, we walked a short distance on flat terrain before ascending a small, pine-covered hill. Halfway up, Joar stopped and turned to us, his lucid dark eyes communicating that we'd reached our destination. Slowly, we entered a thick stand of pines, the trees so close together we crawled on our bellies in serpentine fashion beneath the low branches. Strower and I moved painfully slow compared to Joar, who slithered as if he was transformed into a snake. Bear had told us about his magical ability to approach his prey, but seeing him *become nature* was spellbinding.

The pines terminated at the crest of the hill where Joar stopped, lying flat on his belly, hidden in the dark shadow of the tree-line. Strower and I finally caught up, pathetic snakes, clumsily crawl-dragging alongside him—me to his left and Strower to his right. Peeking beneath the low branches, I was shocked to see a Daggite village, close enough that a spoken word might catch someone's attention.

A peaceful river cradled the encampment within its bend, and several Daggites casually attended their chores along the bank. Between us and the river stood an assortment of huts, strange structures—half tent, half house—with stone foundations and animal skin walls. The four sides reached a peak in the center, where tree-branch corner posts protruded from the skins like upside-down hawk talons. Primitive, but cozy, this settlement nestled like a friendly ambassador between the peaceful river and the imposing mountain.

After gazing for a time, I turned to Joar, seeing his attention fixed on the tall grass a short distance away. Following his stare, I arrived at the object of his focus—a subtle movement in the grass. Suddenly a partridge squawked, flying up with alarming commotion, its wings noisily beating the air, causing my heart to flutter in nearly the same way. Then I heard the belly laugh of a young child, his head now visible above the tall green blades. The bare-shouldered boy of probably five had long brown hair tied tight against his head.

Following the bird with his eyes, the child threw up his hands in playful exasperation before making a quarter turn and pouncing like a cat back into the tall grass. Then I heard a low-pitched grunt and more laughter. With my eyes riveted on the patch of grass where the lad had disappeared, I gasped, as his entire body suddenly shot skyward as dramatically as the partridge's, his legs wrapping the muscular neck of a man, presumably his father.

The boy placed his small hand on the man's chin, wrenching his head backward to make eye contact from his shoulder-perch. The man let out a squawk, identical to that of the partridge, and the boy laughed, attempting a high-pitched imitation of his own. This game repeated itself several times, the patient father offering himself entirely to his young son. Glancing to my right, I saw Joar's face beaming, his white teeth glowing behind a broad smile. The father seemed too enthralled in play to be aware of our presence, and Joar sensed it.

Finally, in the course of their game, the Daggite father turned his back to us for a moment, and Joar used the opportunity to disappear from the scene, pulling out in the same manner he'd entered. Strower and I quickly followed, and the three of us began our journey back to the mining camp.

When we were perhaps a third of the way up the mountain, we arrived at a stream where a collection of large rocks obstructed the water's flow, causing the stream to fray like a worn rope, the separated chords reuniting further down the slope. Joar mounted a large rock with a flat surface. Untying a pouch from his belt, he removed remnants from the camp's breakfast and then extended his hand toward the food, inviting Strower and me to join him.

"Thank you," said Strower, "and thank you for bringing us to see the village."

Joar smiled and nodded as we sat down.

"Were you afraid they'd see us?" I asked. "Is that why we left so quickly?"

"No. They were in *balama*."

"*Balama*? What's that?" asked Strower.

Joar's voice was quiet and solemn, almost a whisper. "It means to *walk with*."

Strower nodded. "Walk with—like we're doing with you."

Joar lowered his brow, indicating Strower's comment didn't make sense. Then, as if he were given the task of describing a color to a blind man, he puzzled for a moment before saying, "No, *balama* is two becoming one."

"I'm not sure I understand what you mean," replied Strower.

Although Joar's speech was surprisingly precise—shaped, I suppose, by the formal manner of our Holy Book—he couldn't find the words to describe *balama*, so he opened his hands and brought them slowly together, interlocking his fingers.

My mind went back to the intimacy between the boy and his father. I'd never witnessed anything quite like it—the complete willingness of a father to join worlds with his young son, and the joy of the son, basking in his father's undiluted presence. Remembering my conversation with the cook—his searching for the right word to describe a truly spiritual person, I uttered the word that he'd used, "Connected?"

Joar's eyes lit, and he nodded.

"Is that how you learned to move like you do—like the animals—from your father?" I asked.

"Yes, but that is a different word, *peecho*—walk like."

I attempted both words myself. "*Balama*—walk with, *peecho*—walk like."

Joar smiled.

Strower asked, "How long does *balama* last?"

"No end. The boy, as he grows, will gain his father's mind. He will share his father's thoughts. The spirit of the father will be his own."

"They were so happy together," I observed. "Did you and your father play that way when you were a boy?"

Joar's eyes met mine, radiating something akin to sympathy, like my use of the word *play* had revealed a crippling ignorance. "Of course," he said. "A young boy has never been a man, but a man has been a young boy. Daggites believe a father must become as his child and *walk with* his son into manhood. This is what *Balama* is. How else can a boy find his way?"

Each time Joar said the word *boy*, the crumpled note in my pocket echoed Carrie's voice. Looking into the Joar's eyes, I could tell his heart was heavy for me. I wondered how he knew.

Remembering the question I'd been asked earlier: *Have you ever met a truly spiritual person?* —I said, "The cook told me that you have great insight into our Holy Book."

"Yes, I've found life there. My Tuvan father tried to explain its pages the way your priests understand it." Joar then made a sour face.

"You read it differently?" I asked.

"Yes, as different as *balama* and *peecho*."

Before I could make further inquiries, Strower interrupted. "Joar, your people are stealing cattle from the farmers around Saleton. Do you know about this?"

Joar's eyes dropped to the water skirting the rock. Then he looked up at Strower. "Have you been told about the Daggite priest?"

"What priest?"

"The men at camp caught the Daggite priest stealing gold. They tied him to a tree."

"Then what?" asked Strower.

"The king's man came—the man who brings supplies."

"What did he do?" I asked.

"He had me ask the priest why he took the gold."

Strower and I waited for Joar to continue, but he never seemed to volunteer more information than the question required. Finally, Strower blurted, "What'd the priest say?"

"He said he was returning it to the ground in the Valley."

"Why would he do that?" I asked.

"The Daggites believe gold gives power to the land. They believe your king is weakening Tuva by removing it."

Sitting forward, Strower guessed what came next, ". . . and if the priest buries the gold in the Valley, he thinks the Daggites will become stronger as Tuva grows weaker."

Joar nodded.

"What'd they do with the priest?" I asked.

"The king's man threatened to kill him and bring his body to the king. He had me tell the priest that the king would bring his army to the Valley and slaughter the tribes, unless—"

"Unless what?" asked Strower.

"Unless he brought him cattle."

"Cattle?" Strower removed his hat, scratching his head. "Why would he ask for cattle? The Daggites don't raise cattle. Do they?"

"No. The people of Dag hunt."

Strower stood up and began pacing back and forth on the rock. "Let me get this straight—the Daggites are hunting Tuva's cattle for the man who brings supplies to the mining camp?"

Joar nodded.

Strower closed his eyes for a moment. Then, looking at me as though he hoped I'd heard something different, he whispered, "This keeps getting worse. We need to see the king. Joar, take us back."

Obediently, Joar scooped up the remaining fragments of food and stuffed them into his leather pouch. Then, jumping down from the rock, he continued leading us up the mountain.

Walking behind Strower, I could see his anger in the way he marched, almost stomping, repeatedly opening and closing his right hand, balling it into a fist. Too numb to feel his rage, I instead felt a sickening resignation—the kind that creeps in when defeat seems inevitable. My mind had stopped trying to circumvent the obstacles. What difference did it make? I was being tossed around on a turbulent sea by a storm that wouldn't go away.

Then I remembered my horse's battle against the mud at Lundgren's place. Like the horses, Strower was still fighting. Unlike me, he wasn't about to let circumstances push him around. I couldn't give up either. We were yoked together.

Still thinking about the new words I'd learned, I began imitating Strower's movements—his marching, the balling of his fist. "*Peecho,*" I whispered to myself, *walk like,* wondering how long it would take to learn to move like an animal, to approach a deer in the forest.

And what about the other word Joar taught us—*balama?* Could that carefree peace be learned? It seemed more grace than skill—*walk with,* sharing a spirit with someone stronger and wiser. I'd seen it now with my own eyes, but for me, it seemed out of reach. *Balama* was losing yourself . . . or was it finding yourself? Whatever it was, I hadn't experienced it. Again, Carrie's voice floated through my mind, "*You're still such a boy.*"

Looking at the fist Strower was practicing, I wondered whom he wanted to punch. Maybe it was me. I'd placed him in the center of a horrible mess. Whether King Thoren knew it or not, he was stealing cattle from his own farmers, and Strower's fist wouldn't fix that.

CHAPTER 23

We reached camp before the miners had returned from their day's work. Standing next to his lean-to, the cook spotted us as soon as we emerged from the trail. "You're back!" he called out. "Will you be joining us for supper?"

Ignoring his question, Strower headed straight for the lean-to—fist still balled—until he stood face-to-face with the cook. "The king's man," he said, "the man who brings supplies—Joar told us he's forcing the Daggites to steal Tuva's cattle. Is that true?"

Before admitting that he knew anything, the cook shot a glance at Joar. Then, stepping backward, he bumped his shoulder on the corner of the lean-to. Evading the question, he asked, "What exactly did Joar say?"

"Is it true?" Strower repeated.

The cook searched Strower's face before responding. Finally, his eyes fell to the ground. "Yes."

". . . and you just let it happen? What kind of men are you?"

"You don't understand. We've been trying to protect—"

"Protect? Protect who? What about the farmers around Saleton? Who's protecting them?"

"Let me explain."

"You can explain it to the king," Strower growled. Then, turning to Joar, he said, "Fetch Carl. We need to go."

Seeking permission to obey Strower's order, Joar looked at the cook, who, after studying Strower for a time, nodded reluctantly. Joar then scampered to the far end of the clearing and disappeared down the trail.

Strower gave the cook one last scornful glare. Then, turning on his heels, he marched to the wagon and mounted the bench, folding his arms across his chest.

Lifting a shaky hand to stroke his beard, the cook turned to me. "He's mighty angry, isn't he?"

"Well, he's a farmer, so—"

"A farmer? He doesn't work for the king?"

"No. William is helping me round up farmers to grow crops for export." Then, unsure if that was still true, I added, "He *was* helping me, at least."

While studying Strower from this safe distance, the cook said, "I know how this looks, but I'm guessing Joar left some holes in his story."

"He didn't really tell us a story. He only answered our questions."

The cook nodded. "That's how he is. He's too humble to tell stories—stories require assumptions, and Joar doesn't make assumptions." Then, looking over at Strower again, he added, "Your friend over there has told himself a story, but he doesn't have all the facts."

"Could be," I replied, "but honestly, I don't think he wants to get buried any deeper in my mess, and I can't blame him."

No longer interested in Strower, the cook turned to face me directly. "You're going to the king with this?"

"What choice do we have?"

With a sad resignation, the cook slumped his shoulders. "Well, we have a little time before your friend returns. Let me tell you what I know—it might help you move forward." He pointed to a pair of stumps next to his boiling kettle of vegetables. "Where should I start?" he whispered while sitting down.

Taking the stump next to him, I said, "You can begin by telling me about the man in charge of supplies."

"Alden Fry? You must know him—if you work for the king."

"No, I'm afraid I've only been with the king a short time."

"Fry has a big job—Minister of Goods—he has several men working for him. But he comes here personally because of the gold."

"Because of the gold? What do you mean?"

"He doesn't just bring supplies to camp; he collects the gold. You can imagine the precautions needed to make sure it ends up in the king's hands and not in someone else's pocket."

"I suppose."

"It's quite a procedure. We have a quota every month. If we don't make the quota, we can expect a surprise visit—the king's guards—they search every inch of the place, interrogate everyone at sword-point."

"How often does that happen?"

"It's happened twice recently. After the first time, we posted guards at the crevice."

"The crevice?"

"It's a deep hole where we keep the gold. At the end of each day, Bear searches every man before going back to camp. Then, all of the gold they mined that day is placed in a sack, weighed, and dropped into the crevice. Alden Fry shows up once a month. They throw a torch into the hole and lower one of the men by rope. When he reaches the bottom, he unties himself, and then one by one ties the rope to the bags. Once they're lifted out, the bags are scaled again—right then and there. Both Alden and Bear place their initials on the king's ledger. When the gold reaches the palace, it's weighed a third time. Alden travels with two soldiers. They oversee the whole process, guarding the gold until it's in the king's hands."

"What kind of man is Alden Fry?"

"Well, when I first met him, he wasn't such a bad man."

"And now?"

"Desperation can make a man cut corners. Once a corner is cut enough times, it becomes a path. Do you know what I mean?"

I didn't nod, feeling like a nod would be a confession of my own cut corners.

Turning his attention to his soup, the cook grabbed hold of a large wooden spoon, stirring while he talked. "Alden walks a path of cut corners. When he comes to camp, he bunks in Bear's cabin. The two guards stay in the carriage with the gold. Once Alden drinks enough rum, he starts talking. Bear's shared some of it with me. I'm not making excuses for Alden, but he has an impossible task. He's not only expected to purchase food and supplies for the palace in the Royal City, but he also feeds half the town of Keenod—both dock workers and palace servants. Most of the workers at the port are from surrounding towns, so they stay in bunkhouses. Hungry dock workers must eat. The thing is, Alden hasn't a large enough budget to buy what he needs. The king's advisors won't approve any spending at the port in Keenod. They have a big say in how tax revenue is spent."

"Yeah, I know how much the advisors hate the port."

The cook continued, "Alden complains to Bear that the king expects too much from him. King Thoren raises money for the port by renting his soldiers to ship owners, but he uses that money to build his port, not to feed his workers. The king lays all that responsibility on Alden. Can you imagine what'd it be like to face a bunkhouse full of hungry dock workers without food?"

"No. How's he supposed to feed them?"

The cook let the spoon handle fall to the side of the kettle. "That's where we come in. We make up the difference by finding more gold. The king purchased the exploding powder from some trader at the port. It's from the East. Thoren handed the powder to Alden like it was a bag of money."

"Ah, so Thoren increased your mining quota."

"Of course. Alden tells Bear that the king makes it sound so simple— 'Find more gold'— 'Buy more food'— 'Stop making excuses'" Pausing for a moment, he added, "I'm sorry. I probably don't need to tell *you* that."

Remembering Thoren's impatience when I suggested his timing might be too aggressive, I shook my head. "What about the king's advisors?" I asked. "Don't they have any say in how the gold is used?"

"I don't think they do," said the cook. It's my understanding that the nobles only receive a share of Tuva's tax revenue. That's why they have the right to reject the king's spending—to protect their payments. Thoren is crafty, though. According to Alden, he has those advisors chasing their tails, always one step ahead."

"Were the men able to make the new quota?"

"Yeah, for a while, they did. The boys were uncovering new veins—veins it would've taken weeks to reach with a pick-ax. But eventually, the weight of the gold began to decrease—"

I finished his sentence, ". . . because the priest was stealing it."

The cook nodded.

"But how did he get to the gold?"

"I suppose he'd been watching from the trees, so he knew where it was. Those Daggites can scale a rock-face with nothing but their fingertips and toes. They don't need ropes. He couldn't carry much weight up the crevice though—otherwise, he'd have cleaned us out. He took just enough from each bag to make everyone suspicious. There were discrepencies between the weight of the bags going into the crevise and coming out. Alden accused Bear of stealing it during his first inspection. Bear knocked him out cold."

"What?"

"Yeah, you don't accuse Bear of doing anything dishonest—not if you want to keep your teeth. When Alden came to, he had the king's guards put Bear in shackles. We tried to tell him Bear was innocent, but he took him anyhow. He brought him to the prison in the Royal City. Alden told the rest of us if we wanted to see Bear turned loose, we best figure out who's been stealing the gold. The men up here really like Bear, so a couple of them secretly started guarding the crevice at night, hoping to catch the culprit."

"And they caught the priest?"

"That's right—tied him to a tree—not knowing if they should kill him or leave him alive. The next day Alden turned up for his second inspection. When we brought him to the priest, Alden had a conversation with him, using Joar to talk back and forth. The priest told him he'd buried the gold in the Valley, but he wouldn't say where. He said it'd curse the ground to remove it now. He said he wouldn't do that to his people. That's when Alden came up with his scheme. He needed that gold to buy meat, so if the Daggite wouldn't give him the gold—"

I finished his sentence again, ". . . he'd have to bring him meat."

Using both hands, the cook rubbed his face, as though trying to scrub off some invisible filth. "I'm afraid so," he whispered through his fingers.

"So Alden Fry told the priest to steal Tuva's cattle?"

"No, he didn't have to tell him that. He just said he wanted cattle— twenty head every full moon—or he'd bring the army to the Valley to wipe out the tribes.

I shivered, seeing in my mind's eye Daggite bodies floating down the river—the young boy and his father now sharing a death. "How long has this been going on?" I asked.

"About a year."

"What about this winter? They couldn't have stolen cattle in the winter."

"That's true, but the king wouldn't march his army in the winter either. They bring the cattle through a low pass just north of here. Alden had some of the miners fence a pasture just below the pass. First full moon after the snow melted this spring there were more than twenty cattle in that pasture."

"Do you think King Thoren knows about this?"

"I don't know," replied the cook. "I don't think so. I've wondered that myself. But I'd be careful if I were you. Whether Thoren is personally involved or not, this will cost him greatly—if word gets out. He might decide to destroy evidence." The cook ran his index finger slowly along his neck, and I realized I had just become *evidence*.

"When did Bear get out of prison?"

"Alden brought him back to camp after releasing the priest. Bear had to swear he'd keep quiet. I suppose he figured if you men found out on your own, he wouldn't have to break his oath. We're making our quotas again, but Alden says the king is still asking about the lean months—he suspects someone up here's been stealing his gold. Alden said if anyone opens his mouth, he'll bring the Daggite's dead body straight to the king."

"How would he do that? He set the priest free."

The cook leaned forward. "Bear asked Alden the same thing." Then his voice fell to a whisper. "Alden said he knew where he could find a Daggite—'one body is as good as another,' he told him.

"What'd he mean by that? He'd kill Joar?"

The cook nodded. "That's why I didn't want you up here. Joar can't go back to his people now. They wouldn't receive him—not after what happened with the priest. Alden's threats came through Joar's mouth. They'd consider him an enemy."

I sat quietly, not knowing what to say. Finally, the old man placed his hand on my shoulder. "Son, after you meet with the king, would you get word back to me—advise me what to do? I need to protect Joar."

"I'll try."

"Be careful," the cook warned. Then, looking me deep in the eyes, he repeated his words. "Be careful."

CHAPTER 24

Anxious to return to Tinsdal, Strower only slowed the horses when they shimmered with sweat, and then just enough to let them recover. Was he pushing for Lundgren's sake? He'd promised Carl that our side-trip to the mining camp would be brief. Maybe he was just keeping his word, but it seemed like more than that. I wondered if Strower was in a hurry to end this chapter of his life—the chapter of Jens.

From my straw mattress in the back of the wagon, I studied Lundgren. He was his old lump-on-the-bench self—quiet, still as a statue. He didn't seem in any great hurry to me. Then, turning my attention to Strower, it was evident he wasn't his old self—tortured, ruminating, stewing. We couldn't talk with Lundgren there. Even when we'd camped alongside the road to get a few hours of sleep, our words were few.

I needed to tell Strower what the cook had confided to me, but I couldn't. Damn Lundgren. Strower was working things out in his head without all the facts, and I was worried. Mostly, I was worried that he'd drop Lundgren off, and then he'd drive the wagon to his farm, dropping himself off— "Goodbye Jens. Good luck." Where would I be then? No beets. No hay. No hope. Would he do that to me? His grip on the reins seemed unnecessarily tight, his knuckles white. Stress perhaps, or maybe the horses were the one thing he could control, and he wasn't going to give them any slack.

It was around noon the day after leaving the mining camp when the wagon finally veered off the road onto Lundgren's obscure driveway. Pulling up to his cabin, Lundgren-the-Lump finally came to life, hopping down and wordlessly scampering toward his porch. Strower and I watched as he traipsed across the squeaky boards and flung open the cabin door. Then, without so much as a glance back in our direction, he kicked the door shut behind him, disappearing into his lair.

Strower looked up at the blue sky like he'd just woken from a long night's sleep. Then a delirious laugh erupted out of his mouth. "Goodbye,

Carl," he said. "I'll miss you too." All at once, the old Strower was back. With an infectious smile, he slapped the bench, inviting me to sit with him.

While straddling between the wagon's bed and the bench, I asked, "What now?"

"Home. A meal. You hungry?"

"Starved," I replied, trying to think of the last time we'd eaten. Cautiously, I continued, "William, I'll understand if you can't pursue this any further, but—"

"What?"

"This situation—it's gotten messy, and—"

"Stop," replied Strower, holding up his hand. "What are you trying to say?"

"Well, you were so angry back at the camp—with the cook. You didn't want to listen. I thought maybe you were trying to wash your hands—"

"Yes, you're right, Jens. I was angry. I'm still angry. I'm angry *for* you. Your friend has you in a bad spot."

"Thoren?"

"Yes, Thoren. He gave you two horses and a painted wagon, expecting you to change the world. Meanwhile, his kingdom is ripping at the seams, and he's sitting in The Crucible, playing ships."

Unable to contain my relief, I began laughing.

"What's so funny?"

"Thoren, playing ships," I replied, "—like a boy in a tub." Then, realizing we'd soon be at Strower's farm and I still hadn't shared what the cook had told me, I added, "William, things are messier than you know. The cook—"

"Wait. I'm sure the cook had a lot to say, but it might be best if I don't know. I don't want the cook's opinion to sway me from doing the right thing."

"But there's a lot to consider, William."

"Not from where I sit. When we visit the king, I'll speak on behalf of the farmers. That's why you want me along, right?"

"Yes, but—"

"No buts, Jens. I'll tell King Thoren what's happening, and the culprits can rot in prison."

"What if that leads Thoren to attack the tribes in the Valley?"

Strower grimaced. "What did that cook tell you?"

But before I could explain, Strower held up his hand again. Then he pulled back the reins, halting the horses in the middle of the road. "Jens, we're almost to my farm. I want to see my children, have a nice meal, and catch up on some work. I'd like to start for Keenod first thing in the morning—before I see one of my neighbors. I don't want to explain this to anyone until it's sorted out. We'll have plenty of time to talk on the way. Let's leave this alone until then."

Nodding in agreement, I shoved my hands into my pockets and my fingers found the crumpled note. What would I say to Carrie? My mind abruptly trading one set of problems for another.

While the horses trudged up the path to Strower's house, I saw Carrie crossing the porch with Magnus and Rasmus in tow and the food basket hooked in her arm. Spotting the wagon, the pirates bounded off the porch, racing to be first to their father. Reaching the wagon, they climbed aboard, engulfing Strower in a chaotic tangle of affection.

Approaching more slowly, Carrie caught my eye, and we used her father's distraction to explore one another's mood. But, try as I might, I couldn't read hers.

Finally, turning her attention to her father, Carrie smiled. "How was your journey?"

"Let's trade stories over a meal," replied Strower.

"I need to feed the men. I'll attend to your bellies when I get back."

Strower held out his arm, reaching for Carrie's basket. "The pirates and I can feed the men. Will that get us fed sooner? Jens here won't last much longer."

Carrie threw a distracted glance my way. "It will," she replied. "Thank you."

I noticed that her freckled nose had been sunburned while we were away, and now the skin was peeling a little. Her unruly hair, loosely pulled back in a disorganized tangle of golden curls, looked like rebellious sunrays. Her eyes were bright and clear and beautiful—so very beautiful. Sitting in private worship, I was suddenly aware that Strower was looking at me. Confused by his attention, I realized that he wanted me to do something—but what? Finally, with laughter in his eyes, Strower shook his head. "You can get down, Jens. We'll be back in a few minutes."

Spastically dismounting, I landed next to Carrie. A moment later, the two of us were standing alone. She turned and began walking silently toward the house, and I followed. Halfway to the door, she said, "Thank you for keeping my father alive."

Her words seemed like a discrete way to discover if I'd found her note, but I wasn't willing to discuss its contents—not yet, anyhow. Answering in the same cryptic code, I replied, "Thank you for sending my jacket."

Seeming satisfied that I'd read her note, she changed the subject. "Did the two of you find what you were looking for?"

"You might say that," I replied, determined to leave it there. By this time, we were walking across the porch, and I didn't know how much Strower wanted Carrie to know. Besides, I had a more pressing matter on my mind— "Carrie, what became of Oscar?"

She stopped, turning to face me. "How would I know?"

"Well, has he returned?"

"No. My brother delivered his final pay the day you left."

"I'm sorry, Carrie. Where does that leave you?"

For a brief moment, her eyes hinted a tear, but then a rush of anger surfaced. "What do you care?" she snapped, turning toward the door.

Without thinking, I grabbed her shoulder, forcing her to face me. "I care," I whispered.

Her eyes probed mine. "All I was to Oscar was William Strower's daughter—a pretty ribbon securing his advancement." She shook her head and turned toward the door.

"What does that mean for me?" I blurted.

With her back to me, she let her head drop. "Why? Are you looking for a pretty ribbon too?" Then, opening the door, she disappeared inside.

Follow her! my instincts screamed. I wanted to tell her how I felt, but something wouldn't allow it. I asked myself if it was fair to fool with her emotions. My work for the king had me plopped into a boiling kettle, and I didn't know if I'd emerge clean or cooked—and whatever end awaited me was likely also awaiting her father. Strower refused to cut and run, and I couldn't keep him safe any more than I could keep myself safe. The truth was I needed Strower to add density to my spine. Like it or not, I was the *boy* her note described, and although I didn't consciously see Strower as my avenue for advancement, our elbows were locked.

Was Carrie the one I longed for when I stared up at the faceless statue? She obviously didn't think she could give weight to my soul. I wasn't so sure, but it was useless to think about it now. There was nothing I could do. Things would have to play out.

It wasn't long before Strower arrived with the boys. Parking the wagon near the barn, he motioned for me to help unhitch the team. When I reached the wagon, Strower instructed the twins to join their sister in the house. When the two of them were out of earshot, Strower opened the tack box and pulled out two brushes. Handing one to me, he asked, "How's Carrie doing?"

"She seems fine," I lied.

Strower didn't seem convinced. "My confrontation with Oscar was pretty hard on her. I wonder if I did the right thing . . ."

Shrugging my shoulders, I chose instead to ask him about the here and now. "Are you sure you want to leave in the morning?"

Strower studied me for a long moment. "Yes, best to leave soon. The boys told me their brother was here—taking responsibility. He and Oscar never got along. In a way, Oscar ran him off."

"Yes, I remember you telling me that."

Strower smiled. "I like that he's returned. Perhaps having me gone is working toward something. Besides, we can't afford to have a neighbor visit. I won't lie if they come around. What we've learned doesn't bode well for the king. If my neighbors knew Thoren was behind the stolen cattle—even indirectly—they'd burn those commitment notes."

I began brushing my horse. "How much of this do you want Carrie to know? She's curious, but I didn't say anything."

Strower stopped working his brush to consider my question. "Probably best we don't tell her about the livestock. That way, she won't have to keep secrets. We'll tell them about spying on the Daggites. That should keep them entertained."

I let out a squawk to mimic the quail.

Strower laughed. "Not bad, Jens."

As we were finishing with the horses, the boys raced into the barn. "Dinner's ready!"

Strower pulled the lead-rope over the last horse's ears and swung the stall door closed. Then the boys each grabbed one of their father's hands and pulled him toward the door. I followed at a distance, watching Strower with his twin pirates heading for the house, thinking of the Daggite father and his son. *Balama.* There'd been plenty of times I'd reached out for the Creator's hand, but always for help. Now, watching the twins *walking with* William, each taking his hand—only because they wanted as much of their father as they could get—I saw another glimpse of what Joar was trying to communicate. Connected.

Inside, the familiar aroma of fresh bread and hot stew greeted my senses like a warm homecoming. After taking his seat, Strower lowered his head, thanking the Creator for our safe return, the protection of his children, and the opportunity to share a meal again. While eating, Strower looked intently at his boys. "Do you want to hear about the Daggites?"

"What's a Daggite?" asked Magnus.

"You remember," scolded Carrie. "We've studied them. They live beyond the mountains to the south and west."

"Oh yeah," replied Magnus, trying to appease his sister.

For half an hour, Strower regaled Carrie and the twins with our foray into Dag, telling how we'd followed Joar to the village. Strower told the story so well, he had me listening intently, too. When he came to the part when the young Daggite sprung after the bird, Strower looked at me, cueing my squawk. When I complied, Carrie nearly fell off her chair. The boys squealed with delight, flooding the farm for the remainder of the day with quail imitations.

Eager to finish his work before morning, Strower kept me busy until sundown, helping him repair a fence. While digging a post hole, I asked him if he'd told Carrie that we were leaving in the morning.

Strower shook his head. "I'll tell her when we get back to the house. I need to spend some time alone with her—once the boys are in bed—to see how she's doing." Then he set down the fence post. "As a matter of fact," he said, slapping the dirt from his trousers, "if you wouldn't mind finishing up here, I'll go put the boys to bed now. She's probably fed them already. They'll want to hear about the Daggites again."

"Of course," I replied, not exactly confident in my ability to finish the job.

By the time the fence was repaired and the tools put away, it was nearly dark. Walking to the house, I saw Strower and Carrie sitting on the porch. The quiet drone of their conversation stopped when I was within earshot, so I quickly crossed the porch in awkward silence.

Once inside the house, Carrie called after me, "There's a plate for you on the table."

"Thanks."

"Get some sleep," Strower added. "We'll need to get an early start."

I found a broken loaf and some strawberry preserves sitting next to a plate. Tearing off a chunk, I smothered the soft bread with Carrie's jam and brought my plate upstairs, hoping the bedroom window would be open so I could hear the conversation on the porch. Reaching my room, or rather, Will's room, I noticed that the door that I'd intentionally left open had been closed. Inside, the room was hot and stale, but I couldn't open the window without Strower and Carrie thinking I was trying to eavesdrop. So I ate my bread in my underpants, sweating on top of the covers.

After a while, I heard the two of them come inside, so I rushed to the window, letting in the evening breeze. Returning to my bed, I reclined on the sheets, welcoming the cool air on my bare skin while listening to the creaks and footfalls on the staircase as Carrie and William stirred about, performing their bedtime rituals.

When the house finally fell silent, I began nodding off, but then I heard something, barely discernable. It sounded like the knob on my door, but the moon didn't offer quite enough light to see if it was moving. Staring intently, I finally concluded that my imagination was running wild. But then the door began opening, creaking ever so slightly. Quietly, a feminine figure entered the room, approaching my bed on tiptoes. Lying there, in only my underpants, I froze.

Cautiously, Carrie sat on the edge of my mattress, whispering my name.

"I'm here," I whispered back.

From the edge of the bed, she reached out, placing her hands on my pillow, one on each side of my head. I could now see her face in the dim moonlight, the muted beams highlighting the unruly gold waves cascading alongside her face, falling next to mine, creating a tent for our faces.

After staring down at me for a moment, she whispered. "I'm scared, Jens."

"Of what?" I asked, reaching my arms around her back and lightly running my fingers down her ribcage like I was playing a delicate instrument. An involunatry shiver ran through her body.

199

"I'm scared of what might happen to my father and you. What you're doing seems dangerous."

I looked up at her, not knowing what to say.

"I'm sorry for earlier," she whispered, using her slender fingers to brush a few of her rogue hairs away from my face. "I know you're not using my father." Then, leaning down, she kissed my lips, barely making contact. As I lifted my head to press in, she moved away in equal measure, finally sliding off the bed and disappearing through the door as quietly as she'd arrived.

CHAPTER 25

I woke before dawn, eager to finish my mission, brave from the kiss—a kiss so light, it almost wasn't. My soul felt different. I'd studied many brave men—my father saw to that—warriors who died for the kingdom's dominion. I'd also studied men made bold by a passion for their work—explorers, artists, inventors—dedicating their skilled hands to realize a dream, fearless of what, or whom, the sharp stick of their imagination might poke. That kind of soul was foreign to me. Whether those men died on the altar of dominion or work, they were driven by passion. I'd never experienced passion like that, which is likely why I'd never felt brave.

But now, something had changed, activated by the kiss. I kept thinking about the light touch of Carrie's lips on mine. As she pulled away, she caused me to sit straight up, chasing her breath across the mattress. She'd changed my posture. No longer lying prone, awaiting my fate, I was eager to forge my destiny. Abandoning my crippling thoughts of failure and success, or life and death, I was now thinking of being worthy of Carrie's hand.

I didn't want to see her face again until my future was unclouded, until I'd cleared a path forward. When I came back, it'd be for her. But first, I needed to fix things.

Without the slightest idea of what time it was, I slid out of bed and dressed in the dark. Then, quietly leaving my room, bag in hand, I headed downstairs, carefully stepping on the outside edges of the treads to keep them from creaking.

Dropping my bag in the hall, I entered the kitchen and lit the candle on the table beside the stove. Then I pulled down the kneading bowl from the cupboard, bringing both the candle and kneading bowl to the dining room table. After ransacking Carrie's school supplies to find a pen and ink, I pulled the crumpled note from my pocket and took Strower's seat at the head of the table. Carefully reading Carrie's letter one last time by candlelight, I then turned the parchment over and wrote her a note.

Carrie,

If you can't give weight to my soul, let me carry the weight of yours.

Jens

After placing the note in the kneading bowl, I returned the bowl to the cupboard, knowing she'd use it to make bread dough before day's end. Then I headed to the barn, hitching up the horses by lantern light. It was still dark when I finished, so I blew out the lamp and reclined in the bed of the wagon, waiting for Strower to wake up.

I must've fallen asleep because I didn't hear Strower until he threw his traveling bag in the wagon's bed, flopping it squarely on my belly. "Uff."

Leaping backward, Strower gasped, holding up his light. "What in the— Jens? Why are you out here so early?" Then, holding his lantern above his head to gain better sight, he noticed the horses already hitched to the wagon. "Huh," was all he said.

I propped myself up on one elbow. "I wanted to be ready this time."

"Uh ha," Strower grunted, not sounding convinced. Then, stepping outside the barn to relieve himself, he raised his voice to span the distance. "You sure you don't want to say goodbye to Carrie? She's up baking bread—seems in a pretty good mood."

My soul took flight, but I didn't know what to say. It would be awkward to see her now, after leaving the note.

Strower returned to the wagon, resting one elbow on the bedrail. The way he studied my face made me wonder if he'd seen what I'd written. "Well? Do you want to say goodbye, or not?"

"No. I'll be back here soon enough. Besides, I left her a note."

"A note, huh?" If Strower had seen what I'd written, he masked his knowledge perfectly. Stepping further into the barn, he grabbed hold of the two horses by the leather straps circling their massive jaws, and slowly pushed the team backward. "Well," he said, as the wagon rolled outside, "I guess that's one way to do it."

After pointing the team in the right direction, Strower climbed onto the bench and grabbed hold of the reins. Moving from the wagon's bed to join Strower, I noticed it was growing light in the east. In the dim glow, Strower turned to me. "You look eager."

"I am eager."

"Then let's go see the king." Strower snapped the reins and made a clicking sound from the side of his mouth, sending the horses up the path.

After we'd traveled quite a distance in silence, Strower pushed back his hat, opening the door to a conversation. "Let's go back to yesterday," he said, "when you told me the king's army might attack the tribes in the Valley."

"That was only yesterday? Seems longer ago than that. I'm not sure where to start. I guess it goes back to when we first met Bear at the inn. Do you remember when he said it'd be a shame if the king turned murderous against the tribes?"

"I remember."

"Well, that got me thinking—somehow, Bear figured out who I was. I think it was because he recognized the king's wagon. For some reason, it made sense to him that I was in Saleton, and I couldn't figure out why. I kept asking myself: *Why would Bear think the king would send the Minister of Agriculture down here?*"

"The king didn't send you down there," Strower reminded me.

"I know, but Bear didn't know that. I was just trying to make sense of what he was thinking."

"I see . . ." replied Strower, like he thought I might be taking him on a wild goose chase.

"Then it hit me—Bear probably thought Thoren wanted farmland of his own. You know—to grow his own crops for export. Bear probably thought I was down there checking the quality of the soil to see if it'd be worth invading the Valley. What better way for the king to acquire land than pushing the Daggites out? It would explain why Thoren wouldn't lift a finger to protect the farmers down there. He'd need things to grow worse, more serious, before Tuva would support a bold move by his army."

Glancing at me from the corner of his eye, Strower said, "Jens, you're babbling. You're making all this up."

"I know, but the logic made sense at the time—like something Bear might think Thoren would do."

Strower squinted like I was giving him a headache. Pulling his hat forward again to shade his eyes, he asked, "What does that have to do with anything? *We know* Thoren didn't send you to Saleton, and *we know* that the man who brings supplies to camp is behind these invasions."

"Just hear me out," I pleaded. Then I recounted to Strower everything the cook had told me. I told him about Alden Fry's impossible task of feeding half the population of Keenod without a budget, and how Thoren had purchased the exploding powder to solve his financial woes. I explained the deal Alden Fry had made with the Daggite priest, Bear's imprisonment, the cattle quota, and finally Alden's threat to bring the king's army to the Valley, along with his threat to kill Joar if anyone at the camp breathed a word about Alden's role in the invasions.

Strower listened without interrupting. Then, after he'd thought for a while, he asked, "Do you suppose King Thoren knows anything about what Alden Fry is up to?"

I shook my head. "If I were a betting man, I'd say he doesn't."

"Then why are you so troubled about the king's army attacking Dag? Jens, Alden Fry has no control over Thoren's fighting men. Most of them are on ships, earning their keep as cargo guards."

"I know. It's just that—"

"It's just what?"

"It's just that I'm worried about you speaking to King Thoren. The only club you hold over his head is your influence with the farmers—that, and the fact that you know the real reason behind the invasions."

"That's right. But that's no small club. If he wants the farmers to grow crops for him, he'll need to protect the farmland around Saleton. It's as simple as that."

"Is it?"

"What do you mean?"

"What might Thoren do when his back is against the wall? Have you ever thought of that? The cook suggested he might decide to destroy evidence."

"What evidence?"

"Me. You. The miners."

"What? You can't be serious."

"Well, put yourself in his shoes. He'd make the whole problem go away. He'd be a hero—just like King Tuva—expelling the Daggites with his army. Then he'd have the land for himself—to grow his crops—and what could his advisors say? He'd be popular with the people, and the advisors are constantly screaming that he needs to protect our borders. That's why they hate the port. William, tell me I'm wrong. Call me a fool for thinking this way. I'll listen. I just can't shake these thoughts."

Strower sat quietly for a moment. "No, you're no fool. The only thing I can't figure is how he'd send his army when they're scattered all over the world? But I guess it wouldn't take too many men, not the way those tribes are separated, and he'd have the element of surprise. So what do you suggest? Do we need to play dumb about this man, Alden Fry? I don't know if I can go along with that."

"Well, I don't think we should mention the mining camp. We should tell Thoren we were in Saleton to buy hay. Leave it at that. That's how we learned about the invasions. We need to ask for his help to protect the farmers—a couple of soldiers stationed at the river crossing. That's all it'd take. We can assure him that his help would gain the trust of the farmers. I think he'll listen to us. He'll soon need to fill his ship with hay, or he'll be in hot water with Sagan's king."

"What if he refuses? What if he won't send the soldiers to guard the river crossing?"

"I guess we'll cross that bridge when we come to it."

Strower tightened his grip on the reins. "What about Alden Fry? How's he going to get what he deserves?"

"He'll probably hang himself by some other means. The miners are making their quotas now, so Alden has the money he needs to buy supplies for the dockworkers in Keenod. He's not desperate anymore. When he hears the king is sending soldiers to protect the border, he'll probably race to the pass to take down his pasture fence."

Strower inhaled a deep breath, slowly letting it escape through a small slit in his lips. "I can't argue with you, Jens. You know Thoren better than anyone. If you think he's capable of killing his best friend, along with the miners—not to mention a valley full of Daggites—we better do this your way."

"I don't know what he's capable of doing, but he's blinded by ambition, and that makes him dangerous."

"Say no more," replied Strower, "you've convinced me."

Nodding gratefully, I remembered the first words Carrie spoke to me when I'd jumped down from the wagon: *Thank you for keeping my father alive.*

CHAPTER 26

We journeyed a day and a half before reaching the rim of The Crucible, where Thoren had stopped his carriage weeks earlier to show me the pottered slope down to the aqua sea. The distant shoreline reminded me of a necklace; a half-circle strung with gray shacks, highlighted against the pale sand, except for one remarkable pearl proudly displayed at the center.

Strower recognized the gem without my help. "Ah, there it is. King Thoren's summer palace."

Nodding, I asked if he was ready.

"For what?" replied Strower. "You're the one with the fancy uniform. I'm to play dumb and let you talk. Remember?"

Looking at the shiny boots that I'd retrieved from my bag that morning, along with the rest of my ridiculous uniform, I exhaled the words, "I remember."

"How about you?" Strower asked. "Are you ready?"

I didn't feel nearly as confident as I did when I'd convinced him to play the supporting role, but what could I do now? "Ready or not," I replied, prompting Strower to flick the reins, sending the horses down the path toward the palace.

The return of the king's wagon caused quite a stir among the servants at the palace. A boy spotted us first, disappearing inside the immaculate stable and returning with two men. After observing our approach for a short moment, one of the men spoke a few words to the lad, who then sprinted toward the palace, probably to notify Thoren of our arrival. Almost immediately, servants appeared around the side entrance, peering and retreating like bees around a hive.

When we drew nearer, the two men from the stable approached, each grabbing a horse and waiting wordlessly for Strower and me to dismount. When we did, they led the horses away, leaving us standing alone, not knowing what to do next. Then a short fellow, who seemed more comfortable in his royal attire than I did, emerged from amidst gathering at the servant's entrance, and briskly approached. I recognized him from my prior stay, though we hadn't been introduced. He was Thoren's Chief of Staff or some such title.

"Come this way," he directed, firing his words in rapid succession, even before reaching us. Then, turning on his heels, he marched quick-step toward the same door from which he emerged, expecting us to follow.

"I'm Jens—the Minister of Agriculture," I said, "and this is—"

"I know who you are," he interrupted, turning his head only enough to show a bit of his profile, "and you can save the rest of your introduction."

"Where are you bringing us? We'd like to speak with the king."

"I'm bringing you to your rooms."

Strower stopped and jabbed his thumb back toward the stable. "Our bags . . ."

Again, without turning or slowing, the man replied, "Your bags will be brought to your rooms—where you'll wait until summoned."

Trotting to catch up, Strower then grabbed my elbow. When our eyes met, he raised his brow, silently asking me what was happening. Of course, I was clueless as well, so I shrugged and kept following. I didn't know if we were encountering the usual disposition of this powerful little man, or if his attitude represented a shunning inspired by King Thoren.

Inside the palace, we quickly made our way down a long hall, the cadence of our clacking boots echoing off the stone floor, sounding like soldiers marching. Knowing Strower wasn't one to blindly follow anyone, least of all this arrogant little imp, I could almost sense his desire to push me aside and take charge. Finally, I blurted, "We'd like to see his Highness now."

"You will not see him now," replied the man, stopping to open the door to a bedchamber. Then, looking at Strower, he pointed to the interior of the room. Reluctantly, Strower entered. When I tried to follow, the man barred the doorway with his arm before closing Strower inside.

"This way," he instructed, continuing down the hall, surging past several doors before reaching the one he intended for me. Expecting me to enter the room, he stood by, surveying the hallway, as if trying to complete my incarceration without being seen.

When I didn't comply, he glared at me. "When can we see the king?" I asked.

Taking hold of my elbow, he tried pulling me toward the open door. "You've been away without corresponding for how long? And now you demand an immediate audience?"

"I wasn't instructed to correspond," I said, jerking my elbow from his grip. "I was given instructions to produce results—results I now need to discuss with the king."

The red-faced man was now at a loss for words. All he could do was accuse me of eluding the king's spy, evil Emil, but why would I feel obligated to report to an innkeeper? Knowing I had the upper hand, he said, "The king will see you when he is ready."

"Will it be today?" I asked, stubbornly planting myself in the hall, folding my arms across my chest, wishing Strower could witness this thickening of my spine. "Does he even know I'm here? There is some urgency, and I'd hate to have this delay be the reason for my failure."

With a hint of fear in his eyes, the little man's self-importance finally gave way to caution, prompting him to share his reason for stealing us away. "We have visitors from the Royal City," he said, with beads of sweat collecting on his upper lip. Then, looking down the hall again, he added, "Advisors . . ."

"Oh, I see," I replied, finally understanding his desire to remove us from sight. The less Thoren had to explain to an audience of advisors, the better. Encouraged that our treatment was perhaps related more to my poor timing than my poor correspondence, I stepped into the room. Immediately, the door closed behind me.

I waited undisturbed in the bedchamber, peering out the window until it was nearly dark. I was watching the orange sun melt into the sea when I heard my door creak open, only wide enough for someone to slide my belongings inside the room, along with a supper plate. Then the door closed again. The plate held a fantastic cut of beef. I glared at the meat suspiciously, wondering if it had once belonged to the man I'd sat next to at the inn in Saleton, the poor farmer who'd lost his herd. Leaving it on the floor like a bloody corpse, I covered the meat with the white napkin and slid the plate under my bed—a respectful burial.

Then I sat down to think. Why did they separate us? And why treat us like prisoners? We were at the king's palace, after all. I doubted they made a practice of sliding their guest's supper plates across the stone floor. They might have only been hiding us from the advisors, but that aside, I could sense Thoren's displeasure from my brief interaction with his Chief of Staff. The innkeeper probably discovered our motive for traveling to Saleton and cast my actions in a bad light.

Maybe Thoren would interview Strower and me separately, checking one story against the other. I'd told Strower that we should play innocent, saying we went to Saleton only because we'd heard there was hay to purchase, but now I was second-guessing my plan. Too many people knew the real reason for our trip—more than thirty farmers attending Strower's planting celebration, many of whom frequently dined at Tinsdal's inn. They would verify that we'd traveled to Saleton to see if the invasions were real—if Lundgren's accusations against the king were true.

I considered sneaking down the hall to Strower's room to adjust our story, but they probably had someone watching our doors. I began thinking about Thoren's state of mind, wondering if one of the visiting advisors was the starched relic who interrogated me the day of my induction. He had a living hatred for Thoren. As far as I knew, all the advisors considered The Crucible a chink in Tuva's armor, an invitation to foreign invaders. Thoren was probably enduring endless criticism, his advisors fuming at having to travel to Keenod to deliver counsel their king wouldn't heed.

Thoren had trouble breathing around his advisors. I remembered chasing him up the tower, whereupon reaching the roof, he could finally inhale properly. I remembered the pile of throwing stones he kept there to unleash his fury, hurling them into the churning water below . . . Churning water— my mother occasionally boiled water in her skillets to release the charred remnants, the blackened scraps that had escaped her stirring spoon. That night, my mind boiled in very much the same way, loosening baked-on dread from the far recesses of my imagination—black, unsolvable problems—churning in rotating boils too swift to fish out for examination, causing me to roll from one side of the bed to the other in a fitful sleep.

I woke in the morning to a loud, authoritative knock. Opening the door, I stood face-to-face with one of the palace guards. "The king will see you now," he said. Then, turning his back, he waited outside my room while I dressed. When I was ready, the guard led me to the same small door where Thoren had brought me weeks earlier—his thinking room with chalk scrawlings on slate walls and windows overlooking the sea.

Standing next to the door, another palace guard had Strower in tow. Now, with the two of us together, one of the guards opened the door, ushering us inside, where Thoren sat at his large table, studying various notes from open scrolls. Finally, he looked up, motioning with four fingers for us to approach. Then, pointing to seats across the table, he waited for us to join him, his bloodshot eyes studying each of us in turn, first me, then Strower.

As uncomfortable as I was, Strower didn't seem to notice the king's visual interrogation at all. I'd been anticipating this moment for a long time, wondering how these two overshadowing personalities would interact. To me, they were two mighty trees piercing the canopy, and I had no idea which stood taller. By position, Thoren rose above Strower. But by the raw force of personality, I wasn't sure.

Rather than submitting to the king's gesture to take a seat, Strower chose to stand, marveling at the breathtaking view of the sea. For a while, Thoren patiently observed his new guest, studying him up and down. Finally, the king peered out the window as well. "What do you think of my view?"

"I've not seen anything more beautiful in all my life," replied Strower, barely able to look away from the aqua sea to address the king.

"Will it be a distraction?" asked Thoren, grabbing a strange vegetable from a wooden crate that sat on the floor near his feet.

"No, Your Highness," replied Strower, turning and extending his hand over the table. "My name is William Strower. I'm a farmer."

Ignoring Strower's gesture, Thoren continued studying his face, waiting for him to sit down next to me at the table. When he did, the king addressed me. "I wonder what reason you have for bringing Mr. Strower here?" The question didn't sound entirely unfriendly, but the words communicated some displeasure, his disappointment that I'd brought a stranger into his intimate space. This transgression would no doubt chill our conversation.

"Mr. Strower has an impressive farming enterprise in central Tuva. He was recommended to me by the blacksmith you sent me to visit. He's extended both hospitality and help. With his aid, I've secured commitments from thirty farmers to grow beets for export."

Thoren's brow lost some of its furrows, "Impressive. Tell me, Mr. Strower, as a farmer, what do you think of this little fellow?" Then, Thoren rolled the strange vegetable he'd been holding across the table.

Picking it up for examination, Strower replied, "It looks like a pale beet of some sort."

"Very good. It is a beet from a distant country to the southeast." Then looking at me, he said, "Akeem brought it to me, along with an interesting story."

"Please tell it."

"Well, I haven't verified its truth, but I've no reason to disbelieve it. Akeem told me a brilliant man from Gladon extracted sugar from beets like these. When his discovery was revealed to Gladon's king, the man was promptly executed."

"Why?" I asked.

"The great country of Gladon has very long tentacles. They occupy a large island in the southern ocean, where they use slaves to grow cane. The cane is refined on that island to make sugar molasses and then shipped north in barrels and sold for a great profit."

"How does that relate to the execution?" I asked.

Strower ventured a guess, "I'd imagine a new source of sugar would be a threat to the king's trade."

Thoren smiled. "Very perceptive, Mr. Strower."

"But the inventor was from Gladon," I protested. "Wouldn't the king benefit from his invention?"

Nodding, Thoren replied, "Perhaps, but the king has already expended a great deal of gold to supply sugar in the current method, and he relies on scarcity to keep the price elevated. If sugar were produced in the north, the king's investment in the south would become worthless. So, you see, it was in his best interest to destroy both the invention and the inventor."

I couldn't believe we were talking about beets—a vegetable I detested. How many nights had I sat alone at the supper table, trying to find the will to swallow one more disgusting bite, wishing they didn't exist? I was surprised enough to learn the alternate uses Akeem had in mind for Tuva's beets in the far reaches of the world—paint, cosmetics, medicine, and even love potions—but now to think that a good man was murdered for finding another use . . . it seemed like a ludicrous dream. "Where did Akeem hear this story?"

"Akeem knew the inventor firsthand. In fact, he was tasked by the inventor to find every variety of beet he could discover in his travels. That's why Akeem visited our commercial district in the first place. The young inventor probably divulged more of his secrets to Akeem than was prudent. Intelligent men of this sort are not always intelligent in other ways."

The king's comment made me think of Lundgren. "That's true," I agreed, "but I wonder how the king learned of the inventor's work."

"Kings have their ways of learning things," replied Thoren, his eyes lingering on me before continuing, "but in this case, it wasn't difficult. Akeem said the young inventor had corresponded with the king, seeking capital, a loan from the royal treasury to build a facility to produce sugar molasses. Not long afterward, the man was found dead, his body destroyed along with his equipment.

Holding the vegetable before his eyes, Strower asked, "What is your intention with this?"

"Only to see how it grows in our soil. Red beets grow well here. Who's to say this variety won't flourish? I'm certain, in time, the invention will resurface somewhere, as progressive as the world is today. Perhaps we could supply beets in the north, just as the island in the south supplies cane. The trick will be to develop a plant perfectly suited for this purpose."

Again, I thought of Lundgren, pondering how his genius with plants had already manipulated a variety of beet for making his rum. The sack of beets he'd taken from me was pathetic in color, compared to our red beets, but Lundgren saw something in those pale beets that made him want them. Perhaps they offered some improvement to his bred-for-rum beets.

"What are you asking of us?" I asked.

Looking at Strower, Thoren inquired, "Is it now too late to plant a small plot of these? Akeem has given me seed."

"No," said Strower, "I don't think so—if we plant them soon."

Nodding at Strower, the king opened his hands, as if to say, "Let it be done." Then, looking at me, he asked, "Are you confident of filling my ship with hay? Sagon's king is counting on me, and I am counting on you."

Wondering what Thoren already knew about our trip to Saleton, I proceeded cautiously. "Well, we've located the hay needed to fill your ship, but I've stumbled upon an obstacle."

Thoren lifted one eyebrow. "What obstacle?"

"Are you aware of the Daggite invasions in the south?" I asked.

"What of them?"

"Well, the raids have left more than a few farmers without cattle, with barns full of hay they could sell to give their families money to purchase supplies this fall—before winter sets in."

Thoren touched his fingertips together. "That doesn't sound like an obstacle to me. It sounds like an opportunity."

"We thought so too, but before we can be persuade the farmers to sell their hay to you, they'd need assurance of your protection against future invasions—nothing drastic—only a couple of soldiers to guard the river crossing."

Thoren folded his hands together, squeezing his fingers tight enough to turn his knuckles white. "You haven't promised my soldiers, have you?"

"No, no, I didn't even tell them who I was," I lied. My statement was mostly true, however—I'd only told Marcus because he'd discovered the crest. Bear had figured out who I was all by himself.

"Well, if you haven't exposed your identity, I have another idea."

"I'm listening."

The king turned to Strower. "Suppose a farmer owning a significant enterprise from central Tuva were to purchase their hay, and I simply supplied the funds? There'd be no request for protection then. Would there?"

The muscles surrounding Strower's jaw flickered before he spoke. "Would you deny their protection? Your Highness, these farmers are your subjects."

"As are you, Mr. Strower." Then, for what seemed like an eternity, the two men stared at each other, lone trees above the canopy, neither refusing to give ground to the other.

Finally, Strower stood up from his chair and turned to me. "I'll be in my room. Come and get me when you're finished." Striding past the guard, he disappeared from Thoren's study, slamming the door behind him.

With piercing eyes, Thoren turned his attention to me. "Why did you bring him here?"

"I'd be nowhere without him. He's helped me secure thirty contracts for beets among his neighbors, and now he's agreed to grow these pale beets for you, and—"

"Enough! You need to secure his cooperation. The money will simply pass through his hands. It's not too much for a king to ask from one of his subjects. You must remember that he has a stake in this too."

"He won't turn his back on those farmers."

Stiffening his spine, Thoren stabbed at the table with his index finger. "Jens, we can't allow Mr. Strower to go back home in his self-righteousness. Now he could just as easily turn the farmers against me as unite them under me. I wish you hadn't given him such a voice. I won't let him dictate what I do—not him, nor you, nor my advisors, nor anyone."

"But he won't turn them against you—not if you send help. Thoren—"

"KING Thoren."

"I'm not asking you as my king. I'm asking you as my friend."

Thoren lauged, "Didn't your father teach you anything, Jens? A king has no real friends. Dominion won't allow it."

Looking into his eyes for a long moment, I finally hung my head, sitting silently, not knowing what to say.

Then Thoren's voice turned tender. "Jens, we do have a type of friendship—of course we do—it secured your post. Did you stand on your conscience when offered a title? I didn't hear you say: 'No, my king. I won't corrupt our friendship.' But now, Jens, you must accept the relationship for what it is."

Looking up from the floor, my heart ached and I was unable to speak.

Thoren placed his hand palm-down on the table. "Finish your work, Jens. Secure Mr. Strower's cooperation, write the contracts for hay, and let me know when you're finished. I'll provide the funds to Mr. Strower, and I'll make arrangements for the transportation of the hay."

"He won't cooperate," I whispered.

Thoren's hand came down violently on the table, and he spoke through clenched teeth. "Do you have any idea how difficult I can make things for him? Do you?" Then, sitting back in this chair, regaining some of his lost composure, he added, "Once those righteous hands of Mr. Strower are a bit dirty, he'll be quite useful to us. Now go."

CHAPTER 27

After leaving the king, I headed to Strower's room, but no Strower. So, assuming he was waiting at the wagon, I hurried to get my things, lugging the crate of beets down the long hallway. Once inside the bedchamber, I threw my bag on the crate and surveyed the floor for anything I might've forgotten. That's when I noticed my supper plate, its edge sticking out from under the bed. I thought of Marcus, the two of us sitting outside the inn. He was hoping that I was the answer to his mother's prayers, the man who could find them some help.

"There's no help here," I said to the walls, kicking the plate further under the bed.

"Have you seen my companion?" I asked the stable boy, after leaving the palace. He was pitching manure from an empty stall, presumably manure from my horses, now hitched to the wagon. Strower's bag was there, but he was nowhere in sight.

Using his forearm to wipe his blonde hair away from his sweaty face, the boy replied, "He told me to tell you he went for a walk."

"Did he say where he was going?"

The boy shook his head and returned to his work.

Leaving my things in the wagon, I walked through the front gate, leaving the palace compound and circling the outside perimeter of the iron fence, finally reaching a cobblestone alley leading to the harbor. Guessing Strower would be drawn to activity, I aimed for the only pier mooring a ship, its cargo being hoisted from the vessel in tight bundles. The dock was crawling with longshoremen, some heaving ropes, others watching and yelling instructions—activities that would draw Strower like an ant to a picnic.

Nearing the beach, I veered from the cobblestone path to walk in the surf. Removing my boots and socks and rolling up my pants, I began wading toward the pier. The sensation was surreal—the tickle of tiny sand particles escaping from underfoot with the receding of the waves, coupled with the screeching gulls fighting for scraps of food—it was like I was reliving a scene from my childhood. Had I been here before? Then I remembered the dream I'd had weeks earlier, the night before Thoren and I set out for The Crucible. Closing my eyes, I let my senses carry me back to the dream, once again becoming the young child at the beach with his father, watching helplessly as the tide leveled my kingdom of sand.

"What have you learned, Jens?" my father kept asking me, forcing me to look into his eyes. *"What have you learned?"*

"Waves are cruel!"

"But they've given you a new beginning, a chance for a fresh start, to apply what you've learned."

Opening my eyes, I half expected to see my father. Was that dream intended to guide me today? I was, without question, reeling from the waves, but what had I learned? Only that friendship and dominion don't mingle well. I'd learned that a man can lose his soul in his pursuits. I'd now seen it firsthand with Thoren and was beginning to feel my soul recede like the sand under my feet . . . but starting over? How could that happen?

Lost in my thoughts, I arrived at the pier, facing one of the gigantic wooden columns on which it rested. Looking up and shielding my eyes from the glare of the morning sun, I saw Strower leaning on a different column further up the pier. He was watching the unloading of the ship's cargo. Captivated as he was, he didn't notice me walking up the dock until I stood next to him, and even then, he didn't say anything.

The longshoremen were arguing with sailors about a bundle—whether it should be swung differently by the sailors, or the cart moved by the longshoremen—neither side giving ground.

"Are you wanting to go straighten them out?" I asked.

"They could use some help in that regard," Strower replied, his attention still fixed on the conflict. Then he looked at me with a strained smile. "Jens, for the first time, I considered walking away from you."

Pretending to share his interest in the ship's unloading, I carefully considered how to respond. I almost told him it wasn't too late, but then I remembered Thoren's threat to make Strower's life a nightmare if he didn't cooperate.

"I lost my poise, Jens, but I had to speak for the farmers. That's why I'm here."

"I don't blame you for what you said or for walking out."

"What did Thoren say after I left?"

"He's upset with me for bringing you here, William. You're a threat to him."

"You weren't able to convince him to send help?"

"No, we're on our own. Thoren wants those contracts for hay as soon as possible so he can make arrangements for transport. He's still expecting to pass his payments through you."

"That won't happen."

"I know."

After quietly watching the workers for another moment, Strower asked, "Do you think he knows that we're aware of what Alden Fry has been up to?"

"I don't know what he knows, but his nerves are as tight as a stretched pelt."

The two of us stood quietly again, Strower watching the men and me watching the waves crashing to shore. They reminded me of fingers reaching for what they could steal from the beach before retreating to the sea with their loot.

"I pray," said Strower.

"What?"

"I pray. I make it a practice."

"I know. I've seen you on your porch."

"Well, I prayed this morning with some fervency. I didn't hear words, but I saw Joar, beckoning."

"What do you make of that?"

"I'm not sure. It was comforting—like the Creator was showing me a soul dispossessed of worry."

"You? Worry? I don't see you as a worrier, William."

"I suppose you don't, but I draw comfort by arranging the future. Nothing better than planning to stave off worry. But Joar has a way of living in the moment."

"Yes. Well, I'm glad you've found comfort. If you have any to spare, I could use a dose."

Strower smiled. "But I'm now wondering if the vision was showing me something more than comfort. We should visit the mining camp before returning to Saleton. Maybe Joar will enlighten us in some way. Perhaps he can show us a way to move forward.

Remembering my promise to the cook that I'd get word back about our meeting with the king, I nodded in agreement, and we returned to the stable.

With Strower driving, I sat as a passenger, my mind spinning faster than the wagon's wheels. I desperately wanted to devote our traveling time to formulating a plan, but Strower refused, claiming it would dishonor his vision. He insisted we speak with Joar first. To make matters worse, Strower also insisted on detouring to Lundgren's farm before heading to the mining camp. He wanted to leave Thoren's seed with the farmer who was best equipped to grow the strange beets. So we traveled in near silence for what seemed like an eternity.

We found Carl a day and a half later, hoeing one of his circle plots. Lundgren's green eyes sparkled with delight when they beheld the pale beets. Without the courtesy of further conversation, he raced off to bury the seeds somewhere in his menagerie of round gardens.

Laughing again at Carl's complete disregard for social convention, Strower shook his head as the two of us watched the hermit disappear into the long grass.

"Now, let's go see Joar," said Strower.

"Aren't we stopping at your farm first? We're so close."

"No. We can't afford to run into anyone else, not until we fix this mess. The next person we come across won't likely be as distractible as Carl."

My heart sank. After the long ride, I was hoping to see Carrie if only for a moment. Strower noticed my drooping countenance. "We left only three days ago," he said, "and you didn't want to say goodbye then."

"I know."

Studying my face, Strower seemed to read everything I was thinking. Placing his hand on my shoulder, he said, "At least she has your note." Then he started for the wagon, chuckling as he walked.

Back on the road, we didn't converse for a long time—me stewing, while Strower's mind ruminated somewhere in his invisible world. Finally, he decided to share his thoughts. "Why don't *we* make sugar from beets?"

"What?"

"Isn't rum made from sugar-molasses? I think Carl makes sugar from his beets already. Carl is probably smarter than that genius from Gladon. That man's product is only Carl's ingredient. Carl has the added problem of turning his sugar to rum." Strower then removed his hat, using it to fan his head.

"That genius from Gladon is dead." I reminded him.

"True. Killed by his own damned king."

We both sat quietly, thinking, listening to the creaks and groans of the wagon and the crunching of gravel. Finally, Strower straightened his back. "I wonder what King Thoren would do if we brought him sugar instead of beets?"

Unwilling to entertain his contemplation, I remained silent as Strower continued on his own. "If we could get Carl to share his secrets, John could build the equipment. It would need to be large, though . . . Jens, what if Tuva could supply sugar to the northern kingdoms?"

"I thought you weren't going to arrange the future until we've talked with Joar. Have you already grown tired of living in the moment?"

"I can't help it, Jens. It's what I do. I need to occupy my mind somehow—with you moping."

"Well, if Gladon's king didn't hesitate to murder a citizen of his own nation to protect his sugar trade, what would prevent him from sending his army to invade Tuva? That's the very scenario Thoren's advisors fear the most."

"Good point, but there is a big difference between the cowardice of murdering one of your own subjects and the bold act of starting a war. Gladon has enemies too—enemies with powerful armies, who'd happily purchase our sugar, and would probably fight for us if it came to that. Besides, I don't think Gladon's king would be foolish enough to destroy the invention a second time. He knows it would only show up somewhere else."

Again, we rode along silently for a time. Then Strower said, "I wonder how many acres of beets it would take to supply Tuva with sugar?"

Before I could respond, he added, "And why wouldn't Thoren export our sugar? He'd make more money than just shipping raw beets."

"I don't doubt that he would export your sugar. Thoren is also vexed with blind ambition."

"Also? Come on, Jens, I'm only passing the time."

"Well, it's not as if we don't have enough problems. Do we need to borrow more from your imagination?"

"Very well, I'll stop. But first, let me ask you this: Do you think a king who steals humans, enslaving them on an island to make sugar should continue to have his way?"

"No, I suppose not."

It was growing late when we ascended the mountain-trail leading to the mining camp. By the time our wagon finally arrived at the nonsensical arrangement of shanties, darkness was setting in. The miners had retired to their cabins but now they came to their doors to see who was visiting. If Carl were along, we might've gained an audience—inspecting the wagon for rum—but the sight of Strower and me alone excited no curiosity. Their doors quickly closed again, keeping out the mosquitoes.

The only man left outside was the cook. The old fellow stood near his lean-to, placing his cookware upside down to dry on a rough table. He noticed us right away but completed his work before ambling over, chattering words before we could hear them. As he drew nearer, I heard him say, ". . . been gone three days now."

"Who has?" I asked. "Joar?"

The cook nodded.

"Do you know where he went?" asked Strower.

Turning sideways, the cook used a sweeping motion of his arm to present the vast wilderness as the only possibility.

Strower slumped his shoulders. "Does he disappear like this often?"

"Not often, but every so often."

"Any idea when he'll return?"

"None," said the cook, snapping his mouth shut, his lower lip disappearing entirely behind his bushy gray mustache.

Strower looked perplexed. I suppose his vision of Joar beckoning had given him the impression that he'd be waiting for us to arrive, eager to reveal a way forward. Now, with Joar out of the picture, Strower was like a hamstrung warhorse, unable to advance or retreat.

"You two can sleep in my cabin tonight, but I have no cots for you. Joar sleeps on the floor."

The cook made his way toward his little shack, expecting us to follow. While he walked, he removed his floppy hat, using it to slap the mosquitoes off the back of his neck. Without turning, he said, "I'll save you from these cursed bloodsuckers at least."

Pulling our bags from the bed of the wagon, I followed the old man while Strower tended to the horses. It wasn't long before all three of us were inside his cabin, trying to sleep.

CHAPTER 28

During the night, I woke to the creaking of the cabin door. At first, I thought either Strower or the cook had gone outside to relieve himself, but I could still hear both of them sleep-breathing. There wasn't the slightest noise inside the cabin to confirm it, but I thought I sensed a presence.

It was very dark. I tried to gain sight from a tiny stream of moonlight trickling in through a small crack between the window frame and the curtain, and after some time, I could finally distinguish dark gray from black. Surveying the room, I wondered if Joar had returned. Who else could it be?

Who else, indeed? Suddenly, two possibilities hijacked my imagination, and every shadow became the knife-wielding silhouette of a killer—first, the Daggite priest, seeking revenge. Then, Alden Fry, sneaking in to murder witnesses to his crimes. Slowly, I lowered my right arm to the floor and retrieved my boot by its toe, holding it in a cocked position while scanning the room for movement. After a few moments though, my panic gave way to reason, and I determined that I must have only dreamt that the door had creaked. If someone had snuck in to do us harm, they'd certainly have made their move by now. Comforted by the rhythmic breathing of Strower and the cook, I reunited my boot with its mate on the floor and eventually fell back to sleep.

I woke to a room glowing pale pink with the promise of dawn, hearing the cook whisper, "No, you stay here." He was heading outside to get breakfast underway, and Joar was trying to follow him. He'd snuck in during the night, after all. Then the cook said, "These men are eager to talk with you."

When the cook left, I feigned sleep, but all the while watched Joar as he moved to the corner of the room and squatted on his haunches, his shoulders resting against the wall, waiting for Strower and me to wake up. He didn't seem to have any thought of disturbing us. Joar had what Strower described as a soul dispossessed of worry, able to live in the moment. Indeed, it seemed to be true. His eyes were gripping to behold in the dim twilight. The whites appeared backlit by an inner luminance, somehow bearing both tender patience and intense awareness. I wondered what he was thinking. Maybe he was simply communing with the unseen.

Suddenly, the Daggite's eyes settled on me, lingering, seeming to sense my consciousness. Sounding rattled, my words came out more like a confession than a greeting. "Uh, good morning, Joar."

Nodding discreetly, Joar remained silent, probably not wanting to wake Strower. Fortunately, the sound of my voice was enough to rouse William from his slumber. Rolling onto his back, he rubbed his eyes, blinking a few times at the rafters before his mind registered what he'd heard. All at once, he sat up, spinning his head, finally spotting the Daggite in the corner.

"Joar. You're back."

"Yes."

"Where have you been?"

"The mountain."

Strower waited for further explanation, but when it didn't come, he added, "In *balama*, I suppose."

"Yes."

Nodding, Strower said, "I'd like to learn more about—"

"Stop, William," I groaned. The words spewed from my mouth like vomited impatience. The two of them turned their heads in my direction—Strower seeming surprised by my interruption, and Joar merely waiting to hear what I had to say.

"Can we please get to the point?" I pleaded. My nerves were too frayed to endure another cryptic conversation with Joar. The last thing I wanted was to sit in the wagon—bound for Saleton—trying to figure out what the Daggite was attempting to communicate. No, we'd either use Joar's *balamistic* insight to uncover a mystical path forward or Strower and I would put our heads together and formulate a logical plan. I couldn't stomach a bastardized blend of the two. If Joar could somehow enlighten us, fine. Otherwise, we needed to be on our way.

Speechless, Strower stared at me. I used his silence as an opportunity to frame a concise question to the Daggite. "Joar, we're heading to Saleton. We need to find a way to protect those farmers from your people. William had a vision that you were beckoning us. Do you have something to tell us, or not?"

"I am to come with you."

"With us?" Strower and I echoed in unison.

"Yes."

Like a terrified critter flushed from its den, a sarcastic laugh escaped my mouth. "You want to go with us to Saleton? Do you even have a plan?"

Joar thought for a moment, probably trying to decide if what he had was a plan. Eventually, he splurged on another syllable to say that he did.

Now, fully awake, Strower walked over to Joar, squatting on his haunches in front of the Daggite. "Joar, you'll need to explain your plan in some detail. The people of Saleton won't take kindly to you—or us—if we bring you along."

"I will move the tribes out of the valley," replied Joar, as if informing us that he planned to relocate a stack of firewood.

Strower cocked his head sideways. "Move the tribes? How will you do that?"

"I will become their priest."

Catching himself from tipping backward, Strower used his right hand to push himself back onto his haunches. "Their priest? I'm afraid I don't understand."

"I will tell them about the Great Sacrifice and help them *walk with* the Creator. I will move the tribes away from Tuva, over the mountains, toward the setting sun."

When Joar said the words *Great Sacrifice*, I suddenly became curious. The term is from Tuva's Holy Book, forming what the priests call the third tenant of our faith.

Tenant #1: The Creator reigns. As image-bearers of the Creator, man reigns.
Tenant #2: The Creator works. As image-bearers of the Creator, man works.
Tenant #3: The Creator sacrificed. As image-bearers of the Creator, man sacrifices.

The third tenant was shrouded in mystery. What was the exact nature of the Great Sacrifice? It was believed sufficient for us, however, as image-bearers, to acknowledge that a sacrifice had been made on our behalf, prompting us to imitate the Creator's generosity by giving the first-fruits of our wealth to the poor and needy. The priests received this offering and distributed it as they saw fit.

When I was younger, I often wondered what the Great Sacrifice could have been and to whom the Creator was sacrificing. I even tried once to pose the question to Thoren, but he had no time for my contemplations. Eventually, I stopped wondering. But now this young Daggite claimed to have insight into the mystery. I remembered the cook telling me of Joar's surprising grasp of our Holy Book, but it seemed far-fetched that he could understand something that had eluded even our priests. And what could it possibly have to do with *balama*?

"What makes you think you understand the mystery of the Great Sacrifice?" I asked.

"It is no mystery to me."

"Why? What makes you smarter than our priests?"

"I understand the death of *balama*."

"What are you talking about? You said *balama* means *walk with*. How is that death?"

"A child cannot have the father's mind without first becoming an empty vessel. *Balama* is both death and life."

"So, what does any of this have to do with the Great Sacrifice?"

The illumination in Joar's eyes intensified. Pushing his shoulders from the wall with a quiver, he replied, "From under the branches, you saw the father with his son. *A father offers his life to his child. Balama* begins with the father's death. We Daggites know the difference between *balama* and *peecho.* You do not."

Offended, my first instinct was to load my sling with some mean words and fire back, but, in my mind, I could still see the Daggite father captivated with his young son, the two interacting like they were the only souls on earth. I'd never witnessed anything quite like it. Could I say I knew the difference between *balama* and *peecho?* No—not in the profound way Joar seemed to. My father once told me that knowing a definition can be profoundly different from understanding the thing itself. *Peecho* meant *walk like,* to imitate. On our journey to the village, Joar had used the word to describe how Daggites sneak up on their prey. Which word best described my manner with the Creator? I didn't know. At best, I was a bastardized blend, someone the Creator probably had trouble stomaching, but that wasn't something I was in the mood to confess.

"How do you know the tribes will follow you?" asked Strower.

Turning his eyes away from me, Joar replied, "I have seen it."

Strower nodded like he was convinced, but I was tired of relying on what these two men were *seeing.* Addressing Joar, I asked, "If you've seen it, why come to Saleton? Why not go straight to the Valley?"

Joar turned to Strower, expecting his help in answering my question, but Strower only waited for a reply. The Daggite's eyes fell to the floor.

"What's the matter?" asked Strower.

"I saw you. As you saw me, I saw you."

"In a vision?"

"Yes."

Strower stepped away from Joar, moving toward the door, and signaling for me to follow. Leaving the cabin, the two of us walked until we stood side by side on the edge of the ridge overlooking the Valley. Strower surveyed the distant mountains for a moment. Then, placing his hands in his pockets, he looked at the ground. "Well, what do you think, Jens?"

"I think it's a foolish plan. If Joar believes he can move the tribes, let him, but why bring him to Saleton? What good will it do? We need those farmers to trust us."

Strower kept his eyes on the ground in front of him. "But what if he needs our help? What if we're part of his plan?"

I shook my head in disbelief. Fate was trying to draw me somewhere I didn't want to go. I knew Strower wished to find his spiritual legs, but this was a dangerous experiment—an experiment at my expense. Turning away from the Valley to face Strower, I said, "I'm sorry, William, but I don't trust it."

"You don't trust what? The Creator? Me? Joar? The visions?"

"Maybe it's that. I know you believe your wife could commune with the Creator, and I know you want that for yourself, but the stakes are too high."

"Exactly," replied Strower. "The stakes are high." Then, for a while, the two of us returned our gaze toward the distant mountains, probably both searching for words to sway the other. Finally, Strower said, "Jens, do you remember when you asked me why I was helping you?"

My mind went back to the night the two of us sat together at the table, Strower looking tired. When I asked him why he was helping, he showed me the verses he'd underlined in the Holy Book—the very morning I showed up. They had something to do with looking after foreigners and strangers. He said that he'd read those words while meditating on his porch, and somehow, he knew they were for him. "Who is the stranger?" he'd asked, and for the first time, he heard an inner voice, "Wait and see." Later that day, I drove my wagon to where he was chopping trees.

"Yes, I remember."

"Did you believe me? Did you believe I'd heard from the Creator? Or were you only pretending to believe because I was helping you, and it served your purpose?"

A tear blurred my eye. "I don't know, William. I guess I wanted it to be true."

Strower placed a hand on my shoulder. "Whether you believe me or not, Jens, I was told to help you, and that's what I intend to do. But bringing Joar is your decision, not mine."

Feeling gutted, I gazed out over the Valley of Ten Tribes, wishing I was someone else. Now, with the decision left to me, I couldn't escape the words from the book any more than Strower could. They seemed to float up from the Valley like an echo. *See that you take care of foreigners and strangers.*

CHAPTER 29

Most of the population of Saleton seemed to be indoors when we arrived in the afternoon, except for a couple of boys, tussling in the dusty street. When they noticed us drawing near, they moved out of our way, eyeing us curiously—first the wagon with the king's crest, then our passenger in the back, clad in animal hides, his long hair blowing across his face. After we passed, the boys raced to a nearby shop, probably announcing the bizarre arrival to anyone who'd listen. Strower and I glanced at one another, sharing the realization that we'd already tripped a snare.

Trotting the horses past the inn, Strower didn't slow the team until we reached the grassy path following the river to the south. Once the horses had turned onto the trail, Strower stopped the wagon, sitting quietly for a moment, taking in the view. To our right were the beautiful purple mountains forming Tuva's western border, and to our left, Saleton's hilly pastureland, dotted with lush groves, the trees now robed in green fluorescence. Dividing the mountains from the pastures, the swift river wound south like a silver ribbon, its eastern bank forming the edge of the trail we now straddled. "Isn't this the path you followed with your friends?" asked Strower.

"Yes," I replied, pointing to the distant tree line. Then I traced an imaginary path with my outstretched finger. "Up there, they drove the herd from the east. The tracks follow the river to that break in the mountains where they crossed into Dag."

"Run back to the inn, will you?" asked Strower, still gazing down the path. "Get a couple of rooms for tonight. Joar and I will wait for you here. I want to follow this trail."

Jumping down from the wagon, I trotted the short distance to the inn, guessing that Strower was probably asking himself the same question I was asking myself: How were we going to explain Joar to the innkeeper? I doubted that he'd board a Daggite. At least this way we'd have the keys and could figure out how to get him safely to the room later.

Entering the inn out of breath, I was relieved to find the innkeeper in a good mood. "Did you run here from Tinsdal?" he asked. "Where are your friends?"

I hoped by *friends* he meant Strower and Lundgren, and that he hadn't seen the wagon pass with Joar in its bed. "Lundgren is back at his farm," I told him, "and William is taking care of some business here. We'll be back later, but I thought I'd secure two rooms for tonight."

The innkeeper pulled out his registry and placed an X on two lines. Then he set the book in front of me. "You might as well sign for William, too."

Picking up the pen, I scanned the page, noticing the last person to register was Thomas Beech. "Is Bear in town?"

The innkeeper smiled. "Indeed, he is. Restocking the camp's rum supply . . . and visiting his woman friend."

I signed our names to the register and exchanged some gold coins for the two keys. As I was heading for the door, the innkeeper asked what time he could expect us.

"Probably around sundown," I replied, swinging the door closed and ending the conversation.

When I reached the wagon, I pulled the keys from my pocket, showing Strower that I'd completed my mission. "Guess who's staying at the inn tonight?" I asked.

In no mood for a quiz, Strower waited for me to tell him.

"I'll give you a hint. It's a big furry animal."

"Bear? How'd he beat us here? He must know a shortcut—I just talked with him at breakfast up at the camp. He told me he comes here almost every week. I asked him why he doesn't buy enough rum for a month. He said the men wouldn't know how to make it last that long."

"That might be," I said, "but the innkeeper mentioned that he visits a woman."

"Ah, it's making sense now. Hah! He has those miners thinking he's doing them a favor." Then Strower elbowed Joar. "I guess we better keep his secret."

A rare smile pushed up the corners of Joar's lips, and his ever-luminous eyes sparkled from whatever he was thinking. Almost to himself, he said, "A bear doesn't need secrets."

"True enough," agreed Strower. "I guess when you're big as he is, you can do as you please."

We spent the rest of the afternoon witnessing Joar's incredible skill at tracking—not only discerning between horse and cow hooves but even distinguishing the tracks of one horse from another, envisioning their number and formation as though viewing a reenactment. But when the mountain shadows began creeping across the river, my mind returned to the problem of getting Joar safely to his room.

"William, those boys we saw earlier seemed eager to announce our arrival. There'll likely be some men waiting for us at the inn, wondering what we're up to. Who knows what kind of ugly mood they'll be in? I've been thinking about how to get Joar upstairs."

"I'm listening."

"Well, for one thing, I think we should hide the wagon on this path—up nearer the road. I'll go on foot and find a place near the inn where I can't be seen and watch for Bear. It might be a while before he shows up, but he's fond of Joar. I think he'd help keep him safe."

"Makes sense," replied Strower.

On our way back up the path, we found a stand of trees just shy of the road, behind which we parked the wagon. I jumped down and trotted toward the inn. Nearing the building, I noticed a stack of firewood alongside a small house across the street. The area behind the house was heavily wooded, so I skirted to my right, circling behind the house in the cover of the prickly scrub, the sharp branches seeming to reach out and poke me in jest. Finally behind the house, I crawled on my knees through the long grass, positioning myself safely behind the stack of firewood.

Peaking over the top, I had a perfect view of the inn's front door. Now, I just needed to wait.

A little while after sunset, I heard a familiar voice—the same low-pitched growl-singing I'd heard the night we met Bear in the stairwell—accompanied by plodding hooves and a squeaky wagon wheel. So far, the men I'd seen enter the inn had arrived on foot or horseback, not wagons. This had to be Bear.

With no time to verify my assumption visually, I scurried off. If Bear made it to his room before we arrived, we'd have no help from him. So while the wagon approached, I sprinted back to Strower and Joar.

"He's here!" I yelled, throwing myself headlong into the wagon's bed. "Hurry—before he gets to his room!" Strower snapped the reins, and the horses made the turn onto the road in full gallop, reaching a speed that required a dramatic stop in front of the inn. The commotion caught Bear's attention just as he was opening the door to go inside. Releasing the handle, Bear leaned his massive body against the doorframe, chuckling in an octave so low I thought I could feel my organs vibrate. "What have we here?" he rumbled. Then, leaning forward and squinting into the dusk, he asked, "Is that you, Joar?"

"Yes."

"What are you boys up to?" Bear asked, approaching the wagon, "You trying to get him killed?"

"No," replied Strower, "That's why we were waiting for you. We might need help getting him upstairs."

"Doesn't seem like you've thought this through very well. Cook told me you were taking him. If I'da knew what the two of you were up to before you left, I'd have stopped ya."

"Joar wanted to come along," replied Strower. "He felt . . . *called*."

"Called, huh?" Then Bear released Strower from his scrutiny and turned his bearded face to Joar. "Is there somethin' you're tryin' to do here, boy? This is a dangerous place for a Daggite. Can't blame 'em either – they don't know you from the men who stole their cattle."

Joar remained silent, and not even the probing eyes of his enormous friend could coax him to defend his decision to join us.

Bear stood looking at the three of us with his brow furrowed. Finally, he slapped the side of the wagon. "Well, get down! I don't have all night." Then he turned and began walking toward the door, mumbling, "I can't sit around here and watch you like children."

Strower jumped down from the wagon. "I'll take care of the horses. You get Joar to his room."

Grabbing my bag, I hopped down too, and Joar and I lined up like ducklings behind their mother. When Bear opened the door, the drunken banter wafted onto the street, blackened, smoky words, each man talking above the other. I heard Bear's name lifted in a few friendly greetings while he lingered for a moment in the doorway, filling it almost entirely. He seemed popular among the throng, or at least respected.

Things changed, however, when Joar entered the inn behind him. A terrible hush settled over the place. The men—the majority of whom were standing in groups—stopped their banter and stared. Those sitting at tables distractedly set down their mugs, their wary eyes following us across the room.

Stupefied, the innkeeper stood behind the counter, alternately gazing at Joar and Bear, the latter of whom he seemed to be expecting an explanation from. Bear didn't oblige, but instead held out his monstrous paw. "I forgot to take my key earlier," he said, his deep voice filling the room like a solo vocalist at a holy gathering.

Finally, as if suddenly emerging from a spell, the innkeeper spun on his heels and pulled a key from a hook, dropping it in Bear's outstretched hand. Then the trance overtook him again, and he commenced staring at the Daggite.

Turning to me, Bear asked, "You need to get set up with rooms?"

"No, we have them already," I replied, pulling the keys from my pocket. This made the innkeeper's eyes narrow a little.

Bear made a quick survey of the men sitting on stools along the counter. Then he looked back at the innkeeper. Elevating his voice for the benefit of the crowd, he said, "This Daggite's name is Joar. He works at the mining

236

camp. He's here to help stop these invasions." No one moved, but the innkeeper gave a slight nod. Then, believing no further explanation was required, Bear asked, "You boys hungry? Maybe you want to take a meal up to your room."

Having eaten nothing since breakfast, I was starving. Pulling some coins from my pocket, I addressed the innkeeper, "Could we get three plates of whatever you're serving tonight?"

One of the men seated at the counter grumbled to the man next to him, "They don't eat from no damn plates."

The man he was talking to answered in a loud whisper, "I know—better feed him though, or he'll be after our cattle."

SWAP. The explosion of Bear's hand slapping the counter nearly bounced the men off their stools. "Enough!" he growled.

Hunching over their mugs, the two conspirators stared straight ahead, becoming stone-cold statues. Pocketing his key, Bear headed toward the front door. He must've only come for the key so he could return later without disturbing the innkeeper. When he reached the door, he turned, scowling, waiting for us to receive our food.

Within a short time, the innkeeper emerged from the kitchen, sliding three plates onto the counter. I handed one to Joar. Then, hooking my bag handle in my elbow, I carried the other two myself. As we walked toward the stairwell, Bear made his exit.

When I reached the door, I was unable to turn the knob—my hands occupied with the plates. Seeing my dilemma, a man sitting at a nearby table jumped up, seemingly to help. "Thank you," I said, thinking he'd open the door. My heart sank, however, when he stuck the toe of his boot against the bottom, holding it closed. I turned to see if Strower had entered yet. He had a way of dealing with people like this. With both Strower and Bear missing, I didn't know what to do. In desperation, I turned to the innkeeper, hoping he'd help, but his eyes were still narrowed from my trickery in acquiring the room keys without telling him about Joar.

The man with his boot against the door signaled for a couple of his friends to take his place. Then he squared up with Joar, chest to chest, and slowly began marching him backward toward the center of the room. Reluctantly, I followed. As we moved, men began forming a circle around us. Out of the corner of my eye, I spotted Marcus sitting with his friends. He looked conflicted, his eyes peering at the men forming the human chord, tightening like a hangman's noose.

The man forcing Joar backward was trying to appear collected, but the twitching muscles in his face betrayed his demeanor. "You ever had anything stolen from you, Daggite?" he seethed, his face nearly touching Joar's. "You ever wake up poor because savages decided to take what's yours?" The man stared hatefully into Joar's eyes, his breathing labored. "No, I didn't think so. Cuz you don't own nothin'. You just take what you want—like an animal. That's what you are – an animal."

The drawstring of hatred was pulling the circle ever tighter. Of course, Joar felt no inclination to defend himself or make any kind of explanation. He just complied with the backward directive of his confronter in remarkable peace, returning the man's gaze without reproach. Stepping around the angry man, I took my place next to Joar, unsure what to say.

Suddenly, the expression on the man's face changed from anger to wonderment. Then it changed again—from wonderment to horror. He was looking beyond us. Turning my head to see what he was staring at, I spotted a man at the far end of the circle, levitating in midair, his eyes nearly as big as the plates I was holding, and his shirt pulled so tight from behind that two of his buttons popped off. Then a booming voice erupted from behind the floating man, rattling empty mugs on nearby tables, "DO WE HAVE A PROBLEM?"

Suddenly the man was thrown forward. To remain upright once his feet hit the floor, he lunged with two gigantic strides toward the center of the circle. Joar and I quickly sidestepped in opposite directions, leaving Joar's angry confronter to receive the full force of the flung human. With a bone-crushing thud, the two men crashed to the floor in a sprawling heap, the bottom man, Joar's confronter, desperately gulping for air to refill his emptied lungs.

All eyes turned to Bear, who now steered his wild gaze toward the men blocking the staircase. Instantly, they abandoned their posts. In the ensuing hush, Strower walked through the door, having bedded down the horses for the night. Taking a silent moment to assess the carnage, he finally asked, "What's going on?"

At a loss for words, I simply looked at Bear, who still hadn't turned his fists back into hands. Marcus broke the silence, "Tell 'em who you are, Jens."

Everyone looked at me. "I work for the king. I'm his Minister of Agriculture."

"What are you doing with a Daggite?" came a voice from the crowd.

Bear piped up, "I told you—this Daggite is part of our mining camp. Anyone who lays a hand on him will have bigger problems than stolen cattle."

Another voice came from the crowd—one of Marcus's friends. "Is the king gonna send help down here?"

I could feel their eyes burning into my face. "No . . . I'm sorry, no soldiers."

Strower squeezed through the crowd, joining Joar and me in the center of the room. Looking around the circle, he said, "Men, I'm a farmer like you. My land is in central Tuva. Jens came to me a while back, sharing the king's plan to ship our crops across the sea. He said the king believes our soil to be the best in the world. He wants to make a name for Tuva—through us farmers."

"Why won't he help us then?" someone yelled.

Strower continued, "Jens and I just met with the king. He's not unsympathetic, but he has all the trouble he can handle right now with his advisors."

"What kind of trouble?"

"In the king's view, the advisors are locked into old ways of thinking. They see the port as an invitation to invaders. They'd instead use Tuva's resources to build up the army rather than investing in farming for export. King Thoren believes the world is changing. He believes Tuva's strength will come through trade. So, you see, he can't very well send his thin troops down here without admitting that his advisors are right about our borders being vulnerable."

"Maybe his damn advisors are right!" yelled a man who'd stationed himself a safe distance from Bear.

"Maybe so," replied Strower, "Thoren is no perfect king, but if we want our farms to be prosperous for our children and grandchildren, I think we farmers need to consider getting behind Jens here." Then, looking at me, Strower said, "He's a good man, and he's been authorized to pay a premium for our crops. The king owes Sagan a shipment of hay before winter. I know some of you have lost your cattle, and you can't feed your children hay. Maybe selling that hay at a good price will give you a way to make it through the winter."

Strower's words were genius. He didn't try to stand behind Thoren's integrity, which he could never do while keeping his own, but he had the farmers thinking about their children and grandchildren, considering their future. He brought them into a mindset that, if navigated correctly, their suffering might have a purpose.

Marcus stepped forward, addressing me, "But what are we going to do about the Daggites?"

"That's why we're here," I said. "We need to work together to come up with a plan."

"We brought Joar," said Strower, placing his hand on the shoulder of Joar's leather smock. "He knows their ways. Maybe we can stop these invasions without getting anyone killed."

Surveying the room, I began seeing hope in some of their faces.

"We're listening," said an elderly man.

"Let's first get some sleep," said Strower, "—get the rum out of our heads. We need clear minds to make a plan. Let's meet here in the morning after chores." Then, looking at me, he added, "The king will buy you all breakfast."

CHAPTER 30

A ghoulish face startled me in my sleep. The specter knew my name, repeating it again and again with growing impatience. At first I thought I was dreaming, and the spirit might go away if I didn't acknowledge it.

"It's me—Lloyd," it finally said.

Lloyd? The name itself was too earthly to be a spirit. He was holding a piece of parchment in one hand and a lantern in the other, up from which glowed a discriminating light, completely ignoring his eye sockets. My terror sat me up in bed, shifting the light just enough to view my intruder without his shadow costume. It was the innkeeper.

"What are you doing in my room?"

"It's my room, actually, and unless you can lay eggs, you better get out of bed."

"What are you talking about?"

"Can you lay eggs?"

"No. Can you? What are you getting at?"

"What I'm getting at is this: You invited at least sixty extra men to breakfast at my inn this morning without asking me."

"And you don't have enough food?"

"Sharp as a spike, aren't you? No wonder the king chose you."

"Is every innkeeper an ass?"

Lloyd held the lantern over my bed, suspending it above our two faces, so we were eye-to-eye. "I don't know, Jens, but I'll tell you what I do know—I take care of my guests. And this morning, my guests will be a room full of men you invited. Now, I can't work in the kitchen and find eggs at the same time, so if you want to keep those men happy, you best stop calling me an ass and drag yours out of bed."

He was right. If I failed on the promise of breakfast, how did I expect to gain the farmers' trust in more significant matters? "Do you have any suggestions where I might go?"

Lloyd handed me the parchment he was holding. "I've drawn you a map. If you leave now, we might have a chance."

Looking out the window, I saw a bit of pink in the sky. It would soon be light. "How many do we need?"

"I think we should prepare for sixty men. Could be more."

I did the arithmetic, "Sixty hungry farmers? That's a couple of hundred eggs."

"Then you better be off. Those chicken farmers have regular customers. They may not have many eggs to spare unless you offer 'em a price that they can't refuse—show 'em some of Thoren's gold. Word of his generosity will spread like a grass fire around here. That should work in your favor."

Like dew on a hot summer day, my reproach evaporated, replaced with gratitude. If Lloyd was hoping for my failure, he only needed to remain silent until his patrons sat before Strower and me with empty plates. True, he was after the king's gold too, but why would I begrudge him that? The hill country around Saleton had never known prosperity. They only knew hard work and hand-to-mouth subsistence. Lloyd was looking out for our integrity, hoping for our success.

"Thank you, Lloyd. Sorry for calling you an ass. Do you need anything other than eggs?"

Yawning, he replied, "I've been frying pork belly for two hours. A couple more batches and I'll have enough for an army."

Without waking Strower and Joar, I hitched up the wagon and set off alone. Truthfully, I feared Joar would have some reason to come along, making my egg-negotiations unnecessarily challenging. The two of them had me feeling isolated anyhow, deciding they'd room together. I guess it made sense that one of us room with Joar, and it made sense it be Strower, fascinated as he was with the Daggite. But that didn't change the fact that I was beginning to feel like the odd man out, especially after sitting alone in my room the entire evening while the two of them stayed up talking. I was glad to get away for a while.

My soul lifted as I headed for the countryside. The morning breeze felt cool on my face, the pale blue sky hinted a beautiful day, and I was finally engaged in a task that I understood—negotiating with farmers. For a little while, at least, I didn't need to be a strategist, a visionary, or an ambassador. I had only to purchase eggs from poor farmers who needed the money. Better yet, Strower and Joar would have to plan the meeting with the farmers on their own, which seemed fitting—since both men were blessed with the ability to *see* what I couldn't and speak like friends with the Creator. Strower couldn't be too upset with me for missing his morning planning session. It was he, after all, who made the promise of breakfast. Oddly enough, neither of my visionary companions could *see* that the innkeeper needed eggs.

Lloyd had four farms marked on his map, which meant I needed to aim for at least fifty eggs per farm to acquire a total of two-hundred. I thought back to the countless occasions the old merchant sent me off with a pouch of money to purchase a particular number of fleeces. When I received his money, he'd already performed his stingy calculations, and I could be sure there'd be nothing extra. My circumstances on this day were quite different. Sure, I was a desperate buyer, but I had all the gold I needed.

I found the nearest X on the map and made my way to a dilapidated shack on the outskirts of town. Jumping down from the wagon, I knocked on the door. No one seemed to be in the house, but as I stood waiting, I heard roosters crowing behind me. Spindly trees had grown up around the house, obscuring my view to the outbuildings, but I spotted a well-worn footpath disappearing into the brush in the direction of the crowing roosters. Then I heard a door slam. After walking a short distance on the path, I spotted an older woman pushing a cart full of eggs in my direction. She was bent low, laboring from the weight of the cart, wearing a frumpy dress and untied boots that drug along the ground like muddy anchors. In contrast to her disheveled appearance, her eggs were neatly crated, and she was too distracted with counting to notice me.

"Twenty-one, twenty-two. . ." I assumed she was counting dozens because the cart was full. Standing on the path, I waited for her to reach me, but when she failed to look up, I worried that she'd walk right into me and I'd scare her witless.

"Good morning," I said in my most pleasant voice while she was still a safe distance away.

Stunned, her head jolted up and her mouth made an unintelligible utterance.

With the hope that she could supply all two-hundred, I said, "I see you have an abundance of eggs."

Dropping the cart handles, she nervously wiped her dirty hands on her even dirtier apron. "Who are you?"

"My name is Jens. Lloyd-the-innkeeper thought you might sell me eggs."

"I have none for sale."

I pointed at her heaping cart. "But what of those?"

"Spoken for," she replied. She began pushing the cart again, requiring me to step off the path. As she passed, I pulled out a handful of gold coins from my pocket. Trying to sound more polite than desperate. "Could you at least spare fifty? I'll pay you generously."

"I told you—they're spoken for. Good day, young man."

Perplexed, I followed her down the path toward her house, hoping she'd stop and reconsider. When she didn't, I reluctantly mounted the wagon. I had three more farms to visit and now needed to average sixty-seven eggs.

Scanning the map, I discerned the nearest X was only a short distance up the road, but before I could flick the reins, a sense of helplessness came over me. Moments earlier, I'd been enjoying the fact that while Strower and Joar sought the Creator's counsel, I could occupy myself with activities easily accomplished without disturbing the heavens. Now, I wondered if I'd stepped into a trap set for the arrogant. Looking to the sky, I whispered, "I could use some help too," wondering as the words left my mouth if my lowered voice reflected the intimacy of someone who *walks with* the Creator, or if I somehow thought that whispering was required to sneak up on omnipotent prey. I shook off the thought and flicked the reins.

At the next farm, I didn't bother going to the house because the barn door was open and the man inside saw me approaching. After watching the majestic horses for a moment, he set down his bucket and sauntered out to meet me.

"You must be the man who works for the king," he said, patting one of the horses on the chest. "What magnificent creatures."

"Yes, they do attract attention."

Finally, the man moved his focus from the horses to me. "I thought you'd be at the inn. I'm heading there myself as soon as I milk these cows."

"Excellent. Then you know about the meeting."

"Yes, my neighbor stopped late last night—all rummed up. He poked his head inside the door, yelling my name. Scared my wife half to death. He said you'll be talking about stopping the raids. Said you brought one along—a Daggite, that is."

"All true. But it won't be much of a breakfast without eggs. Lloyd said you might have some to sell."

"How many you need?"

"Couple hundred."

"How much you payin'?"

"How much you asking?"

The man thought for a moment, looking the horses over again. "Sure could use a new plow horse."

The expression on my face must have been priceless. I opened my mouth, but nothing came out.

The man grinned. "Ah, I'm just playing with you, but the eggs ain't mine to sell."

"They're not?"

"My son and daughter handle the eggs. They have a route." Then, pointing in the direction of the old lady's farm, he added, "They sell Hazel's eggs too. She's a widow up the road. She has a big flock."

"I know. I met her this morning."

"You try to buy eggs from her?"

"Yeah, but she wouldn't even discuss it."

"Good for her. She's loyal to my children. Honestly, I don't know what she'd do without us. Those eggs are her livelihood, but she can't get around to sell 'em." Then, turning his head toward the barn, he yelled for his son.

Almost immediately, a spry boy of about ten came running out. "Yeah, Pa?"

"This man wants to buy two-hundred eggs. Can ya help him out?"

"Guess so. Hafta short some people, though."

"I'll make it worth it for you," I said, pulling out a handful of gold coins. The boy's face lit up.

"Son, put your eyes back in your head. That's the king's gold. You can charge him a little more, but charge him fair, and make sure the leftover eggs go to the people who need 'em most."

"Yes, Pa."

"Now get over to Hazel's. She's probably got 'em picked already. And bring those eggs to the inn right away. They need 'em for breakfast."

As we watched the young lad trot off, the man said, "I even made 'em a donkey cart for deliveries. His sister helps too." Then he turned and started back to his barn, talking as he went. "I better get back at it if I'm gonna make your meeting. They'll have the eggs there shortly."

CHAPTER 31

When I returned from my egg-mission, the inn was bustling with farmers, appeasing their post-chore appetites with buttered bread and tea while waiting for a real breakfast. A line of men caught my attention, standing at the counter with cups in hand, waiting for Lloyd to top off their tea with Lundgren's rum. Stationed at the spout of the barrel, Lloyd shot me an embarrassed glance, shrugging, as if to say, *Sorry, but if I had eggs* . . . Questioning his substitution, I looked away, deciding to ignore it. Now that some of the dangerous liquid had escaped the barrel, it was probably more hazardous to shut it down than to let it flow.

From the entrance, I searched for Strower and Joar, but they were nowhere in sight. Then I heard the door open behind me, the hinges creaking timidly. Turning, I spotted the innocent face of a young girl, wide-eyed and curious, poking her head through the small crack she'd created. When the girl noticed me looking at her, she pushed the door open further, making room for her brother, whose skinny arms strained to carry all two-hundred eggs at once. Behind him, on the street, their little donkey rested from what must have been a frantic journey.

"Let me help you with those," I said, relieving the boy from his load. He followed me to the counter.

"Here's your eggs," I shouted over the noisy farmers.

"To the kitchen," Lloyd instructed, abandoning his post at the barrel to lead the way. The three of us passed through a door, where a woman—probably Lloyd's wife—stood working in ridiculous heat, adding a sweaty accent to the heavy aroma of pork fat. When she saw the eggs, she pointed to the stove and pulled a large skillet from its hook on the wall.

After placing the eggs near the stove and settling my account with the boy, I asked Lloyd if he'd seen William.

"No," replied the innkeeper, already heading back to service his rum-line. "I think he's up in his room with your Daggite." Before leaving the kitchen, Lloyd pointed at a giant tea kettle. "Why don't you bring him up some tea—tell him breakfast will be ready shortly."

Grabbing two cups from the shelf above the kettle, I poured the tea and left the kitchen, intending to head upstairs. But before I was half-way across the crowded room, the door to the stairwell swung open, and out stepped my companions, casting a spell of silence over the inn—first on the men nearest the door, and then quickly spreading like a plague to the far reaches of the room. For some mysterious reason, Joar had decided to adorn himself with paint, feathers, and jewels. Stunned, I held out my arms, extending the two cups in their direction, but my stubborn boots refused to advance any closer to the spectacle.

Acting like nothing was out of the ordinary, Strower approached and took both cups from my outstretched hands. Then he led our strange little party to an empty table in the corner. "Where have you been?" he whispered.

"The innkeeper sent me after eggs."

I could tell by Strower's expression that he wasn't impressed with my excuse for missing his planning session. Deciding not to make a defense in front of our quiet audience, I instead glanced at Joar, whose countenance was unsettling, to say the least. Encased in black paint, his lucid eyes glowed like sunlight through a knothole in a dark barn. Feathers strung together from various birds, large and small, wrapped his neck, arms, and thighs, giving him a hawkish nature. Gems embedded into leather straps—the same type of stone Thoren had traded with Akeem—banded his forehead, wrists, and ankles.

"Why is he dressed like that?" I whispered. "He looks like he's ready for war."

"Not war," Strower whispered back. "He's dressed as a priest."

"But why?"

"There's no time to explain this now. If you'd been here earlier, you'd know."

"Just tell me why he's dressed like a priest."

"He's dressed like a priest because he *is* a priest," Strower replied, no longer caring who heard.

Self-consciously, my eyes scanned the room, meeting other eyes, darting, peeking around each other to see the Daggite. Of course, Joar felt no compulsion to explain why he dressed the way he did. Feeling like I might wretch, I excused myself under the pretense of checking on breakfast.

My mind raced as I made my way to the kitchen. Joar had brought a leather satchel on the journey, and I'd been curious as to its contents. Mystery solved—paint, feathers, and jewelry. Ironically, I'd considered asking him to dress in my clothes since I was again wearing the king's uniform. I thought it might help make him look more like one of the farmers and, more importantly, remove the stigma of a savage. But as Strower had already reminded me, I'd skipped the planning session in favor of purchasing eggs, so it was too late now.

Part of me felt passively numb, like a criminal making peace with the gallows, powerless to change his sentence. But a larger part of me was still scrambling for safety, wanting to distance myself from the two of them and whatever plan they'd concocted.

I reached the kitchen just as Lloyd's wife was spooning eggs onto plates and handing them to Lloyd to pile on strips of pork belly.

"Need help in here?" I asked.

"It's your show," Lloyd replied, handing me a large tray to set plates on. "Serve 'em up."

My show? It was a show, no question, but it wasn't my show. Lloyd clearly felt more comfortable in his blazing-hot kitchen than out socializing among his patrons. Angrily, I tossed six plates on the tray. *So be it*, I thought— passing plates to farmers was far better than sitting at that miserable table in the corner. But if I had my druthers, I would've stayed in the kitchen with cowardly Lloyd and his wife. If this plan went wrong—which I was pretty sure it would—I'd need every inch of separation I could find. For once, I was glad to be wearing the king's uniform—not to impress anyone, but if things turned ugly, perhaps my clothes would make the farmers think twice before stringing me up.

After countless trips to the kitchen to reload my tray, it seemed I'd finally served breakfast to everyone. While standing amid the men and surveying the room for anyone I might've missed, one of them pulled on my shirt sleeve. "Son, we need to get back to work. Can we get on with this?"

Strower happened to be watching me from across the room, so I gave him a nod, which he returned. An eery hush muted the crowd as Strower and Joar pushed out their chairs and stood up, walking together to the center of the room.

With a soft voice, Strower began his speech: "Men of Saleton, thank you for coming this morning. I hope you've enjoyed your breakfast. As I told you yesterday, my name is William Strower, and, like you, I am a farmer. I farm in Central Tuva near Tinsdal. I'm here with Jens." At that, he extended his hand toward me before continuing. "Jens is Tuva's Minister of Agriculture. King Thoren commissioned him to find farmers to grow crops for export. The king believes our nation's future lies in our rich soil. He's discovered markets for our crops in distant lands—kingdoms willing to pay a handsome price for our beets, using them for odd things such as dyes and medicine—even a potion, I'm told, that causes a man and woman to fall in love." Strower smiled broadly, adding, "If I'd known beets could do that, I'd have spent more time as a young man in the kitchen, working on my recipes."

A few of the farmers chuckled, while others narrowed their eyes. All of them, however, listened carefully, hanging on every word.

Strower continued, "I believe the king's efforts will provide great opportunities, especially for future generations."

One of the farmers who had his eyes narrowed said, "You may have good soil, Mr. Strower, but we don't have your soil down here. We have pastureland and hay-ground. So maybe you're barkin' up the wrong tree."

Other narrow-eyed men began nodding in agreement, grumbling at their tables, making muffled comments like, "Who does he think he is?" and "What kind of potion is he trying to sell us?"

Raising his hand, Strower elevated his voice above the grumbling. "Please hear me out." The room again grew quiet, and Strower continued. "Not long ago Jens and I visited your town. The Daggite raids had come to our attention, and we traveled here to verify the truth of the reports. While here, the man you know as Bear invited us to the mining camp to meet this young Daggite." Strower placed his hand on Joar's shoulder, saying, "This is Joar. He has lived among the miners for almost three years. The cook at the camp took him under his wing after an injury left him crippled. The cook became like a father to him, teaching him our language—not only to speak it but to read it. Joar has read our Holy Book from cover to cover more than once."

Pausing, Strower again gave the crowd a disarming smile. "How many of us can make that boast?" he asked. When no one responded, Strower continued, "Granted, it was the only book at camp—the miners not being much for reading." Some of the farmers laughed at that, probably having met a few of the miners on their rare but raucous retreats to Saleton, the town nearest camp.

One of the farmers yelled, "He musta blew some dust off that book!" Now, most of them were laughing.

Taking advantage of the growing goodwill, Strower pressed on. "I won't say that Joar has adopted our religion exactly. There are passages he's interpreted through his Daggite upbringing—things written in the book his people would embrace differently than we do. But he's been greatly impacted, and he desires to become a priest among his people."

"He don't look like no priest to me," came a voice from the crowd.

"To me either," agreed Strower, "but to his people, he will. He wants to move the ten tribes west, away from the Valley.

Strower paused, looking around the room, studying their faces. It was remarkably quiet, and the eyes of his audience moved back and forth between him and Joar. By the length of his pause, I suspect Strower thought someone would interrupt, but no one did.

Now Strower's voice took on that energizing quality he usually reserved for his porch meetings. "Men, if Joar is successful, the Valley of Ten Tribes will be open for farming. It's good land. I've seen it—probably better than mine in Tinsdal. I propose that those who've lost cattle in the raids be given equal tracts as payment for their loss. This new ground could be broken by your sons—those willing to work hard to create a new future for Tuva."

Strower then stopped, waiting while his words soaked in. Finally, the man who'd angrily confronted Joar the previous night stood up. "I have two sons," he said, his voice cracking with emotion. "They both work hard."

Strower nodded, his compassionate eyes lingering on the man until I thought he might shed a tear himself. Then, surveying the room, he asked, "Are there any objections to my proposal?"

Someone shouted, "What proposal? I ain't heard no proposal."

Strower corrected him. "You mean, you haven't heard a plan. My proposal is this: If the Daggites abandon the Valley, the land shall be broken into parcels and occupied by members of those families who've lost herds in the raids. Does anyone dispute this proposal?"

Another long silence ensued. Certainly, some who hadn't lost cattle to the Daggites must've secretly wished to get their hands on a parcel. However, with the man who'd threatened Joar still standing, teary-eyed, an overriding spirit of sympathy seemed to carry the room. As I looked around, the majority appeared to be on-board with Strower, but a few still had their eyes narrowed. One yelled, "What's in this for you, Mr. Strower?"

This question must have been on everyone's mind because the entire crowd seemed to lean forward.

"Selfishly," said Strower, "I support the king's plan to export our crops. It will be good for my farming operation. But I worry that Thoren's advisors will find a way to close his port if Tuva's people don't get behind him. And men, if that port closes, your opportunity to prosper goes with it."

 Strower looked around the room, meeting the farmer's eyes with his own. Then he added, "And on a less selfish note, you men are my brethren. Whether we farm in Tinsdal or Saleton, we are all farmers, and I don't take kindly to seeing my brothers suffer. Neither do my neighbors."

Strower's magic was starting to work. I could feel it—like I was back on his porch, sensing the collective energy piercing our souls like an invisible needle stitching us together.

"If there are no objections," said Strower, "I would ask Lloyd to pass around a document for signature, attesting to your agreement in this matter."

Lloyd, who'd been listening from behind the counter, quickly pulled a sheet of parchment from his registry, took up his pen, and started writing.

"Why do you need signatures?" someone asked.

"Because you'll need a record of every man's agreement," said Strower. "Greed has a way of clouding a person's memory. The Valley needs to go to those who've lost their herds. It's that simple."

The man who'd initially asked to hear a proposal now spoke up again. "What's your *plan* then, Mr. Strower? This all seems pretty far-fetched."

"Today, I am only hoping to arrive at a general agreement and learn the names of those who've lost their livestock. We'll meet with each of those families separately to see if they're willing to join our effort."

"What about King Thoren?" someone asked. "Will he honor our ownership of those parcels?"

"I believe he will," said Strower, "particularly if you intend to grow beets for export, but it'll be up to Jens to make that argument to Thoren." Everyone's eyes turned to me. Little did they know I was hearing this for the first time.

"Why hasn't this plan been brought to the king already?" someone yelled from the back of the room.

Strower and I looked at each other, neither knowing how to answer that question without revealing our own fear of what Thoren might do. After an uncomfortable pause, Marcus stood up and said, "Why give Thoren time to think about how he might use that land for himself? If we occupy the Valley before Thoren even knows it's deserted, what choice will he have other than to accept our ownership? Think about it—he'll have a new source of taxes and crops dedicated to his port. He wouldn't kick us out. It's a good plan." Then, looking at me, he said, "I trust Jens. He grew up with Thoren. He'll get it done."

Marcus returned to his seat, and Strower asked, "Are we in agreement then?" Heads began nodding, some quickly, some reluctantly, but eventually everyone was nodding. Then a man stood up—the drunken man I'd sat beside at the counter on our first trip to Saleton. I didn't recognize him at first because he was no longer as white as a sheet.

"Excuse me," he said, "but did you say last night that the king is willing to purchase hay?"

Strower looked at me.

"Yes," I said. "King Thoren needs to fill a ship. I'd pay handsomely for any hay you can spare."

Others raised their hands, probably wanting to inquire how much *handsomely* was. The room was growing louder. At a nearby table, I heard two men—fortunate farmers, who hadn't lost their herds yet—discussing how they might, through me, sell their cattle to the king. Others were talking about the Daggites in the Valley—where they might head next. I even heard one man ask another, "Are you believing this?"

Taking back the floor, Strower spoke loudly. "We can't discuss all the particulars now. I know you men need to get back to work. I would ask that Lloyd stand by the door, collecting every man's signature as you exit. If you've lost cattle in the raids, give Lloyd your name, and we'll visit you at your farm."

The meeting appeared to be over, so Strower turned to discuss something with a farmer who'd tapped him on his shoulder, but then a loud voice stole everyone's attention. "Hold on!" He was a large, barrel-chested man. "It's likely gonna take all of us to fight those savages," he said. "I ain't lost no cattle, but I sure ain't afraid to fight alongside those who have!" Several others voiced their agreement.

Strower held up his hand, quieting the crowd. "Our plan doesn't include fighting."

"You're a fool to think you'll take that Valley without a fight," spat the farmer. "Feathers and paint ain't gonna do nothin'."

"Let us try," replied Strower, "If we fail, the next plan can be yours."

Not exactly pacified, but at a loss for words, the man sat back down, pulling off his hat and scratching his matted scalp. Seeing he had nothing left to say, the rest of the crowd stood and filed out, Lloyd enlisting their signatures before they disappeared through the door.

CHAPTER 32

After the meeting, I slipped off to my room while Strower discussed farming with an old-timer who didn't seem in any hurry to get home. Rather than feeling hopeful about the morning's progress, I felt guilty, and I needed some time alone.

Sitting in the corner of my room, I contemplated where bravery came from in men like Strower and Thoren. What made them so willing to risk everything? What made them discount the probability of failure or defeat? Carrie came to mind. Sure, I felt brave around her, but she was a woman, not a crutch. *I can't give weight to your soul*—that's what her note said. She didn't want to be the one to give me substance, but I didn't know where else to find it.

I started thinking about Carrie's visit to my bedroom that night, her light kiss, and how she'd pulled away before I could press in. I thought of the note she'd left in my pocket. *Keep my father safe*—that was her only request. I wondered if that kiss suggested a covenant—her father's safety in exchange for a future with her. That's what I wanted, but my actions certainly didn't prove it. I'd spent most of the morning trying to distance myself from her father to protect my own hide.

I began pacing back and forth between the window and the door. Perhaps bravery was nothing more than being oblivious to circumstances—setting your jaw like flint in a given direction and moving forward. That's what Thoren and Strower seemed able to do—plow through their obstacles. Wishing I could have the morning to do over, I vowed to be braver in spite of my fear. That was, after all, the kind of man my father thought I'd become. Perhaps obstacles were more intimidating to me than they were to men like Thoren and Strower, but that made it even more crucial that I hit them with force, with less time to worry.

Then I heard a tap on my door, and Strower poked his head inside my room. "We'll be off in a couple of hours to start visiting farmers."

"What will we do until then?" I asked.

"I need to spend some time with Joar," Strower replied. "You know—figure out how to go about this."

"Shouldn't I be part of that?"

Strower paused while his face silently filled the small opening in the door. Reluctantly, he entered my room, making his way to the wooden chair in the corner. Once he'd sat down, he leaned the chair back on two legs, lifting his hat off and setting it on his lap. "Jens, I think we need to leave you out of this."

"What are you talking about?"

"It's best that you're not involved."

I could feel a prickly rash racing up my neck. Was he punishing me for missing his planning session? "What do you mean by *not involved?*"

"Jens, if we include you, this will become the king's plan."

"No it won't. We can tell them it's not when we meet with them."

"About that—I don't think you should come along to these meetings with Joar and me."

"You want to leave me out of everything?"

"Just hear me out, Jens. Joar's plan is—"

"Joar? Now that he's a priest with some face paint and feathers, you don't need me?" I started pacing again. "William, this is my mission."

"I know it is. Sit down and let me explain."

I walked to the bed and sat on the edge.

Receiving my icy glare, Strower tried to radiate assurance. But when he couldn't melt me, he began speaking in measured words. "Joar's plan isn't something Thoren would want his name attached to, not without being consulted. It's unconventional, to say the least."

"I suppose he has you painting your face too."

Strower tried to squelch a smile. "No. It's nearly that strange, though. But strange as it is, I think it might work."

"If you think it'll work, why are you scared to have me involved? Thoren doesn't care how things get done. You know that."

"I'm not exactly scared, Jens."

"What is it then?"

Strower stood up from the chair, letting it fall back on all four legs. Walking to the window, he placed his hands on the sill, pretending to be looking outside. "The way I see this, Jens, having you involved is bad either way. If Joar's plan goes wrong, you'll be an embarrassment to the king. Who knows what he'll do? Your friendship might not be enough."

"Yes, but you said you think it'll work."

"If it works, Thoren is likely to take ownership of the plan. You're his Minister of Agriculture—his right arm. If you're involved, he's involved. I've seen how he operates. He'd justify taking the land for himself, leaving these farmers with nothing. That's why you can't be part of this, Jens."

I sat quietly for a moment, allowing Strower's words to sink in. As much as I hated to admit it, he was probably right. Thoren needed to think the farmers around Saleton had solved their own problem. If he could somehow take credit, he would. Then he'd treat the farmers like squatters on *his* land. He wouldn't need them to grow crops. He could use prisoners to work his fields if he wanted. I shook my head at the irony—now Strower was distancing himself from me.

"So I have to sit around here while the two of you visit farmers? That will take days."

"No, you need to follow us—but one day delayed. You can write contracts for their hay. I'll tell the farmers you'll be around to see them. They have no cattle, Jens. The soil in the Valley won't help them survive *this* winter. If Joar succeeds in moving the tribes, it'll take all summer to clear those fields. There won't be a crop this year."

"How do you expect me to get around?"

"In your wagon. Lloyd has a wagon we can use. He'll take Joar and me around to visit the farmers. He wants to help, and he knows where they live. We'll map our route each day for you. It's best to use the king's wagon for the king's business."

"Will Joar be going around in feathers?"

Strower laughed at how ridiculous the question sounded. "Yes, I think it's best he wear his feathers. Stories are more believable when the characters are in costume."

"That may be true, but his costume might cause someone to come after him with a club."

"I won't let that happen, Jens."

"That's what I'm afraid of . . . William, you have children at home. You didn't see the hateful eyes of the man who confronted Joar at the inn—you were out with the horses. If Bear hadn't been there . . ."

Strower studied me for a moment. "Carrie has you looking out for me, doesn't she?"

"She's worried about you, William. She wants the twins to have their father, and she needs her father. Are you sure there isn't a better way?"

"I'm sure," replied Strower, heading toward the door. Then, placing his hand on the knob, he hesitated. Without looking at me, he said, "Joar and I will be clearing out of our room when we leave today. We'll sleep across the street at Lloyd's house. I'll have Lloyd's wife bring you a map each morning. I'll see you when this is over."

With that, he left my room, closing the door behind him. I sat on my bed for a few moments, trying to get my bearings. If Strower was right about the farmers being willing to sell their hay, the next few days would be a dream come true. Strower would make the suggestion to the farmers, and I'd only need to sit down and write contracts. What could be better? I'd have nothing to explain to Thoren other than parting ways with Strower so I could attend to business. He'd be glad to hear that.

Still, I hated being left out. Not that I wanted to be seen with Joar—I didn't—but I didn't trust him alone with Strower either. He was too different, too unpredictable. He captivated Strower, though, and the two of them were becoming thick as thieves. *Keep my father safe*—the words kept floating through my head. Regardless of what Strower wanted me to do, I couldn't neglect my obligation to Carrie. Not again.

Quietly, I opened my door. I could faintly hear the drone of their voices inside Strower's room, so I tiptoed across the hall and stood at the threshold, placing my ear next to the door. The first voice was Strower's. "So all we need to do is get the farmers to form a circle and chant those words?"

"Yes," replied Joar. "They summon Bito, their judge. The warriors will fall to their knees and wait for the priest's judgment. The circle must then close, everyone holding hands."

Strower spoke again. "That will be hard for the farmers to believe. Once they get them surrounded, they'll want to run them through with pitchforks."

Joar's voice came softly through the wood. "Farmers will die if they fight."

"I know," agreed Strower. "I'll need to convince them of that, but are you sure the Daggites will honor you as their new priest?"

"Yes, I have seen it."

A period of silence ensued. I waited, wishing I could see Strower's face. Finally, he said, "Good—so when we meet with each farmer, we only need to give them the chant to memorize. We can explain the circle once we have them all together, but we won't be able to tell them when, or where, this is going to happen."

"I know when. In two more nights, when the moon is full, the spies will come. They will choose a herd by the light of the moon. I will follow them."

"How are you so sure they'll come in two nights?"

"The Daggite god of battle is Barta, their moon-god. They spy when Barta's light is brightest. They hunt when Barta's light is but a sliver. That is their way."

"Will the spies come on horses or on foot?"

"They will spy on foot. They will hunt on horses."

"How will you know where they'll cross the river?"

"They will cross between the mountains, where we saw the tracks disappear. I will wait behind the rocks to follow them."

"I wish you'd let me come along."

Joar's response was immediate, "Too loud." It didn't surprise me, remembering how Strower and I tried to follow the Daggite down the side of the mountain, thudding our boots on roots and kicking walnut-sized rocks down the mountain face.

"How will you know which herd they choose?" asked Strower.

"I will see as they see, and I will think as they think."

Strower piped in. "Maybe we can take some of the thinking out of it."

Joar must have silently waited for Strower's explanation. I brought my ear closer to the door, thinking I was missing something. Finally, Strower continued, "What if we brought a large herd someplace where they couldn't resist stealing them—a place near the river, where they'd be easy to rustle? Would that help?"

Joar must have given him one of his silent nods.

"Very well," replied Strower. "We'll borrow a herd and drive the cattle to the most tempting pasture we can find that's close to the river. We'll just need to find a farmer willing to lend us his cows. Are you sure you know when the Daggites will come for the cattle?"

"Eight days past the full moon," Joar replied. "That's when they hunt—when the moon is a sliver."

Quietly, I returned to my room, closing the door behind me. Pulling out the maps Thoren gave me, I began familiarizing myself with the area around Saleton. Before long, I heard Strower's boots, skipping down the staircase in his familiar horse-trot cadence. *Ka-thunk, ka-thunk, ka-thunk, Ka-thunk.* Not surprisingly, I couldn't hear the Daggite's footsteps at all.

Had Joar's isolation from the Daggites driven him to madness? Strower and Joar's spiritual connection was the only thing causing William to embrace this hair-brained plan. Moon-stages, mystical chanting, gods, and a circle of judgment—what chance did it all have of working? Perhaps Strower could convince the farmers to give Joar's plan a try. They were desperate, after all—grasping for hope—and Strower could be mighty persuasive. But could it work? It was too illogical for my rational mind to accept.

Then I remembered an incident from my childhood. One of the king's disgruntled subjects stabbed his knife through a Tuvan flag. It happened in the Royal city, in front of the palace. The man was apprehended by the palace guards, sentenced to death, and hanged by his neck from hastily erected gallows at the very spot of the infraction. There was a dispute between my parents as to whether I'd be allowed to witness the hanging, my mother's voice prevailing in the end, protecting my eyes from the disturbing scene.

I remembered my confusion. The man had only cut fabric. My father explained that he had disrespected the symbol of our nation, and by association, the king. My father—the most rational man in the kingdom— had justified an illogical consequence. I suppose a nation's rituals and customs could explain all sorts of strange occurrences throughout history. Who was I to say Joar's plan wouldn't work? He was the Daggite, after all.

The thing that bothered me most was that every facet of this plan hinged on Joar—his integrity, his perception, his motive, his sanity—what if Joar had Strower under some kind of spell? Or, what if his plan was a hoax? What if Joar secretly arranged for more warriors to sneak in behind the rustlers and wipe out Strower and his gullible circle of judgment? They'd ride off with the largest herd yet—and Joar would be back in the good graces of the Daggites after living among the enemy for three years.

Then I had a thought: What would prevent me from spying on Joar while he spied on the spies? If I saw him making contact with the Daggites, I'd know he was up to something. I now knew where and when he'd be waiting for the spies. All I needed to do was get there first.

CHAPTER 33

The next morning, as I hung precariously from an evaporating dream, I heard the sound of parchment sliding under my door. In my dream, I'd been searching everywhere for Carrie's note, frantically checking my pockets, hoping it hadn't fallen into her father's hands. Now, in my half-conscious state, the crackling of parchment had me thinking Strower was returning the note.

When I opened my eyes, I saw a map lying on the floor. Breathing a sigh of relief, I scampered barefoot across the room and held the parchment toward the window, where fresh morning beams fought through dirty glass. It looked as though Strower and Joar had visited five farms the previous day. Not bad, considering their late start. Now, with my marching orders in hand, I simply needed to retrace their route.

By the end of the day, all five farmers had sold me their hay. Three of them repeated Strower's comment from the meeting— "My family can't eat it." Two of them told me they hoped, with frugal living, they might have enough money remaining in the spring for breeding stock, allowing them to begin the process of rebuilding their herds. The five visits consumed my whole day, mostly because the grateful wives set food before me, and my eating slowed with each successive visit.

On the second day, Strower's map included seven locations. This was the day when Joar would watch for the spies at the river-crossing. I needed to get there before he did so I could find the perfect hiding place. Without being rude, I did my best to cut the meetings short, getting down to business and politely refusing the food.

By early afternoon, I'd finished all seven meetings and returned to the inn to lock the contracts in my room before heading to the river. The place was empty, but Lloyd's wife must've heard me enter from the kitchen. Peeking her head out, she caught me trotting through the menagerie of tables on my way upstairs. "I'm making roast beef for supper," she said. "Will you be joining us?"

Her question caught me off guard because I wanted her to believe I'd be spending the evening in my room. "No ma'am. I need to finish my contracts from today and then prepare for tomorrow's meetings. If you don't mind, I'll take some bread and jam to my room."

"Nonsense. I'll bring up a plate when it's ready. It's no problem."

It was a problem, though, because she wouldn't find me in my room later, and then she'd tell Lloyd, who'd surely tell Strower—and Strower didn't want me nosing around in their plan.

"Good as it smells, I'll have to pass on the roast beef. I visited seven farmers today, and they all offered me food," which wasn't a lie—they had *offered*. Then I placed my hand on my belly, inflated my cheeks and groaned, "I suppose it'll be the same tomorrow."

Lloyd's wife laughed. "Goodness, seven meals? I'll fetch you some bread and jam for later." She disappeared into the kitchen and then reappeared with a full loaf, along with a jar of strawberry preserves and a knife. "Just bring down whatever you don't eat in the morning," she instructed.

Racing to my room, I threw my bag on the bed and set the food on the nightstand, tearing off a corner of the loaf and wedging it into my mouth. Then I snuck back down, stopping on the last stair to crack open the door. The room was still empty, and I could hear Lloyd's wife humming in the kitchen. When her knife went to work on the chopping block, I seized the opportunity to rodent-scamp across the room, squeezing through the front door without making a sound.

The hike to the river-crossing seemed a lot further on foot than by wagon. I started out running, but it wasn't long before I was trotting, then walking. I was glad I wasn't going to follow the spies. If my clumsy feet didn't get me discovered, my panting certainly would. No, I'd learn everything I'd needed to know when and if Joar met the spies at the river. If they communicated in any way, I'd know Joar was in cahoots with the Daggites. If the spies didn't show up, I'd assume Joar was out of touch with reality, living in some kind of fantasy world. Or, if Joar didn't show up, I'd know his whole story was fabricated.

When I reached the place where the Daggites had crossed the river with the cattle, I pulled off my boots and pants and waded into the fast-moving water, holding my clothes high above my head. The river quickly became waist-deep, then chest-deep, making me wish I'd taken off my shirt as well. The soft mud wrapped my ankles like moldable shackles and fought for possession of my feet, the current threatening to uproot me like a weak tree in a flood. Upon reaching the other side, I didn't bother to put on my pants and boots until finding the perfect hiding place—a huge rock, half the size of a house—a stone's throw from the river. Waist-high squatty brush skirted the boulder, giving me the perfect cover with visibility to the crossing.

An arm's length of space separated the outward-sloping rock and the thick brush, providing a tight corridor for me to move. With the afternoon sun pounding down, I leaned against the cool stone, taking advantage of its growing shade. According to Joar, the Daggites wouldn't show up until the moon was out, so I was pretty sure I had a few hours before Joar arrived. Settling back, I stared up at the cloudless sky, waiting in relative comfort for evening. That's when a strange sensation came over me—something I'd never experienced before, and certainly didn't expect now.

As far back as I can remember, my constitution had been one-part ambition and two-parts worry. I only possess enough ambition to strike out on an adventure, but it's my anxiety that sustains me along the way. That's the whole reason I sat there so early—better safe than sorry. I suppose the gift of worrying came from my father, the advisor: "Have you considered this?" or "Have you thought of that?" and "What if so and so happens?" Some men need worriers in their life—men living in the open sunlight of hope, relying on worriers to splash them in the face from time-to-time with cold reality. I've always wanted to live under the warm rays of hope. But unfortunately, I'm more prone to shiver in the shade of fret.

The point is, my constitution doesn't tolerate relaxation very well. It seems like daytime resting provides the most tantalizing opportunities for the buzzards of worry to perch on my carcass. That's why I've always avoided naps. I use my precious daylight hours to chase down my fears and club them in the head. When I spend the day clubbing my worries, they tend to nest elsewhere at night. But any kind of relaxing during the day tempts the damn buzzards to perch on my soul and pick away at my peace.

On this day, however, something was different. Maybe there were simply too many things to fret over, the consequences too awful to contemplate. Or, perhaps it was a special gift from above, but that afternoon the buzzards of worry left me alone. I suspect when a soul becomes convinced that a foul scenario will play out, it finds a perverse serenity in that certainty, which is what I was experiencing—serenity. It came the same way my worries usually did—as a question—but phrased oppositely: What if this hair-brained plan works?

Suddenly, I felt another kind of winged creature perch on my soul, roosting there, not to scavenge its light, but to deposit joyful thoughts. Instead of enduring a list of dreads, I began entertaining pleasant possibilities. I saw a ship full of hay, launching from Thoren's port toward Sagan. I saw Joar leading his people over the mountains to the west, starting a new chapter in their history. I saw farmers planting beets in the soft black earth in the Valley. I saw Carrie and me together on the porch, enjoying a sunset, my arm around her neck.

Then came an invitation to sleep—not seeded by exhaustion, but rather by a desire to throw off the tight garments of consciousness and wade naked in the stream of the future. The invitation bid me to lift my feet from the muddy shackles and let the current take me downstream. With hours before dark, and without the voice of anxiety to counsel me differently, a short nap seemed like the perfect way to pass some time, now that I was safely in position. Slowly, I drifted off . . .

When I opened my eyes again, the sky was dimmer, and an evening breeze was skimming over the scrubby brush. I'd taken off my shirt to let it dry, and the cool air moving across my chest heightened my senses. Suddenly, I was aware of a presence. Attempting to sit up, I plunged my face right into Joar's hand, now cupping my mouth, his gentle eyes watching me, waiting for my panic to subside.

When I finally nodded, he removed his hand. "What are you doing here?" I whispered.

Joar looked at me as if the question made no sense, which it didn't. The real quandary was: What was *I* doing there? Of course, Joar was too unassuming to ask it. He gave people the freedom to do what they do.

I rephrased the question. "How did you find me?"

The Daggite looked at me with a hint of humor in his eyes.

"Oh," I whispered. I was a city boy, and although I'd often traveled country roads, I'd never learned to track or hunt. And I'd certainly never been hunted. A chill ran up my spine when I realized I could have just as easily been jarred awake by the Daggite spies, standing over me with knives drawn.

"I'm sorry, Joar."

He looked at me as if the word were unfamiliar, so I stammered an explanation. "I . . . I shouldn't have come. I just wanted to see . . ."

Joar's eyes met mine. Behind the fierce paint, I could see his kindness. At that moment, my suspicion of any ill-motive melted away. He wasn't capable of that kind of deceit. The only question that remained was his sanity. He was a man who receives visions, who speaks with the Creator as a child speaks with his father. Strower trusted him because he saw something similar in his wife—but a man in grief is no reliable measure of sanity either. After a moment, Joar broke eye contact with me, peeking around the boulder toward the river crossing.

"Joar, what if the Daggites find my tracks?"

This time he didn't turn toward me but kept his eyes fixed on the crossing. "Your tracks are no longer there."

"Thank you."

"You must stay here," he whispered, still peering at the river.

"I know."

Remaining motionless, we squatted behind the rock while the curtain of darkness fell over the land. Not long after, a gigantic moon climbed the horizon. I'd never seen it this impressive. Then again, I'd never staked my life on a plan featuring the magnificent glowing beacon. Joar's eyes remained fixed on the river. Then suddenly, like a snake, he vanished, slithering silently through the low foliage.

I quietly assumed his place, barely poking my left eye around the corner of the boulder, and there they were—two shadows obscuring the moon's glint on the water, moving steadily toward the far bank. Reaching the other side, the shadows moved quickly, disappearing into the distant darkness.

I kept my eyes fixed on the river, looking for Joar, but I couldn't see him. He must have belly-crawled into the river and swum underwater because the surface remained undisturbed. He was a snake, and he'd become a wolf when he reached the far bank, running tirelessly in pursuit. At that moment, I wasn't quite sure if he was human, but I was sure of one thing: He wasn't crazy.

CHAPTER 34

As I walked back to the inn, the bright moon cast eerie shadows, and I heard noises in the trees. I'd stop to listen, but the gurgling river made it hard to tell where the sounds were coming from. It was unnerving to share the night with the spies. My logic said they'd skirt Saleton, veering east halfway up the path, retracing their route from the last raid, but my nerves imagined them moving with me in lockstep, flanking my right shoulder inside the tree-line, where gnarly oaks cloaked the forest in blackness.

When I finally reached the inn, I heard the banter of men inside. The unrestrained voices were strangely soothing. Standing outside the door, I looked across the empty street at the lamp-lit windows of Lloyd's house, imagining Strower sitting inside, waiting expectantly for Joar to return. I considered walking over and knocking, but then I thought better of it. He didn't want to see me until this was over. I wondered if Joar would tell him that I'd nearly foiled their plan by showing up at the crossing, but that was a problem for later. At the moment, I needed to focus on getting back to my room without being seen by Lloyd's wife.

Just then, a man's frame entered the canopy of light from the posted lantern. He was walking from the village. I waited for him by the door and then swung it open for him. "After you," I said. He gave me a suspicious look but honored my gesture. I followed on his heels, head lowered, using his body to shield me from view. When the man stopped to greet his friends, I tried to skirt around him and make my way to the staircase, but someone grabbed my wrist. Instinctively, I jerked my arm free, spinning to see Marcus sitting with his friends at the same table where I'd met him on my first trip to Saleton.

Without leaving his seat, Marcus reached across to another table and grabbed the backrest of an empty chair, spinning it around with his thick wrist. Then, pulling the chair alongside his, he slapped the wooden seat, inviting me to sit down.

Still trying to evade attention, I slunk into the chair, happy to be situated with my back to the counter. Marcus patted my shoulder and stood up, yelling for Lloyd's wife to bring over a drink. When he sat back down, he leaned forward, addressing our little group in a way that couldn't be overheard by the surrounding tables. "You boys remember Jens, right?" They all nodded. Then, turning to me, Marcus asked, "Where've you been?"

Feeling my face redden, I decided to give the most unspecific answer I could get away with. "Just buying hay," I said, hoping I wouldn't have to say more, but they all continued leaning in to listen, so I added, "Thoren promised a shipload to Sagan's king, so I'm talking with the farmers who've lost their herds. I wish I could do more, but this at least puts some money in their pockets before winter."

Marcus nodded. "It's a good thing yer doin'. None of us can afford to buy another man's hay. It's about the only thing we can grow for ourselves down here."

Lloyd's wife approached from behind and set a mug on the table. Surprised to see me, she asked, "Are you down for a break?"

Nodding, I said, "Yeah, it was getting lonely up there."

"Charge this to your room?" she asked.

"I've got it," said Marcus, placing some money in her hand.

"Next round's on me then," I instructed Lloyd's wife. She forced a wry smile, seeming annoyed by having to remember such things. When she moved on, Marcus leaned in again. "Are you part of Mr. Strower's plan?"

"No." The word came out more abruptly than I wanted.

Marcus studied my eyes. Then, smiling, he said, "Well, there's a twist. Now I have a secret from you."

"Well, I know Strower and Joar have some sort of plan," I confessed, "but he hasn't shared it with me."

Taken aback, Marcus hesitated. "I probably shouldn't say nothin' then," he finally said. But after looking around the room, he blurted, "I bet half the men in here are talkin' about it—Strower's setting a trap for the Daggites."

"A trap?"

Marcus leaned back in his chair, interlocking his fingers behind his head. "Yes, a trap, and I'm the bait." His friend laughed at his antics.

"What do you mean by that?"

"Remember how I told you the Daggites drove the last herd right through my family's property?"

"Yeah."

"Well, Strower's Daggite friend has a plan, but he needs to catch the thieves in the act. So they've decided to set out a real tempting herd near the border, where they'd be easy to steal. They chose a field on our property, where we grow hay for cutting. We don't use that field for pasture, so a bunch of us spent the day putting up a fence. From there, it's a straight path to the river trail."

I took a sip from my mug, staring at the table, amazed at what Strower had already accomplished. Then a chill ran down my spine as I realized how close Marcus's farm was to the path I'd just walked. The spies were likely only a short distance away. Regathering my wits, I asked Marcus, "Strower has you grazing *your* cattle in that field?"

"Half of 'em are mine," replied Marcus. Then, pointing to one of his friends across the table, he added, "The other half are his."

"What if the Daggites somehow make off with them?"

Marcus smiled. "That was my question too. That's why we split up the herd, so neither of us will lose everything. But listen to this: Mr. Strower promised both of us a plot in the Valley for helping out—if that priest can get the Daggites to go west."

"You think it'll work?"

"Hope so," said Marcus, staring at his mug. Then looking up, he added, "At least it's a plan. I figure they'll probably get my cattle sooner or later— might as well give it a try. It feels good to do something." Then he hoisted his mug, finishing it in two big gulps.

"Well, I hope it works too," I said. "When will all this happen?"

"I don't know yet. We're all waiting to hear from Mr. Strower. He said we'd likely not hear anything until it's time to come together. He doesn't want half the village finding out the time and then showing up. It'd scare off the Daggites. Smart man, that Strower."

Suddenly, I felt an urgency to get back to my room. I was worried about what I'd say if I started drinking. "Marcus, I have to get back upstairs and finish writing contracts. It was good to see you again." Then, nodding at his friends, I added, "I'll have Lloyd's wife bring over another round."

"It ain't that late," Marcus protested. "Have a cupla drinks with us."

"I'm sorry, but I need a clear head for tomorrow—meeting with farmers all day."

Marcus stood up with me. Pressing in close, he kept his voice barely above a whisper. "Don't tell Mr. Strower what I told ya. We're not supposed to be talkin' about this."

"I won't breathe a word of it," I assured him.

Entering my room, I lit the lantern and noticed Strower's map lying on the floor. Picking it up, I studied my assignments for the morning, marveling at Strower. Everyone, including me, was now moving to his cadence. And Strower got his wish—no one was calling this the king's plan. Under Strower's guidance, the farmers were uniting to solve the problem on their own.

I hacked off a thick slice of bread and smothered it with jam, shoving it in my mouth with no thought of tasting it, my mind occupied with what would happen in eight days when the Daggites rode across the border. If Strower's trap had worked, the location of the raid was secured.

Now that I knew the time and the place of the confrontation, it tortured me that I wouldn't get to see it. I contemplated sneaking over to Marcus's grove and perching in a tree to witness the ceremony, but the Daggite had already proven I wasn't very sneaky. Shuddering, I remembered how he'd settled next to me while I slept. Would he tell Strower that I'd shown up at the river? Joar wasn't one to volunteer information, but Strower would be asking plenty of questions. Then I wondered if Joar had noticed me walking the river-path back to Saleton. Marcus's farm was very close to that trail. What if the spies saw me? I might've made them skittish, causing them to bypass the decoys. I'd know soon enough.

I threw off my pants and crawled into bed, half-expecting an angry Strower to startle me awake.

CHAPTER 35

I didn't rise until well after sunup. Grabbing my trousers off the floor, I stabbed one foot through a leg-hole, then sat on the bed to insert the other. I was in a hurry to get going, but as I sat there, an odd question entered my mind. *Which Script?*

Taken aback, I let go of my trousers, suddenly intent on exploring those two words. My mind was always scripting tragedies, and then I'd spend my energy trying to keep them from happening. I'd gone to bed thinking I'd ruined Strower's plan, and that he'd be knocking on my door in the middle of the night. But now, the morning had arrived, the birds were happily chirping, and the scene hadn't played out. It rarely did.

The two words came again. *Which script?* At the river, my mind had experienced a different type of story. I'd imagined lifting my feet from the muddy shackles and giving my body to the current. No longer trying to forge my own path, I was enjoying the scenery, trusting the destination.

Which script? The question felt like an invitation to rest. Perhaps it still lingered from the previous day but it wanted an answer before I dressed. *Which script?* Would I continue trying to make my own way? Or, would I surrender to the current?

Then I heard the clomping of hooves. With one leg still in my trousers, I hopped to the window, poking my head outside just in time to see Lloyd's wagon heading east. Lloyd was driving with Strower beside him. In the wagon's bed, Joar sat sideways, his back resting against the sideboard. Like an owl spotting a field-mouse, the Daggite's head snapped in my direction. From his forehead to under his eyes, black paint covered his face, and bright streaks of color ran diagonally from his cheekbones down his jawline. Neither of us broke the stare as the wagon passed.

Once they were out of sight, I turned and sat on the window sill, contemplating this mysterious Daggite, wondering if he was as bewildered by me as I by him. No, I probably wasn't much of a puzzle. It felt the opposite—like Joar knew things about me that I didn't. My thoughts went

273

back to the river. I had panicked when he covered my mouth with his hand, but when I looked into his eyes, the fear melted. I saw only peace.

Slowly, these thoughts began to reframe my understanding of the last two days of solitude, stripping away my anger at being left out. Perhaps my time of seclusion had a higher purpose. Growing more and more convinced that it did, my cloak of loneliness began to fray, finally falling off altogether, gradually replaced with a sense of privilege. I'd been plucked up and pulled aside by the Creator, invited into a restful intimacy. The proposal was gentle but powerful, and my heart was begging my weary soul to let go and accept it. I was tired of slogging through the mud.

Which Script?

Strower had described Joar's soul as one dispossessed of worry, but when I looked into Joar's eyes I saw more than the absence of worry—I saw a presence. And although I'd never met Amanda Strower, I was sure her eyes radiated the very same presence.

Then I remembered Joar's words, *"A child cannot have his father's mind without first becoming an empty vessel. Balama is both death and life."*

Die to live? Was that the invitation before me?

Which script?

The river's current wanted to take me, but my feet were stabbed into the mud, refusing to forfeit control of my life. What was I holding on to? Becoming empty meant letting go, releasing the familiar in exchange for something entirely new. The promise of peace stood before me, rock-solid, but unreachable without first letting go.

Maybe I'll wait, I thought. It would be easier to exchange the old for the new later, after having some time to think about it. Then the words came again. *Which Script?*

No, I couldn't wait. Waiting was choosing—choosing the old, the familiar. The invitation was upon me. I had tasted the promise. If I didn't take hold of it now, I likely never would.

I needed to be brave, but for some reason I couldn't will myself to surrender. "Help me," I finally said. "Help me let go."

Then I felt it—a release. Suddenly, I was swept into the current, but I was too heavy to float. I was sinking under the weight of my pride—my belief that my life was mine to spend as I pleased. With one leg in my trousers, I collapsed to my knees. "I'm sorry," I said. "Forgive me for going alone. I need you."

Then, in my mind's eye, I saw the Creator's offering, the Great Sacrifice—the image of a man glowing in splendor—reaching for me. Extending my arms, I cried, "Please, take me." And just like that, the swirling stopped, and an indescribable presence flooded my heart. Then, like a lost child who'd finally stumbled upon the path home, I began weeping.

For a long time, I sat quietly on the floor, then on the edge of the bed, contemplating what I'd done. My world had shifted, and I didn't dare stand until I had my bearings. I'd always thought my conduct was the key to pleasing the Creator. I suppose it came from the guilt welling up when I'd break a rule. One time, to save my hide, I lied to my father. I'd stolen a coin from his bedside table, thinking he wouldn't miss it. When he confronted me, I panicked and lied, avoiding punishment, but feeling alienated, like the Creator had seen it and turned away in disgust.

I thought of my stiff lessons in the virtues. I'd been instructed by the priests in generosity, kindness, protecting the weak, and many other good behaviors. They'd been sewn carefully into the fabric of our religious lives, and starched with rules of conduct. We gave offerings to the priests, from which they fed the poor. We exchanged kind greetings on the street. We included the sick in our prayers, but I had a selfish reason for practicing these things. I was investing in my name. It had been drilled into my head: A good name opens doors. A good name takes you places. For me, a virtuous life had been self-serving. Suddenly, I saw my religion as what Joar called *peecho*, walk like, a feeble attempt to approach the Creator by imitation, only to get what *I* wanted. Remembering my goosebumps in the chapel, I realized that I'd always sensed there was more. Finally, I knew what it was.

Now I was in a strange place. To *walk with* the Creator, I needed to turn my back on my self-serving ways. It wouldn't do to critique my past, tallying my virtues against my shortcomings to see if perhaps, with extra work, I could tip the scale in my favor. Instead, I needed to concentrate fully on the Creator's presence, the Divine's grace-filled desire to *walk with* me. This presence wasn't a tool for my advancement, nor a platform to step over obstacles. No, *balama* was intimacy, pure and simple. Everything else would need to flow from a humble soul, seeking fulfillment from above.

As the trailhead of my new path came into focus, I wondered how I'd missed it for so long. I thought back to my lessons in religion, the priests explaining that my offenses were far too great to amend on my own—that I didn't possess the standing or the resources to cover my debt. I'd always sensed *that* to be true. I remembered the priest's voice trailing off, a strategy he used to prompt his students to lean forward and listen. "The Creator himself has paid the price for your sins," he told us. I could see his pointy gray beard moving up and down with his words. "Now, it is your task to repay the Creator by giving to others in the same way."

There it was—*peecho*, walk like.

I stood up from the bed, pacing the room, one stray trouser leg trailing behind me on the floor, wondering if the priests themselves understood the Creator's motive behind the Great Sacrifice. They seemed to believe it was a lesson in morality—a prescription to follow rather than an invitation to intimacy.

In his perfectly simple way, Joar had convinced me that the Great Sacrifice was nothing less than the doorway to *balama*, an invitation to *walk with* the Most High—as Father and child—and I had finally accepted that invitation and surrendered to the current. Lifting my feet, I'd now focus on my Companion rather than my destination.

What now? Joar hadn't given me anything by way of practical instruction. I wasn't about to paint my face. Looking down, I realized that my trousers were still one leg in, one leg out. Grateful for the simple task, I stepped into what seemed like new clothing. Then, rolling up the map, I vacated my room.

While heading for the front door of the inn, I heard Lloyd's wife humming in the kitchen. *Something* compelled me to stop and greet her. When I pushed open the kitchen door, I saw her standing by the stove, cooking breakfast for her patrons, too occupied with the sizzling meat to notice me. Intending to slip out unseen, the same *something* prompted me to acknowledge her.

"Good morning."

She jumped. Then, seeing it was me, she placed her hand on her heart. "You scared me. Good morning, Jens. What can I get you?"

"I just wanted to thank you for the bread and jam. I'm keeping it—if you don't mind—for tonight."

"Oh, goodness—don't do that. I can bake fresh."

"Not necessary. What's your name?"

"M-Me?" she said, like she was seldom asked that question. "Corinne."

Examining her tired eyes, I wondered why I hadn't noticed them before. They were intelligent, trustworthy, kind—eyes that didn't miss much. She was a person continually looked to and seldom seen, always responding to the needs of others. Now, viewing her in that big kitchen, it occurred to me that she wasn't just picking up Lloyd's slack at the inn, but my companions had invaded her home, and she was no doubt caring for them as well.

Suddenly, I sensed an unreasonable distance between the two of us. Overwhelmed with gratitude, I approached, and without thinking, embraced her. "Thank you for everything you're doing, Corinne," I whispered, my voice choking on a strange emotion.

Stiffening, she patted my back with her small hands. "It's fine," she replied, "You better be going. Go see your farmers." Then, pushing me away, she smoothed her apron and looked up at me. "My friend Annie was in town yesterday," she said, her eyes growing moist, "buying supplies. You met with her husband, Calvin. The shop owners are giving the farmers credit on their contracts with the king. Annie hasn't been able to buy sugar or tea for months, and Calvin won't let her take charity." Then she paused to wipe away a tear before adding, "You're making a difference."

With that, she forced a tight-lipped smile, patted my forearm, and returned to her snapping skillet of pork belly.

CHAPTER 36

The ensuing days worked themselves into a routine. I'd receive a map under my door, visit the farmers, and purchase their hay. Now, grateful for the solitude, I used my spare time to establish the discipline of *balama*.

Since my visits didn't take the entire day, I began leaving the inn a little later, dedicating an hour or two each morning to reading the Holy Book. I'd tossed it in my bag when I left home but hadn't cracked it open until now. I tried to read it conversationally like I'd seen Strower do on his porch in the wee hours of the morning. When I didn't understand something, I'd say so out loud. Then, reading the words again and again, sometimes my understanding congealed like milk whipped to butter. Other times, I'd slide the question to the back of my mind, knowing there'd be opportunities throughout the day to carry on the conversation.

Outwardly, it didn't seem like I'd changed much since falling to my knees, except for an occasional hi-jacking of my senses. I suppose I didn't know what to expect. I thought perhaps I'd be more like Strower—the winsome leader—or Joar—the cryptic prophet—but instead, I was becoming a sensor.

One day, a farmer wanted to show me the hay he had stored in his loft. His son, whom I guessed to be twelve or thirteen, was at the age when a young man's hands and feet are full-sized, but the limbs themselves seem artificially long, stretched, girth unfavorably traded for length. He was in the loft with us, throwing down hay for the horses—a clumsy spectacle—high-stepping in oversized boots to keep from tripping. He kept looking our way as we talked, curious as to what we were doing. So I asked his father, "Can your son join us?"

Taken aback, the boy's father replied, "My son? Why?"

"He seems interested."

As if waking from a long coma, the man stood gazing at his son, perhaps just now noticing he'd aged, probably entertaining the idea that this young man might now have the capacity to be interested in adult topics. I'd seen the same kind of thing with many of the farmers, and it grieved me—their shame from losing their herds causing them to detach from their families, enfolding everyone into a damp blanket of isolation, an itchy-coldness I could now feel.

Finally, the farmer said, "Jason, come and join us."

The boy clodded through the deep hay, his eyes large and eager.

I reached out to shake his hand, but rather than offering me his, the boy looked at me like I was asking for something he didn't possess. Embarrassed, his father said, "Shake his hand, Jason," which the boy did with the intentionality of someone learning to use a new tool.

"Jason, my name is Jens. I work for the king. I'm here to purchase hay from you and your father if you'll sell it. I need to fill a ship bound for Sagan."

The boy looked at his father, who smiled and said, "What do you think, son?"

After staring at his boots for a moment, the boy looked at me with surprising conviction. "I don't see why not. We ain't hardly got any cows."

"That's what I was thinking too," said his father, placing his left hand on Jason's shoulder and extending his right hand to me for a gentleman's handshake. "I guess that seals it, Jens."

When I drove off, the farmer and his son were standing side-by-side like two men. It was all I could do to keep a lid on my emotions. I waved, quickly turning away, trying to hide the joyful tear running down my face.

And so the days piled up, one upon another, along with the contracts. I kept them separated by the date they were written, each stack lying on the floor, topped with its respective map. There were now nine piles—two piles made before the spies came and seven since. That meant it was now the day of Joar's grand performance. I'd received Strower's map under my door, on which he'd written, LAST DAY. It didn't surprise me that he'd coordinated his visits in a perfect sequence leading to Joar's climactic final scene, providing me one last day to finish my final three contracts.

By early afternoon, I'd concluded the last of my meetings, and I didn't feel like going back to the inn to lie around. Sitting in the wagon, I scanned one of the large scrolled maps that Thoren had sent with me and noticed I wasn't far from Marcus's property. Veering south on a road that looked seldom traveled, I kept my eyes fixed to the right, hoping to run into my friend.

Nearing the south end of Marcus's property, I spotted three men removing a tree stump on a hillside. They'd secured one end of a chain to a horse and the other to the stump. Squinting, I thought I recognized Marcus standing in a shoveled hole surrounding the stump. He was ferociously swinging an ax at the roots, sending a blizzard of wood chips flying through the air. A gray-haired man, presumably his father, held the horse by its bridle, coaxing the beast forward, keeping the chain taut. A third man, probably a brother, wore a huge hat and stood uselessly between the horse and the tree, wringing his hands.

I pulled back the reins to watch, wondering how long Marcus could swing with such fervor. He seemed to be gaining ferocity as the roots held their claim to the soil. Finally, a loud crack filled the air, and the horse lunged forward, jerking the stump from the ground. Marcus collapsed onto the grass at the edge of the hole, wiping sweat from his brow while staring up at the sky. When he finally sat up, he spotted my wagon and came running over. Upon reaching me, he was too winded to talk, so he rested his forearms on the foot-board until he could push out some words.

"Jens, why are you here?"

"I just finished writing the last of my contracts. I'm heading back to town. Thought I'd come by your place on the way."

Still finding it hard to breathe, Marcus nodded, turning away momentarily to spit in the grass. "Well, our farm ain't exactly on the way to anywhere, except Dag." Then grinning, he added, "Maybe you just like watchin' a man work."

"Sounds fascinating. Where might I see something like that?"

Shaking his head, Marcus ran his fingers along my wagon's hatchet-scar. "Would you like to see what my ax could do to this buggy?" he asked, making his eyes large and deranged looking. Then, slapping my leg, he pointed southwest. "See 'em?"

I glanced in the direction he'd indicated, spotting a patch of pasture in the cleavage of two hills. Although most of the cattle were out of sight, I could see at least a dozen. As far as I could tell, they'd be a tempting herd, grazing out there like honey smeared on a bear trap. Though I couldn't see the river from where I sat, I knew it was only a short distance from the western border of Marcus's property.

"How many head?" I asked.

"Seventy-five altogether. It took some thought to come up with that number. Strower didn't want the trap to seem too obvious, but this herd matches their biggest take so far. It'll be hard to resist."

"No doubt."

Marcus then turned his eyes from the pasture to me. "You plannin' to come tonight?"

"No. I wasn't invited."

"Huh. I'm surprised. This day will go into our history books—if it works—something we can tell our grandchildren we saw first-hand."

Marcus was right. My father had shared all sorts of Tuva's stories with me, but this would be the most incredible tale of them all—if it worked. The thought of being barred from witnessing an actual historic event sewed a seed of resentment in my heart, and I could already feel it sprouting.

Marcus must have read my thoughts because his eyes suddenly lit. "I have an idea."

"What?"

"My brother over there—he's as shy as they come. He's skittish. Everything makes him nervous. He don't want nothin' to do with this. Daggite warriors? He'll wet his pants before they even get here."

"What does that have to do with me?"

281

Marcus poked his thumb over his right shoulder, pointing at his brother. "Well, just look at him. He wears that big hat all the time. He won't look no one in the eye. He keeps that brim pulled down."

"Yeah?"

"He's been begging Pa to stay in the house tonight, but Pa won't hear of it. He wants him out there helpin' earn our share of the Valley. Toby couldn't care less. He ain't never gonna move from this place."

"I still don't see what all this has to do with me."

"What if we hid Toby in your room at the inn and gave you his clothes? With his hat pulled down like that, no one would know. It's gonna be dark anyhow. Toby'd be grateful. Heck, I'd be grateful too. He'll be climbing up my back tonight. It's gonna be hard to concentrate."

I sat quietly for a moment, contemplating, wondering how much I'd regret not taking Marcus up on this offer. Then I asked myself how angry Strower would be if he found out. He didn't want me to play any part in this production. I tried to put Strower in my place, asking what he'd do with this opportunity. That's when the scale tipped. I didn't know if he'd be as sneaky as this, but I was sure if Strower were in my boots, he'd find a way to be there.

For a brief moment, I felt a catch in my spirit. I suppose the part of me communing with the Creator was trying to say something, but the other part of me—the worldly part—was squealing like a spoiled child having a tantrum, muffling the much quieter voice of *balama*. Reflexively, I stabbed my feet back into the proverbial mud.

"How will I get Toby's clothes?"

"You're gonna need what he's wearing or Pa will wonder why he changed." Then Marcus's eyes lit again. "How about this? I'll have him sneak off to the inn during chores. Toby usually feeds the calves while Pa and I do the milkin'. If he ran off then, no one would notice till supper. Then I'll tell Ma he's with the animals. They calm him."

It sounded like it might work. Toby would be safe in my room, and I could watch the ceremony from under the brim of his shy hat. If Strower caught us, I'd have the flimsy excuse that I was protecting Toby as a favor to Marcus. It wasn't much, but it was something.

"Let's do it," I said, "I'll be at the inn, sitting at the table nearest the door leading upstairs. Does Toby ever go there?"

"I've brought him a time or two, but he never goes there by himself. You should make it seem like he's on an errand for me, so you have an excuse to go to your room. Then, when you come here, find me in the crowd. Toby hides behind me when people are around, so just act nervous and stay in my shadow."

Looking over his shoulder, Marcus saw his father was coming our way. "You better be going," he said, backing away from the wagon.

CHAPTER 37

When I returned to the inn, I was surprised to see Lloyd behind the counter. Greeting him with a nod, I commented that I hadn't seen him in a while.

"Strower told me my work is finished," he muttered.

"Oh, I bet Corinne will be happy to have things back to normal."

"Yeah, back to normal."

Something was off with Lloyd. I suppose he'd relished his short season as Strower's right-hand man and was now resentful that he'd been cut loose before the big ceremony. *I know the feeling*, I thought, hurrying past the counter. I didn't have time for him now. Already, a few of the tables were occupied with patrons, and I wanted to lay claim to the one nearest the stairway—where Toby would meet me.

Racing to my room, I collected all the contracts and brought them down to the table where I could perform some calculations while waiting for Toby to show up. I didn't know exactly how much hay it would take to fill a ship, but I had stepped off the dimensions of each of the farmer's lofts and estimated the average depth of their hay. I wanted to compare my totals with what I thought to be the size of a ship's hold to see if I had enough.

While scribbling my calculations on the back of a map, Lloyd approached with two mugs, setting one in front of me and keeping the other for himself. Then he plunked down in the chair opposite mine and held up his mug, saying, "Here's to a successful venture."

Reluctantly, I grabbed the handle of my mug, inspecting its contents. "Little early to be drinking, don't you think?"

"Nooo," Lloyd purred, "two hours ago was a little early." Then, chuckling at his own wit, he added, "You've got some catching up to do. Looks like we'll be keeping each other company tonight."

"I'm afraid Lundgren's rum doesn't go very well with arithmetic," I said, setting the mug back on the table without taking a sip.

Lloyd stared at the mug. "The least you could do is drink with me after all I've done for you."

"For me? Strower told me you wanted to help the farmers."

Ignoring my comment, Lloyd scooped up my contracts and held them in front of my face. "You don't think you'd have these without me, do you?"

Refusing to reward his audacity with gratitude, I continued my calculations, quizzically asking, "So you're taking credit for all of this?"

"Well, me and Strower. I roped 'em and Strower tied 'em—Strower and that Daggite friend of yours. All you did was smoke their ass with the king's brand." Then he belched, trapping the gas in his mouth before expelling his rancid breath through a fake smile. Dropping the contracts back on the table, he said, "Go ahead then, do your arithmetic. I'll drink by myself."

Foolishly hoping he'd go away if I ignored him, I continued my calculations under his abiding scrutiny. "How'd you like the maps," he asked.

"Fine."

"Ever get lost?"

"Yeah, a couple of times."

"Where?"

"I don't know, Lloyd. I was lost." I felt guilty for being rude, but I was trying to starve the smoldering conversation of fuel, hoping to snuff it out altogher.

In the ensuing silence, Lloyd sat watching me, belching digestive gasses in my direction. I didn't want him there when Toby arrived, but I couldn't figure out how to get rid of him. Finally, he decided to explore another topic.

"Lundgren makes some good rum, don't he?"

I didn't look up from my work. "Yeah, good rum."

"How long you known him?"

"Who? Lundgren? Only since he threw a hatchet at me. The man is insane."

Seeing he was now on a touchy subject, Lloyd decided to inquire about the contracts. "Have you enough hay?"

"Hope so," I replied. Then, wondering if he was only lingering until I'd acknowledged his efforts, I added, "Thank you for your help, Lloyd, I really appreciate it."

Lloyd eased back in his chair. "If that's true, would it be wrong to assume the king might want to show his appreciation in some way?"

There it was. He was looking for money, but I wasn't going to make it easy for him. "What do you mean, Lloyd?"

Plunging in, he began his rant. "Have you not noticed my absence from this inn? You've been using my wagon. I've fed your friends."

"I never used your wagon. I have my own wagon."

"You imp."

"Listen, the whole reason Strower accepted your help was to keep King Thoren and me out of this. That's why I've been working on my own. Now you want to send Thoren a bill? What would Strower say to that? He'd skin us both."

Lloyd leaned in. "Strower don't need to know—neither does the king. I've seen that bag of gold you carry around."

"Tell you what, Lloyd, why don't you charge me for the maps that your wife delivered to my room each morning? Itemize them. That's something I can explain to the king without telling him what the three of you were up to."

"Fine," he growled, pushing his chair from the table and meandering back to the counter. Each time I looked his way, he seemed to be scowling at me, so I kept my eyes on the contracts and waited for Toby to arrive.

Around supper time, Corinne showed up, disappearing into the kitchen while Lloyd stumbled around to his patrons. With Lloyd's attention elsewhere, I set my work aside and kept my eyes fixed on the front door, waiting for Marcus's shy brother to appear. Just as Lloyd began clearing the gravy-smeared plates from the tables, a young man with a monstrous hat snuck in, making a bee-line to me.

Unfortunately, Lloyd saw him too, and came walking over, both of them arriving at my table at nearly the same time. Disinclined to speak, Toby stood in front of me like a piece of furniture, a hat-rack, waiting for me to take him to my room.

"What's *he* doing here?" asked Lloyd, inspecting the young man as if he were some sort of animal rarely seen up close.

"He came to pick something up," I replied, gathering my contracts.

"What's he here to pick up?"

"A book," I blurted. It was the first thing that came to mind.

"A book? What's he gonna do with a book. He don't even talk."

"Lloyd, you of all people should know that talking has nothing to do with a man's intelligence. Hasn't Lundgren's rum taught you anything?" Then, giving Lloyd a friendly pat on the back, I disappeared with Toby upstairs.

Once in my room, the only words Toby was able to utter was, "Don't stretch it," referring to his hat. My head was a little bigger than his, and he seemed indignant that I would still try to pull the brim down to my eyebrows. Who could blame him? Once he had it back, it'd probably fall over his eyes, but I wasn't going to chance being recognized, so I pulled like mad until we heard fibers snapping.

As I was leaving the room in Toby's clothes, he sat on the corner of the bed in his undergarments, staring out the window. "Don't know when I'll be back," I told him, "but I'll try to bring Marcus with me, so you don't have to walk home alone."

Making no attempt to acknowledge me, Toby continued staring out the window. "Did you hear me?" I asked. He cast his eyes to the floor and gave me a slight nod.

Before leaving the room, I noticed my Holy Book lying on the table, open from my morning conversation with the Creator. I quickly turned away, trying to escape the guilt it evoked.

Then, remembering I was now Toby, upstairs collecting a book, I walked back to the nightstand and tucked it under my right arm. Before leaving the room, I reminded Toby to stay put, almost laughing at the way he looked at me in response.

Reaching the door at the bottom of the stairwell, I paused. How would Toby do this? He'd probably open it cautiously, which is the very thing I wanted to do. Pushing the door open a crack, there sat Lloyd, occupying my table, awaiting my return with two full mugs. I suppose he'd noticed that I'd cleared the contracts from the table and figured I was finally ready to drink with him. He seemed hell-bent on the two of us—the cast-offs— keeping each other company on this momentous night.

Pushing the door open a little further, I stepped into the room, nervously pulling Toby's hat down even further over my eyebrows, snapping more fibers. Grateful for the poor lighting on this side of the inn, I slowly approached Lloyd, beginning my long journey to the front door. Fortunately, he seemed less concerned with looking *at me* then he was looking *around me*.

"Where is Jens?"

I didn't answer but stared at the ground the way Toby did when asked a question.

"Well, is he coming down, or not?"

I shook my head that he wasn't.

Looking aggravated, Lloyd leaned back, now inspecting me. "What've you got there?" he asked, pointing to what I had tucked under my arm.

I showed him the book.

He took it from me. "I see what's happening," he said. "You're scared of the Daggites showing up at your farm tonight."

I gave him a slight Toby-nod, staring at the floor.

Lloyd laughed, tapping the book's cover with his index finger. "I ain't saying this book can't do you good . . . over time. But boy, you ain't got time. Let me give you somethin' that works real fast."

Grabbing the handle of the mug meant for me, he said, "Since Jens ain't comin' down, we can't let this go to waste." Extending his arm, he commanded me to drink it, promising it would make me braver than a grizzly bear.

Receiving the mug, I took a sip, recognizing the taste of the rum-ale concoction, but much stronger than I remembered. Lloyd must have been serious when he said I needed to catch up. I tried to set it back on the table.

"No, no, no, no, no," droned the drunken innkeeper. "If you want to be brave, you gotta drink it all."

Unfortunately, the brim of Toby's huge hat didn't give me enough room under its canopy to tip the mug, so I turned away from Lloyd, cocking my neck enough to guzzle the fiery liquid. Then I spun back around, set the mug on the table, and Toby-trotted for the door, leaving Lloyd with my book. I hadn't eaten anything since breakfast, so, like a cloud of black smoke rising through a chimney, the effects of Lundgren's rum immediately billowed up my chest and exploded into my head.

CHAPTER 38

At first I was the only one who could hear the pounding. I wondered why the others couldn't. My thumping heart seemed loud enough to get their attention. Baboom, baboom, baboom . . . and it grew louder, more urgent, making the fabric of my shirt quiver with each beat. Still, no one noticed. Strower and Carrie were conversing with the twins, enjoying supper like nothing was wrong, even though the vibrations caused Carrie's fork to clatter on her plate. BABOOM, BABOOM, BABOOM. Finally, I tore my shirt open, revealing my chest. Now I had their attention.

"Papa, why is his chest doing that?" asked Magnus.

"Jens," Carrie scolded, "don't open your shirt at the table."

Looking at my chest, Strower tried to appear calm. "Hurry children, get to the porch."

"No! Don't leave," I yelled, my voice piercing the fragile veneer of the dream and exploding into the quiet room, where it seemed to echo off the walls until I was at last, fully conscious. I let out a long sigh—another strange dream.

Squinting at the morning through thin slits, my head was thumping in much the same manner my heart had thumped in the dream. At first, I couldn't separate what was real from what wasn't.

I remembered leaving the inn wearing Toby's clothes, but after that, the rum had compromised my faculties. While wondering if my memories from the prior evening were only a part of my strange dream, I rolled over in bed and gasped. My right shoulder felt like someone was extracting an embedded spear. Carefully unbuttoning Toby's shirt, I discovered a massive bruise, sickly yellow, framing a crimson scrape. "Son-of-a-school-teacher— I didn't get that in bed," I whispered to myself. Propping my right arm under my pillow to relieve its weight from my sore shoulder, I closed my eyes, trying to piece together what had happened. . . .

I remembered leaving the inn, struggling to walk a straight line. After ambling a short distance down the road on foot, I had turned back to get the wagon. Obviously, I wasn't thinking very well, but I planned to drive the wagon to a wooded area along the river trail, tie the horses to a tree, and walk the short distance to Marcus's farm.

But when I drove past the inn, I saw Lloyd relieving himself in the bushes on the west side of the building. He had watched me pass and yelled for me to stop, but he was in no position to give chase. I remembered him shifting his weight from one leg to the other, trying to speed things up. How stupid of me to take the wagon. I was supposed to be Toby. Lloyd must have thought I was stealing it.

I had yelled for the horses to go faster, and when I turned to look back, Lloyd was running down the street, still trying to fasten his trousers. I snapped the reins, and the horses finally responded, leaving Lloyd in a cloud of dust. When I turned again, he'd given up chasing me and was stumble-running back toward his house, where he kept his own wagon.

Thankfully, I had enough sense left to realize the foolishness of engaging in a chariot race, cantering our horses down the very trail where Strower was expecting the Daggites to travel. So I stopped at the trailhead, abandoned my wagon in the road, and sprinted for a cluster of trees, intending to hide from Lloyd, whom I'd incorrectly assumed to be hot on my trail. Unfortunately, the large oak I was aiming to hide behind seemed to move at the last moment. Trying to avoid a collision, I instead veered right into its unforgiving trunk. . . .

"Good grief," I whispered to the ceiling, taking a break from the painful memories to ease my weight to the left side so I could resituate my pillow. Then I noticed my book missing from the nightstand. Wincing now from a worse kind of pain, I realized how completely I'd abandoned my Companion. "I'm sorry," I whispered.

Closing my eyes again, I tried to remember what happened next. The details of my journey to Marcus's farm were hazy, other than being poked in the face by unseen branches and tripping on things. I must have fallen more than once because my hands were sore and swollen. Examining my right palm, I found a large sliver buried just below the skin. I spent a few moments pulling it out, trying to think of how it got there. . . .

I'd fought my way through a dense stand of trees and I remembered entering a clearing, where I saw Strower standing on a field cart, addressing the gathering of farmers. I didn't know whether to hide in the woods or join the group, so I stood there like an idiot, doing neither. The farmers had their backs to me, but Strower saw me and nodded, causing the entire crowd to turn and look. It was then that Marcus emerged from the sea of faces, running to meet me.

"Where've you been?" he spat in a low scold.

I told him I didn't know. What I meant to say was I didn't know what happened to the time, but Marcus interrupted the sentence before I could finish it.

"What do you mean *you don't know?*" he said. Then, "Have you been drinking?"

I confessed that I had, but, for some reason, I didn't tell him that Lloyd had forced it on me.

"Where's Toby?" Marcus then whispered.

I said he was in my room. Then I told him how unhappy Toby was because I'd stretched his hat. At the time, I thought it was hilarious, but Marcus didn't. He told me to shut up and keep my head down. Then, grabbing my arm, he led me to the group like a naughty child, saying to Strower, "He's just nervous. Keep going."

Obediently, I stared at Toby's boots, letting the brim of his giant hat hide my identity. I don't remember much of what Strower shared with the crowd—something about hiding and chanting. My head was buzzing from the rum, making it difficult to pay attention.

By the time Strower asked if anyone had questions, it seemed to be growing dark. I was incredibly sleepy. I remember staring at the dimming ground, wondering if the sun was disappearing, or, if I was losing consciousness. Then I heard someone say, "Who's that?" Everyone, including me, turned toward the road, where Lloyd's wagon was approaching. He had someone with him, and both Marcus and I knew who it was.

"Don't worry," Strower told the mumbling crowd. It's Lloyd and Jens. "I'll send them back to town. Everyone take your places. Go!"

At that, the crowd scattered into the woods. Marcus again grabbed my arm and led me toward the trees, whispering cuss words along the way. I turned my head to see what would happen when Strower reached the wagon. To my surprise, Strower didn't even allow Lloyd to stop. He grabbed the horse by the bridle and led it in a wide arc, sending it back toward Saleton. That's when I turned to Marcus and told him we were safe.

My comment, however, didn't sit well with Marcus. "Safe?" he spat. "You don't think Strower knew it was Toby in that wagon? How dumb do you think he is? Dammit Jens, if I lose my share of the Valley because you botched this . . ."

Pulling the pillow from under my arm, I used it instead to cover my face. Then, lying as still as a corpse, I tried to recall if I'd resolved my conflict with Marcus. . . .

I remembered him slapping my face, but it wasn't because he was angry. He was trying to wake me up. I must have fallen asleep while waiting for the Daggites. "Jens, they're here," came his urgent whisper. When I tried to say something, he placed his hand over my mouth.

By this time, it was dark. My head still wasn't right, but the nap had helped. Struggling to my knees, I peeked around a tree. Sure enough, the muted sound of horse hooves thumped the ground in the pasture, along with the distressing sound of bellowing cattle, but it was too dark to see much other than stirring shadows against a gray backdrop.

"Follow me to the edge of the trees," Marcus commanded. "Then lie down and keep your mouth shut. You got that?"

I remembered following Marcus like a puppy through the trees on my hands and knees. When we reached the perimeter of the woods, I collapsed to my belly. Crouching on his haunches, Marcus waited next to me. Suddenly, an eerie scream pierced the night, and the hair on the back of my neck stood up. I'd never heard anything like it. It ranged from a high-pitched trill to a low gurgling sound, like the last utterance of a drowning animal, then back to the trill again. At this, the horses stopped, and the air was absolutely silent, save the occasional bellowing of a terrified cow.

"What's happening?" I whispered to Marcus.

"Shhhh."

Marcus had stood up, readying himself. Suddenly, from the pasture, I heard the sound of a drum, a rhythmic thumping, like a heartbeat, starting slow and soft, but growing louder and more urgent. . . .

I sat up in bed, my mind revisiting the dream that woke me up—Carrie scolding me for opening my shirt at the table, the one article of clothing that would keep my innards from splatting against the walls. Exhaling slowly, I released the ridiculous images to the abyss of nightmares, but in the back of my mind, I could still hear the cadence of that drum—*baboom, baboom, baboom*. Resting my head against the headboard, I reclosed my eyes, returning to the prior evening. . . .

There was no movement in the pasture. Like icicles awaiting spring, the Daggites were frozen by the eerie scream and held motionless by the rhythm of the drum. Then a flame went up, igniting a huge pile of brush near the cart where Strower had addressed the farmers. By the light of the fire, I could now see the menacing black silhouettes of the Daggites—eight dark statues. Then Joar ascended the platform, his body brilliantly lit by the hungry flames and colorfully adorned with shimmering beads. Even from a distance, his eyes glowed like they too had been ignited by the fire.

Joar let out a howl, and when he did, the black images dismounted their horses in unison. A chant went up from the surrounding woods. Marcus was chanting too. He had placed his hand on my shoulder but kept his eyes on Joar as he droned strange Daggite words.

As the chant continued, Joar jumped down from the field cart, marching slowly toward his Daggite brethren. Then Marcus stepped out of the trees, along with the other farmers, and began forming a circle around the invaders, still chanting to the beat of that drum.

A few farmers had blades strapped to their belts that shone in the firelight, but they were for cutting weeds, not flesh. I wondered how they'd fare against the trained spears of the Daggites. I remembered the way Marcus had attacked that stump with his ax and imagined the carnage of such an onslaught to flesh and bone. . . .

I drew up my knees in bed, subconsciously protecting my vital organs. Could this have really happened? The shimmering colors and surreal sounds belonged in the domain of dreams. Shrugging, the pain in my shoulder reminded me that I was visiting an actual memory. . . .

Joar continued his advance, holding a flaming branch that he'd pulled from the fire. As he strode, the circle of farmers grew tighter. The warriors, seemingly in full cooperation with the ceremony, moved toward each other, leaving their weapons with their horses. Then Joar let out another short yelp, and the circle of farmers reached out their arms and held hands. When they did, the chanting stopped.

Encased within the circle, Joar advanced ceremoniously toward the warriors, who were on their knees in a perpendicular line to his approach. He stood above each warrior, using black ashes from the torch he'd extinguished on his leather smock to smear a streak across each of their foreheads while he spoke in the Daggite tongue.

When Joar had finished marking their foreheads, he backed away, lifting his arms in the air. The warriors stood to their feet. When Joar let his arms fall, the farmers released their hands and quietly retreated into the trees, like a pack of wolves after gnawing clean the bones of an elk. Then the warriors lined up single file behind Joar, who led them on a march toward the river. Quietly, they disappeared into the night, leaving their horses behind. . . .

From my bed, I whispered to the walls, "I think it worked." Then more loudly, "I think that crazy ceremony actually worked." I had no idea what happened once the Daggites reached the river crossing. For all I knew, the warriors might have drowned Joar in the river and let his carcass float downstream, but the ceremony had gone off without a hitch, and no farmers had been injured or killed. I left the remaining memories to fend for themselves. Suddenly, it didn't matter how I'd gotten back to the room, or what had happened with Lloyd and Toby. The ceremony worked.

"Thank you," I whispered to the empty nightstand. "Thank you," I repeated, easing my sore body out of bed. Then, while heading for the door to retrieve my book from Lloyd—hoping I could go back to being the man I was becoming—Strower himself burst into my room.

"Good morning," he chimed, grinning ear-to-ear.

"Good morning," I replied, suddenly realizing how much I'd missed his smile.

Practically dancing across the room, Strower mounted the wooden chair backward, as if riding a horse. Like a victorious general, he pulled his steed back on two legs.

"Well?" I asked.

"Well, what?" replied Strower. "It worked." Then, seeing Toby's hat on the floor, he added, "You know, Jens, you look good in a hat."

Closing my eyes—partly from shame, and partly to remember my excuse—I said, "I can explain that."

Waving away the offer, Strower changed the subject. "We have things to do. Are you ready to head back to the mining camp?"

"The mining camp?"

"Yes, Joar asked me to check on the cook. We need to let him know how it went. I don't suppose they'll see each other again."

"But how will we know if the rest of Joar's plan worked?"

"That's my other reason for visiting the camp. We know the location of one of the tribes. We can hike down the mountain and see for ourselves."

"And if they're gone?"

Strower stood up and spun the chair back into place. "If they're gone, I'll head home and let my neighbors know the Daggites are no longer a problem."

"What about me?"

"You'll need to meet with Thoren. Having the Daggites gone will stop the raids, but it does little good for the families who've already lost their herds. You'll need to convince the king to give the Valley to the farmers. They're all willing to grow beets for him."

"You want me to go alone?"

"We've no choice. My neighbors are waiting to hear from me, and we can't afford to let word of this get back to the king before you've met with him. He'd take the Valley in a heartbeat. You know that."

Reluctantly, I nodded.

"Besides," Strower added, "the king is cautious around me. My presence would only aggravate him. You, on the other hand, have a fistful of hay contracts and the Valley to be planted in beets—if the Daggites are gone—not to mention the beets you'll collect this fall from my neighbors. Jens, you have all the ammunition you need to make your request."

Strower was right. But as I looked at him, a sadness crept over me. I knew my season of being mentored was coming to an end. I'd been weaned and given a new Companion, but that didn't change the profound bond I felt. This man had sacrificed everything to lay success at my doorstep. Now it was up to me to finish the job on my own.

"I don't know how to thank you for all you've done," I whispered.

"Don't thank me yet," replied Strower. "Let's first see if there's anything to thank me for."

CHAPTER 39

Strower and I set off for the mining camp, quiet in each other's company. For most of the way, Strower seemed lost in his thoughts, driving the wagon with his body hunched forward, his elbows resting on his knees. It seemed odd that he'd be downcast now, after being so lighthearted at the inn. Finally, I asked, "What's bothering you, William?"

"Joar," he said, sitting up straight, as if suddenly realizing he wasn't alone. Then he added, "I feel guilty for what I said this morning—for calling the plan a success. I have no way of knowing that. We left Joar alone with those warriors . . ."

"I don't think he was alone," I said.

Strower nodded. "You're right. He wasn't alone."

Again, we rode in silence. I couldn't discern if Strower was tortured by worry over what might have happened to Joar, or if something else was bothering him. I knew the two of us wouldn't be together for much longer, and I didn't want to spend our precious time in silence.

"I've adopted your practice with the Holy Book," I said.

"What practice?"

"Reading in the morning, asking questions . . ."

"Oh. What caused you to start?"

"Well, that's a long story."

"We've got time," Strower replied, stretching his legs and hooking his heels over the front of the wagon. "Besides, I could use the distraction."

"Well, I overheard you and Joar talking one day through the door. Joar was telling you exactly when the spies would cross the river, so I went there myself to witness it."

"You did?"

I nodded. "At the time, I wasn't sure Joar could be trusted. I wanted to see for myself if he was telling the truth."

"And?"

"Well, I fell asleep next to a big rock, and Joar found me, but I had no idea he was sharing my hideout. I was dreaming that I was trying to cross the river, and my feet were sinking into the mud. It felt like I might drown. Then a voice bid me lift my feet and let the river take me downstream. When I did, my worries fell away. I had an overwhelming sense that I could trust the current. I've never before felt such rest. When I woke, Joar had his hand over my mouth. He must've been worried I'd cry out when I saw him. Not long after that, the spies crossed the river, and Joar followed."

Strower pulled off his hat, using the brim to scratch his scalp. "He never told me."

"Hah! Does that surprise you?"

Strower smiled and shook his head. After we'd driven a little further, I asked, "Do you remember the Daggite boy who rode on his father's shoulders?"

"Of course."

"That's how it felt, William—in my dream, floating down that river. I felt like I was riding on the shoulders of the Creator. Do you remember the two words he taught us?"

"*Balama* and *peecho*," replied Strower. "*Walk with* and *walk like*."

"Yes, *balama*. Lifting my feet from the mud and letting the river determine my course—it felt like *balama*." When Strower didn't reply, I added, "I probably sound like I've gone mad."

"Not at all, Jens."

"Well, mad or not, that's when I started reading the book. I've been conversing with the Creator ever since. It's changing me, William. At first, I thought I'd be more like you—more of a leader, but it's different for me. I notice things now—mostly little things. I've always been too absorbed in my worries to see what other people are going through. I don't know if that makes sense to you—you're not a worrier."

"You're right. I'm not a worrier, but I deal with the current in my own way. I guess I'm more apt to build a dam and try to harness its power, tame it like a saddle horse. Once my imagination attaches to a pursuit, I know I can make it happen. I've always been that way—feeling destined to lead, to accomplish things."

"What's wrong with that?"

Strower thought for a moment. "You say you've been too focused on your worries to notice other people. Well, I've used people as tools to get what I want. It's no better—probably worse."

"I think you're being hard on yourself, William. You're a great leader. Look what you've accomplished."

"That's just it—what *I've* accomplished? I find myself lured by pride to take credit for what I could have never done on my own. Those farmers were practically falling at my feet last night, calling me their savior—and I received it—while Joar humbly disappeared into the night. If anyone deserves credit, it's him. But he'd never claim it. It's the difference between those two words he taught us. This morning, I said, 'Let's see if there's anything to thank me for.' The moment I said it, a little voice spoke up, saying, 'Should you be thanked?'"

"The voice of *balama*," I mumbled, almost to myself.

"Yes, the voice of *balama* . . . Jens, I believe the Daggites have left the Valley, and I believe they'll follow Joar as their new priest. But from the moment Joar marched those warriors into the night, I've been throwing rocks in the river, building a dam, thinking how I can harness its current for myself. It's no wonder Joar calls our religion *peecho*. I thought I had more in common with him, but now, I don't know."

"I think I understand what you're feeling," I said. "Last night was no better for me."

Strower placed his hand on my shoulder, and the two of us commiserated to the rhythm of horse hooves.

"What now?" I finally asked.

"We get back on track. If there's one thing I've learned, it's when I can't sense the Creator's presence, I'm the one who has turned away. Think of the Daggite father. If his son wandered off, would he abandon him?"

The answer was obvious. In my mind, I saw the young boy propelled through the air on his father's shoulders. I looked up at the sky and whispered, "I'm back."

Strower looked at me. "What?"

"Nothing. You'll miss him, won't you?"

Strower nodded. "The last few days have been hard. Old memories. Joar's intimacy with the Creator—I haven't seen anything like it since—" He pinched off his sentence and looked off toward the mountains. After a few quiet moments, he continued, "Amanda held the same light, Jens. I know I can't *walk with* and go my own way at the same time, but I keep trying. The voice of *walk like* is mighty loud. I wonder if I'll ever learn."

"I think we're learning together, William."

We reached the mining camp by early afternoon, finding the old cook standing alone next to his lean-to. With dozens of wet plates drying in the sun, it appeared that he'd just finished washing dishes after the noon meal. When he saw the wagon, he took one step in our direction, then hesitated, as if bolstering himself for what might be bad news. Strower quickly jumped down from the wagon, yelling a happy greeting. "Hello, my friend!"

The lightness of Strower's words seemed to buoy the old man's spirit, at least enough to allow him to raise his arm, reminding me of a wounded soldier calling for medical attention. "Do you bring good news?"

Reaching the cook, Strower said, "Yes, I think so. Things went well in Saleton—as far as we can tell. The warriors accepted Joar as their priest. He led them back to Dag. After that, we don't know what happened."

The cook looked off to the west, then knelt. I thought his knees had buckled, but then he started arranging his cookware. Without looking up, he said, "If he's still alive, he'll move them out of the Valley."

"Ah," replied Strower, "he's shared his plan with you. I wondered if he had."

"Yes, we discussed it every night—so far as moving the tribes west, that is." Then, using his index finger to flick a beetle off the side of a skillet, he asked, "What will become of the Valley?"

Strower lowered himself on his haunches until he and the cook were face-to-face. "If Jens can convince the king, the Valley will be deeded to the farmers who've lost their cattle. We're hoping to sneak down the mountain this afternoon and see if the Daggites have abandoned the nearest village."

The old man rubbed his whiskers. "I'd like to go with you, but I've got supper to cook."

"We'll bring you a report," replied Strower, "but if they've abandoned the village, we might roam the Valley for a while. Do you have a tent and some food you could send with us?"

"Staying the night?" asked the old man, curling his lower lip disapprovingly. I was having a similar reaction. Why not sneak down and then return to camp? We could be back by supper.

Before I could question his strategy, Strower began explaining himself. "I want to see the lay of the land. The farmers expect me in Saleton in a few days. They'll want to explore the Valley with me. We'll need to parcel it by family. I'd like to draw a simple map so I can think about how to divide the land before I have the farmers whispering in my ear. If they start fighting over boundaries, we could still have a war on our hands."

"You'd better be on your way then," said the cook, his aged eyes admiring Strower. "The men were damn hungry today. They've eaten everything I cooked, but I can send dried beef and raw vegetables."

"That'll do just fine. How about a tent?"

The cook pointed to the back wall of the lean-to. "There's three stacked right there."

Strower took a long look at the old man, probably realizing the torture we'd put him through by tarrying in the Valley while he waited—once again—for news. "On second thought," said Strower, "We'll come back this afternoon to let you know what we find. We can explore the Valley tomorrow."

"No," the old man replied. "If you're still gone come nightfall, I'll know you're exploring. That's all the news I'll need."

The journey down the mountain was much slower without Joar. Not that we didn't know the way, but Daggites move quickly, in absolute silence. With no such ability, Strower and I settled into a pace we could travel in relative stealth.

Finally reaching the Valley, we ascended the small pine-covered rise and crawled under the boughs, just as we'd done with Joar. As we neared the pinnacle, my heart pounded uncontrollably. Strower, who'd been crawling a half-body length ahead of me, stopped just shy of the crest, probably immobilized by the same thought I was having—*What if they're still there?* That would likely tell us the plan hadn't worked. It might also mean that Joar was dead. Until now, I'm sure Strower hadn't thought much about that possibility, but I had. So, in a snake-like fashion, I propelled myself past Strower, reaching the top first.

Peering down at the clearing from under the pine boughs, I scanned the village for movement. Other than the river flowing obliviously in the background, all was still—no women doing chores, no children running about, not even wild critters staking a claim. It was eerily quiet.

Strower crawled alongside me and stared down. "Look at the huts," he whispered. I'd been too busy watching for movement to notice. The Daggites had removed the animal skin roofs, leaving the branch rafters naked on the half-walls, like a herd of roped cattle with skeletal legs pointing to the sky.

No longer whispering, Strower proclaimed the obvious—"They've cleared out."

CHAPTER 40

While together, Joar had provided Strower a vivid description of the Valley of Ten Tribes, explaining that the ten villages circling the outer perimeter of the Valley are equally spaced from one another. He also described the river, which he said flowed southwesterly from the high slopes of the border-mountains into the Valley's center and then back toward the southeast.

The village near the mining camp was in the northeast corner of the Valley, so Strower and I decided to walk in a southerly direction, avoiding an immediate river crossing. Strower had me counting paces from specific landmarks while he scrawled a rough diagram on the back of one of my maps. He wanted to plot the Valley like a wagon wheel, with property lines as spokes. That way, every parcel would meet at the hub, all touching at the center—in theory, forcing everyone to be neighbors. Obviously, with me counting steps, Strower and I weren't conversing much. I concentrated on walking a relatively straight line in uniform strides while Strower concentrated on drawing the map.

Unusually flat, the Valley had small wooded areas interrupting what was mostly a sea of shoulder-tall grass, bowing and standing in helpless tribute to the respirations of the overlording mountains. I guessed that the farmers would soon log the wooded areas to produce more cropland for farming and lumber for building and that the worshipful grass would quickly change to squatty beets—that is, if I could convince Thoren to deed the Valley to the farmers.

In the center of the Valley stood a strange rock formation, tall and straight as a spike. As we moved along, I noticed that its flat head never seemed any closer or further away, making it the perfect hub for the wheel.

By the time we reached the river on the south end, the sun was beginning to disappear behind the western slopes, shading us in a gigantic mountain shadow. We'd found three other villages by this time, all abandoned in the same manner as the first, the paces between each remarkably equal.

I was quietly watching Strower add the southern leg of the river to his map when a hawk descended, screeching an eerie announcement of nightfall, sounding to me like a final warning to evacuate. Strower paused from his map-making and looked up at the bird, which surrendered its body to invisible currents, hoisting it higher and higher on motionless wings. Then Strower again took notice of the tall rock and said, "That rock over there would make a great lookout over the Valley, wouldn't it?"

"Yes," I agreed, thinking he was merely speaking theoretically. "Have you noticed that it stays the same distance from us?" I asked. "It must be almost perfectly centered."

"Odd-looking thing," said Strower, now giving the rock his full attention. "It's level on top, almost like a giant's supper table." Then, with a wild gleam in his eyes, he wondered aloud if it could be climbed.

"Climbed?" I said, fighting off the image of my body being placed on a giant's table—at mealtime, no less. "You don't think we can make it back to the mining camp before nightfall?"

"Why would we do that? I'd rather make camp down here. It doesn't make sense to climb up the mountain just to come back down in the morning?"

Mumbling an incoherent complaint, I followed Strower along the riverbank toward the freakish formation. Now, with its top illuminated by the setting sun, the rock resembled a stage set for the final scene of a tragedy.

The closer we drew, the more the rock looked like an altar, and the more it looked like an altar, the more reverent our steps became until we finally stood at its base, staring up at its unscalable walls. From where we stood, we could see three sides, more or less. But Strower wouldn't give up on the idea of making it to the top until he'd viewed the fourth side.

Behind the rock flowed the river. There was barely enough room to walk between the riverbank and the rock wall, but Strower found an obscure path through the thicket and moved along the rock's edge until he found a partial shallowing of its slope. I stood off to the side, watching as he slowly made his way higher and higher. Twice, it appeared that he'd exhausted his options to continue, but both times he found a handhold and enough footing to keep climbing. Finally, he was at the top, pumping his arm triumphantly, and then gesturing for me to follow.

I climbed much slower than Strower, frequently waiting for his instruction from above. Slowly, I ascended the face, trying to keep my eyes in front of me. Only once did they venture downward, making my knees weak and my back-foot quiver at the ankle. When I finally neared the top, Strower reached out his hand and pulled me the rest of the way up. My sense of relief was quickly replaced with awe as I turned a slow circle, taking in the panoramic view. From where we stood, we could see all ten of the abandoned villages.

After a moment of silence, Strower pulled the folded map from his trousers and spread it open against the half of the Valley we hadn't yet surveyed. "I could almost finish this map from up here," he said. Then he started placing the abandoned villages and more significant landmarks on the yellow parchment. When he'd finished his crude drawing, he looked up, saying, "I wonder if we dare start a fire up here?"

"Up here?" I moaned. As beautiful as it was, the place still gave me a foreboding sense of dread.

"Sure. You can't make a safer camp than this—unless you roll around in your sleep."

"But we didn't bring up the tent," I protested, looking down at the bundle lying next to the stream.

"I'll get it," said Strower, already starting his descent. It wasn't long before he was again at the top with the tent on his back, and after searching to find four cracks suitably placed for tent pegs, we had made camp.

"I guess we can do without a fire tonight," said Strower, handing me some dried beef. "I'm too tired to go back down for wood." He was looking at me, probably hoping I'd volunteer, but when I didn't, he sat down and leaned against the pack, removing his hat and stretching his neck in all directions. "Maybe we can make a little fire next to the stream in the morning," he suggested, examining a small pouch the cook had sent along containing tea leaves. "Wouldn't a little tea taste good in the morning?"

"Yes, I guess it would."

After we finished eating, Strower surveyed the Valley one last time and then retired inside the tent. The tent-pack, which we'd stuffed with food and some of our belongings, now sat by itself. I opened the flap to see what else I might eat, but instead found Strower's Holy Book. Forgetting my appetite, I thumbed through the pages, feeling like I still had unfinished business with Creator. Examining the underlined verses, I wondered if the markings were made by Strower or his wife. Finally, I arrived at this verse:

My child, there is no valley too deep or too wide for you to escape my loving eyes.

The verse was underlined twice, presumably by both Amanda and William. But regardless of their personal motives for underlining it, I had the sense it was marked twice for my benefit. The sun had now totally disappeared behind the western summit, leaving the faintest pink halo to illuminate the beautiful Valley, where rugged mountains encircled us like kings seated for a conference. A shiver ran through my spine. "My Father," I whispered, carefully searching for the right words. Then I remembered Strower's response when I asked him what to do after abandoning *balama*. "You turn back," he said. Those three words almost rang audibly, and I sensed a Holy Presence. "Thank you," I whispered. It was all I needed to say.

Sleeping outside the tent, I awoke to the sound of stirring at the base of the rock. Knowing Strower to be an early riser, I assumed morning was near, and he'd probably climbed down to start his fire by the river. When I heard a metallic clanking, I imagined that Strower was pulling out the cookware. Then I realized that my head was propped against the pack containing the utensils.

My eyes shot open. It was pitch dark. Lying motionless, listening, I tried to comfort myself with the fact that even a tiny creature can make quite a stir in the stillness of the night, but there it was again—a metallic clank. Reaching my right arm through the flap of the tent, I swept my palm across the floor, hoping my hand wouldn't find Strower's leg, but it did. I sat up, wondering whether I should slap the leg and wake Strower, or crawl quietly to the edge of the rock to explore what was happening below.

Then I imagined that someone might be climbing the rock face, the metallic clanking being their sword hanging from their belt, banging against the stone. I had no instinct to fight, but I did have the realization that there'd likely be a brief moment when even a sure-footed man would be vulnerable to falling, and, just as Strower had lent me a hand to pull me up,

I might have an opportunity to use my hand to push the intruder backward off the ledge.

I crawled to the edge and peered down, but I couldn't see anything through the darkness. Relying then on my ears, I discerned that the noise seemed to be coming from the rock's base. I crawled back to the tent, reaching my arm inside, again locating Strower's foot and squeezing his big toe, whispering for him to wake up.

"What?"

"Shhh . . . Listen."

Another metallic clank reverberated through the night, and I could hear Strower sit up. "What's that?" he whispered.

"I don't know, but it sounds like metal. It can't be an animal."

Strower opened the flap and emerged. Together, we crawled to the edge. I nearly jumped out of my skin when Strower barked, "WHO'S DOWN THERE?"

A silent moment elapsed. Then we heard something drop into the rocks, followed by the snapping of brush and a splash. Once again, the night was quiet.

Strower and I looked at each other, still compelled to whisper. "What do you suppose it was?" I asked.

"I've no idea, but it'll be a long night now. Try to get some sleep. I'll keep watch for a while. We can take turns. I'll wake you when I'm tired."

Retiring to the tent, I had a terrible time falling back to sleep, but at some point I must have dozed off because it was light out when Strower finally woke me, quizzing me from outside the tent.

"Jens, listen to this . . ." CLANK. When I heard the noise, I poked my head through the flap to see what it was. Strower was standing there, smiling like a stage magician, using both hands to present the crude leather sack that he'd just dropped near his feet.

"What's in it?"

"See for yourself."

I crawled from the tent and untied the leather band that gathered the sack at the top, pouring out several chunks of gold. "What in the—"

"It's the king's gold."

"I can see that," I replied, remembering that Joar had told us that the Daggite priest had buried the gold he'd stolen from the mining camp in the Valley. "So this is where he hid it," I mused. "I knew there was something strange about this place. It's probably their holy ground."

"There's more down there," said Strower. "I found this sack inside a little cavern at the base of this rock. The entrance is right next to where we started climbing—another three paces and we'd have found it last night. The priest must have planned to haul out as much as he could carry. I suppose he abandoned the sack when he decided to swim for his life. He probably thought he was surrounded."

I picked up a nugget, feeling its weight. "Yeah, this would make a pretty heavy anchor. So you think it was the priest?"

"Think about it, Jens. If Joar is now their new priest—"

I finished the sentence—"The old priest is without a position, and he's likely the only one who knew where the gold was hidden. I wonder why he's still here."

Strower shrugged. "I don't pretend to understand the Daggite customs, but you can bet he's been humiliated. Maybe he wanted to harness the gold's power somehow."

"Could be . . . Or, maybe he wanted to plant the gold in their new land."

The two of us sat on our haunches, staring at the treasure. Soon, the morning sun was peeking over the eastern ridge, and the nuggets shimmered in the yellow beams. "What should we do now, William?"

"I've been contemplating that very thing."

"And?"

"I've been thinking about sugar," replied Strower, standing up and surveying the Valley.

"Sugar again?"

"Yes. Lundgren has a way of making it from beets, remember?"

"Yes, but what does that have to do with this gold?"

"Somewhere on his property, Lundgren hides his rum-making equipment. What if we used this gold to hire John to make the same equipment, only larger? There's a river right here."

I laughed in disbelief. "After our conversation yesterday, you *literally* want to build a dam on this river?"

"I know what you're thinking," said Strower, realizing his *peecho* metaphor from the prior day had now materially manifested, "but hear me out—"

"Lundgren owns that design," I interrupted. "He'd never release it—not for Thoren's benefit, and not to John. He already thinks John stole the design for his plow."

"You're right—he wouldn't do it for Thoren or John, but he'd do it for Carrie."

"Carrie?"

Strower smiled. I was too timid to inquire any further about his daughter, so I continued my questioning, "If Lundgren could be convinced to help us—"

Strower finished my thought—"The farmers could sell sugar at the port instead of beets. Remember what Thoren told us? Sugar is shipped to Gladon from that island in the south and sold at huge profits."

I remembered Thoren's story about the man from Gladon who'd been killed by his own king because he was close to the very same invention Lundgren had already perfected for making rum. "That could mean war with Gladon," I reminded him.

"Or, it could mean a future for Tuva. Think of those poor farmers who will occupy this Valley. Think of how much you—their Minister of

Agriculture—could pay them for sugar. Jens, we could use this gold to purchase a future for those families." Then, to convince me that his motives were pure, he added, "This isn't a dam I'm trying to build for my glory. I have a heart for these farmers, Jens."

"I know you do, but it's not our gold, William. It belongs to King Thoren."

As if snapping out of a trance, Strower stepped backward one stride and stared up at the sky. "You're right. You need to bring this gold back to King Thoren. Its weight will match the records of what's missing. It will clear Bear and his men of suspicion."

"Yes, but Thoren will want to know how I acquired it. Should I tell him about Alden Fry and the Daggite priest? We still don't know how much Thoren knows."

Strower shrugged like he was too distracted to think about Alden Fry. Assuming he was still scheming over how to make sugar, I said, "Maybe there'll be another way to purchase the equipment later."

Strower smiled, holding up both hands as if surrendering his dream on the stone altar. Then, pointing down at the river, he said, "This isn't my dam to build, Jens. I need to let it go. At least I have a rough map of the whole Valley now. The farmers can help me step-off the rest of it when I come back. I need to get to Tinsdal and secure those contracts with my neighbors, and you need to meet with Thoren."

"Agreed. How much gold is down there?"

"I think we can carry it out if we distribute it equally and travel slowly."

"What about the priest?" I asked. "I imagine he's still lurking down there somewhere."

Strower pointed to the northeast. "That's the direction of the mining camp. I think we should load up and head straight toward it. There's two of us and only one of him."

"True, but he's probably armed, and we know he wants this gold."

Strower laughed. "Well, I guess we could stay up here until someone rescues us. I just hope they get here before the buzzards."

He was right. With my stomach in a knot, I turned and started kicking out the tent pegs.

CHAPTER 41

I've heard tales of men overtaken by super-human strength in the throes of fear. I won't say my strength was super-human on that hike back to the mining camp, but maybe partially so. I was surprisingly nimble, even though I was lugging a hefty amount of gold up the side of a mountain. Even Strower was jumpy, his head swiveling at every twig-snap. To our relief, we made it back to the mining camp without incident while the day was still young.

Upon noticing our emergence from the wooded slope, the cook seemed anxious for details. Jumping to his feet, he abandoned the pot he was scrubbing and attempted one clumsy step forward before stopping to slap his trailing leg, which must have fallen asleep while he was working on his haunches. While he was trying to revive his appendage, I whispered to Strower, "How much should we tell him?"

The question seemed to catch Strower off guard. "Let me do the talking," he said.

As the cook approached, my pack's weight announced itself loudly to my bruised shoulder. Easing my right arm through the strap, I swung the pack around, letting it crash to the ground. The nuggets made a clank, which caught the old man's attention. But he only glanced at my pack for an instant before his concern for Joar stole back his focus.

"They're gone?" he asked.

"All ten villages—completely abandoned," replied Strower. "They all followed your son."

The cook turned his face, hiding his emotions. "I knew he'd do it," he sniffed, looking longingly toward the western slopes.

Strower approached and threw his arms around the old man's neck, letting out a long sigh. This tender display of understanding invited the cook to release his emotions fully, and he started moaning like he'd lost a child. I stood awkwardly off to the side, waiting for the tide to recede.

Finally, the cook pulled away from Strower, wiping his eyes with his shirt sleeve. "What will you do now?"

"Well," replied Strower, chuckling at the absurdity of what he was about to say, "I've been wondering about your rum supply."

"Rum supply?"

"Yes, I'm wondering if Bear is planning to make a trip to restock?"

The cook shrugged. "Bear goes when Bear goes. We still have rum, but it disappears fast. What are you thinking?"

"Well, I know Tinsdal is a good bit further away than Saleton, but if we could entice Bear to take a trip to Lundgren's farm, I could catch a ride home, and Jens could take his wagon straight to the port without losing a day. Time is of the essence. I'll donate the rum myself—a whole barrel."

"As I said, Bear goes when Bear goes. It's not up to me. We'll hafta ask him."

Strower looked at me. "Get your wagon ready." Then placing his arm around the cook's shoulder, he added, "Let's go wrestle the Bear."

I didn't respond. I had a mighty craving to see Carrie, so I was hoping to drop Strower off myself. Her kiss had my soul reaching for her. It felt like a promise, a down payment—*keep my father safe, and you'll have my lips again.* Now, here we were—our mission accomplished, her father safe—and I wanted to collect before I went to The Crucible to see Thoren. I needed her strength. I wanted to feel our hearts pounding together again.

Strower must have sensed my conflict. After he'd walked a few paces with the cook, he stopped, instructing the old man to keep going, telling him that he'd catch up. Then he came back and asked me if something was wrong.

Hesitating, I said, "It's just . . . you know. . . I think you forget that Bear has a woman in Saleton that he likes to visit when he goes for rum."

Strower cocked his head, eyeing me curiously. "Well, that's true, Jens, but sometimes when there's important work to do, that has to wait. I think Bear is man enough to understand that, don't you?" Then he winked at me.

Now, desperate to change the subject, I said, "You never told me how much to share with Thoren about Alden Fry. Somehow, I need to explain this gold."

Strower placed his hand on my shoulder, speaking barely above a whisper, "You know those conversations you've been having in the morning?"

"Yeah."

"Well, that would be a great topic to bring up." With that, he trotted off to rejoin the cook.

Not surprisingly, Bear agreed to Strower's plan, and I found myself alone in the king's wagon, driving in the warm summer sun toward Thoren's palace in Keenod. Before long, though, a dense cloud crawled across the sky, drizzling a warm mist. The cloud had the appearance of a thousand sopping wet rags suspended from the sky, the tips nearly touching the ground. I kept moving, and the rain kept falling, only hard enough to keep me miserably damp.

Trying to distract myself from my annoying circumstances, I remembered the day I'd departed from the palace in Keenod, only weeks earlier. The farmers were plowing then. Now, their crops were coming up, transforming the landscape from black to green, death to life. I had no idea then what kind of adventure awaited me. I slid my fingers across the scar on the king's crest, remembering how I ran for my life after discovering Lundgren's base of operations— he, blazing a shortcut through the tall grass, giving himself one last opportunity to inflict terror.

I reflected on my time at Strower's farm, smiling at the thought of Carrie teaching me to milk a cow. I revisited my wrestling match with Oscar, and relived my experience with Carrie afterward, whispering my secret in the soft hay, telling her about my feelings for a woman made of stone while she rested her pretty head on my shoulder.

I thought of the note she left me—saying she couldn't give weight to my soul—and the hot anger it induced. Now, I felt like I needed her for that very purpose.

Then, I remembered *balama*. If I was trying to find my substance in Carrie, had I once again strayed?

I thought about the days I'd spent cocooned at the inn. Suddenly, it occurred to me that perhaps my present solitude was for the same purpose. The Creator, who seemed to have a jealous side, didn't want me looking to Strower for courage, or to his daughter for comfort and strength.

I was still a full day's travel from The Crucible when it began to grow dark. I pulled the horses off the road near a stream, unhitching them from the wagon so they could drink. Then I tied them to a tree to lazily graze the night away. Thankfully, the rain had finally stopped, and a cold breeze was pushing the low gray cloud speedily across the sky. I made my bed in the back of the wagon, munching leftover dried beef from our trip to the Valley. Before darkness had entirely covered the land, I tore a piece of parchment from one of my maps, using the backside to scrawl these words:

> *It's a fantasy of emotion,*
> *creatures, offering life to one another.*
> *We can only offer companionship*
> *on this hard journey.*
>
> *Her body is not food.*
> *Her blood is not drink.*
> *The destination for my soul*
> *lies beyond her arms*

Lying on my back, I stared at the words until it was too dark to see them anymore.

The wind grew even colder during the night, and then the rain returned. I threw on my coat and wrapped myself in a blanket, but it wasn't long before the relentless drops soaked through the material. Freezing, I cursed the sky, looking east for what seemed an eternity, until finally, I could see the slight glow of the reluctant dawn. With barely enough light, I jumped from the wagon, frantically hitching up the horses to get underway.

Before I'd traveled very far, I began shivering uncontrollably. Every so often, I'd stop the wagon, dismounting in the rain to run back and forth on the road, doing my best to restore heat to my body. As the day wore on, my knees, elbows, and neck began stiffening, as if coated with rust, and my skin, corpse-blue, grew so cold that the frigid rain felt warm by comparison.

Then my mind began playing tricks on me. Brick-heavy, my eyelids coaxed my body to lie down on the wagon seat to rest, allowing the horses to continue onward, not even realizing the foolishness of such a decision. I don't recall seeing landmarks—not even the panoramic view of The Crucible. I don't remember the ride down the winding road toward the palace. The only thing I vaguely remember is the commotion of arriving, being lifted from the wagon by two strong men, who were asking stern questions and shaking me for answers. But there didn't seem to be a path from my jumbled mind to my quivering lips.

I remember my face being slapped over and over, my back pressed against a wall, held in place by the two men so a third man could interrogate me. This made me sleepier still, and I kept dozing off. My warm blood, coaxed to the surface by the mean hand of my abuser, felt strangely comforting against my cold skin, giving me the perverse assurance that I was alive.

Finally, they threw me into some kind of carriage and tossed a blanket across my body. The last thing I remember hearing was a woman's shrill voice screaming something about the king, but the voice quickly grew distant as the carriage began moving. At the time, I wasn't sure it was real, and I didn't care. The cramping, the screaming, the pain in my clenched jaw—I didn't care about any of it. My mind pushed it all away. I only wanted to sleep.

CHAPTER 42

A carriage wheel must have fallen into a rut, rolling my sleeping body into the sidewall and startling me awake. My eyelids were stuck together, crusted in matter, and my throat was too sore to swallow my spit.

My only view to the outside of the carriage was a tiny barred window in the front, so I pushed off the blanket, attempting to stand erect, but instead fell backward. Fortunately, my shoulders caught the sidewall, saving me from toppling to the floor. I'd never been so stiff and weak.

Hunched like an old man, I shuffled with pathetically small steps until I could take hold of the bars in the window. Gripping with all my might, I hoisted myself straight, surprised to see the backside of a man's stubbly head only inches away. The head sat atop a neck resembling the trunk of an oak. I craned to see who was with him on the bench. To his left was the driver, whose neck, by comparison, was as slender as a sapling. To his right was another headed-stump with long dark hair. Then, looking off in the distance, I saw the Royal City perched on its high hill, glimmering orange under the last rays of the setting sun.

Not wanting to draw my captor's attention, I released the bars, turned my back against the wall, and slid to a seated position beneath the window. I was having difficulty with my sense of time. To have traveled this far, I must have slept for more than a day. While I collected my thoughts, the men began talking.

"It'll be dark when we arrive," one of them said. "That's good. I'll put you two up at my house tonight, but before I take you back to Keenod, I have one more assignment for you."

"Yes, Mr. Fry," one of them replied.

Mr. Fry? Alden Fry? Now realizing I was locked in the same carriage they use to transport gold from the mining camp, I wondered if the two headed-stumps were the king's guards or if Fry had recruited these men from the docks in Keenod. Why were they taking me to the Royal City? I couldn't understand what was happening, and my sickness was making me so sleepy it was nearly impossible to think.

After a short time, I realized that the stubble-headed man might try to observe me through the small window. Sitting as I was, I'd be invisible to him, and they'd probably stop the carriage to see what I was doing. So I crawled back under the blanket, pretending to sleep, but all the while exploring my surroundings through one squinted eye.

There was a bundle laying lengthwise along the other side of the carriage that looked like a rolled rug. Although it was dim, I thought I recognized the pattern from the carpet in Thoren's study—the rug Akeem had brought from the East. Then I noticed what looked like a golden lock of hair protruding from the end of the roll.

Startled by the thought of sharing space with another prisoner, my mind began imagining what sort of man they had me caged with. Lying very still, I tried to remember what questions the men were asking while they had me pushed against the wall, but try as I might, I couldn't recall even one.

Then I heard one of the men say, "Does it stink back there yet?"

For a moment, darkness muted my surroundings while the stubble-headed man's face covered the window. "It smells like piss," he replied, "but the king isn't rotting yet."

The king?

Slowly, I reached down and touched the crotch of my pants. He wasn't wrong about the smell. I looked again at the golden lock of curly hair, recoiling like a spring as the carriage bounded along the bumpy road. Gradually, the unspeakable truth gnawed its way into my mind—I was traveling with Thoren's corpse.

A wave of nausea crawled from my stomach to my throat. Holding back the vomit, I hoisted myself to my hands and knees, trying to stop what was about to happen, but I couldn't. Heaving violently, I spat out what was mostly bile. Between heaves, one of the men slapped the front wall of the carriage. "Clean that up, boy," he growled, "or I'll feed it back to you with a spoon."

I slid the blanket over the puddle, falling on it, too weak to find a better way to deal with the mess. With my back to Thoren's corpse, I faced the wall, shivering and weeping, wishing the awful ride would end, but terrified by what might come next.

The carriage rattled along the cobblestone streets of the Royal City in darkness, finally coming to a halt. Peeking through the little window, I could see the dark stone walls of the palace. Suddenly, a menacing face filled the window. "Boy, if you make one sound, I'll slit yer throat right here."

The men unhitched the horses, and I could hear the hooves clomping on the cobblestone, growing fainter and fainter until the street was once again quiet. I didn't dare to yell for help, fearing one of them had stayed back. It didn't seem likely that they'd leave the king's dead body unattended, but I feared they'd deal with me first.

Soon, I could hear chains rattling and voices whispering. Then the side door swung open, and a large hand reached into the darkness, finding my ankle and jerking me toward the door. With my feet protruding from the carriage, they placed shackles on my ankles. Then my body was pulled outside, and my wrists shackled as well. Too weak to resist, and nearly too weak to stand, I wondered if I'd be able to walk under the weight of the chains.

When he had me fully bound, the stubble-headed man took hold of the chain connecting my wrists and led me stumbling like a half-dead animal toward the northwest corner of the palace—the dungeon. Reaching a small door, he knocked with one knuckle, ever so lightly, and the door opened immediately. Placing his hand on the back of my head, the man pushed me inside. I tripped on the threshold, falling to my knees, where another guard grabbed the chain and jerked me back to my feet before the door slammed behind me.

In front of me was a narrow hall, dimly lit by wall-mounted torches on each side. Between the torches were barred cages, separated from one another by thick stone. As a boy, my father had once brought me to the dungeon with the chief warden, and I'd never asked to see it again. It was cold and damp, and the pungent odor of rancid flesh, along with the stench of human excrement, seemed to have permeated the very stone from which it was constructed. I went stiff when the awful smell reached my nostrils, but the guard jerked the chain, coaxing me along in helpless obedience.

320

From the tour, I remembered that this wing was separate from the rest of the dungeon—reserved for prisoners awaiting execution.

The guard placed a hood over my head and led me to a cell to blindly sit on a bench.

"Leave us," came a familiar voice, but whose?

The door swung closed, creaking on its hinges before latching, and the guard walked away.

"Why am I here?" I croaked, pushing air through a throat that was nearly swollen shut.

"Why, indeed," answered the voice. "You're awaiting execution, of course. Isn't that what happens to murderers?"

"Murder? What are you talking about?"

"Don't play games with me, young man. We found the gold in your belongings. As Thoren's so-called friend, you have private access. Now we only need to know who paid you to kill him."

"You're mad. What evidence do you have?"

"Well, the gold, of course. Not a bad price. But still, for the life of a king? I would think you could have demanded more. Tell me, Jens, who paid you to kill young Thoren?"

"I didn't kill him."

"Then how do you explain the gold?"

I started to speak, then stopped.

"Just as I thought—you can't explain it. Well, Jens, you best give me names. You don't want to die alone for this. Honor your father's legacy and come clean. Tell me who paid you."

When he mentioned my father, I recognized the voice. It was the advisor who approached me on the day of my induction ceremony. He spoke of my father then with the same tone of contempt he used now.

"I'm telling the truth. I have a witness who can attest to where I was and where that gold came from."

"A witness? Who?"

Again, I opened my mouth, but something made me close it again. For one thing, there was too much to explain. Strower and I had done many things behind Thoren's back, and I wasn't sure the truth would serve me very well. But beyond that, nothing made sense. Why had they brought me here in the dark? Why didn't they want me to see the face of my accuser? Why was I being held where there were no other prisoners? I knew this snake hated Thoren.

Realizing my life depended on my ability to think, I tried to clear the cobwebs. Was I being set up all along? No. No one knew I was traveling to Keenod except Strower and the cook, but perhaps I became a convenient scapegoat once I arrived. If Alden Fry and the advisor had something to do with the king's murder, they'd want to know if I had an alibi before publically accusing me. Otherwise, after my execution, someone might come forward and point a finger at them. Strower was the only witness who could testify where the gold came from, but if these men were already guilty of murdering Thoren, they wouldn't hesitate to kill a witness. Strower was the only man who could clear me, but I didn't dare speak his name.

The advisor was growing impatient. "I asked you once. Don't make me ask again. Who can attest to where the gold came from?"

I remained silent.

"Very well. Perhaps you'll talk with some persuasion. I'll return after Eric has knocked loose a memory or two. Sometimes they attach themselves to teeth." With that, he strode off, sending the guard back to do his dirty work.

The cell door opened and my hood came off. The guard standing before me was large, but he looked less menacing than I expected, his eyes sad—like he didn't want any part of this. But even if he didn't enjoy doling out pain, I knew he was bound to oblige the advisor or suffer himself. Taking hold of the chain that bound my wrists, he used his weight to anchor himself and spun me in a circle until my feet couldn't keep up with the rest of my body, which wasn't long, sick as I was. Then he let go of the chain, sending me flying into the stone wall and tumbling to the floor. Stunned by the impact on my shoulder and head, I lay face-down. The guard approached and took hold of my hair. Lifting my skull off the floor, he knelt and whispered in my ear. "You better tell him what he wants to hear, young man, or I'll be back for another dance."

Then, using my skull to push himself up, he ground my face into the stone floor. I heard a sound—much like a spade piecing hard soil—and I knew he'd snapped my front tooth. Finally, the door creaked closed, and he was gone. With considerable effort, I crawled back onto the bench, spitting out part of my tooth and feeling the jagged edge with my tongue. My shivering returned, convulsing my stiff joints. Now, completely quiet in the secluded wing, I sprawled on the bench, allowing a steady drip from somewhere unseen to enfold me into a merciful trance. Eventually, I lost consciousness.

With no way to see the sun and nothing to do but wait for more questioning and another beating, I lost track of time. Over and over, the advisor asked who else knew about the gold. The only variation was the eventual promise of a blanket if I named names. Every so often, the guard brought stale bread and water, but I was too sick to swallow anything other than a couple of soaked crumbs.

At one point, I reached into my pocket and found the note I'd written on my journey to Keenod. Slowly, I reread the words:

It's a fantasy of emotion,
creatures, offering life to one another.
We offer each other only companionship
on this hard journey.

Her body is not food.
Her blood is not drink.
The destination of my soul
lies beyond her arms.

For the longest time, I stared at the bread in the corner of my cell—more food I couldn't eat. Then, looking down at my blood-stained shirt, it occurred to me that I was now experiencing my most terrifying nightmare, yet somehow, I was strangely at peace. Death seemed likely, either by hanging or sickness, the latter spreading like mold in the cold, damp cell. Being executed for Thoren's murder would bring everlasting disgrace to my family, but even that thought couldn't rob me of the strange serenity. The current held me in its flow. I could trust it.

Remembering a conversation I had with Strower about the Great Sacrifice—what it might have been—I contemplated what price could buy an adoption, allowing a flawed human like me to be the Creator's child, to ride on His neck. Looking down at the parchment, the words *body* and *blood* glowed for a moment, and I suddenly realized the source of my peace. In my suffering, I sensed a fellowship. At that moment, I knew my adoption was somehow purchased with a life. And now that life—that mysterious presence—was alive within me.

CHAPTER 43

I heard the guard's boots tramping toward my cell. Bracing myself for another beating, I was surprised when he passed, continuing toward the door to the outside. Then, for a brief moment, everything was quiet again until I heard a much lighter set of footsteps, tip-toeing down the hall from the same direction the guard had come. Whoever it was, stopped before reaching my cell.

More time elapsed. Then, I heard a knock at the door, which opened to a cacophony of shuffling feet, grunting, and cussing.

When the tangle of humanity reached my cell, I was shocked to see Bear, bruised and bloody, but not as bruised and bloody as the pair of headed-stumps that had hold of him. The guard was pulling on Bear's wrist-chain from the front, while Alden Fry's men pushed from behind. All three of them were keeping their faces and vital organs as far from the writhing giant as possible. But when they had him near my cell door, the guard stopped for a moment, giving Bear a chance to notice me. When he did, his rage turned to confusion, but before he could utter a word, the guard once again began pulling, and Fry's men resumed pushing, and the four of them continued wrestling their way down the hall.

Once they finally had Bear corralled in a cell, his captors passed before me again, accompanied by the guard. The outside door creaked open, then closed, and the guard passed a third time, now walking the length of the hall and retreating into the other wing of the dungeon.

"Why are *you* here?" Bear shouted.

Intending to shout back, but only achieving a loud whisper, I said, "Someone is listening. They've accused me of killing King Thoren."

"Same here."

"Don't say any more. They want to destroy our alibi." I used the word *alibi*, hoping he would realize I was talking about Strower, but I knew the code was probably too cryptic.

"What do you mean?"

"Just stop talking."

With Bear arrested, I was more convinced than ever that Alden Fry and the advisor were behind Thoren's death, and that they'd used my appearance in Keenod opportunistically to concoct the story that Bear had paid me that gold to murder the king. No doubt they'd also dreamt up a motive of some kind, and since Bear had already sat in prison under suspicion of stealing the king's gold, people would probably believe their story. I was now sure that my withholding of Strower's name was the only thing keeping the two of us from being formally accused and executed. But they wouldn't wait long. A dead king requires expedience, and sooner rather than later, they'd have to chance a damning witness at-large and make their accusations formal. Time was running out.

For what seemed like hours, Bear and I sat quietly in our cells, neither of us saying another word. Then, I heard the door to the other wing open, and the guard's boots—a sound I dreaded—once again marching down the hall. His steps hesitated momentarily in front of the cell next to mine, where I imagined the eavesdropper was shaking his head that he still didn't have the information he needed.

This time, the guard angrily entered my cell. "You'll talk today," he said. "I'm finished playing games with you."

Suddenly Bear's voice boomed through the entire wing. "YOU WANT TO FIGHT? YOU COWARD! COME HERE, COME HERE, COME HERE . . ." He kept repeating those two words louder and louder, rattling the door of his cage as he yelled.

Finally, the guard turned his face toward Bear's cell, evaluating the giant's threats through the safety of several stone walls. Realizing his attention had momentarily shifted from me, I dove at his ankles. I'm not sure what I was hoping to accomplish, but somehow the valor in Bear's thunderous voice resounded in my soul like a war-drum, pumping momentary strength into my sickly limbs. Wrapping the guard's ankles with both arms, I pushed against his shins with my shoulder, kicking the wall for leverage. Having nothing he could reach to balance himself, the guard gradually began falling backward like a felled tree. His rump hit the stone floor first, then his shoulders, but his head clanked against the iron bars and remained in that propped position as if he'd fallen asleep reading a book.

Staring expectantly, I thought the guard's eyes would at any moment pop open, but instead, his knees drew up spastically before stiffening straight as a spear. I didn't know if he was dead or only unconscious. Before stepping over his body, I pulled the ring of keys from his belt. Then, exiting my cage, I swung the door closed behind me, peering into the next cell, where the sour-faced advisor was sitting on the bench, his mouth agape. I lunged for the door to his cell and pushed it closed before he could escape. Realizing the tables were turned, and that he was now *my* prisoner, he began demanding immediate release.

Ignoring him, I slowly made my way to Bear, who'd grown quiet after hearing the advisor's tantrum. When Bear saw me with the ring of keys, his jaw fell open too.

"How did you—"

"Doesn't matter," I whispered, trying various keys in his cell door. I was winded and could barely get enough air through my swollen throat to breathe, let alone talk.

Bear couldn't hear me over the din of the advisor. To silence the old man, he issued a threat. "Shut your mouth. That cage is keeping you alive."

The dungeon was instantly quiet again. When I finally found the right key, Bear emerged boldly from his cell, striding a few paces to lay eyes on the advisor, who had shrunk into the corner.

"Should I beat some answers out of him?" Bear asked.

"No. I doubt that he'd survive it. Then we'd be in a worse mess."

Reluctantly, Bear turned away from the advisor. "Let's get out of here."

When we reached the door to the outside, we discovered it too needed a key. Once again, I tried various options from the ring while Bear began asking questions.

"Fry told me they found the missing gold. He said it proves that I paid someone to kill the king. Are you that *someone* they're talking about?"

Placing my index finger on my lips, I signaled for him to keep his voice down. I knew the advisor would be straining to hear us. Then I whispered as softly as I could, "Strower and I found the gold in the Valley. We discovered the priest's hiding place. I was bringing it back to Thoren."

"Was he alive? Did you see him?"

"I don't know when he was killed. They nabbed me before I could see him." Then, jabbing my thumb over my shoulder, I pointed to our prisoner without taking my eyes off the key ring. "That's one of Thoren's advisors. I think he and Alden Fry had something to do with Thoren's death. They're working together. Strower's the only other man who knows where that gold came from. I told this advisor that I had a witness, but I wouldn't tell him who. I think they'd kill William if they knew he could clear us. We know too much. They're desperate to discover how I acquired that gold."

Bear looked back toward the advisor's cell as if reconsidering whether to pay him a visit. Just then, I found the right key, and the door opened. It was broad daylight outside. Bear took a couple of steps toward freedom and then stopped, waiting for me to follow. When I didn't, he came back inside.

"What are you waiting for?"

"You're too big, and I'm too sick to escape when it's light. I can hardly walk, let alone run. I don't know who knows about us, but if the guards do, they'll catch us before we're off the grounds."

Bear reclosed the door. "So be it. We'll wait until dark."

Several hours elapsed. Periodically, Bear cracked open the door to see if the sun had set. Sitting on the cold stone floor, I began coughing. Sore as my throat was, the coughing was nearly as torturous as the beatings. In the midst of one of my spells, Bear suddenly stood up, turning his ear toward the hallway. He'd heard something. When my coughing subsided, I heard it too—boots marching.

"Let's go," Bear whispered.

"No. You go."

"What about you?"

"I'd only slow you down. Besides, if we're together, we'll look like we're conspiring. Go."

Bear hesitated for an instant, then he opened the door and disappeared into the night.

Seconds later, four men stood before the advisor's cell, two of them wearing guard's uniforms. One of the men in plain clothing saw me sitting by the door and came running over, yelling my name. To my surprise, it was Marcus.

"He's been beaten," Marcus yelled to the others.

In no time, the men had released the advisor and came rushing over to me.

"He murdered the king," spat the advisor.

"Nonsense," Marcus replied, helping me to my feet.

When the contingency reached us, I recognized the warden. He'd aged, but it was the same man who'd given my father and me a tour of the dungeon.

"Do I know you?" he asked.

"Yes, my father was Jacoby Berrit."

"Sure. I can see it now. You look like him."

"Lock him up," commanded the advisor.

The warden turned, glaring at the old man. "This is my dungeon, sir, and this man is down here without my knowledge. I'll conduct this inquiry."

The advisor stiffened. "Your own guard lies on the floor of this man's cell."

The warden gave the nod to one of his men, who went to check. A moment later, the man yelled from my cell, "He's dead!"

Now, the warden's brow furrowed, erasing the affection he'd shown me a moment earlier. In a low voice, he asked, "What have you done?"

"He was beating me," I whispered, almost inaudibly. "I pushed him backward, and he hit his head."

"Why was this man being beaten?" the warden asked, staring at the advisor.

"To learn who else was involved in the conspiracy to kill the king. The safety of Tuva is at stake."

Taking a step backward, the warden gazed at the floor, presumably deciding what to do next. Finally, he turned again to the advisor. "You sir, have no authority to use this dungeon to interrogate suspects. Guilty or not, you've kidnapped this man, and you've obviously enticed my guard to do your bidding behind my back, and now he's lying dead in one of my cells." Then, still glaring at the advisor, but pointing at me, he added, "My guard's death is as much on your head as it is his."

"But—"

"Stop! Don't forget where you are. I'm in charge down here." Then, looking at Marcus, he said, "Young man, tell me again why you're here."

Marcus blurted his words in rapid succession. "I rode to Keenod from Saleton because I have the fastest horse. I was sent by the farmers to deliver this map to Jens—it's the Valley of Ten Tribes. The Daggite's ain't there no more. The farmers around Saleton want it. We're plannin' to grow beets for export." Marcus then unfolded the map, showing the warden.

Displaying no particular interest in the details of the map, the warden turned to the advisor. "I've heard nothing about Tuva occupying the Valley. What do you know of this?"

"Pff. Young Thoren has been involved in a thousand forms of mischief, never informing us of any of it. It's no wonder he's dead."

Returning his attention to Marcus, the warden asked what happened when he went to Keenod.

"Well, half-way there," Marcus began, "I stopped at an inn. I had to eat and rest my horse. People were all up in arms, saying the king was dead.

They said the port was closin' to protect our borders. They were talking about the Daggite invasions in the south, and how Thoren couldn't protect Tuva because all his soldiers were off guarding cargo. They said it served him right that no one was there to protect him."

The warden repeated his question, trying to keep Marcus's story from straying too far. "What happened when you went to Keenod?"

"I couldn't find anyone who knew Jens. While I was thinkin' what to do, I asked the stable boy at the palace if he could spare a little hay for my horse. The two of us got talkin', and he recognized my description of Jens from that wagon he drove and the big horses. He said the wagon mysteriously showed up at the stable, but no Jens. I saw the wagon myself. The stable boy sleeps in that fancy barn. He told me he woke up hearing a commotion in the middle of the night—the same day the wagon showed up, the same day the king died. He snuck outside and watched a couple men throw a body in the back of a locked carriage and then leave in the dark. He figured they were taking Thoren's corpse to the Royal City."

"Why did you decide to come here?" asked the warden.

"Well, a man can't just disappear, can he? I wondered why they'd be sneaking around in the middle of the night. I figured maybe the king's corpse wasn't the only body locked in that carriage. I knew Jens and the king were close. I asked around at the docks, and someone told me that carriage hauls gold between the mining village and this palace. They said it only comes to Keenod once in a while to bring supplies for the dock workers. So I figured if there was gold or a dead king in that carriage, it'd be comin' here."

The warden shook his head. "What a tale. By my word, I thought you were insane when you came to me with that story, wanting to see my prisoners. I only half-listened. The only reason I agreed to come down here is to find my missing guard. He hadn't returned from his rounds."

Then, turning to me, the warden asked, "Why were you in Keenod?"

"To ask King Thoren to deed the Valley of Ten Tribes to the farmers."

The warden's forehead seemed to grow more wrinkled as the story took on more wrinkles. "Did *you* have something to do with clearing the Daggites from the valley?" he asked.

"No," I croaked, finally grateful that Strower hadn't allowed my involvement. "I was only there to purchase hay from the farmers who'd lost their cattle in the raids. Thoren needs a ship full of hay for the king of Sagan."

"Did you see the king?"

"No. I'd grown sick on the way and was sleeping on the wagon's bench when they took me."

"He's lying," said the advisor. "A large payment of gold was found in his wagon. He killed King Thoren."

"What motive would he have for killing his friend?"

"One of the palace guards in Keenod will tell you that he visited Thoren several days ago. He brought a man along with him. Some sort of dispute broke out between that man and the king. The man stormed out of Thoren's study, angry as a wasp." Then the advisor pointed his bony finger in my face. "Do you deny it?"

"No," I whispered, realizing he'd been busy building his case.

"Who was that man?" asked the warden.

Reluctantly, I whispered, "His name is William Strower. He can tell you where that gold came from."

"No, he can't," said Marcus.

"What?"

"I'm sorry you have to hear it like this, Jens, but Mr. Strower is dead."

"What?"

"Someone slit his throat on top of that big rock. Mr. Strower called it the Giant's Table. After the land was divided, the farmers made camp and started celebrating. Mr. Strower wanted to be alone, so he hiked off to that rock. When he didn't come down in the morning, I climbed up to see if he was okay . . ."

Marcus kept talking, but I couldn't hear him anymore. My mind stopped racing. I was no longer worried about staying alive. I stopped caring about my innocence. My best friend was dead, and I was guilty of breaking the one promise I'd have died to keep. Carrie's request repeated itself over and over in my mind—*Keep my father safe.* Being accused of Thoren's murder suddenly seemed like backdoor justice, and the sickness I'd been trying to hold off now seemed like a friend, showing up to take me away. Releasing myself to it fully, I was overtaken by the dizzying lethargy, robbing whatever strength remained. I collapsed onto the floor.

CHAPTER 44

"Would you like to talk about it?" asked my mother.

I couldn't count how many times she'd asked me that question, nor how many days I'd been lying there, but from the first time she asked it, my answer was always the same. Rolling over in bed, I gave her my back.

It was the third morning since my fever broke, and the hallucinations stopped. That much I knew. The hallucinations were sometimes terrifying and other times wonderful—nothing I could recall now, just raw emotions in full costume, prancing about in my mind without a script. I'd have snippets of coherence when my mother set a fresh rag on my forehead, and cold water ran down my temples and into my ears. But then the characters whisked me off again.

When the fever finally retreated, I couldn't close my eyes without seeing Strower lying on the Giant's Table. Preferring the hallucinations, I kept hoping that if I kept quiet with my eyes closed, maybe he'd wake up. But now, on this third day since the imaginary characters packed up and left, I could no longer hope for a different ending. Why was I spared, while a better man lost his life?

"Wait," I blurted, as my mother was leaving the room, "I lost a friend."

"I know," she replied, probably thinking I was referring to Thoren, "And I nearly lost you."

Slowly, I sat up. "How did I get here? Why did they release me?"

"Thomas brought you here."

"Thomas? Who's Thomas?"

"The warden," she replied, making her way back to my bed and feeling my forehead with her hand. "He hauled you here in that cart they use to transport prisoners." Then she smiled a warm smile. "I've had some explaining to do with my neighbors."

Taking a deep breath, I said, "Then explain it to me."

She pulled up a chair next to my bed. "Thomas was an old friend of your father's. He doesn't live far from here. Well, perhaps they weren't friends in the usual sense, but at least they admired one another. I think they both understood the weight of their responsibilities, and neither of them used their position selfishly. That's a very small fraternity among the king's staff."

"But why did he release me? That advisor wanted me tried for Thoren's murder."

My mother frowned, her face turning cold and judicial. "That advisor was hanged by his neck, along with Alden Fry and two others."

"Huh?" I grunted. With the dead now at six, I wondered how long I'd been in bed, but I didn't ask. I was too eager to hear more. "How is that possible?"

"Thoren's brother Gabriel has taken the throne," she replied, her face softening again. "Remember him? He was always such a serious boy."

"Of course I do. Thoren and I were never very good to him, though— we didn't include him. He was always left alone."

"Well, in Thomas's opinion, he'll make a fine king. Perhaps his character is better off for having been left alone by his brother."

"No doubt . . . but how was I released?"

"I was getting to that. Even bedridden, you're terribly impatient."

My mother's stories usually contained more details than I thought necessary, so I made a habit of hurrying them along. I'm sure she'd been carefully curating the specifics of my ordeal until I was ready to hear it, and she wasn't one to skip over things. I propped my pillow against the

335

headboard and tried to lean back and relax.

"I'm sorry," I mumbled.

Closing her eyes to remember where she'd left off, she continued, "King Gabriel placed Thomas in charge of investigating the accusations against you. He told me privately that Gabriel didn't know who else he could trust. It's a good thing, too. Thomas was no admirer of Mr. Penton."

"Who's that?"

"The advisor behind all of this. Your father didn't like him very well—and Penton despised your father."

"Oh yes, I'm aware of that."

"Well, I suppose I know more than I should. Thomas has been here twice to check on your health, each time giving me more details. He must feel we're owed that much."

"Tell me."

"He said your friend, Bear, returned to the palace shortly after escaping the dungeon—a huge man, I'm told. He couldn't leave you, Jens. He came back to sort things out. That's a good friend."

I nodded. It seemed odd to hear my mother call Bear my friend. We'd hardly spoken to one another before our imprisonment. I remembered the old cook saying, "Bear goes when Bear goes." Like his namesake, Bear was a creature of instinct, and like Marcus, his instincts led him straight to the palace at just the right time. As thankful as I was for the two of them, I was even more overwhelmed with gratitude to the One who seeded their instincts.

My mother continued, "Thomas separated Mr. Penton, Alden Fry, and the two worthless men from the port, interrogating them individually. With no loyalty to one another, they began tattling like children, each trying to make himself look innocent at the expense of the others."

I shook my head. "What a spectacle that must've been."

"I'm sure. Anyway, piecing together their stories, Thomas was able to arrive at the truth—especially with your two friends explaining things from their side. The four were found guilty of either murder or treason. I can't remember now who was convicted of which. It doesn't really matter—the penalty for both is hanging. King Gabriel made short work of their execution. Thomas said Gabriel wanted to send a message to the other advisors."

"Why? Were others involved?"

"Thomas believes so. He couldn't conceive that the rumors of the port closing and the spreading of fear throughout the kingdom could've been accomplished by so few. Who knows if the advisors are really concerned about our safety? Thomas thinks they're more concerned about protecting their allotment than our borders."

My mind was racing to keep up. Almost to myself, I said, "I suppose the other advisors will distance themselves from Penton's crusade now. They won't want a rope around their necks."

"Yes, according to Thomas, that's what Gabriel is hoping. Whether they were involved or not, Gabriel doesn't want his advisors thinking they can push him around. The port seems to be here to stay, and honestly I think Gabriel will make a much better king than Thoren. He's more level-headed, more like his father."

"Did Thomas find out how they birthed this plot?"

For some reason, this question made my mother laugh. "Oh goodness, yes," she said, "Penton had apparently been paying Alden Fry to incite the invasions along the southern border." Then she shook her head.

"What's funny about that?"

Sensing I was in no mood for laughter, she turned serious again. "Oh, it's just something Thomas told me: The invasions were already occurring when Alden Fry offered to incite them for pay."

"I don't understand. Why would Penton pay Fry to incite invasions that were already happening?"

"Penton didn't know they were happening."

"Oh, I see. Fry was being an opportunist."

Nodding, my mother continued, "And Penton wasn't happy to learn it. Once Thomas pulled on that snagged thread, their whole quilt began unraveling—both men wanting so badly to see the other hanged."

"Well then, I guess they both succeeded," I mumbled, gazing out the window, slowly fitting the pieces together in my mind. "But why was Penton willing to pay Fry to incite the invasions in the first place?"

"He thought that if Tuvans began fearing invasions, he'd have an easier time swaying sentiment against the port. He was only trying to create fear."

Nodding, I waited for her to continue.

"Penton also tasked Fry with finding the right opportunity to take the king's life, promising to make him very wealthy if he did. That's one of the reasons Thomas believes more advisors were involved—it would likely have taken the help of others to compile the sum promised to Mr. Fry."

"That makes sense, but I still don't see how they managed to get me involved."

"Thomas told me that Fry happened upon you while you slept in your wagon alongside the road outside The Crucible. Apparently, Fry had just left the mining camp, where he'd discovered that Bear had set off for Tinsdal with a farmer—and you for Keenod. One of the miners told Fry that the farmer Bear was traveling with was the same man who'd gone to Saleton days earlier with you and a Daggite."

My mother paused from her story. "Is that true? Were you traveling with someone from Dag?"

It would have taken far too long to explain Joar to my mother. "Yes," I said. "Please go on."

"Well, I don't know many more of the details, but finding that gold in your wagon is what inspired Alden Fry's plan. He thought he could tie you together with Bear and that farmer—make it look like the three of you were conspiring with the Daggites against Tuva—but he hadn't learned the farmer's identity. Bear told Thomas about the gold—how it was stolen from the mining camp by a Daggite priest." Then she paused again. Wanting to clear up her confusion about my involvement with Dag, she asked, "Was it the same Daggite who traveled with you to Saleton?"

"No mother," I replied, realizing how strange the story must have sounded to her, "different Daggites."

"Oh . . . Well, Thomas still wants to ask you about the gold. He told me it was a hefty sum, and they can't rightfully return it to the king's treasury until you verify where you found it. I think he was hoping you'd be awake the last time he stopped, but at least he knew it wasn't a payment for murdering the king."

Then she paused a third time, waiting for me to tell her about the gold. "We found it in a little cavern," I said, remembering Strower's mischievous smile when he dropped the sack outside the tent. The memory made me incredibly sad. My mother nodded eagerly, obviously hoping for more details, but I couldn't continue. A nauseous wave of grief was working its way to the surface, and I knew her questions would be endless once I started explaining things. "I'm sorry, mother, but it's a long story, and I'm exhausted. Can I explain it to you later?"

"Of course, but I haven't even told you about the farmers yet."

"What farmers?"

"The farmers who drove their wagons here from Saleton—full of hay."

"Here? To the Royal City?"

"Yes, to the palace grounds."

"Why?"

"When they heard the rumors of the port closing, they came in protest with their contracts in hand."

"How many?"

"I've heard thirty came with hay, but they've collected sympathizers along the way. Rumors say hundreds have arrived so far, and more coming. Thomas told me that the young man from Saleton—the one who came to find you in prison—has been meeting with King Gabriel, negotiating on behalf of the thirty to have the Valley of Ten Tribes given to them for growing beets. Gabriel will sign the documents tomorrow. The palace is planning a celebration and a parade, sending the farmers off to The Crucible with their hay. Thomas thinks it's a wonderful diversion for Gabriel. It will endear him to his subjects." Then my mother's eyes grew moist. "You must have played a big part in this, Jens. Your father would have been so proud of you."

"I'm happy for them," I replied, staring numbly out the window.

Probably sensing my conflict at having Marcus finish my assignment, my mother's voice sounded artificially upbeat. "The new land will be called Strower Valley," she announced. "The farmers insisted. They say it's named after that man from Tinsdal. Did you know him well?"

I didn't answer. I couldn't.

She placed her hand on my wrist. "I'm told he died. The king is bringing his family from Tinsdal for the ceremony tomorrow—to honor their father's sacrifice."

A cold spear stabbed through my heart, and hot tears began streaming down the side of my face as I imagined Carrie and her brothers taken to the Royal City in the king's carriage—props to embellish Gabriel's popularity—to celebrate their father's death. Seeing my anguish, my mother whispered, "You must have been close with Mr. Strower."

"He's the friend I lost," I whispered. Then, turning my face, I stared blankly at the wall.

After a long silence, she said, "I'll let you rest."

CHAPTER 45

I woke the next morning feeling some of my energy returning. My mother had left for the market, giving me the rare chance to have the house to myself. So I ambled into the gathering room and sat in my father's chair with the Holy Book on my lap. Then, remembering how Strower had situated himself on his porch, I pulled up a second chair for a conversation with the Creator. But just as I was settling in, I heard a knock. I shuffled to the door on weak legs, surprised to see to the king's courier standing outside, dressed in royal attire.

"Jens Berrit?" he asked, when I opened the door.

"Yes."

"I have a dispatch from King Gabriel."

After signing a ledger of some sort, the courier handed me the correspondence and was on his way.

I returned to my father's chair and broke the wax seal.

To Jens Berrit,
I thank you for your faithful service to my brother, the king.
I hope you will understand that as Tuva's new king,
I feel obliged to appoint new ministers.
In light of recent events, a fresh start seems the best way to move forward.
As such, I've given the post of Minister of Agriculture to Marcus Patch.
He is uniquely qualified to represent Tuva's interests—both the interests of the crown
and also the interests of the farmers.
Once again, thank you for your service to Tuva.
My blessings on your future.

I sat for some time, silently staring at the note. My reason for sitting in my father's chair and opening the Holy Book was to seek guidance on how to move forward without Strower, but now I had no place to move.

Crumpling the letter, I threw it in the fireplace, where it could serve as kindling for the next chilly morning. But then I retrieved it again, using both hands to flatten the parchment before placing it between two pages of the book. For all I knew, this letter of gratitude, shallow as it was, might represent the only accomplishment I could someday share with my children.

I tried for a while to read from the Holy Book, hoping to find comfort, but I couldn't concentrate. Like a thousand butterflies on a vast prairie, the words seemed to float about on the page. "How should I feel?" I inquired of the chair. I wanted to be angry, but with who? Marcus? Gabriel? I couldn't dispute either of their decisions—and Marcus had saved my life. How could I be angry with him? Gabriel was simply cleaning up his brother's mess—a mess that had splashed all over me. Besides, against all odds, I was alive and free. "I should be grateful," I told the chair.

For a long time, I sat there, trying to gather my thoughts. My future aside, I was glad that Gabriel was embracing Tuva's farmers. William would've been thrilled that our new king had hoisted his sails to capture the prevailing wind, endearing himself to those who worked the land. Although Gabriel was using Carrie and her brothers to bolster his popularity, I couldn't resent him for making their father a hero. William Strower was a hero—a man for future generations to admire. I only hoped the historians would capture his essence—not the swagger of a conqueror, but the humility of a man surrendered to his Creator and called to a purpose.

Joar deserved half the credit for Tuva's progress, but like me, he'd probably be left out of our history altogether. The king's historians would write it as they preferred, preserving the dignity of the king and retelling only the noble parts. Thoren would be the visionary of Tuva's rebirth, Gabriel, its implementer, and Tuva would continue to be—in Joar's word— *peecho.*

I was deep in thought when my mother returned from the market. "You're looking better," she said. "Was someone here?"

"No," I replied, suddenly feeling embarrassed for having pulled up the chair. She was holding a bowl that she'd retrieved from the nightstand in my bedroom.

"You didn't touch your soup last night," she scolded. "I made it in celebration of your accomplishments."

"You know I hate beets."

Waving off the remark, she looked out the window. "I wish your father were here. It's an important day for Tuva, and his son played a huge role."

I stared at the chair.

Still gazing out the window, she continued, "I heard at the market this morning that Gabriel has commissioned a statue of Mr. Strower to rest on the palace grounds. He obviously wants to win the hearts of the farmers." After she said it, there was a long pause. I couldn't tell if she was looking at something out the window, or if she was contemplating what to say next. Finally, she turned to me. "Do you feel strong enough to attend the parade? It's only a short walk to the route. The fresh air would do you good."

Was I strong enough? That question had already presented itself in my ruminating. I was now physically strong enough to walk the short distance to the wide cobblestone street—but to see Carrie's face? I didn't feel like I'd ever be that strong. I needed to see her, though. I needed to see her moving forward without her father—and I needed to find closure for myself. My soul had attached itself too possessively to the memory of her kiss. In order for me to find a path forward, that memory needed replacing with something less intimate. I was hoping that by gazing at her anonymously at the parade, nestled among a throng of my countrymen, knowing that my eyes were just two of thousands admiring her, I might be released from her sway. She'd asked one thing of me, and I'd failed to deliver it. Because of me, Carrie and her brothers were trading a living father for a dead hero— and sharing him today with the rest of Tuva. Now, my affection for her— so heavily concentrated—needed diluting, so it could be shared with Tuva as well. It was only fair.

"Yes, I'm strong enough."

Sauntering down the dusty avenue, my mother held my elbow to steady my wobbly legs. As we neared the great street, I could hear the growing clamor of the crowd. Tuva loved cutting loose and celebrating. I wondered if this memorial would become an annual event. Thanks to Strower and Joar, Tuva was now a little larger.

As happens at every parade, the libation vendors from the merchant district brought their goods, and I could hear them crowing above the tumult, "ALE! ALE!" Another voice cried out, "RUM! TUVA'S FINEST!"

I scoffed at that, causing my mother to turn and look at me. *If Strower had a say in the matter,* I thought to myself, *they'd be selling Lundgren's rum.*

When we reached the main avenue that leads to the palace, the crowd was too large for us to see anything. If I'd been healthier, I could've elbowed my way to the front, but in my current state, I barely had enough strength to stand on my own. After surveying the situation, my mother suggested we walk north, where the property facing the street was elevated. She had a friend living on that hill, on whose steps she thought we could sit.

When we arrived at the house of my mother's friend, we discovered that her steps were already full of people. Fortunately, we found seating on the hillside, and no sooner had we settled in, than the jugglers arrived, dressed in brightly colored costumes with exaggerated smiles painted on their faces. One of them actually juggled beets—four at a time—probably honoring Tuva's new export crop. Another threw clay jugs into the air, spinning them with perfect rotation, their narrow necks racing around just in time to be reached by the juggler's outstretched hand.

A mean-spirited spectator pushed his drunken friend into the street in front of the jug thrower, upsetting his timing and causing all three jugs to smash on the cobblestone. Clay fragments flew in every direction. Some people laughed, while others chastised the bewildered culprit, who was frantically trying to nuzzle his way back into the crowd. Undaunted, the performer invited onlookers to throw something else he could juggle and was soon barraged with a storm of hats. Someone decided to toss a shoe, which hit the juggler on his shoulder. A cane followed close behind, barely missing his head. The crowd roared with laughter. Finally, the resourceful juggler chose two hats and the shoe and was off juggling again.

Next came the drumline, pounding their sticks, first on the stretched leather, then on the drum's wooden frame, BOOMITY BOOM, then CLICKITY CLACK, BOOMITY BOOM, CLICKITY CLACK. The drums seemed to capture the crowd's energy and release it in spurts. I caught myself holding my breath, the pulse feeling like my own heartbeat. I held my hand to my chest, remembering the absurd dream I had after Joar's ceremony.

Behind the drummers, the captain of the guard yelled his cadence. The soldiers marched in formation, their red jackets and white trousers impeccably pressed, swords gleaming in the sun, and boots pounding the street in perfect unison.

Following the guards, the royal chariot rolled down the street with Gabriel, Tuva's new king, standing next to the driver, waving to the crowd. The horses pulling the chariot seemed to understand the pomp of the event, hesitating between majestic strides and raising their hooves high in the air.

I hadn't seen Thoren's brother since he was a boy. Now, every bit as handsome as Thoren had been, he wore the purple cloak, and his blonde hair shimmered with oil, forming golden ringlets below his crown. The young girls screamed when they saw him, probably dreaming of one day being his queen.

The king's chariot had so captivated the crowd that no one gave much attention to the next carriage until it was almost upon us. It was, in fact, King Gabriel who shifted our focus by turning and extending his right arm toward the Strower family, inviting the crowd to honor them. Cheers filled the air as Will, Carrie, Magnus, and Rasmus passed by, waving hesitantly. Dressed in their best outfits, the twins stood, one on each side of the bench, seeming uncomfortably separated from their threadbare play clothes.

Will and Carrie sat on the bench together, Will's arm wrapping his sister's shoulder. She was beyond beautiful, wearing what I guessed to be one of her mother's dresses, emerald green and fitted attractively to the sleek curves that she normally kept hidden beneath looser clothing. With her long golden curls, bright eyes, and sunbaked skin, she looked like a jewel, set in place by her brother's strong arm.

"She's beautiful, isn't she?" observed my mother, whom I sensed to be studying my face, appraising my reaction, but I couldn't look away. I hated sharing my affection with the crowd. I hated having her beauty on display. I hated the men who'd stepped into the street to gain a better look, causing her to bury her face in Will's shoulder. I hated it all—but I couldn't turn away. I drank it like awful-tasting medicine.

Following the Strowers, a long line of farmers pulled dilapidated wagons full of hay behind tired horses. The farmers pumped their fists like they'd won a great battle. The crowd cheered wildly. I recognized all thirty—I'd sat at their tables, drafting the very contracts they were now redeeming. Watching all of this anonymously from the crowd made it seem like a dream.

When the parade ended, my mother and I sat for a long while, waiting for the people to disperse. "Are you ready to go back?" she finally asked.

Back? I felt a pit in my stomach. Back to what? In my mind, I saw the bearded face of the wool merchant. I saw my cramped apartment above his shop. Was I ready to go back? "No," I replied, with an intensity that surprised my mother.

"Do you need to sit a while longer?"

"No. I'd like to walk to the palace. I want to see Strower's statue."

"But it's not carved yet. It's only a block of granite."

"All the same."

"Alright. It is a beautiful day for a walk."

"I'd like to do this myself," I said, turning away from my mother and looking up the street toward the palace.

"Hmmm, I think I should come along. You're not very strong yet."

"I'm stronger than you think." Then, turning, I saw her helpless expression. Placing my arm around her shoulder, I gave her a quick squeeze. "I need to be alone for a while. I need to sort some things out."

"You're so much like your father. I share my thoughts while I'm thinking them, but your father, he'd never share anything until he'd quietly worked it through his brain. I suppose I shouldn't expect anything different from you."

"I suppose not."

"Well, go then. But don't think I'm not going to watch you walk. If you collapse in the street, someone will need to roll you off to the side."

I stood, summoning all my strength, trying to make a good show of it. I needed to walk confidently until she couldn't see me any longer. Then I could hobble, limp, or crawl the rest of the way. "I'll be home for supper." I said.

I was exhausted by the time I reached the palace. From a distance, I could hear the sculptor's hammer and chisel, so I followed the clanking until I came upon a group of people gathered around the grumpy artist. He was muttering foul words under his breath. Apparently, he didn't like working under the scrutiny of a crowd. As my mother had predicted, the statue was, thus far, only a block of granite with a few edges knocked off.

"What will it be when it's finished?" asked a curious onlooker.

The sculptor gave no response. Another man in the crowd, who'd perhaps imbibed libations at the parade, shouted, "It looks to me like a statue of a rock!" The crowd laughed, inviting a reproachful glare from the artist.

On the other end of the green courtyard stood the white marble statue— my faceless lover, her outstretched arms calling me away from the crowd, away from the granite Strower, and away from my depressing thoughts. She, too, was alone. I walked to her and stood for a long time, looking at her elegant white arms and the smooth curves of her breasts. She was still beautiful to me, but it felt different now to gaze at her. Gone were the intense longings she conjured. Gone was the promise of eternal comfort. She no longer embodied my desire. Now, she was merely a fellow soul reaching for something more.

At that moment, I realized that I'd found *something more*. Standing next to the statue, I closed my eyes and focused on *balama*. Gradually, the sadness of returning to my old life fell away. I realized I could no longer allow circumstances—which can change in a heartbeat—to dictate my happiness. Nor could I let my fellow creatures determine my worth. An invisible King had adopted me, and that singular act would now rule my soul. Lying in the grass under the smooth face of the white statue, I closed my eyes and let the sun's radiance kiss my face.

Then I heard her soft voice, "I hoped I'd find you here."

Opening my eyes, I looked up to see Carrie admiring the woman I'd described to her in the hayloft. She had now replaced her mother's emerald dress with one of her own, but she was no less breathtaking in my sight.

With one hand sliding across the smooth while stone, Carrie looked down at me. "She is quite beautiful."

"Where are your brothers?" I stammered, scrambling to my feet.

"Will has the twins inside the palace. They're having a tour—if you can imagine. Magnus and Rasmus are wearing terribly on our guide's nerves, though—interrupting with endless questions and touching what they were told not to."

She smiled, which made me smile. When she saw my chipped tooth, she touched my face. "Jens, what happened?"

I squelched the smile. "Oh, I spent some time in the dungeon," I said, immediately hating how sorry for myself I sounded. "It was nothing," I added. "Everything worked out."

"Jens!" she gasped, now inspecting me up and down, "You're nothing but skin and bones. Tell me what happened."

"It's a long story. I've been sick, but I'm better now—just weak."

Carrie glanced at the palace. "I need to get back. I was watching for you. Every time the tour brought us by those windows, I looked down. I'm sure my brothers thought I was watching the sculptor." Then, glancing again at the faceless statue, she said, "I hoped to find you with her." Then, bravely fixing her eyes on mine, she added, "I have something for you." Pulling a folded piece of parchment from the waistband of her skirt, she then handed it to me.

"What is it?"

"It's what my father was working on the night that big man dropped him off. He told me he was making a map. I think he drew it on this scrap first, before making the final document."

"Why are you giving it to me?"

Her eyes fell. "I don't know. If nothing else, it can be a reminder of him."

I unfolded the parchment. It was torn on the edges and ill-shaped, but the drawing was what Strower had described—a wheel, with property lines for spokes, and names scrawled between the lines. The only difference from what I had imagined was a small round hub in the center of the wheel, circling the Giant's Table. Holding the map between us, Carrie studied it while I studied Carrie. I'd have the rest of my life to examine that scrap of parchment, but I knew my time with her was coming to an end.

"Thank you," I whispered.

"Well, I'd better get back. I've abandoned the tour without announcement." Then she held out her arms, striking a very similar pose to the statue, waiting for me to claim her embrace. I hesitated, not wanting to lose sight of her eyes, and not wanting to say goodbye.

Finally, I fell in and buried my eyes between her shoulder and neck. "I'm so sorry," I groaned. Then her shoulder began convulsing against my forehead, and her lips, which were touching my ear, emitted a pained sigh. Suddenly, she pulled away, and without looking up, ran toward the palace.

I stood watching, hoping that she'd turn to look back, but she didn't. Within moments, she was gone—vanished around the corner of the gigantic building. Leaning against the statue, I slid to a seated position in the grass, staring off into the distance. The tide had now leveled everything.

"Waves are cruel," I whispered.

I don't know how long my reverie lasted, but I finally looked down and noticed the parchment in my hand. The spokes of the wheel, like arrows placed on the map to direct my eyes, all pointed to the hub—the circle drawn around the Giant's Table—where Strower had met his end.

Strower had measured the circle sixty paces in every direction from the Giant's Table and labeled it with the words *sugar mill*. Tears filled my eyes. He couldn't let go of that dream. He'd drawn the river on the west side of the rock, running southeast, with dark lines spanning from one bank to the other. Above those lines, he'd written the word *dam*. Next to the dam, he'd drawn a square, and inside the words *Lundgren's contraption*. Next to that, a simple diagram of a house—just a rectangle with a peaked roof. Staring in disbelief, I read the words he'd written on the inside. *Jens and Carrie Berrit.*

I looked up at the palace again. Then, closing my eyes, I listened for that still, small voice from deep within my soul. *"Waves can be cruel,"* it finally said, *"but they've given you a new beginning."*

ABOUT THE AUTHOR

There were five of us boys in the first grade at Manchester School. With two rooms and four grades, this school was the last of its kind in our neck of the woods. When it closed the following year, I was the only boy to advance to the second grade at a newly erected school in Albert Lea. For social reasons, I begged my mom to hold me back with my friends, but I'd soon discover what would have been a better reason—I hadn't learned the basics of reading. This disability haunted me until my third year of college, where I'd plow through one page in the time it'd take my roommate to read a chapter. That's when I had the privilege of taking an Efficient Reading course on the St. Paul campus of the University of Minnesota. It changed my life. On the last day of class, the instructor challenged us to read books for fun over the summer—a foreign concept in my world. So while running a conveyor in a dusty gravel pit, I read a book that I found on a little shelf built into the headboard of my parent's bed, *Kramer vs. Kramer*. It's hard to describe the experience of finally having the tool to burrow into someone else's imagination and share their treasure. And since my own imagination was incredibly fertile, I remember thinking how rewarding it'd be to invite others to cozy up to a tale of my telling. This book is the culmination of that desire.

Made in the USA
Monee, IL
09 September 2020